King

The Branded Trilogy
Book 2

J.A. Guynn

Acknowledgements

Thank you to my wife for the continued support and for convincing me this book is better than I thought it was.

Thank you to Emily Armstrong for her continued efforts as a beta-reader. Your input improved this story in ways I could not see by myself. Also, I can't wait to see your story come into the world!

ISBN: 979-8-9856947-2-7

Library of Congress Control Number: 2022918045

Cover Design: 100covers.com

Editor: Charlie Knight at cknightwrites.com

Proofreader: Mark Schultz, the Hyper-Speller at www.wordrefiner.com

Publisher: 3220 Group, LLC. Alvin, TX

Publisher Note:

Chapter 1

I picked at my breakfast, knowing I should eat but not feeling hungry. Each riot brought the possibility of civil war and the end of Croy. Thanks to Eirickson, no one knew the Satran were dug into our country like ticks on a deer...and were proving harder to remove.

Each group we cut out seems to give rise to three or four more soon after.

Agrim hurried through the courtyard. I recognized his pace easily.

"Come in!" I yelled, before he knocked.

A streak of dried blood ran down his gray beard and continued to his leathers.

"Good news?" I asked.

He bowed. "Jarl—"

"King," I snarled.

I've corrected him at least eight times over the past six weeks.

I thrust my finger toward him. "How do you keep forgetting? Croy no longer has a jarl. I refuse to use the title soiled by my father and half-brother. Don't make me correct you again."

Cringing, he lowered his eyes. "Apologies, Sire. I'm not thinking clearly. We put the last group of resistance down near sunrise. I wanted to report our success before getting some sleep."

"You're certain *all* Satran influence is gone? I've received similar reports before, yet here you stand, bloodcd again."

After a sigh, he nodded. "It's not just Satra causing unrest. As much as I appreciate having the Varian soldiers aid us, it looks bad."

"What do you mean? Other than helping your company, Elias makes sure his men keep to themselves."

He shrugged. "Varian soldiers spilling blood in our capital bothers people. Eirickson's claim of a planned attack from the north reached many ears. A company of Varian soldiers inside the wall, camping where the Council of Thanes used to meet, makes many influential people uncomfortable. Rumor has it, some of our own warriors suspect Elias and his men are scouting for an invasion."

I shook my head. "Varia is our *ally* against Satra; they are *not* invading. Why do so many people have difficulty believing the truth? Put out the word: I'm calling a meeting of the commanders—again."

Someone knocked on the door.

"I'm busy."

They knocked again, harder.

"This better be important! I yelled. "Who is it?"

"It's Roi," my mentor answered.

I jumped from my chair, a smile spreading across my face, and rushed to open the door. Gripping his offered hand, I pulled him into a hug. "Thank you for coming. I need someone with good sense."

"I'm glad to see you alive. Until Albin got word to me, I had my doubts."

"Agrim," I barked. "Why are you still here? I told you to gather the commanders."

"Of course, Ja—, Sire." Judging by his pace, he kept his calm until he thought I couldn't track him.

"We need to talk."

Roi nodded and followed me to the table.

"Where are Grima and Einns?" I asked, taking my seat.

Dropping his backpack, he took the seat across from me. "We didn't know how safe it would be here, so they stayed in Swinter. I'll send for them after I have a place to stay."

"Everyone expected me to take Eirickson's home, but I leveled it. The land will be turned into a memorial when I have time. Living in the Thanes' compound makes it easier to keep an eye on Porsey and Boril. Not all the guards I assigned to watch them agree on the meaning of house arrest. Sooner or later, I'll have to move them somewhere; they have too much influence here."

"Where are the other two Thanes?"

"I killed one after killing Eirickson. Roald, the eldest, made himself useful enough to earn some amount of freedom."

"I almost forgot. Before he left to find his brother, Albin asked me to give you this," Roi said, pulling folded parchment from his pack. "He said you needed to know."

"Hopefully, it's good news," I said, placing the pages on the table. "I'll read it soon, but I could use some of your wisdom."

"Ruling not as easy as you thought?" he asked, smiling.

I ran my fingers through my hair and sighed. "Nearly two months of non-stop madness. Other than Elias and the rest of the caravan guard, I haven't received any support from Varia. I still don't know who I can trust."

He pressed his lips together.

"Generals were openly conspiring against me. I had to face one in combat before they understood I shouldn't be taken lightly. Not long after that, Satran-led insurgence started. Thankfully Roald kept information on them. He didn't know all of Eirickson's schemes, but he knew enough to help me."

"Sounds like you trust him," Roi said.

I nodded. "Along with Agrim and the men under him, but the majority of the people around me are suspect. It's likely one, or both, of the other Thanes are behind the power plays I've faced. Trying to get the merchants and workers to support me, or even cooperate, has been its own battle."

My shoulders drooped. "What have I done?"

He patted me on the shoulder. "What you thought was right. Change is never easy. Did you expect the people to welcome you with open arms?"

"Eirickson sacrificed my land, our people, to keep Satra from taking the whole country. How long do you think that will last? I'm saving them from—"

"From a hidden threat. I'd be willing to bet the average Croian felt like they had nothing to fear once Satra stopped at the central forest. They conquered your skati and seemed content. Eirickson becoming Jarl displeased a few, but everyone felt safe with his leadership. Now, a branded, disgraced half-Varian ex-Skald stormed his wedding with a group of Varian criminals, killed him, and declared himself King of Croy. Did you expect no one to contest your claim?"

"I've told everyone who would listen that Varia will help us against Satra," I said.

"And their jarl declared Varia the enemy. He cautioned everyone to expect an attack from the north. Don't your actions look like a Varian invasion?"

I glared at him. "I can't take the fight to Satra if I'm still struggling to keep my country stable."

"You know how this business works," he said. "Build trust. Listening to you, all you've told me about is chaos and bloodshed. Very few people want to live in that situation, so show them that life is going back to normal."

"I miss Crum," I said.

"His people skills could come in handy...and I've rarely said that," Roi said, with a grin. "Speaking of people with questionable ethics, how's Tindra? Albin said she lost a hand in the fight."

I nodded. "Haven't visited her in almost two weeks. She's mostly recovered physically but having a hard time dealing with the injury. I suspect how she lost it weighs on her more."

"Do you think she meant to kill Stina?"

I shook my head. "Tindra's loyal to her king. Someone attacked me, she reacted. I think she would've killed her own mother in that situation. But I have enough to think about; I'd rather not relive that moment."

Reaching for the pages, I asked, "The message isn't sealed. Have you read it?"

"No. I figured it was meant for the King of Croy."

I chuckled. "I'm sure it is. Any idea where you'll stay?"

He shrugged. "Came straight here, haven't had time to look."

"There's plenty of room here until you have your own place. Make yourself comfortable."

"Sounds better than sleeping outside," he said. "Which room should I use?"

I waved toward the back of the building. "Mine's straight down the hall, meeting room's the first door on the left. You can have your pick of the others."

He nodded, grabbed his pack, and walked to the last room on the right.

The message had two pages, one from Ander, and the other from Kurt. Considering what Eirickson said about killing the Varian royal family, I read Ander's first. He opened the letter congratulating me on the successful attack. The details on Eirickson's agents were sparse. Ander's arm was broken when they struck. Ines did not fare as well. She took three knives to the chest before Crum got between her and the assassins. His quick thinking kept Jesca out of harm's way. After disarming one attacker, he killed them and kept watch over Ines. He ignored his own injuries until an herbalist treated her. An herbalist closed the deep cut in his left hand, saving his thumb, but he couldn't move it until the stitches were removed. The royal guard considered him a hero for his actions and dedication to their queen. Ander noted his willingness to accept Crum as a suitor to his daughter. Aerison had five hundred volunteers ready to help me secure my country. They were mine for the asking.

I noted he didn't mention Stina until the end. He wanted to meet, face to face, about what happened and her death.

Kurt's letter was short, down to business. He questioned my reasoning for banishing Sebast, insisting we would talk about the situation after visiting Tindra.

Plans were for him to accompany Aerison.

I rubbed my temples, trying to avoid getting a headache.

Crum did what I would have expected. He protected those around him as best he could. As proud as I felt, I really wanted him by my side. I needed him here, in his homeland, helping me reassure the people.

Where would I house five hundred Varian soldiers? As much as I knew I needed them, Croy needed them, no one would believe they were here to help. If I let them stay in the capital, my detractors would call it an invasion. If I set them up outside the walls, it would be called a siege. *Hopefully, I can find a workable solution. I need to talk to someone with better insight into the situation.*

Chapter 2

A short walk across the courtyard took me to Roald's quarters.

I raised my hand to knock when the door opened.

"You need me?" the eldest Thane asked.

"I need some insight."

"I do believe that's why I enjoy my freedom," Roald said. "Come. Sit. Let's talk."

"You remember Roi, my mentor?"

He looked at me for a moment. "I know of him...and your history with him."

"He's here, ready to advise me again, but you know things he doesn't."

He nodded. "What's on your mind?"

"Lots of things," I said, frowning. "Right now, the issue of trust. How should I go about building trust with those who currently oppose me?"

"You're asking about a long list of people...from what I hear. To some, you've shed a lot of blood for no justifiable reason. That breeds a large amount of distrust; some may even want revenge. Others see you as a temporary ruler and make moves to position themselves to take your place. Though the Satran no longer operate in the open, it will take time to remove their influence. Ultimately to gain trust, you must give it. Perhaps lift the house arrest of the other Thanes. Give them the same freedoms I have."

I stared at him for a moment, collecting my thoughts. "I have reason to believe they may still conspire against me. If Porsey and Boril are free to move about, what keeps them from inciting another uprising? Even a passive resistance to my rule keeps resources I need out of my hands. How can I justify freeing them?"

He shrugged. "You asked for my insight. That's a start. Maybe their freedom buys you some goodwill."

"But you told me the council couldn't control Eirickson. You feared him. Why do they resist me?"

"You stripped them of their standing and their freedom. What's next? Are you going to kill them? Their deaths would further anger their supporters, giving them more reason to resist you. With nothing to lose, they don't fear you."

I pointed my finger at him. "Can you persuade them to support me because I plan to let them live?"

He frowned. "They never listened to me when they had power. Why bother now?"

I stroked my beard, considering Roald's wisdom.

"That reminds me," he said. "You look like a wild man. It wouldn't hurt your image to clean up. Long hair and an unkempt beard...not a good look on a Croian ruler. Both Eirickson and your father were clean-shaven with closely cropped hair."

I leaped from my chair, knocking it over. The thick wooden table cracked when I slammed my fist into it. Clenching my jaw, I said, "Do not ever tell me I should look like either of them. I know the truth. I know what they did with their power. If I could get the people who believe Eirick and Eirickson could do no wrong to understand how those two abused their power and this country, they would curse their names."

Roald raised his hands, stood, and backed away. "I—I meant no insult. Please, I beg forgiveness."

"I'll forgive your mistake this once. Make it again, and it might cost you your head. I'll send for you when I think you may be of use again."

He bowed. "You are ever understanding."

To burn off some anger, I walked the perimeter of the courtyard instead of going straight home. Since the wall around the courtyard was more ornate than secure, I had ordered four guards for the entrance gate. Only two stood there now.

"Where are the other two guards?" I asked.

"Sergeant Vegar said there should only be two guards here," one of them said.

I sighed and shook my head. "Who does he answer to?"

"Commander Agnor."

"Thank you. I'll take it up with him. See to it that no one else comes in without my knowledge."

Neither acknowledged my order.

"Did you not hear me?"

"Sergeant said not to take orders from you."

"I am not in the mood for games. If I find anyone inside the walls who doesn't belong here, I will personally deliver your heads to Vegar's bed. Is that clear?"

The silent guard turned pale and swallowed before nodding. The other showed his wisdom by bowing.

Closing the metal gate behind me, I sythed the stone around it so it wouldn't open without someone fixing the wall.

I sighed while walking past the pile of clothes I'd removed from Auti's quarters. They were too small for me, and his body lay rotting in the tunnels next to Eirickson. Still, someone could use them if the guard would bother to take them away as I ordered.

My disappointment continued when I noticed the name and likeness of the dead Thane still remained on the door to my quarters. *Are there no woodsyths to spare? Something else I have to address with the commanders.*

Roi sat at the dining table, eating an apple. "At least you have some food," he said, after swallowing.

"Only men under Agrim's command are allowed to bring me food. I'd probably be poisoned otherwise," I said, taking a seat.

"I'm getting a better idea of what you're dealing with. You have to eliminate the willful disobedience. Seems you have Agrim's trust. Why isn't he helping?"

I nodded. "He's doing what he can, but what are thirty men against most of the country?"

"What about Nikulas? You don't have his support?"

"I've been too busy taking care of problems here to contact him. I'm not sure if he'll be happy with me when I do."

"Why?"

"I'm going to change his responsibility. He'll be our ambassador to Varia."

"Again, why?"

"He's already surrounded by Varian agents, might as well let him openly coordinate with them to shore up the allegiance."

"Makes sense to me, but won't your detractors see that as another step in a Varian invasion?"

I shrugged. "Roald thinks I should free the other Thanes as a show of trust."

"But you don't trust them, do you?" Roi asked.

"Only to stab me in the back."

"Why have you kept them alive?"

"You're full of questions," I said. "I asked you here to help me find answers."

He frowned. "Can't give answers without understanding the situation. Albin told me you originally planned to kill the Thanes."

I nodded. "Roald said something...changed my mind. Sparing them meant I was better than Eirickson. I wouldn't let myself be as evil as he was."

"He's right, but they don't seem to appreciate your mercy."

I pressed my lips together and took a deep breath. "Exactly, so what do I do? If I free them, what keeps them from encouraging more resistance? So far, the small flames of rebellion haven't joined together. If those two unite my detractors, I won't live to see Croy fall."

"Get them away from the people they influence. Send them to Nikulas."

I shook my head. "That won't work; he's accustomed to doing the council's bidding. But it does give me an idea. I'll think about it while working on a response to King Ander and Kurt."

"What did they have to say?"

He rubbed his chin while I gave him a summary of the two messages, smiling at Crum's heroics. "No less than I would expect from him," he said. "Varia sending five hundred men sounds like a good show of support."

"I would agree if I wasn't so worried about the problems they may cause,"

"Varian soldiers have a reputation of discipline and professionalism."

"Yes, but the fear of a Varian invasion is alive and well around here. Where am I going to house five hundred men that doesn't instill more concern in the people of Croy?"

"Maybe weave them into your army, put them under the Croian commanders."

"I doubt that will go over well with either faction, but I'll consider it. I already have to meet with the commanders, might as well deliver bad news along with a fresh tongue lashing."

Roi smiled, "That's not how you make friends."

"No, but I'll have more cooperation for a few days, at least."

"What are you going to say to Kurt?"

"The truth. Until I know Tindra can defend herself, or I can keep her safe, Sabast is not allowed in the capital."

"Why do you care?"

"She kept telling me she had my back. She was ready to die for me. She said she'd show me she was trustworthy. I didn't believe her. Halmar took some blows, and had to get some stitches, but Tindra was the only one who really got hurt, and she did it defending me. How could I not care?"

"Guess I owe her a little trust too then," he said. "Considering you're getting five hundred men from Ander, do you need the council's support?"

"At this point, I'm more concerned with not making another enemy," I said. "The Varian war council would be a dangerous opponent."

"Then choose your words wisely. Is it safe for me to take a walk? I'd like to visit some of my former haunts."

"I doubt anyone would threaten you," I said. "You'll have to fix the wall around the gate so it will open. I don't trust the guards to keep people out."

"Thanks for the advice," he said. "Have fun writing."

Chapter 3

I heard the door close as I made my way to the meeting room. After taking a moment to admire Auti's taste in quality ink and selection of quills, I wrote to Kurt first. Much like his letter to me, I wrote little more than a note, starting with an open invitation to visit Croy when he wanted. Before addressing the situation with Sabast, I gave him an update on Tindra's condition based on what I knew and said I looked forward to talking with him.

Next came the letter to Ander. I expressed my concern for his wife and wished her a speedy recovery. It took some time to come up with the right words to express my gratitude for sending Aerison and so many men. I told him I would do my best to have accommodations ready when they arrived. After several hesitant strokes of the quill, I spelled out how much I regretted Stina's death and how I wished the situation had not played out the way it did. I ended the letter by offering any help I might be able to provide once I had stabilized my country.

I pulled out a third page and wrote to Crum. It felt necessary to tell him how proud his actions made me feel and included Roi's praise. I asked for him to continue working to strengthen the relationship between Croy and Varia by being a good example of how Croians are willing to aid our neighbors. The letter ended with a reminder that I missed him and he would always have a place to stay in his home country.

After folding each letter, I addressed them, sealing each with wax, and secured them in a pouch. I had sythed my own seal, using a mirror to make a copy of the brand on my face. *If I'm going to wear it for life, might as well own it.*

With the letters finished, I considered how to deal with Porsey and Boril. House arrest wasn't having the effect I wanted, and Roald was right about the outcome of executions. I needed to get them out of the country, away from their supporters, ideally in a way that would get people on my side. The beginning of an idea came to mind, but I needed to talk to someone first. Hopefully, she'd be awake and willing to talk business.

After stopping by my room to put on my hammer, I left my quarters. Exiting the compound grounds, I found a single guard at the gate.

He stood a couple of fingers shorter than me with a little more bulk. The color of his stringy hair reminded me of sun-faded hay. At first, I thought the dark, half-moon-shaped mark near his right eye was a fading bruise, but it had a distinct border against his fair skin. *Tattoo or birthmark?*

"Why are you alone?" I asked.

"Paulans said he wasn't going to waste his time standing around here if anyone could come and go as they pleased."

My eyebrow twitched, and I shook my head before running my hand down my chin. "What's your name?"

"Sigric. Sir."

"Sigric. Why are you still here?"

"I want to keep my head."

I pressed my lips together and nodded. "Nice to hear you can pay attention. Do you believe I want to take off heads?"

"Rumors say—"

"To the fire with rumors. What do you believe?"

He turned pale when I interrupted. "I...well, I—"

"Spit it out!" I shouted.

"Sergeant Vegar told everyone that he met with Porsey, and the Thane told him you were planning to kill anyone who resisted the coming Varian invasion."

I clenched my jaw and pulled two chairs from the ground. "Sit."

The startled guard looked around before quickly moving into the chair.

My hammer made a dull 'thunk' against the stone chair as I sat. "Have you seen me kill anyone?"

"No, but everyone knows Agrim's company is your personal assassination troop."

"Everyone?"

"Vegar said Agrim and his men helped you get into the council building the day you attacked. He said Agrim's men slit throats to give you and the Varians a clean path inside."

"Are you afraid of me?"

He nodded.

"Why?

"Jarl Eirickson branded you a traitor after you attacked the Thanes. He exiled you from Croy, but you killed him and took the country. You're going to let Varia take over."

I stared at him until he squirmed. "Some of what you say *is* true. Before I tell you more, I want you to answer one more question. If I am a bloodthirsty, murderous traitor intent on giving this country to Varia, why are you still alive?"

"What do you mean?"

"You've insulted me. If I am the man you believe me to be, why haven't I killed you?" I reached for my hammer. "After all, this is the hammer I smashed Eirickson to death with. I could do the same to you and no one would know."

"I...yes, you could."

I nodded. "Do you want to hear the truth? Do you want to know what happened to me in the council chamber? Why I was there to begin with?"

He glanced around. "How will I know you're telling the truth?"

"Because you'll live to tell others the truth."

"Couldn't hurt to listen," he said, shivering.

"No, but it might hurt not to," I said, with a smile. "I'll assume you know Eirickson was my half-brother, and I governed the land conquered by Satra. I traveled from my skati seeking aid from the Thanes. Satran soldiers were raiding Croian farms, and I needed warriors to protect my people and secure the border. I didn't attack the Thanes; I threatened them. Eirickson did brand me for that, but he didn't exile me. He did much worse. He threw me into a lightless maze of tunnels with no exit. His judgment alone sentenced me to wither away under the capital while he sacrificed Croian lives to pacify the barbarians to our south. Instead of fighting the Satran like the powerful jarl everyone believed him to be, the coward let them slaughter our countrymen. Worse than that, he met with them, working out plans for invading Varia. He offered Croian warriors to the Satran cause."

Sigric sat, silent, his mouth hanging open with an expression made of confusion and disbelief fixed on his face.

"Take your time. Think about what I said and what has happened this past year. I'll gladly answer any questions you have."

"You admit to attacking the Thanes?"

"No," I said. "I threatened them. Just like I threatened to remove your head earlier. Had I attacked them, someone would have been injured or killed."

He nodded. "I see what you mean. But if those tunnels had no exit, how did you get here?"

"I worked hard to get out while fighting to live and protect others. A man I trusted died so I could rescue a woman and escape. I made my way to Varia, nearly dying when Satran soldiers found us in the woods, and found people who would listen. They swore to help me as long as I promised to keep Satra from winning. What do you know about Satra?"

"Jarl Eirickson had us preparing to fight off a Varian invasion from the north. Our commanders told us to not worry about Satra. They told us they wouldn't come through the central forest."

"Why would Varia invade from the north? Think about it—there's an open passage on our eastern border. Why risk traveling through mountains on foot when you could drive wagons full of soldiers and supplies through the pass?"

"I'm a warrior; I don't question my commanders."

"Yet you don't listen to my orders," I said.

"Sergeant told us to only do what we must to stay out of trouble."

"I'll address that soon enough. Do you believe me yet?"

"I'm not stupid enough to call you a liar," he said, looking down.

"I appreciate your honesty," I said, with a grin. "Can I trust you to not stab me in the back?"

"I like living."

"Close enough. I'd like a second set of eyes with me while I make my way to herbalist Abi's house. Since Agrim and his company are resting, I'd like for you to walk with me."

"And if I refuse?"

"It's not an order, it's a request. You can stay here guarding the gate. I'll know you still don't believe me, and I can't trust you. However, honor my request, and I'll consider it a show of trust which could benefit both of us."

"Who will make sure the Thanes don't leave the compound?"

"That's my problem," I said, with a smile.

Sigric looked around again as if he expected someone to be watching, waiting to trap him. "Are you leading, or am I?"

"I'd rather we walk side by side. Trust is important."

Chapter 4

I noticed people staring at us as we walked to the herbalist's home. More than a few sneered or frowned, and some spat at us as we passed. While the attention didn't bother me, Sigric's shoulders drooped, and he let his gaze fall to the ground.

I know some people are unhappy with me, but what has he done?

"I'd invite you in, but I'm not sure Tindra wants company," I said, before knocking on the door.

He nodded. "I'll wait here."

"Thank you."

Abi opened the door. "How may I help—oh, I apologize. Please, Sire, come in."

She had the calm, soft voice of a loving grandparent but wasn't much older than me. Her curly, brown hair, tangled with leaves and stems, partially hid warm, brown eyes. More plant debris clung to her rough, woven dress. *She must have been harvesting this morning.*

"Thank you," I said, closing the door behind me. "How's she doing?"

She shook her head. "Still more bad days than good. Hardly touched breakfast. Maybe you can cheer her up."

The thin herbalist was a little shorter than Tindra but walked with rapid strides. I hurried to keep up with her as we walked deeper into her odd, round house. The closer we got to the center and the outdoor space the home surrounded, the more greenery climbed the walls.

Abi stopped at a door. "She's sitting in the garden. I'll give you your privacy."

I walked out, following the trail to a table. Tindra sat, staring at the three candles. The flame flared and jumped from one to the other, causing shadows to dance.

"May I join you?" I asked.

She flinched before looking at me. Her tawny skin had an ashen look. Dark rings circled her amber eyes. Her black hair had grown shaggy and lost its shine. *Wonder when she washed it last.* She'd lost more weight since my last visit; I could see it in her cheeks.

"It's nice of you to visit," she said, with a blank expression.

Approaching the table, I saw a spoon resting in a bowl of boiled grains next to a plate of sliced fruit. "Abi said you didn't eat. Don't try convincing me you're still learning to eat with your left hand. We both know that's a lie."

"She doesn't believe me when I tell her I need meat," she growled, sounding almost feral.

"We went over this last time I visited," I said. "You agreed to follow her orders. She's doing everything she can to help."

"Everything but feeding me a decent meal. I can't take any more of these bland grains. I'd settle for some Varian spices." The flame grew higher as she ranted.

"I'll talk to her, give her a few suggestions. Do you feel up to talking about something else?"

"You know what happened—you were there. We don't need to talk about it," she said, and lit all three candles.

"That's not why I'm here. I've got news from Varia. Kurt's coming. He wants to see you."

"Why? To gloat? To tell Sabast where I am?"

"Don't worry about Sabast. I've got that situation handled," I said. "I'm not sure why Kurt asked to visit you, maybe to see how you're doing. That's not the only reason I'm here. I also need your opinion on something."

"What?"

"I have an idea to solve a problem, but I need your take on it. You're the only person I know who can tell me how to best approach this."

"No. I told you before, I'm out. I'm done."

"Get over yourself. You're the one who told me every scar is a lesson. Well, you have a big scar—learn from it."

"I can't do my job anymore. I'm no good to anyone like this," she said, waving her right arm at me.

I grabbed the bandage above her wrist. "I'm not asking you to be a spion. I'm asking for information you already have. Regardless, you're wrong. There's plenty good you can do if you'd just do it."

She pulled away. "It itches."

I looked at her for a moment. "That's not unheard of. Wounds itch when they heal."

She pointed toward where her hand should be. "Not the wound. My hand. It itches between my thumb and first finger, but I can't scratch what's not there."

My eyes opened wide. "Oh, I don't... Have you talked to Abi about it?"

"No. She'd tell me to chew on some leaf or something."

I nodded. "I'll talk to her for you and tell her no leaves. Will you discuss this problem with me? It might do you some good to think about something else."

"I'm not going to promise I'll answer, but I'll listen."

"I have an idea of what to do with Porsey and Boril," I said. "I want to——"

"Kill them."

"No, that would cause more problems. I want to send them away, and I think I know where they can do some good."

"Send them to Satra for slaves."

I shook my head. "That would be as bad as killing them. I want to send them to Daufi."

She rubbed her forehead for a moment. "Let me get Abi. I'm sure she has some leaves you can chew until you understand why that's a ridiculous idea."

I smiled. "I had a feeling you might not see the wisdom in my idea."

"So, convince me you haven't lost your mind."

"Sending them, and their families, on a special, long-term diplomatic mission to the capital of Varia makes them seem important again. It gives the appearance of me trusting and respecting them. The people at Daufi can keep Porsey and Boril on the grounds, away from anyone they might use to gain power. Their families can help, maybe even give goods from Daufi a place in the markets, to generate money for the house. I could give King Ander a warning to make sure the Thanes don't influence anyone in the Varian court."

I saw a flicker in her eye. "Underhanded deception for your own gain...I didn't know you had it in you. Might work, but how long would my parents have to hold them?"

"Ideally? Until the Thanes die. Realistically, only until they have no way to influence anyone in Varia."

"If my father thinks it will work out for his people, he'd likely agree to take them in. When are you going to send them?"

"I have to decide how I'm going to get them there first. And shouldn't I ask Mikael before dumping them at his gate?"

"Bring me some parchment; I'll dictate a letter to Abi. Sooner or later, I have to learn to write left-handed," she said, with a weak smile. "It's well past time I let my parents know I'm alive anyway."

"Thank you. I have news from King Ander if you want to hear it."

She sighed and closed her eyes. "My life is his for the asking," she said, blank expression returning.

"He didn't call for your life. I think he has more on his mind anyway. Ines was gravely injured before Crum killed the attackers. Ander's arm was broken, and Crum's hand is in bad shape—"

"Oh," she said, frowning. "I know how that feels."

I smiled. "Humor?"

She shook her head. "Reality. Is Jesca hurt?"

"Unharmed," I said, and patted her leg. "Eat. You need your strength. When I come back with parchment, I'll bring some meat. Do you mind if I bring Roi?"

"When did he get here? Does he know?"

"Earlier this morning," I said. "He knows enough."

She lifted the spoon. "I won't turn you away if he's with you."

I nodded and left her to eat.

It took some searching to find Abi, but I wanted to talk to her before I left. "Tindra says her missing hand itches. Any idea how to help with that?"

The herbalist shook her head. "Why didn't she tell me?"

"She didn't want you telling her to chew more leaves."

Abi smiled. "I recommend what I know works. I don't know anything about ghostly itches. I'll ask some of my friends."

"She wants meat to eat."

Her face lost a little color, and she frowned. "I've eaten nothing but fruit and plants my whole life. The meals I make are good for her. She'd recover just fine if she'd eat."

"You won't protest if I bring her some meat?"

She shrugged. "Not if it gets her to eat. I don't mind the company, but I'm not going to let her stay only to starve and waste away."

"She had started eating when I left. I'll bring her something else when I come back," I said. "I'll see myself out."

As I turned, Abi said, "You're welcome to come and go as you like, Sire."

I looked back. "Ignoring how impolite that would be, I have enough people accusing me of terrible things. I don't need more rumors or accusations."

She nodded, and I left.

Chapter 5

I hadn't been confident Sigric would wait, but he came to the door as I stepped outside.

"Do you still require my services, Sire?"

I cocked my head for a moment. "Sire, instead of sir?"

"Thought about what you said before—trust. I figured respect was a necessary part of it."

"So, you *can* think for yourself," I said, with a smirk. "Good quality for a man to have. I recommend keeping it up. Do you know if there are any Varian cooks on the way back to the compound?"

"You're asking the wrong person. I've never tried Varian food," he said, with a shrug.

"Fair enough," I said. "Who cooks the best meat?"

"Depends. What are you in the mood for?"

"Meat. The more flavor, the better."

"It's still early for lunch, but Grith runs a butcher shop and does some cooking. I can't say if the best or not, but it's not too far off the path back to your home."

"Perfect," I said. "Lead the way."

He nodded and took me to a market square I wasn't familiar with. The farther we walked, the more attention people paid to us. Soon my head turned toward every noise.

Sigric noticed. "Relax. They're more worried about me than you."

"Why?"

"Most of the shop owners know I'm under Vegar's command. He throws his weight around sometimes, takes things."

I guess all the sneers and spit before weren't just directed at me.

"Something else I need to address," I muttered, then cleared my throat. "Is there a reason you brought me to *this* butcher?"

"Because Grith is good people. I try to get word to him when Vegar might be coming by. Like I said, I've been thinking...I may not question my sergeant, but I don't have to agree with him."

"How do I know you're telling me the truth?"

"Ask the butcher. I'll introduce you and leave if you'd like. No reason he'd lie if I'm not there."

"I'm still wondering if this is a trap."

"You killed Jarl Eirickson, and General Hallfrid may never walk again without crutches because of what you did to him. I don't want to get on your bad side."

"I want you to trust me, not fear me."

He shrugged. "The outcome's the same."

"Only in the short term. Leading by fear never works for long. I'll talk to Grith. If you're telling the truth, I'll make sure Vegar understands I don't approve of his activities."

We turned a corner, and he pointed to a shop with several skinned goats hanging from the porch. "Right there."

"I'll go in alone to see what he says. I trust you'll stay nearby."

He nodded. "Go ahead. I'll watch your back. You'll see I'm telling the truth."

Keeping my eyes and ears open, I hurried to the shop and stepped inside.

WHACK! A hatchet struck a block of wood.

A thickly muscled, nearly bald man, wearing a blood-stained apron looked up from the headless rabbit. "Can I help you?"

I held out my hand. "Grith. From what I hear, I think we can help each other."

He squinted, staring at me, and didn't bother to wipe the sticky blood from his hand before shaking mine. "Haven't seen you around here before. I'd remember."

"King Fitzeirick. I'd like some cooked meat, but I want to talk first."

He pulled his hand back and wiped it on his apron. "Excuse my lack of manners. Not often we get royals here."

I bobbed my head to him. "I take no offense. Think nothing of it."

He stepped back and looked me over. "I've heard you'd beat a man for less."

"Vegar?"

He nodded and looked past me.

"So, what I've heard is true?" I asked.

"Depends on what you've heard...and who's talking."

"I've heard one of my sergeants takes liberties with some of the shops in this market."

"And you've come looking for the same?" he asked, gripping the hatchet. "Vegar's smart enough to have men with him when he comes."

I tapped my coin purse hanging from my belt. "No, I'm here to do business. Do you have any cooked meat left from breakfast?"

"I've got a little roast pork, but it's too dry to eat now. Planned to throw it in the stew pot for dinner."

I nodded. "How much?"

"I wouldn't feel right taking coin for it."

"Price isn't important. How much meat do you have cooked?" I asked.

"About enough for two people. Why?"

"Sounds like Sigric brought me to the right place. I'm looking for some meat, something that would be good in a soup or a stew, and about enough for two people."

"Sigric?" he asked, looking past me again. "Did he tell you when Vegar's coming by?"

"Don't worry about Vegar. He's my problem."

"I'll give you all the meat you want if you get Vegar to leave us alone."

I shook my head. "You won't *give* me anything. I'm here to do business. How much for the dry pork?"

"I wouldn't feel right selling it to you. I'll wrap it, and you take it. Buy fresh from me later."

I crossed my arms. "Name your price."

He wiped his brow. "Freshly cooked, it's a silver single per person. I'll take one for all of it."

I'm not carrying any silver.

Nodding, I grabbed two coins from my purse and held my closed fist out. "You're more than fair; here's your payment. Wrap it, and I'll leave you to your work."

He wrapped the pork in a piece of burlap and tied it closed with well-practiced ease.

Taking the bundle, I placed coins on his table and turned to leave.

"Two gold doubles is too much by far," he said.

I glanced over my shoulder, smiling. "Consider it payment for valuable information. Spread it around if you don't want to keep it all."

The butcher squinted and tilted his head before nodding.

I reached Sigric, and said, "You're not going to serve under Vegar much longer."

"What are you going to do with me?"

"Have half a mind to send you to Agrim."

"I don't want to be an assassin," he blurted out.

I pinched the bridge of my nose and sighed. "Agrim's men aren't assassins. He's proved his loyalty, so they act as my right hand. Do they kill for me? Yes, but only when necessary and never in secret. Regardless, I haven't made my mind up, but I do have a job for you when we get to the compound."

"What if my sergeant sends someone looking for me?"

"Tell them you're doing my bidding. If they have a problem with you following my orders, they can talk to me."

"Yes, Sire," he said, with a smile.

Chapter 6

The compound gate stood open and unguarded.

"I need to get a few things from my quarters. Would you mind looking in on Porsey and Boril? I'd like to know they're where they're supposed to be."

"Of course, Sire. Should I alert you if they are gone?"

"I won't be long. Wait for me at the gate. I'll give you your assignment before I go back to Abi's."

He nodded before turning to Porsey's home.

It didn't look like Roi had returned when I entered my quarters. I grabbed the pouch with letters bound for Varia, jotted a quick note for Agrim to let him know why I sent Sigric to him and sealed it before grabbing some parchment for Tindra's letter. I also selected a nice quill and a couple of ink jars. *She said she needs to practice.*

I almost ran over Roi as I stepped out.

"In a hurry?" he asked, and chuckled.

"Wasn't expecting anyone," I replied. "I'm going to drop some things off for Tindra. Want to walk with me?"

"Don't have anything better to do. Wanted to talk to you about something anyway."

"Be nice having you at my side," I said, "like old times."

He chuckled.

"Nothing out of the ordinary to report, Sire," Sigric said, as I approached the gate. "Boril seemed in good spirits. Porsey didn't like having his nap interrupted."

"Thank you," I said. "If plans go my way, their lives won't be so dull soon."

Handing the note and the pouch to Sigric, I said, "Agrim's probably asleep in his quarters. When he wakes, give him this note and wait for him to decide how to handle the pouch."

He gave me a strange look but nodded.

"Afterward, relax. Get something to eat. Perhaps Grith might have something interesting to say. Above all else, stay out of trouble."

"Yes, Sire."

"What's on your mind?" I asked Roi.

"Ran into some people I hadn't seen in a long time, heard a disturbing rumor."

"Rumors about me run rampant, don't believe them."

"Not about you, about my father."

"Someone's seen Rorec?" I asked, stopping.

"I've known Engli for as long as I can remember. Swore he saw my father during the invasion. Said Rorec wore a Satran officer's uniform," he said, frowning.

"Your friend had to be mistaken. Fear clouded his mind. You don't believe your father's fighting for Satra."

"Engli's solid under pressure. He'd recognize my father in a crowd. I don't think he's mistaken."

I looked around, suddenly aware of all the people looking in our direction. "We'll talk about this later. Let's get to Abi's now. I'd like you to talk to Tindra. Maybe you can help her see life isn't over."

"Why me?"

"You suffered a greater loss than her and managed to live through it. That kind of experience taught you things I can't know."

"I'll try."

When Abi's home came into view, Roi said, "I recognize this place. My parents were good friends of Yrsae and Ulfar. They treated me a few times when I was young. I haven't thought about them in ages. How did Abi come to live here?"

"Don't know."

"Mind if I ask?"

"Not at all, but don't press if she doesn't want to answer."

"Wasn't planning to be impolite," he said, grinning.

Abi opened the door shortly after I knocked.

I introduced her to Roi as we stepped inside.

Roi looked around the entryway, pressing his hand against the wall. With a childlike smile, he said, "It's the same as I remember."

Abi cocked her head.

"He knew Yrsae and Ulfar."

She smiled. "Oh, they were wonderful people. It seems like they were here yesterday."

"What happened to them?" Roi asked.

"Yrsae got sick, so sick. Ulfar worked day and night to help her get better. I did what I could to help. All the herbalists within a day's ride looked in on her, but nothing worked. She withered away to skin and bones before she died. He died not long after. His mind was still sharp, but he lacked the will to live without his wife."

He pressed his lips together tightly and sniffled a couple of times. "How did you meet them?"

She frowned. "Father died fighting for Jarl Eirick in the far east. Yrsae took me as their apprentice, and they raised me after my mother died."

He hugged her. "I didn't mean to bring sorrow to your door."

She shook her head. "I understand. You didn't know. Tindra's still in the garden."

"Before we go see her, I brought some meat for her lunch, but it needs to be used in a soup or stew. Are you comfortable with that?"

"I can try," she said. "I've never cooked meat."

"I'll do what I can to help. Do you have any peppers or spices ready?"

She looked at me and furrowed her brow. "Are you not feeling well?"

"Not for a cure, to add to the soup."

"I don't use peppers or spices in my food," she said.

"I know, and that's one of her complaints," I said. "Roi, would you go talk to Tindra while I help in the kitchen?"

He nodded and walked toward the middle of the house.

"He's a herbalist?" Abi asked, as we walked.

"No, stonesyth. He's suffered loss. I thought his experience might help her figure out how to get past her self-pity."

"Oh," she said. "What do we need to make this soup?"

"Let's start with what you normally use in soup."

She nodded. "Roots, carrots, and potato or beets usually."

"This is pork. A little sweetness will go well too. Do you have any dried sugar beets?"

"No. I don't grow sugar beets."

I nodded. "Get a pot of water on to boil. We'll work with what you have on hand."

While the pot heated, Abi chopped carrots and potatoes before dropping them in.

"You wouldn't happen to have horseradish, would you?" I asked.

"Never heard of such a thing. What is it?"

"A root...popular in Varia. I've had it once; it's hard to describe. Think about a spice you don't taste, but it hits your nose instead."

She wrinkled her nose. "Doesn't sound very good."

I chuckled. "Used sparingly, it makes an interesting flavor. How about dried peppers?"

She shook her head. "All the peppers I have are fresh."

"Mortar and pestle?"

She looked at me like she questioned my sanity. "Not in here. Who would keep one in the kitchen?"

"I'd like to grind up some fresh peppers to spice the meat."

"Oh. I'll go get one. Peppers are in the jar on the shelf behind you. The dark red ones carry the most heat."

I nodded and picked five, firm, red peppers from the jar. I'd removed the stems by the time Abi returned.

"Are you sure she's going to like this?" she asked.

"More than the bland Croian food she's had so far," I said, while grinding the peppers into an oily paste. My nose burned as the smell filled the air.

Abi coughed a couple of times.

While coating the meat, I had an idea. "Abi, do you have any ripe pears?"

"No, only dried, cubed pears. Why?"

I dropped the pork in the boiling pot and smiled. "Would you mind if I used some?"

She looked sideways at me before walking into a nearby pantry and returning with a jar.

I reached inside, grabbed a handful of tan-colored, shriveled cubes, and dropped them in the mortar. "Leave them to soak up some oil. We'll add them to the soup shortly before it's ready."

She scrunched up her face. "I don't think that's going to taste good."

"It's not traditional Varian cooking, but I'm willing to give it a chance. Tindra and I ate some Satran food with pear in it before. I'm hoping she'll remember and maybe cheer up a little."

"Where did you eat Satran cooking?"

"An eatery in Varia run by a friend of Tindra's. His family left Satra long ago."

"It was good?"

I nodded. "For a meat-eater. Tudal used more earthy flavors compared to the fiery Varian cooking."

"Earthy flavors," she repeated, while scratching her chin. "I wonder what plants give earthy flavors to food."

"I don't know much about cooking and spices. Roi's son's a pretty good cook. When he gets here, maybe you can talk to him about it."

"Isn't Roi Croian?"

I nodded. "He lived with Grima and Einns in Varia for a while. Einns uses a combination of techniques. Doubt he's picked up any Satran influence but wouldn't be surprised if he could figure it out...especially with the help of an experienced herbalist."

Abi blushed at the praise. "I do what I can."

"Speaking of which, are we paid up? You've done a lot for Tindra, and I know she can be a handful."

"You're fine. She's been a good patient until lately. Guess she's finally got enough strength back to be uncooperative. I don't mind; it's nice to have some company in this lonely house." She stirred the pot. "How do we know when the soup is ready?"

I took a deep breath and couldn't smell the peppers. "Let it boil until you smell the peppers in the steam. Then we'll take it off the fire and drop the pear cubes in."

"I can do that if you want to go out to the garden. Take a pitcher of water and some cups. I'm sure your friends would like a drink."

I grabbed a tray and cups while Abi filled a pitcher from the water barrel.

"Let's see how Roi and Tindra are getting along," I said, with a grin.

Chapter 7

"...once you've decided to do that, the rest is easy," Roi said, and turned to look at me.

"I'm not interrupting anything, am I?"

"Roi said you brought meat," Tindra said.

"Soup's not ready yet. Abi thought you two could use some water."

"Sit," she said, pushing a chair out with her foot.

I placed cups on the table, filled them, and took the offered chair after putting the tray and pitcher down. "Make any progress?"

"She's a good listener," Roi said, before taking a drink.

Tindra swallowed. "I appreciate your honesty. You gave me a lot to think about. I don't talk much when I'm thinking. What's for lunch?"

"Have a little patience—it's cooking," I said. "I also brought some parchment, a nice quill, and ink for your letter, and so you can practice writing."

"Thank you, but what's for lunch?" she asked again.

I shook my head. "Carrot and potato—"

"Meat!" she shouted.

I smiled. "Soup with peppered pork and a surprise."

Her mouth dropped open, and a little drool ran out of the corners. "You talked the plant-eater into cooking meat? I don't mind a salad on occasion, but I need meat."

"I got some here as soon as I could," I said. "Can you wait for it to get to the table?"

Roi chuckled.

"What choice do I have? I can't carry it for myself."

"Not like you used to," Roi said. "But you aren't incapable. It would only take more trips."

Abi placed the pot on the table before setting a tray with bowls and spoons down next to it. "If you don't mind, I won't be joining you. I need to make my lunch."

"I didn't mean to make you uncomfortable in your home," I said.

She shook her head. "No worry. I can't stomach that smell much longer."

I stood, grabbed a gold double from my purse, and put it in her hand. "Thank you."

She nodded and rushed out of the garden.

Tindra ladled her bowl full before using her spoon to find a piece of pork. Jamming it into her mouth, she closed her eyes and hummed. The corners of her mouth turned up in a disturbing smile. She chewed quickly, swallowed, and sighed before dropping her shoulders.

"Meat," she said. "And some spice. Not like home but a vast improvement over bland plants."

"You've had fruit too," I said.

"I can't eat fruit for every meal," she replied.

"What are these sweet, spicy, white cubes?" Roi asked.

"The surprise," I said.

Tindra scooped one of the cubes out of the soup and sniffed it before popping it into her mouth. "Tastes like spiced pear."

Roi furrowed his brow. "What made you think of that combination?"

She grinned. "I know. Tudal and Hampus."

I nodded. "Mostly Tudal."

She smiled for a moment. "That seems like a long time ago."

"It does, doesn't it?" I said, then remembered the conversation with Abi in the kitchen. "Roi, when you send for Grima and Einns, would you mind if he spent some time with Abi? Adding the spiced pears made her curious about cooking with other plants."

He nodded. "I'll ask once they get here and get settled. Wouldn't hurt for him to learn a little of the herbalist trade either."

I turned back to Tindra. "What are your plans for the rest of the day?"

She cocked her head. "I'm going to eat as much of that soup as I can and rest. Maybe a stomach full of real food will help me feel better."

Roi chuckled again.

"I can't talk you into joining me in a meeting this evening? I could use your skills," I said.

"How many times do I have to tell you I'm out before you believe me?"

"I'm not asking you to act as my spion. I could use another pair of wary eyes and ears. I'll have Roi but having you there would be helpful. I'm meeting with the generals, again, because I can't get anything done with nearly fifteen hundred men working against me. General Hallfrid already wants my head, and I'm sure the other four don't disagree. Sergeant Vegar is telling his men to ignore my orders on top of taking advantage of merchants. Such behavior reflects poorly on me. It makes people doubt my leadership ability. We can't take the fight to Satra if I'm not certain my warriors will fight for me. Right now, Agrim's company is the only one I can rely on. Thirty men against all of Satra? I'm not that stupid or crazy."

"Put it off a week, see how I feel then," she said.

"I can't. Plus, assuming Sigric did what I asked, Aerison will be here with five hundred Varia soldiers in two weeks or so. Kurt's coming with him. You don't want to look vulnerable to him, do you?"

She raised her eyebrows and swallowed another mouthful of soup. "No. I don't want anyone seeing me like this."

"Then take what I told you to heart," Roi said. "It's the quickest way to move forward."

She nodded and ate faster.

I finished my bowl and drank more water, waiting for her to eat her fill. Roi patted his stomach and belched, but Tindra kept eating.

Maybe I imagined it, but it looked like some color returned to her face as she ate. *Probably the peppers.*

When she started her third bowl, I said, "We can leave you alone if you'd like."

She shook her head and swallowed. "I don't mind the company, but if you need to leave, go."

"I would like to talk to Roi about the meeting before it starts. Maybe develop some strategy."

"Would be a wise idea," he said.

"Then go. I'll be fine," Tindra said.

"About the letter to your parents. Can I pick it up the day after tomorrow?"

"Only if you promise to bring more meat," she said, with a smile.

"I promise."

Before he stood, Roi put his hand on her shoulder. "Thank you again for what you did. I'm sorry it cost you so much, but you *can* get on with life."

She nodded, mouth full of soup, and looked toward the door.

Chapter 8

We left the garden, said goodbye to Abi, and headed home.

"I don't recall you mentioning a meeting before," Roi said.

After glancing left and right, I shook my head. "Rather talk inside—too many eyes and ears around."

He nodded, and we hurried back.

I sighed in disappointment at the unguarded gate to the compound. *Why is it so hard for warriors to follow simple orders?*

Instead of sitting at the table, I led Roi to the more comfortable seating in the meeting room.

"By now, Agrim should have told the generals I wanted to meet with them and their commanders after sunset. I want them to trust me, respect me, but if the only way I can get cooperation is through fear, so be it."

Roi raised his eyebrows. "How many men?"

"Five generals, each with five commanders."

"That's a full room you're trying to intimidate," he said, with a grin.

I shook my head. "I don't want to intimidate them. I want to *lead* them."

"Sounds like one big boulder to crack. What do you have in mind?"

"First, I'm going to exile two of my biggest detractors, but I'm not going to tell them, or their supporters, they're being exiled."

"I see why you want Tindra at the meeting; you really need Crum too," he said, smiling.

"Hear me out. Tindra's writing a letter to her parents. I'll send Porsey, Boril, and their families to live in the House of Daufi in the Varian capital. It's a long-term, diplomatic mission to investigate the truth behind all the rumors of Varia invading from the north. The idea is everyone will see my actions as freeing them, trusting them to work in Croy's best interest. The people living in Daufi will keep the Thanes on the grounds while their families help the House."

"Two questions come to mind. How are you going to get them there, and how long do you think they'll cooperate?"

"I'll send them back with Kurt. His men can keep them from causing trouble until they reach their new prison. As far as I'm concerned, those two can die in Varia but the longer they stay out of contact with their support here, the fewer problems they can cause."

"No one will expect reports from them?"

I smiled. "All reports will come to me. Also, once I have the army under control, no one will care about Varia after I order forces east to take back my skati."

"I see how the plan for the Thanes could work, but it's not addressing your immediate disobedience and misconduct problem."

I nodded. "I'll just have to take direct action on that. Starting with telling the generals about the Varian soldiers coming to help us. I expect an uproar of resistance, but once I've calmed them, I'll ask for suggestions on how to integrate the extra men into our force."

"You expect your generals to believe these Varian soldiers will fight against a Varian invasion?"

I shook my head. "I'm ready to counter that argument. I'll specify that the Varians take front-line duty. King Ander would not send men to die fighting their countrymen."

"You're overlooking the fact that Ander's men could let more Varians through the front lines instead of fighting."

"I'm going to play up the general's pride to fight that argument. If my generals don't believe our fifteen hundred men can foil a treacherous maneuver by five hundred Varians, how could they hope to survive against the whole Varian army?"

He rubbed his chin. "That might work, but I still haven't heard anything about quickly gaining trust and obedience."

I nodded. "The more I think about it, the less I expect to gain any trust soon. Some people—Sergeant Vegar, for example—are going to try to force my hand. I'll make an example of them, as each situation arises, until everyone understands such behavior will no longer go unpunished. The average Croian doesn't understand they were oppressed by Eirickson. The leaders see my attempt at kindness as weakness. If I have to get tough for a while..."

"I told you before I wouldn't like what you had to become to do this. That still stands."

I nodded and smiled. "I won't be that person for any longer than necessary...especially not with you at my right hand."

"Fair enough. I—"

A knock at the door interrupted him.

"I wasn't expecting any visitors," I said. "Hope it's not more bad news. I'll be right back."

Sigric had his fist positioned to knock again when I opened the door.

"S—Sire," he stammered. "Sergeant Agrim told me to update you. He has men looking for Albin to send your pouch back to Varia. He spoke to General Jomar personally about the meeting. He also mentioned that I am to attend as part of his company. Sergeant Vegar will protest."

"I expect General Hallfrid will voice your ex-sergeant's displeasure. If Hallfrid could lead half as well as he voices dissent, he wouldn't need crutches to get around. I'll be sure to remind him of that fact."

"As you say," he said, and bowed. "Is there anything else you need?"

"Not until the meeting. You're dismissed until then."

"Thank you, Sire," he said, before bowing again.

I closed the door and returned to Roi.

"All is well?" he asked.

"Getting better," I said. "This evening's meeting should be interesting, entertaining even. Make sure you come armed."

He coughed. "Armed? After everything you said about building trust, you want me by your side with my sword?"

"I expect at least one challenge to my rule. There might be bloodshed before everyone is satisfied."

"'Come back to Croy. Bring your wife and her son; they'll be fine. Just make sure you come armed to meetings with the military commanders. They tend to cross lines and have to be beaten into submission,'" Roi quipped, imitating my voice.

I chuckled and wagged my finger at him. "Not every ruler would be so accepting of such blatant disrespect."

"I can still take you," he replied.

I smiled. "I know."

"Just make sure you don't forget it," he said, returning the smile. "It's still a while before dinner. How are you going to pass the time?"

"Let's go for a walk. I'd like to visit a market."

"Should I get my sword first?" Roi asked, eyeing me suspiciously.

"Probably, but only because we might eat in the market and go from there to the meeting."

He nodded and left to get his blade.

It took a little time to retrace the path back to the market I'd visited with Sigric earlier. It was busier than when I had visited earlier but not overly crowded.

Roi said something about picking up a few things for Grima and Einns and left me outside a weaver's shop. I looked over some clothes on display without attracting much attention.

"Excuse me," I said to a woman working a loom. "Do you have any cloaks? I used mine in a burial and haven't had a chance to replace it."

She turned and looked at me. Sweat stuck her straight, brown hair to her reddened forehead holding it just out of her blue-green eyes. "Sorry," she said, "I couldn't hear over the—Oh, it's you." She stood and curtsied.

I looked around, wondering if anyone saw her. "I'm looking for a cloak...dark, maybe sheds water. Have anything like that?"

"Grith said the king stopped by his shop this morning. We didn't believe him. I'm Fastan."

I gave her a slight bow. "Well met, Fastan. I didn't see any cloaks among your wares. Do you have any?"

She shook her head. "I make dresses and shirts. You should see Thorgault. He's a tanner but also makes cloaks. Shop's across the way, to the left. Is it true?"

I raised my eyebrows. "Is what true?"

She looked over my shoulder. "What Grith said. You're going to make Vegar stop."

"Seems I have several problems needing my direct attention. Rest assured, his behavior will be addressed...soon."

"Many of us will be appreciative. I know someone tries to warn Grith before Vegar comes, but we don't always have time to hide our best wares."

"Is Vegar the only one?"

"Some of his men help. Seems like different ones every time."

I reached into my coin purse and pulled out a silver single. "A gift from someone who cares and will make things better."

"I couldn't. Wouldn't be right. Others have suffered more than me," she said, looking away.

"In that case, this is payment for information."

"I won't keep it. Others here need it more."

I nodded. "It's yours to do with what you wish. You said Thorgault's shop was close?"

She pointed. "Yes, across the way, to the left."

I bowed again, "Thank you."

The smell of leather and tanning fluids assaulting my nose as I got close led me to my next stop. Stepping inside, I saw a bulky-looking man with a long, thick braid of gray hair hanging down his back, stirring something in a barrel.

"Well met. Are you Thorgault? Fastan said you may have some cloaks for sale."

"I might," he said, without turning away from his work. "But I'll see ta ya once I'm done. Can't ruin this skin."

"Apologies. Didn't mean to interrupt important work."

He nodded, but his big arms never quit moving. I considered going to look for Roi and returning later when he pulled the stick out of the barrel and placed a lid on it. "Whatcha lookin' fur again?" he asked, turning.

"A cloak. I'd prefer something dark that sheds water."

His blue-green eyes opened wide as the thick, gray mustache above his lips followed them into a frown. "Beg pardon, m'lord. Didn't know it was you."

"No offense taken. I like doing business with a man who takes pride in his work. Are you related to Fastan?"

He shook his head. "People think she's a sister with our eyes bein' the same color. Life's funny like that."

"It can be. Now—"

"Helped her out once, though. Some sweet talker wouldn't leave her alone. She ran ta me, called me her pa. One look at me, he never came round again."

I smiled. "Sounds like you did a good thing. Now, about the cloak? Do you have anything fitting my needs?"

"Believe I do," he said. "Hooded?"

"Perfect."

He walked to a stack of wooden boxes. "Leather or cloth?"

"Cloth, if you have it."

He nodded and moved the boxes until he could reach inside the one in the middle. "How dark?"

"Something good for hiding in the woods at twilight."

He squinted. "Why wouldja need that?"

I shrugged. "No reason right now. Memories mostly. Used to have one, and I'd like to have another."

He pulled something out of the box and held it up. It didn't look like any cloak I had ever seen. If I had to guess, it belonged with a small tent.

"Wrong box. Gimme a minute."

"Take your time. I'm in no hurry."

He shuffled several more boxes around before finding what he was looking for. "This is more like it." He showed me a cloak almost identical to what Crum brought us when we left Vekel's for Varia.

I smiled again. "By any chance, do you have another, sized for a woman? Top of her head's close to my chin."

"You sure you're not upta no good?"

"Why would the King of Croy be involved in anything illegal?"

"Grith said I should trust ya if ya came round," he said. "Let's see what I got."

Cloaks piled up before he showed me another one. It looked a little short for Tindra but close enough.

"I'll take them both," I said. "How much?"

"Take 'em. They're yours."

I shook my head. "That's not how I do business. Name your price."

"A silver single for yours and a copper single for hers."

I reached into my pouch and pulled out a coin. "How about a gold single for both?"

"Too much by a copper."

"Consider it payment for me interrupting your work."

"I gave ya a fair price."

"Very, and I gave you a more than fair counteroffer."

"That ya did, and I'm just smart enough ta take it. Pleasure doin' business wit ya," he said, folding the cloaks into a bundle.

"Things are going to get better around here, I promise," I said, on my way out.

Working my way through the crowd, I found Roi leaving Fastan's shop with a pack over his shoulder.

"Would you mind if I put these in your pack?" I asked.

"Of course not," he said, turning his back to me.

"Let's see about dinner," I said, after tying the pack closed again.

"You have someplace in mind?"

I nodded. "Butcher shop close by. If he doesn't have anything ready, I'm sure he'll tell me where we can eat."

"Sounds good."

I smelled meat cooking before we reached Grith's shop. We had to wait for some customers to leave before we could get inside.

He saw me, and asked, "Back so soon, Sire?"

I smiled. "Needed to do a little shopping. What's for dinner?"

"A rabbit and goat stew, probably not the meal you're used to having."

I held up a gold double. "If it tastes as good as it smells, I'm sure I've eaten far worse. A bowl for myself and my mentor."

"For this, I'll throw in some ale from my personal supply to wash it down."

"Told you Grith would take care of us," I said to Roi.

"Good to see you remember it's important to make friends," he said.

"Never forgot," I said. "It's *who* I'm trying to befriend that's changed. If the elite won't side with me, I need to get the commoners on my side."

Roi nodded as Grith placed full bowls on the counter; large wooden mugs followed soon after.

The butcher's stew was simple and unseasoned, light on broth and potatoes but loaded with meat. The slightly bitter ale went well with the unseasoned meal.

I tried to get his attention before we left, but he was busy with other customers. I left a copper single next to our bowls, but Roi picked it up.

"Don't make him think you're trying to buy his loyalty."

"I'm not. The extra's for his ale."

He handed me the coin. "Trust me. Besides, the sun's starting to set. How far to the meeting?"

"No need to hurry. We'll get there in plenty of time."

"I'm following you."

His words brought a smile to my face. *Now to get my military to fall in line.*

Chapter 9

A crowd of warriors stood outside the officer's dining room, my chosen meeting place. Most of them didn't look happy to see me.

"Who's he?" one challenged, as I reached for the door.

"Roi, my mentor and right hand," I said. "Expect to see him around more often."

The stocky man stepped back.

The scene waiting for me in the large, lantern-lit hall made me smile. A single, round stone table with seven chairs, pitchers of water placed in the middle, and a cup for each chair sat in the center of the room. Sergeant Agrim sitting with his men in rows of chairs on the left side of the room. Chairs for the commanders were lined up on the right.

Good to see someone can follow directions.

Agrim stood when he saw me. His men followed soon after. "I trust all is as you ordered, Sire."

"You did well, Agrim. I appreciate your attention to detail. This is Roi, my right hand. Unless his order conflicts with mine, he speaks for me."

"Understood."

I looked over my shoulder at the empty side of the room. "Guess we're a little early."

"Jomar told me Hallfrid would hold everyone back and make you wait. I tried to explain that's not in anyone's interest, but how often does a general listen to a sergeant?" Agrim said.

"Changes are coming," I said.

He bowed, and the warriors didn't return to their seats until Roi and I sat.

If not for the flickering lanterns, I'd have sworn time stood still as we waited.

Roi laced his fingers together, closed his eyes, and breathed slowly.

Figures he'd take a nap.

He didn't move when the door creaked on its hinges but the click-scrape sound of General Hallfrid entering on his crutches caused him to open his eyes and yawn.

The general's short, gray hair did not complement his round head. He had a scar running from above his left eye toward his ear. In a way, he reminded me of a much taller and thinner version of a thug I killed in the Varian capital.

I'll never understand how either man received any respect.

He glared at me while taking the seat across the table. Commander Agnor, his favored lackey, took the general's crutches and sat behind him. "The others will be here shortly," Hallfrid said. "I wasn't expecting an audience."

"Anything you need to say, they can hear," I said, returning his stare.

He flicked his hand at me and looked toward the door.

General Jomar entered next, alone. He looked more like a Croian than Hallfrid, with short blond hair. He had dark, almost black, eyes and the well-muscled body one expects a warrior to have.

He bowed to me and took the chair to Hallfrid's left.

Several commanders came in together. Agrim and his men stood when Ottar took the seat behind Jomar.

Generals Heming, Gudmann, and Nothri came in together, leading a large pack of commanders.

Standing, I glanced at the rows of seated men and noticed an empty chair where Sigric should've sat. "Generals and commanders, I appreciate your attendance. Before getting to the meat of this meeting, I want to introduce Roi, my lifelong mentor and right hand. You should show him the same respect you afford me."

When I said his name, Roi stood and bowed.

"General Hallfrid," I said, returning to my seat. "One of your men is missing. I specifically invited Sigric, a warrior in Sergeant Vegar's company. Do you, or Commander Agnor, know why he's not attending?"

Hallfrid gave me a toothy smile. "I saw no reason for a lowly warrior to attend this meeting."

The other generals nodded their agreement.

Jomar added, "I question why Sergeant Agrim and his company are here when none of the other sergeants are attending."

I pointed at Hallfrid. "I left nothing open to interpretation. It was not for you to decide or even consider. I *ordered* Sigric's attendance."

He sneered. "You're lucky I bothered to attend. I'd considered sending Agnor in my place and finding a better way to spend my evening."

Slamming my fist on the table and knocking water out of several cups, I turned to Agrim. "Send men to find Sigric."

The sergeant stood and bowed. "Yes, Sire. We will return with all haste."

Commander Ottar stood. "Sergeant, if you leave this room, do not return."

I pointed to Jomar. "I gave an order. Control your man."

Hallfrid laughed. "No one cares about your orders. We don't follow unqualified, traitorous half-breeds."

Roi growled.

I put my hand on his shoulder and glared at Hallfrid. "Do you not remember what happened the last time you challenged me? Do I need to remind you? Maybe break an arm this time?"

Hallfrid put his hands on the table and pushed himself to his feet. He wobbled a couple of times before looking me in the eyes. "You were too weak to finish the job."

I stared at him for a moment, not believing what I heard. *I've tried being nice, and they see me as spineless. I don't want to rule through fear, but if all they respect is strength, I'll show them what I'm willing to do to get their cooperation.*

Pulling strength from the floor, I shoved the table, knocking him back into his chair. "Weak?" I bellowed. Rising to my feet, the room trembled. "You call me weak?" I gripped the table so tightly, my fingers sank into the stone, and I roared, "How *dare* you call me weak!"

My voice rang out from the table, the walls, the floor, even the ceiling. Dust fell from above as my rage filled the room.

Everyone in front of me had their hands over their ears. Some cringed, turning away from me, while others looked stuck in slack-jawed stares.

My body quaked so hard, I didn't dare let go of the table. *How did I do that?*

I flinched when Roi tapped a finger on my arm.

"Sit," he mouthed, wide-eyed.

I looked at him, ears ringing as my voice stopped echoing. After several breaths, I felt more in control. "Now, do I have everyone's attention?"

No one answered. Those not still staring at me were looking around the room with expressions of disbelief.

"Can we continue?" I asked, returning to my chair.

"S-Sire," General Heming stuttered. "I-I...that is..." He coughed. "I think I speak for everyone here when I say you have our attention."

Hallfrid nodded slowly, eyes wide.

"Good," I said. "I think it best if I talk and everyone listens. You'll be free to ask questions or voice objections when I'm done."

A few more heads nodded.

"First, Agrim, find Sigric...quickly."

"Of course, m'lord," he said.

I waited for the door to close behind him before continuing. "Soon, five hundred Varian soldiers will arrive to support us in the upcoming battle to take back the far eastern skati. No doubt this is shocking information and looking at you all convinces me that you need time to think this over. Don't take too long to decide where they will stay and how the extra men might benefit our country. I'm willing to listen to reasonable suggestions, but I will house them and use them as I see fit if you leave the decision to me."

More slow nods answered me.

"Nothing else I have to tell you should need more than simple agreement on your part. Assuming most of you can listen and think at the same time, I'll continue."

After pausing for a drink, I continued. "There are those among you holding onto the belief that Varia intends to invade Croy. Despite my repeated attempts to convince you otherwise, I have changed few minds. I'm working on a solution to this dilemma, though it is too early to be completely confident all parties will agree. I want to send Boril and Porsey, with their families, to the Varian capital on an extended diplomatic investigation. The initial request will leave for Varia soon. I will not send them until I know they will have housing fitting their status and all necessary support to confirm what I know... Varia is our ally. Any questions?"

Jomar and Heming looked at Hallfrid but said nothing.

"I haven't spoken to Boril or Porsey about this trip yet. But if and when they depart, it will be with my full support and confidence. Anyone who wishes to accompany them will be accommodated if at all possible. The final two items I wish to present directly affect Sergeant Agrim, his company, and Sigric. Any objection to waiting for them to return?"

"Not an objection to waiting," General Gudmann said. "A question about the proposed diplomatic visit."

I turned to him. His short, red hair and bright, green eyes stood out against his pale face. I hadn't seen him enough to know if that was his natural complexion or if his color had not returned from the earlier surprise. "I'll do my best to answer any concerns. Speak freely."

"How will they travel, and who will see to their safety if we don't send guards?"

"Excellent questions. The safety of our countrymen is always my concern. Those issues are part of the support that must be arranged. I plan to speak with Skald Nikulas soon. If the Varian trade caravan has not left, I imagine we could offer to buy passage for them or send wagons of our own. Valuable cargo will be well guarded. If that isn't an option, I'll ask for volunteers to accompany them on their mission."

"I'd heard rumors you were doing away with Nikulas' title, yet you still call him skald. Which is it?" General Nothri asked.

The first time I saw Nothri, I thought he may be half Varian. His brown eyes showed a hint of turned-up corners, and he wore his black hair long enough to conceal his higher than usual cheekbones. "Am I correct guessing you are from his skati?"

He nodded. "My father joined his guard not long after I was born."

"So, you are a second-generation warrior?"

"Third. My grandfather also served."

I nodded to him. "I'll discuss my plans with Nikulas at the appropriate time. Only then will anything change—with his support, of course. Ignore rumors. Better yet, bring them to my attention."

"As you say," he replied.

Hallfrid looked at me. His jaw twitched as the door opened, and men marched into the room. Agrim and his company returned, escorting Sigric.

"Thank you, Sergeant," I said. "Sigric, please come to the table."

Hallfrid's eyes narrowed.

"Agnor, would you stand?"

The commander looked around and blinked a couple of times before rising.

"I've done some investigating today, spent time among the commoners. Since General Nothri brought up rumors, I've heard one myself. It's a particularly nasty rumor concerning someone under your command, Agnor."

His face turned red as he balled his hands into tight fists. "Whatever Sigric is accused of, I'll make sure he's punished. We don't tolerate criminals in our ranks."

Sigric's eyes opened wide.

"I never said Sigric was accused, nor did I mention anything criminal."

"Yet here he stands," Hallfrid said. "Surely that means he's involved."

"Oh, most certainly, and I'll explain everything after hearing what Commander Agnor has to share."

"Nothing, Sire," Agnor said, "I just assumed."

I nodded. "Just like you assumed there are no criminals in your ranks?"

"Are you accusing one of my commanders?" Hallfrid asked.

"Perhaps you know something you aren't sharing, General," I said.

"My men do as they are told."

"Correction: your men do as *you* tell them," I said, smiling. "Some under your command are telling their warriors to ignore my orders. Does that come from you? Do you think you outrank a king? You've called for me to step down more than once. Did our last confrontation not settle this matter?"

"I tire of this game. If you are going to accuse someone, name them and what they did," he said through a scowl.

"I will soon, but I have one more question to ask...of everyone," I said. "Isn't intentionally undermining the authority of a ruler committing treason? Earlier, Hallfrid called me treasonous, yet his men tell their warriors to ignore their ruler."

Hallfrid's jaw clenched.

"Hallfrid, before you say anything, I'll share what I've learned, and you will hear testimony from a trustworthy witness. It has come to my attention that a sergeant under Commander Agnor abuses his authority. Sergeant Vegar tells his men to ignore me and steals from merchants. He does not act alone in the theft; he uses warriors under his command to back him up." I turned to Sigric. "Would the witness please testify?"

The warrior stood still as a stone.

"He's after a promotion," Agnor said.

"Considering how he follows orders, I'd say he's due one. Don't speak again until Sigric has spoken," I said. "Sigric, you have my permission to speak freely."

"Thank—Yes, Sire. I stayed at my post, the gate to the Thanes' compound, this morning when Vegar told Koll and me to ignore the king's request for four guards at the gate. At King Fitzeirick's request, I escorted him through the city. We stopped at a market square—one Vegar frequents and takes goods from."

Agnor pointed at Sigric and yelled, "Baseless accusation!"

I shook my head and pushed my talent into the floor. Stone flowed up Agnor's legs, hardening and encasing him to just below his nose. "I told you to be quiet." I felt the commander shaking. *Right now, I don't care if it's from fear or anger. At least I'm getting a response and everyone knows I am serious.*

Hallfrid's lips curled into a snarl at my treatment of his bootlicker.

"Sigric, please continue," I said.

The warrior nodded. "The merchants are afraid of Vegar. He's hurt people who don't cooperate, especially those he catches hiding valuable items."

Pointing to the empty chair, I said, "Sigric, I am moving you to Sergeant Agrim's company."

The warrior bowed to me.

Hallfrid sputtered for a moment. "You can't do that."

"I'm the king. I can, and *will*, move men at my whim. Those serving this nation should set the example of Croian honor." I used the stone around Agnor to force him back into his chair before releasing him.

"Sergeant Vegar has one chance to avoid punishment. Commander Agnor, you *will* make certain the men under your command behave honorably at all times. All reports of misconduct will be investigated immediately and thoroughly. Punishment will be determined by me based on the severity of the behavior. Baseless accusations will also be punished; I will not tolerate liars. General Hallfrid, any further disobedience will be considered a willful act of treason. Judgment and punishment will be swift and harsh. Everyone before me will voice their understanding of what I said."

Heads nodded.

"I said *voice*," I barked. "Speak."

An unenthusiastic chorus of 'Yes, sir' echoed quietly through the room.

Not ideal, but at least they are responding. I nodded. "My final business is to announce Sergeant Agrim and his company no longer report to Commander Ottar. Effectively immediately, Sergeant Agrim is head of my personal guard, and his company is said guard. He and I will discuss his duties, and I will arrange separate housing for them soon."

I looked around the room, waiting for someone to protest. Both Jomar and Ottar's faces were dark red but neither said anything.

I stared at Hallfrid. "No one? It's your chance to speak freely."

"Why are you taking men from my command?" Ottar asked. "The Croian warriors have always kept the thanes and the jarl safe."

I chuckled. "Considering the recent death of Eirickson and a Thane, both by my hand, I'm not willing to risk being that safe. Does anyone else have a question?"

"I will contact you later," Hallfrid said. "After I've had time to discuss this evening with my fellow generals."

"In that case, everyone except my guard is free to go. Enjoy your evening, but keep in mind, I want an answer regarding the Varian soldiers soon...or I will take matters into my own hands."

Dust fell from Agnor's clothes when he stood to help Hallfrid to his feet. Everyone paraded out behind the click-slide cadence of Hallfrid's crutches.

Chapter 10

"Captain Agrim, please move your men to the other side of the room. We need to talk."

"Captain?" he asked.

I turned to him. "You are no longer a part of the Croian army. You answer to me."

"Yes, Sire. Men, you heard him."

While they moved, Roi leaned close and whispered, "What did you do earlier?"

I shrugged. "Later."

"Agrim," I said, after everyone settled into a chair, "you've served me without question from the moment we met. Your men have worked hard to keep order following my takeover. I have made many enemies this evening; your job will not be easy."

"It has been my honor to serve you, Sire," Agrim said. "You will find we're up to anything you ask."

"Your company seems to run well, but I do have a request. Select two men to act as your proxy, call them lieutenants, in case you are indisposed when I call for you."

"I will consider it."

I nodded. "All I can ask. I want a guard rotation at my quarters. Four men at the gate at all times. No one, except those in this room, goes in or out unchallenged."

"Understood. Four men will see you home safely this evening and remain while I work out the rotation."

"Tomorrow, I will ride to visit Nikulas. I want guards with me, at least four. Roi will be in charge while I'm gone. As I said before, he is my right hand and speaks with my authority."

Turning to Roi, I said. "I do have a job for you. Find suitable quarters for my guard before I return. Build it if you must."

He nodded. "I'll start after breakfast."

"Captain, if you have any requests, give them to Roi."

"Yes, Sire."

"My final order applies to everyone: you are my eyes and ears. If you are not on an assignment and not asleep, be alert. You will investigate any and all claims and complaints. Vegar will stop for a little while, but sooner or later, he'll return to his old habit. I can't build trust among the commoners if my men are abusing them. Despite how badly I want to avoid more bloodshed, I will make a public example of him. No doubt Hallfrid's already plotting against me. If I can catch him in a conspiracy, I can move on him. Does everyone understand?"

My new guards responded in unison, "Yes, sir."

"This meeting is adjourned. Who's escorting me to the compound?"

"Myself, Sigric, Hedin, and Skegg," Agrim said.

"Putting the new man to work so soon?" I asked. "He guarded the gate this morning."

"No better way for me to get to know him," Agrim said.

"I knew I made you captain for a reason," I said, with a smile. "Lead the way."

Agrim slowed as we got close to the compound. "Sire, there are men at the gate. Four by my count."

Vegar walked toward us. "A word, if it pleases the king."

"Certainly," I said, stepping closer to him. "I'm guessing you have questions about Sigric."

"No," he replied. "I'll pick a replacement warrior from the next batch of recruits. I'm more concerned about the accusations against me. Why wasn't I allowed to address them?"

"Do you not trust Agnor and Hallfrid to have your back?"

"I trust them with my life, but they do not know what I do day in and day out. What's it going to take to remove this tarnish from my reputation?"

I looked at him, trying to read his face. *Is he serious?* "As I told your superiors, I expect every warrior, regardless of rank, to carry themselves as an example of Croian honor. First, I'd recommend you stay clear of your accusers. Next, stop telling your men to ignore my requests. Assuming you can do those things, we'll revisit this subject later."

He glared at me for a moment before bowing. "I plan to start now. Me and three from my company are guarding your gate tonight. Four will replace us at sunrise."

I smiled and swept my arm toward Agrim and his men. "Thank you for the initiative, but I have my guard. You and your men are free to enjoy the evening. Get a good night's sleep; you never know when I may call on you."

He nodded. "If it's all the same to you, Agnor told me to take this post."

"If your commander gave you this assignment, then see it done to the best of your ability," I said. "I hope the evening goes smoothly for you. Sigric, see Roi and me to my quarters."

Vegar's face reddened when I called on Sigric.

"Of course, Sire."

I put my hand on his shoulder when we reached my door. "Agrim will keep you safe. Remember what I said: you are my eyes and ears. Don't provoke Vegar or your former company-mates but watch and listen."

"Thank you for the advice, Sire. Sleep well."

Roi and I entered and sat at the table.

"What do you think that's all about?" I asked.

"I haven't the slightest idea. I'm more interested in how your voice came from everywhere. That gave everyone a fright."

I shrugged. "Don't know how I did it. I've seen King Ander do the same thing, but he seemed much more in control."

"I've never seen anyone do such a thing. For a moment, I thought you were going to bring the hall down on us."

"You have to admit, it had the desired effect."

He chuckled. "You did make an impression. I'm assuming that's the most cooperation you've received from those leaders."

I nodded. "By any measure. Last time, I broke Hallfrid's leg. You'd think someone that thin would know better than to challenge a hammerman to combat."

"He's going to strike, sooner or later. Once the shock wore off, I suspect he cooperated only to give you a false sense of accomplishment."

I smiled. "I agree with you there. But now I have a company loyal to me gathering information. Given a little time and ample opportunity, corrupt men will expose themselves. I can clean up the mess then and gather more support at the same time."

"It seems I have a busy day ahead of me—and you to thank for it. I'm going to bed," Roi said.

"I have one more favor to ask."

He yawned. "What?"

"If you find yourself with nothing better to do tomorrow, try to figure out how I control pushing my voice through stone."

He laughed. "Any other near-impossible puzzles you'd like me to solve in my spare time?"

I joined him in laughing before wishing him a good night.

"Things are going to get better, at least until I start my warriors marching east. Then things may get much worse," I said to no one.

Even if Nikulas accepted his new responsibility and the Thanes went willingly to their new prison, I was going to be working harder than ever to get my country ready for war.

· · · ● · ● · · ·

I woke sitting up. Looking around the room, I realized I'd fallen asleep at the table. *How'd I manage to do that with my hammer across my back?* My legs and back cramped when I tried to stand. I ignored the discomfort when the door opened.

"Wondered if I should dump water on you," Roi said. "Hungry?"

The smell of roast goat filled the room.

"Nice of you to get breakfast."

"Grith sends his regards."

"At this rate, I'm going to be the reason he stays open," I said, sitting back down.

"It's good meat, nearby, and he seems to be good people," Roi said, placing a pitcher and a bundle on the table. "Threw in some goat milk."

"And you paid for it," I said.

"Generously. You need to eat quickly if you're going to get to Nikulas' hall before lunch. I'll get cups."

"Thank you for letting me sleep. I have a lot on my mind."

"Ruling's not as easy as you thought it would be?"

I tapped my finger on my chin and looked at the ceiling. "I think I've heard that before."

"I'd bet you're going to hear it again," Roi said, smiling.

I dropped the subject and peeled a strip of meat off the goat. Compared to the bland stew we'd eaten yesterday, this was a meal fit for a king. Still unseasoned, but it had a rich, smoky flavor. After swallowing a mouthful of meat, I took a drink. Milk is not good combined with smoky meat. Still, it beat going thirsty.

Once I'd eaten my fill, I headed for my room to change clothes into something more practical for riding. Soft leather pants and a long-sleeve, woven, wool shirt, along with tall, thick-soled boots. After strapping my hammer back on, I stopped by the washbasin and splashed water on my face.

I passed Roi on the way to the door. "Don't make a mess of things while I'm away."

His laughter followed me out the door.

Chapter 11

Approaching the gate, I noticed only six men stood watch. Agrim and his three were still there but only two of Vegar's company. Vegar and one of his men were gone.

I asked Agrim to come with me to the stable.

His hand moved to cover a yawn before he nodded.

"I take it everyone behaved last night," I said, as we walked.

"I kept Sigric away from Vegar. The sergeant stuck around for a little while after you got in. He took Egil and left after mentioning he remembered a special duty Agnor had for him."

"So be it," I said, placing my saddle on Andale. "Before you go to bed, remind my guard they are my eyes and ears. I want to know about anything suspicious or out of the ordinary."

"Of course, Sire. Let me know if you don't have plenty of volunteers when you stop by the barracks to get guards for your journey."

"I will," I said, cinching the saddle and double-checking everything before mounting my horse.

Passing the training grounds, I stopped for a moment to watch several recruits practicing swordplay. It reminded me of training with the Varian guard, especially Sabast putting so much effort into attacking me.

Riding past the warrior's barracks, I received a mix of stares and glares; some men didn't bother to look my way. I dismounted outside Agrim's company barracks and tied Andale to a post.

I stepped inside to find the room more orderly than I expected. "Nice to see you men take some pride in your quarters," I said, to two warriors seated at a table, playing cards.

"Of course, Sire," one replied, before showing his hand and taking a pile of copper.

I cleared my throat. "I need four men to ride with me to Skald Nikulas' hall. Volunteers?"

Every man in the room stood.

"Enthusiasm is a good quality, but I only want four. If you expect to be assigned to guard my gate today or tomorrow, you cannot go."

That left about ten men standing.

"How many of you are not well-rested?" I asked. "If you need sleep, go to bed."

Six men were still on their feet.

"Still too many," I said. "Raise your hand if you're an archer."

Three hands went into the air.

"The two best swordsmen of you three, step forward."

They looked at each other.

One shrugged and sat down.

The first man stood tall, about the same height as Roi, with a muscled frame. His slicked-back, red hair and alert, dark eyes reminded me of a hawk.

The second stood about half a head shorter, with a bulky build. His hair reminded me of a few days' beard growth. A deep scar across his left cheek drew attention away from his blue eyes.

After eyeing the nearly bald man for a moment, I asked, "You're an archer?"

"Otkel doesn't say much, but he's almost as good as I am, Sire," the hawk said.

"And your name is?"

"Svan, my lord."

"If you were to pick two fighters to go with you, who would you choose?"

"I'd want Sibbi at my side and his brother, Bior, in front of me, sword at the ready."

When he said their names, two men stepped toward me with smiles on their faces.

"Which is which?" I asked.

"I'm Bior, Sire." the closest one said. The faint streaks of silver in his coarse, curly, black hair were either from age, or possibly he had some Satran blood in his veins. His light-blue eyes stood out against his darker skin, another hint at Satran ancestors.

"That means you're Sibbi," I said, looking at his brother. He had similar hair, just not as curly and slightly darker eyes. Both stood about the same height as Otkel.

He nodded. "I am, m'lord."

"Good. Gather your gear and get horses. I'd like to eat lunch with Nikulas," I said.

"I'll grab rations for the group and meet you at the gate," Svan said.

"Don't bother," I said. "I don't want to spend a night away from the capital."

"You expect trouble?" Svan asked.

I shook my head. "I expect the trip and meeting to go smoothly. Nikulas will understand I need his support to help fix what's wrong with Croy. It's unlikely he'll deny my request or spend much time debating but, if we get delayed, he'll extend appropriate hospitality."

"If you don't expect trouble, why ride with four guards?" Sibbi asked.

I rubbed the brand on my cheek. "I carry a reminder that trouble pops up when you least expect it. I'd rather have you with me and not need you than need you and not have you."

Svan patted Sibbi's shoulder. "We understand, Sire."

I smiled. "Good. I'll wait for you outside, but before I leave, I have one more thing to say. With your help, we *will* fix what's wrong with Croy, and we'll get the far eastern skati back."

Heads bobbed in agreement as I spoke.

"Understood, Sire," Svan said, when I finished. "You heard King Fitzeirick, get your stuff and get moving. Those working outside, keep his words in mind and take them to heart. A better Croy starts today."

"Here, here!" several men shouted, as I walked out of the barracks.

Soon my escort jogged out, dressed in brown, leather armor, Svan in the lead, heading for the stable. Sooner than I expected, I heard hoof beats heading my way.

"Otkel, you and Bior take the lead. Sibbi and I will follow the king," Svan ordered, when they stopped.

With a quick nod, I fell into their formation.

I couldn't help but compare the reaction I received leaving the capital as king today to when I left my hall as a skald just over a year ago. So much had changed. Instead of bows, the warriors glared at me. Most people who paid any attention to my group tended to scowl.

Things will get better.

Chapter 12

After exiting the southern gate, I motioned for Svan to ride next to me. "I'm going to ask you something, and I want your honest answer."

"Of course, Sire."

"Do you know why Agrim has been so loyal to me when the rest of the warriors go out of their way to disrespect me?"

"I wouldn't want to put words in my sergeant's mouth."

"He asked if you know. He didn't ask you to speak for anyone but yourself," Bior said.

Svan looked into the distance for a moment before nodding. "Sergeant never liked Eirickson. After you killed the jarl, you treated Agrim with respect. That first evening, Sergeant Agrim told us he'd cut down any of us if we crossed you."

I chuckled. "You need to get used to calling him Captain Agrim now."

"Old habits, m'lord."

"I understand. He still slips and calls me jarl, but I don't let him get away with it. What about the other men? Why do they disobey? They seem to take my kindness as a weakness."

"That trick with your voice may have changed some minds," he said, and shivered. "Truth is when you killed Eirickson, you humiliated General Hallfrid. The plan to hide warriors under the courtyard, leaving fewer visible guards near the jarl, came from the general. I'm not sure how you knew where they were, but those were his men you killed."

"Why does he speak for all the generals? It seems to me any of them could beat him in combat."

"He cheats," Svan said. "Finds a weakness and holds it over you. Do what he wants, or he'll strike when you aren't expecting it."

"So, I should expect him to strike back in secret?"

Svan's lips pressed together and twisted into a tight smile before he covered his mouth and coughed. "No, Sire. In your case, when he comes at you, it will be out in the open with as big an audience as he can gather. I've heard his commanders talking. He wants to humiliate you, make you beg and offer your power to him, before ending your life."

"Are you telling me I don't have to worry about a knife in the back?" I asked.

"Not from him. Agnor, on the other hand, could take offense to being bound. He won't act but, if he's of a mind to, he'll order one of his men to get revenge for him."

"Perhaps that's why Vegar came to the compound gate last night," I said.

"A smart man might bet a few doubles on it," Svan replied, with a smile.

"Some might say a smart man wouldn't want to rule in the first place," I commented.

Svan shook his head and laughed. Before too long, the other three joined him.

"I appreciate your honesty and openness, Svan," I said, after the laughter died. "You've given me a lot to think about—as if I didn't already have quite a bit on my mind."

"I'm honored by your praise, my lord," he said. "I get the impression no ruler's burden is light."

"I'm figuring out governing a quiet skati kept me blinded to the corruption in the capital. I got a glimpse of similar problems in Varia. Truth be told, I have to walk a thin line between supporting criminals to benefit Croy and turning said criminals into enemies."

"Far be it from me to tell you how to rule, Sire, but maybe better to have criminals you know than criminals you don't. At least you know how to find the ones you know," Bior said.

"That's very close to what some criminals told me in Varia," I said, smiling. "Should I have the guard keep an eye on you, Bior?"

"What? No, Sire. I'm not involved in anything except some friendly wagers on cards and the like. My own brother would vouch for me."

Svan chuckled. "Of course, he would. He knows you'd take it out of his hide if he didn't."

"That true, Sibbi?" I asked.

"No, Sire," he answered. "I mean...yes, I would give a good word for my brother but not because he can best me. He hasn't been able to take me in years. Well, not in a fair match anyway."

"Are you calling me a cheat?" Bior yelled.

"Never," Sibbi replied. "I'm just saying you're getting too old and slow."

Svan snickered. "My king, maybe you should move them apart. I'd hate for the brothers to call a duel."

"You two, save the fighting for Satra," I said.

"Yes, Sire," they said together.

We turned east, toward the Carved Scar, and entered the crowded trade path. Svan moved to a position behind me, and all the guardsmen turned more serious.

Our progress slowed, sometimes to a snail's pace, as we wove our way past wagons and foot traffic. Other than a few glares and some choice words thrown our direction, we made it through the Scar without incident.

There seemed to be a few more buildings near The Trader's Cup than I remembered from my last visit.

Turning to Svan, I said. "I take it Geri's doing good business."

He nodded. "Renting houses to refugees from the east from what I hear."

"I need to settle with him one day," I said, thinking out loud.

"What do you owe Geri?" Sibbi asked.

"It's a long story, but maybe my life. He took me in, fed me, and clothed me after I escaped those tunnels. I returned his kindness by killing one of his workers. Like I said, long story."

"I didn't mean to trouble you, m'lord," Sibbi said.

"You didn't know; no harm in asking. Still, let's give The Trader's Cup a wide berth. No sense stirring up trouble if I don't have to."

Sibbi nodded and spurred his horse to a trot, speeding us past the inn.

I noticed the crowds on the trade path grew steadily thinner the farther east we rode. We were almost alone before turning north toward Nikulas' hall. I couldn't help but remember riding in that wagon with Mam and the haircut I'd inflicted on her. Was life better or worse then? I guess the only safe thing to say is it was different. *So much has changed in a year.*

"Sire, not to sound disrespectful but are the rumors true?" Svan asked.

I laughed. "Which rumors?"

"You're going to remove Nikulas' title and take his land."

I turned to look at Svan. "Most rumors have at least a grain of truth. Nikulas will be the last man called skald in Croy. One could argue when I leave, he'll have more influence than he did when I arrived. I'm planning to appoint him as ambassador to Varia. He'll be my voice to the Varian crown, manage the relationship between our countries."

"But Eirick drove Varia out, beat them on their own land. Surely that means they are weak," he said.

"I used to believe the same as you," I said. "Then I met with King Ander of Varia. Eirick betrayed their trust and ambushed them after convincing the Varian royal court he was their ally. Worse, he had their daughter kidnapped while the royal family fled. I'd expect that kind of behavior from Satra. What my father did disgusts me. Believe me when I say Varia is vitally important to the future Croy. At the same time, they know if Croy falls, they fall soon after."

"I don't understand," Sibbi said. "Satra hasn't pushed past the forest."

"They haven't pushed past it *yet*," I said. "No one listens when I tell them Eirickson conspired with Satra. The Thanes claim he gave them my skati to keep them out of the rest of Croy. That was simply part of a bigger plan. Also, with Satra in control of so many of our resources, it's only a matter of time until we can't sustain a war against them. When that day comes, they'll take everything."

"I want to believe you, Sire," Sibbi said. "Your words sound true, but the whole thing...it doesn't make sense."

"Think about everything that has happened. If Varia had plans to invade, why pull the warriors from the eastern border? That's the perfect point for them to start the war, not some unknown path through the mountains. Why did Satra start raiding only after Eirickson took my defenses away? Their hit-and run-tactics were too fast, too random for my guard to respond to. The Thanes existed to keep Croy functioning and safe, yet they refused to secure my territory."

"You've given us a lot to think about, m'lord," Svan said. "Perhaps it's best if we concentrate on our duty and get you to Nikulas safely."

"Looking for a promotion, Svan?" I asked, smiling.

"No, Sire," he said. "Simply trying to do my assignment the best I can."

"That's a good start toward a promotion," I said, with a chuckle.

"As you would, my lord," he replied flatly.

Bior snickered behind me but didn't say anything.

Chapter 13

The sun had not quite reached its peak when the gate to Nikulas' hall came into view.

"No sudden moves as we approach the gate," I said. "Considering how close Satra is and the unrest in the capital, I'd hate for someone to mistake us for scouts or attackers."

"Agreed," Svan said. "Everyone mind your manners."

Sibbi chuckled for a moment. "Should I ride ahead and announce you, Sire?"

"Not a bad idea," I said. "A lone man presents less of a threat."

He bobbed his head once and pushed his horse to trot.

I watched as he reached the gate and spoke with the four men standing ready. He pointed back toward us before one of them nodded. His horse pivoted, and he waved to us.

Almost in unison, we urged our horses to trot.

"Tobias is waiting for us at Nikulas' hall with men ready to see to our horses."

I nodded to the guards. "Thank you for keeping everyone safe."

"Least we could do, Sire," the one nearest me said, while waving us through the gate.

The attitude inside seemed much less tense than what I'd seen every day in the capital. People smiled and waved at us. Several bowed once they realized who I was.

I felt some of my gloom leave my body at seeing the smiles. *This is what it's supposed to feel like to be a king.*

A man ran down the steps and greeted us. "So good to see you, King Fitzeirick. I trust your journey went smoothly."

"Tobias?" I asked.

He nodded.

"Well met," I said. "We made it here without any problems."

"Music to my ears," he said, with a smile. "If you would, please dismount and come with me. Stable hands will be out shortly to take care of your horses. One will show your men to the dining hall, or they are free to find food for themselves. I hope you don't mind having a traditional Varian lunch."

My mouth watered. "A Varian lunch—what a pleasant surprise."

"As we expected," he commented, as we climbed the stairs.

"We? Are there councilmen here?"

He shook his head and opened the door. "Not at present. But they send their regard. From what I know, Kurt is anxious to visit. Rumor is he has gifts for you."

"He should receive his invitation soon," I said. The scent of spices in the air grew stronger as we walked.

Tobias led me to a door, knocked, and stepped aside.

Nikulas stood just inside with his hand extended and a smile on his face. "I guess I have to get in the habit of calling you king instead of skald. Please, join me at the table."

He still carried a little more weight than he should, but at least the wrinkles around his bright, brown eyes had not deepened, and he'd had a chance to groom the mess of curly hair. It looked like a pile of dried straw if you caught him at the right, or wrong, time. I shook his offered hand. "I appreciate everything you did for me. To some extent, you made this possible. I'll also thank you now for everything you may do in the coming days and years."

"May we put off serious discussion until after we eat?" he asked.

"Of course," I said, following him to a small table with two chairs. Sunlight streamed in from an opening in the roof. The decorations were as I expected, bright cloth and paint. If I didn't know better, I'd say he belonged to a wealthy Varian family.

A servant placed a bowl of salad in front of me shortly after I sat. A pungent, smoky smell hit my nose when I plunged my fork into the greens. I looked at Nikulas.

"A recent creation of one of my Varian cooks. Mix it up, he layers the horseradish, spiced pear slices, and dried bread between smoked mustard leaves. I'm sure you've never experienced anything like this," he said, smiling.

"Horseradish? I didn't think it could be found in Croy."

"One of the advantages of having connections in Varia."

Mixing the greens around, the burn of horseradish joined in the smoky mustard. I took a bite and immediately decided it tasted better than the salad I'd had at the fancy eatery in the Varian capital. "This could be served in the Varian capital," I said, after swallowing.

"Only the best for our new king," he said.

I nodded. "How about something to drink?"

"I'm sorry. The spiced apple ale was still cooling when you arrived. I expect it will be ready shortly. I can call for some water if you'd like."

"I think I can wait a little longer. Gives my tongue a chance to get used to the idea of flavor again anyway."

He chuckled. "As much as I love my country, we have a lot to learn when it comes to cooking."

I nodded and continued eating.

I had nearly emptied my plate when a servant entered, bringing a pitcher and cups.

The ale was warmer than I would have liked, but the combination of sweet, spice, and bitter complemented the salad well.

As I refilled my cup, the servant returned carrying a tray. At first, I had a hard time recalling the smell layered with roast pork but, as he put the tray on the table, I remembered. Garlic. Mother had used it with a few dishes.

"Do you ever wonder why Croians don't use many of our native herbs in our dishes?" Nikulas asked.

"Honestly, no," I replied. "Probably because I grew up around so many Varians."

"True. I occasionally forget," he said. "You've had garlic before, I trust."

I nodded. "Not in a long time, though. This is an unexpected treat. When are we getting plates?"

"We aren't," he replied. "You eat this by peeling meat from the pig." He demonstrated by digging a finger into the soft flesh and pulling up a strip.

The garlic aroma rose from the opening, and my mouth watered more.

Following his example, I pulled off a piece and took a bite. Not as good as the red stag I'd had, but very tasty.

Between the two of us, we stripped quite a bit of meat from the pig, but at least another meal's worth remained when we'd had our fill.

"My guests will eat well this evening," Nikulas said. "I forget, are you staying the night?"

I shook my head. "I dare not stay out of the capital overnight. One of my generals may lock me out if I do. I'm here only long enough to discuss your future."

He frowned. "My future. I've heard rumors. What if I'm not willing to go along with your plans?"

I shrugged. "Ignore any rumors you've heard; I'm sure they're not entirely true. I'm trying to make your life easier...and more difficult, at the same time."

"You're not doing a good job of selling what you brought me," he said, still frowning.

"When I leave, one way or another, Croy no longer has skalds."

He nodded.

"Instead, you are the first Croian ambassador to Varia. I'm not taking your holdings, but you will no longer rule this skati—that's my job as king."

"What am I to do?"

I smiled. "Almost the same thing you're already doing. Meet with Varian representatives and occasionally travel to their capital. You are my voice in Varia. You maintain our relationship, looking out for Croy's best interest, of course, and keep the alliance strong when we start fighting Satra."

He eyed me suspiciously. "Why me?"

"Why not you? Other than me, you're the most familiar with their culture, and you're already in contact with Varian agents."

"I am not," he exclaimed. "That would have been treason under Jarl Eirickson."

I nodded. "You are, trust me. For example, how much do you know about Tobias?"

"He's served for me for years now. Started as a lowly errand boy and worked his way up. I trust him. He negotiated the trade agreement when the caravan arrived."

"The same caravan I traveled with, posing as a Varian guard?"

"I—" He stopped, mouth opened, and stared at me.

"The same caravan that left with King Ander's permission? The idea for that caravan started with a group called the war council. It's a group of criminals in Varia who operate with Ander's consent. The group came into being after Varia lost the far eastern skati. Their goal is to advance their country's ability to wage war."

He blinked. "What does that have to do with Tobias?"

"Before I answer that question, are Sabast and Halmar causing any trouble?"

"No. Sabast has voiced his anger at being banished here, but both men have offered their assistance if I need. I still don't understand what they have to do with our discussion."

I nodded. "Has anyone ever approached you about your desire to rule Croy, to be jarl?"

He crossed his arms and looked up at the sky. Several moments passed before he looked back at me. "Yes, years ago. A young man, Kurt, came with some other, older Varians to visit. Over drinks, in the middle of discussing a business deal, he brought up the idea. I told him, without hesitation, that I would not be party to treason. They left not long after that conversation. I never saw any of them again."

I pursed my lips for a moment. "I've met with Kurt. He's the one who sent Tindra after me. He's coming to visit me soon. I don't know if Tobias works directly for him, but he's connected with the war council."

"That's not possible," he exclaimed. "I've known him for so long. He's loyal to me, indispensable."

"Doesn't mean it's not true," I said. "Sabast came with me to act as Kurt's man in Croy, and Halmar is to be his right hand. I'm telling you this because they are already here. Varian agents are all around you. I'll bring Kurt for a visit when he's here if that will help convince you."

"If you're telling the truth, why do you need an ambassador?"

"Because I don't want them gathering power in Croy as they have in Varia. I know I won't be able to keep them out, but I'll do everything I can to keep them under control."

He shivered. "How can I help?"

"Gain their trust. Get them to let you in on their plans and feed me information so I can do what's best for Croy."

His shoulders sagged. "If that's what my country needs of me."

I stood and moved next to him, putting my hand on his shoulder. "Don't think of this as losing power. You will provide an increasingly valuable service to your people, this country, and me. Without you, I won't know what Sabast, Kurt, Tyres, and the rest of the council are trying to do here. They are coming. I can't stop it, and we have too much to gain from using them. What I can do is keep them from causing too much trouble or hiding their activities from me. That's what I need you to help with."

"Spying is a young man's game."

"You aren't a spy. You're an ambassador, hosting Varians and negotiating with them for the benefit of both nations. I'm not asking you to dig up secrets. Just report back what you learn."

He looked at me. "I keep my land?"

"The only thing you lose is the responsibility of ruling your people. I'll shoulder that burden."

He stood and offered me his hand. "Then Croy has its ambassador."

"Thank you. Your work will be appreciated. I trust you will spread the word to your people?"

"Yes, but who is going to tell Varia about this?"

"I'll inform Kurt when he arrives and send a letter to King Ander explaining your position. Obviously, neither of them will know your true purpose."

"Speaking of King Ander, how's your relationship with him now?" he asked. "His daughter *was* killed during your attack."

"I haven't spoken to him directly, but I don't think he holds me or Croy responsible. Also, he has bigger concerns. Eirickson had agents in place to kill him and his wife."

Nikulas' face lost color. "Please tell me they failed."

I frowned. "Not completely. Crum did his best to save everyone. Jesca is unharmed, but Ander has a broken arm, and Ines was severely wounded."

"When you talk to King Ander, please tell him I hope for the queen's recovery. Hard to believe Crum protected them. Even harder to believe Princess Jesca stood in front of me, and I didn't know it."

"*She* didn't know who she was then. How could you?"

"True," he said. "I still feel terrible for everything she went through."

"You contributed to getting her back home," I said. "Take pleasure in that."

He nodded and smiled weakly. "I know you want to get back to the capital. Thank you again, King Fitzeirick. I trust you to do what's best for our people. I'll send someone to bring your horses and find your guards. Travel swift and safe."

I thanked him again for accepting his new position and left. It didn't take long for our horses to arrive. The stable hands said my guards weren't far behind. I mounted and waited for them.

Another step toward fixing what's wrong with our country. I had expected Nikulas to accept my proposal, especially after pointing out how it would help our people. I hadn't considered what I would do if he refused. I couldn't afford to make another enemy;

those were stacking up faster than I could get rid of them. *Hopefully, Roi can guide me, help me see other possible outcomes. Perhaps I'm too optimistic.*

Before I could continue that line of thinking, my guards arrived. They all had silly smiles on their faces.

"I trust you enjoyed your visit?" I asked.

A chorus of enthusiastic, "Yes, Sire," answered.

"Did you partake enough that I should fear for my safety?"

"Of course not, m'lord," Svan said, suddenly serious. "It's not often we get treated so well. Made for a nice change."

"I know what you mean, but it's time to head home. Sibbi, Otkel...on you."

They wheeled their horses around and led us out of town at a brisk pace.

Chapter 14

The sun hung low in the sky as we passed The Trader's Cup.

"Sire, are you sure you want to ride all the way back this evening?" Svan asked.

I nodded. "Even if I didn't, stopping at the Cup would not be a good idea."

"As you say, Sire. Sibbi, let's get a move on."

The sun shined bright in our eyes as we entered the Scar. Something whizzed past me, and Bior cried out in pain. I saw a blur before something struck my left shoulder. Pain raced out from the blow. I blinked and looked down. An arrow stuck out of my chest.

"Ambush!" Svan yelled. "My lord, get behind us."

Andale pivoted when I yanked his reins.

"Run!" someone bellowed. Since I didn't recognize the voice; I assumed it was Otkel.

"I can't see them," Svan said. "Cover the king. Sire, get to safety."

I heeled Andale twice. He wasn't built to run fast, but he moved. *Safety. Where can I find safety? The Trader's Cup.*

I hated to run. An icy cold swept through me as I considered my men seeing me as a coward. Looking over my shoulder, I saw them not far behind me, arrows flying toward them.

People jumped aside as I sped past, toward the inn and Geri's wrath. I guided Andale to the back of the building. Grunting when my feet hit the ground, jarring my injured shoulder, I hurried in the back door.

Luta gasped, then yelled, "Who are— It's you! How dare you show your face around here?" She grabbed a nearby pan.

I raised my hand and tried to keep some distance between us. "I know I shouldn't be here, but I'm hurt. My guards and I were ambushed in the Scar. I don't know if they made it out. Please, help me."

I felt her pull strength from the floor, and she raised the pan higher.

Geri ran into the room. "What's all the— You! You may be king, but you're not welcome here. Leave."

I pointed to the arrow. "I'm hurt. Roi said you were a good man. Prove him right."

"How many others have you failed to protect?" he asked.

"Failed to...what? I met with Nikulas over lunch. Archers ambushed us at the Scar. My guards may be dead, I don't know. Please, help."

"Someone on your tail and you lead them here?" he said, face growing red. "Luta, keep the pan ready while I go see if anyone's outside."

Her chest heaved as she snorted breath in and out, her knuckles white from keeping a tight grip on the pan's handle. At least I had something to focus on other than the throbbing pain in my shoulder.

"Luta, I'm truly sorry for what happened with Slode," I said. "Didn't Geri tell you I tried to keep the peace?"

"This isn't about Slode," she said, harshly. "Geri curses your name daily for all the trouble you caused. All the people you endangered and left homeless."

I furrowed my brow. "What are you talking about? I got rid of my half-brother. I'm trying to make things better."

She spat at me. "Stupid. Useless. You declare yourself king and sit safe on the throne. All the while, Satra takes farms in the south."

"I know about the raids in *my* skati. That's what started all this mess."

She shook her head and spat again. "Not your skati—this one."

Geri returned before I could say anything else. "I don't see anyone. Guess you weren't followed. If you can still travel at night, I suggest you leave after dark. If not, you can sleep in the stable. I want you gone at first light."

"Is what she said about attacks in the south true?" I asked.

"Luta doesn't lie."

"Satra is on this side of the forest?"

"Has been for weeks," he said.

"And no one thought to tell me?"

"We've sent messengers to the capital every day since it started. Just like your brother, you don't do anything," he said.

"I'm nothing like Eirickson! No one has said anything about messengers or raids. I *will* do something as soon as I return to the capital, but I can't get back without help. I need an herbalist and men."

"I might be able to find an herbalist willing to help you, but you won't find any men here interested in fighting for you," he said, and left through the back door.

"Luta, you can put the pan down. I'm not going to hurt anyone."

She and I both turned toward the great room when someone banged on the inn's front door.

"Are you going to see what's going on?" I asked. "You're in better shape to fight than I."

"Coward," she barked, walking past me and still gripping the pan.

The door slammed against the wall. "Is the king here?" Svan shouted. "Has anyone seen King Fitzeirick?"

Ignoring the growing ache, I hurried from the kitchen before Luta did something we might all regret. "I'm here," I called out. "Geri's not happy about it, but he's looking for an herbalist."

Everyone in the room turned to look at me. The crowd wore a mix of surprise, disgust, and fear on their faces. All four of my guards came inside. Bior, with an arrow in his arm and another in his leg, leaned against his brother. Svan had blood running down his neck from a cut on his cheek. Otkel nodded to me before turning to look outside.

Svan smiled. "We feared the worst." He glared at Luta. "You, woman. We need a room. Now."

She spat at him. "Stable's out back."

Svan clenched his jaw, and the muscles in his sword arm flexed.

Several men rose from their seats, ready to fight.

"Stop!" I yelled. "Otkel, keep watch. You three, in the kitchen with me."

"We have a prisoner," Svan said.

My eyes opened wide. "A prisoner?"

"Best not talk about it here," he said.

"Stable's out back," I said, holding back a laugh. "I'll meet you there."

Andale grazed on the grass nearby. I grabbed his reins and guided him to the stables. Soon, my guards joined me with an unconscious, dark-haired, Satran soldier gagged and secured across one of their horses.

"How did Satrans get this far north without anyone seeing them?" I asked.

Svan shook his head. "It's Wary. He's in Vegar's company."

"You're sure?"

"We grew up with him," Sibbi said.

"Otkel, find some rope and tie him to a pole in the back of the stable. I'll talk to him after we rest," I said. "Wait, what's his talent?"

"I've seen him firesyth," Sibbi said.

"Then he can't work wood. What about stone?" I asked.

"I don't remember," Sibbi said. "Maybe."

"If he can draw strength from the ground, he'll get free. Find a bucket and a plank of wood. Fill the bucket with water, put it on a plank, and put his feet in the bucket."

"Good thinking, Sire," Sibbi said, and hurried out of the stable.

"Sire, no need to dirty your hands. I'll question him," Svan said.

I shook my head. "There's a bigger problem. I want you to watch the entrance. Did you know Satra's taking farms in the southern end of this skati?"

"No," he said, after looking at the other guards.

"Have you seen any messengers bringing word of attacks to the capital?"

"Again, no, but we've never guarded the southern gate," he said.

"Who has?" I asked.

"That gate is General Hallfrid's. Any of his commanders could have men there."

I frowned. "We need to find out where the refugees living here are from. Send Sibbi to the refugee houses to politely find out what's going on."

"What are you thinking?" Svan asked.

"I'm thinking not everything is as it seems. We saw many houses here, yet Satra left almost no one alive when they raided my skati. Geri accused me of not taking action on information from messengers I never heard from. Everything seems fine in the north; Nikulas didn't mention any raids. We're attacked by a Varian warrior wearing Satran armor. Did you see any of the others in the Scar?"

"I'm sorry, my king. We did not. The only reason we captured Wary is he decided to give chase. One man chasing four is a doomed man," Svan said.

"I'll save any other questions for him when he wakes. Odds are, we're sleeping out here, so get some straw down for bedding."

Svan shook his head. "I can't believe you're letting Geri get away with this."

"I have my reasons," I said.

"Of course, m'lord."

"Luta said I'd find you out here," Geri said, sticking his head into the stable. "Who's going to fix my front door?"

Svan growled.

"Calm yourself, Svan," I said. "Who's the best woodsyth?"

Otkel grunted from a dark corner in the back of the building.

"See to Geri's door."

He nodded to me as he walked past.

"Geri, did you find an herbalist?" I asked.

"Asdi's brewing something right now, be here when it's ready. Who's paying for this?"

"I've got gold in my purse," I said. "Once I'm back home, I'll send more if it's not enough, but I'm not paying a copper single until our wounds are treated."

"She'll be here when she's ready," Geri said.

"I'll also pay for a modest meal," I said.

"If Luta's willing to bring something down, we'll feed you," he said, and left.

"How dare he?" Svan said. "You're the King of Croy."

"Don't cause trouble. If everyone in his great room gets angered, we can't hold them off. They're upset with me—for good reason, it seems," I said. "If we haven't eaten by the time herbalist is done, I'll send Sibbi after food when he gets back from talking to the locals."

He nodded and moved to watch for anyone coming toward the stable.

Sibbi returned, talked to Svan for a moment, and set about keeping our prisoner separated from the ground. Once he finished, he hurried out of the stable, and I heard hoofbeats as he rode away.

Without anything to distract me, the throbbing pain in my shoulder got my full attention. I needed something else to focus on. "Bior, you going to make it?" I asked.

"Doing the best I can, Sire," he said. "Hope that herbalist gets here soon."

"You're worse than I. She'll see you first."

"No," he said. "You're the king. It's my duty to give my life for yours."

"And I won't let you...this time," I said. "Talk to me. What happened after I turned?"

"Neither Svan nor Otkel could get their bows ready; the arrows came too close together. We turned to leave the Scar. Soon after, men shouted, and I heard hoofbeats behind us. Svan signaled for us to split away once we got out. Wary rode out alone and chose to chase me and Svan. My brother and Otkel came after him. Sibbi clubbed him with the butt of an axe. He hit the ground, and his horse kept running."

"Why would one man chase four?" I wondered aloud.

"Didn't make sense to me either," Bior said.

"Lantern heading this way, low to the ground," Svan said, quietly.

I heard his sword scrape against its scabbard.

"Who goes there?" he yelled.

"Me," Otkel said.

"You alone?" Svan asked.

"He's helping me," an old woman's voice replied.

"I don't recognize your voice," Svan said.

"Asdi, herbalist," Otkel said.

"Put your sword away. See if you can help her," I said.

"Yes, Sire."

A short woman, not much more than half my height, entered the stable with Otkel close behind carrying a basket.

Svan shrugged and returned to watching outside the stable.

The golden-red light from the lantern made strange shadows across the herbalist's wrinkled face. "Who's hurt?"

"I have an arrow in my shoulder, but one of my guards took two—one in his arm and the other in his leg. See him first," I said.

"Sire, no," Bior said.

"I've lived this long and with worse injuries. See to him," I said.

"I've never treated a king," she commented, as she walked by.

"Croy never had one. At least not officially," I said.

Asdi called Otkel to her, "Bring my basket. And can you break the arrows for me?"

He grunted, and soon after, Bior moaned. I heard sticks hit the floor.

"I can't treat the wound," Asdi said. "He has to take his armor off."

More moaning and shadows danced on the wall.

"You might want to have something to bite on," she said. "I'm going to wash the wounds with the tonic I prepared. It's going to hurt."

I shivered, sending a bolt of pain down my arm, at the memory of the last time an herbalist told me to bite down on a musty piece of leather. No doubt she saved my life, but the cure was almost worse than the injury.

I heard popping as Otkel sythed the arrows apart.

Bior moaned while the herbalist slid the shafts out of his body.

"Done," she said. "Otkel, hold this cloth firm against the holes in his arm. I'll sew his leg closed first."

Screams replaced the moans.

"Hold still," she said, sharply.

"Now for the arm. Help him lay down on his side."

Sharp breaths hissed through Bior's teeth.

"Almost finished," she said. "Otkel, get the small clay pot and some bandage cloth from my basket while I tie this off."

I heard Bior hiss and moan again.

"Leave those bandages on and tied tight at least a day. Two would be better," Asdi said. "Try to sleep on your side to keep the bandages off the ground. Do not get them wet."

"Th—Thank you," Bior said weakly.

The herbalist studied my face before setting her lantern on the ground. "You're familiar with pain."

"Yes," I said. "And my head's been stitched before."

She nodded. "Then you know what to expect. Otkel, the arrow please."

The wooden shaft grew warm, popping when it split at my back.

I drew a sharp breath as he slid the arrow out of my shoulder.

"Sorry," he muttered.

"Shirt off," Asdi said.

"I'm having trouble lifting my arm," I said. "Can you cut my shirt off?"

Otkel pulled a knife from his boot and carefully slit the front of my shirt before peeling it off my bloody shoulder.

"Sit," she commanded.

"I know what's coming," I said. "Get it over with."

Otkel offered me a piece of the arrow. "Bite."

I nodded and let him slide it across my teeth. I closed my eyes and crunched the wooden shaft.

I'm sure I made the same sounds that came from Bior as she worked, but I kept my focus on the wood slowly splintering as my jaw tightened.

"All done," she said. "Same as him, leave that bandage on, two days if possible. Keep it clean and dry."

I spat out the stick and asked, "How long should we leave the threads in?"

"Ten days would be ideal but at least seven."

"Good to know. What do I owe you?" I asked.

"A silver and a copper."

I reached into my purse and handed her a gold double.

"I don't have coin with me," she said.

"Treat Svan's cheek, and we'll be even," I said.

"No need," he said. "It's already stopped bleeding."

"Consider us even anyway. I'm sure you had something better to do this evening than work on us," I said. "Thank you for your service. Many here would not have helped. Otkel, see her home safely."

"Of course, Sire."

"Svan, any sign of Sibbi?" I asked.

"No, m'lord."

I took more coins from my purse. "Take five gold doubles to the inn. Get food for us, even Wary, a shirt for me, and clothes for Bior."

"I have coin, my lord."

"I'm sure you do, but this is for all of us, and I gave you an order."

"Yes, Sire," he said, and took the coins.

Ache and fatigue were taking their toll. I'd started to nod off when Svan returned carrying a pot.

"Luta thickened the last of the stew broth with some grains. It's not even warm," he said.

"I've eaten worse," I said.

"Geri didn't send any bowls, just spoons. He said he'd have a shirt ready in the morning."

"You and Bior eat first. I'll stand watch," I said.

"You're hurt, Sire. Rest," he argued.

"I've lived through worse, and I'm a stonesyth," I said. "I can hold anyone back until you get here. Don't make me order you."

"Yes, Sire."

Standing near the stable's entrance, I pulled some stamina from the ground before pushing my talent out, searching for anyone moving in our direction.

Before long, I noticed something heavy moving at a steady pace and called for Svan.

Chapter 15

"Good timing—I can't stomach that slop," he said. "What do you need?"

"There's a horse heading this way. Hope Sibbi's on it," I said.

He looked out then back at me. "How can you tell? It's too dark for me to see anything."

"A wise king always has some tricks he doesn't share," I said, grinning.

"Of course, m'lord. Go eat. I'll greet whoever arrives."

Before I sat to take my share from the pot, I checked on Wary. I patted his cheek but got no reaction. Sagging against his bonds, he took shallow, unsteady breaths.

I shoved a spoon into the bland grains, flavored with cold chicken broth. *I have eaten worse.* You didn't chew the thick mass, more like softened it enough to swallow. Each bite hit my stomach like a pebble.

"Sibbi's back," Svan said, as I swallowed the last bite I could stand.

"Come eat, then tell me what you found," I said.

He sat next to his sleeping brother. "How's he doing?"

"Herbalist said we'd both live," I said.

"Good to know. What's for dinner?"

"It's food. Not sure what else to call it. Cold grains and chicken broth," I said. "There's plenty for you and Otkel when he gets back."

I couldn't see Sibbi in the dark stable, but based on the sound he made, I could imagine the look on his face when he tasted dinner.

"That...that is terrible," he said.

"Like I told Svan, I've had worse."

"I can't image what tastes worse than this."

"You probably wouldn't believe me if I told you," I said. "Eat. I want to hear what the refugees had to say."

He moaned and grumbled but choked down some food, then said, "Most of them didn't want to say anything to me. Seems they don't much trust anyone from the capital, especially warriors. The few who did talk said they came from the south of this skati. Not a single person said they were from the far east."

"Who's there?" Svan yelled.

"Me!" Otkel bellowed.

"Did you leave enough for him?" I asked.

"More than," Sibbi said.

I chuckled then groaned when my shoulder reminded me laughing was a bad idea. "Continue."

"Not much else to say, Sire. The people around here aren't happy with us."

Otkel sat and took the pot.

"It's all yours," Sibbi said. "Enjoy."

He mumbled something and started eating. Unlike the rest of us, he didn't seem to mind the taste—or lack thereof.

"I know," I said. "Seems like things are getting worse faster than I can fix anything. Truth be told, I think Eirickson allowed, maybe encouraged, the ill behavior of the warriors in the capital. Scared people are easier to rule, at least until someone gets brave." I rubbed my forehead. "I have to get the warriors behind me, somehow. I fear heads are going to be lost before the generals and commanders understand how serious I am."

"Sounds a lot like ruling by fear," Sibbi said.

"I know. Exactly what I'm trying to avoid," I replied. "I can't fix anything without knowing who's causing the problem, though, and it seems I can't get any answers without threats or worse." My eyelids drooped by themselves. "It's been a rough last half of the day. I'm going to sleep."

"As you will, Sire," Sibbi said.

"Otkel, syth the doors shut. We all need to rest," I said, taking my hammer from my back so I could lay down.

"Yes, m'lord," he replied.

· · · ● · ● · ● · · ·

Nickering horses disturbed my sleep. The sound of creaking wood and a bowstring drawing taut brought me wide awake.

Light streamed through gaps between the boards in the eastern wall, and Svan stood, his bow ready. "Open the doors at your peril!" he shouted.

The other guards bolted up. Bior groaned.

"Svan? That you?" Agrim asked, through the door.

"It is," he said, relaxing his bow.

"Is King Fitzeirick with you?"

"Yes, but he's hurt. So is Bior. How many men are with you?"

"Five," Agrim said. "What happened to the king?"

"I'll let you in, and he can tell you," Svan said.

Sunlight flooded the stable. I jerked my hand up to cover my eyes, and pain burst from my shoulder. Gritting my teeth to keep from yelling, I forced myself to stand. I'm sure I didn't have a pleasant look on my face.

Agrim rushed in. "Sire, what happened?'

"Ambush in the Scar late yesterday," I said. "Your men did a fine job of getting me out alive. An arrow caught me in the shoulder, but Bior's worse. He took one in the forearm and one in the leg."

"And we have a prisoner," Svan added, pointing to Wary. "It's not good news, though. One of Vegar's men wearing Satran armor."

"What?!" Agrim yelled. "Our warriors dressed as Satrans and tried to kill our king? What has he said?"

"Nothing," I said. "He hasn't regained consciousness."

"And he won't be," Sibbi said. "He's dead. Guess I hit him too hard when I knocked him off his horse."

"Never saw how many there were in the Scar," Svan said. "Only caught Wary because he got stupid."

"Or greedy," I commented. "I'm sure whoever put him up to the ambush is paying plenty for my death."

"Give me the word, m'lord," Agrim said. "I'll bleed Vegar myself."

I raised my hand. "Calm yourself. This will not go unpunished, but we have to gather more information first. We don't know enough to accuse anyone yet, and that can come back to bite us. Why did you come anyway?"

"Roi had us leave at first light when you didn't make it back by high moon," Agrim said. "If I'd have known, we would have ridden out immediately."

"If I'd expected an attack, I'd have brought more men," I said, smiling. "Svan, Otkel, go ask nicely for the shirt I paid for last night and see if Geri is feeling generous enough to provide some breakfast."

"We came prepared to search; we have rations," Agrim said.

I nodded. "Forget the food, but I want what I paid for."

"I'll get it, Sire," Svan growled. "One way or another."

"No," I said. "Ask nicely. Geri has his reasons. Causing more anger here won't help. If you can't do it, I'll send Sibbi with Otkel."

"It will be done, m'lord," he said.

"Captain, food and water. We ate a meager meal last night," I said.

He turned and yelled, "Ingo, Lopt! Food and water. Now."

The two men jogged in with saddlebags over their shoulders. They dropped the bags at my feet, handing me a hard roll, a handful of dried meat, and a bulging waterskin.

I quenched my thirst before chewing a piece of meat. *A vast improvement over my last meal.*

"We're in no hurry," I said, after swallowing. "Take your time to eat."

About halfway through the hard roll, Svan returned carrying something that looked like a cloak made out of a root sack. "Your...*shirt*, Sire," he said, and chuckled.

I shook my head. "I'll put it on after I finish eating."

I slid my right arm into the shirt's sleeve and draped the left side over my shoulder. It wasn't made from any cloth I recognized. I decided it must be woven straw or the like. The rough fibers scratched into my skin. "Agrim, put my hammer sling on to hold this closed."

After he buckled the strap across my chest, I guided my hammer to the magnets. It stuck in place with a comforting click.

"I'm going to get some fresh air while the rest of you finish eating. Sibbi, help your brother and see to his armor. Agrim, walk with me."

Chapter 16

Turning my face to the sun, I walked a little way past the stable. I stepped into a small dip in the ground. *Must be where I buried Slode.*

Coming to a small tree, I leaned against the east-facing side of the trunk. "Have you heard anything about attacks on farms in this skati?"

Agrim tilted his head. "Attacks here?"

I nodded.

He raised his eyebrows. "Not a word."

"No messengers from here have spoken to you?"

"No, Sire. I swear it," he said. "If even a rumor of more attacks had come to my attention, I would have told you directly."

"Relax," I said. "I'm not pointing blame, yet, simply asking a trusted source for information. Satra, or someone acting like them, has established a foothold in the south."

"Not that I doubt your word," he said, "but how do you know?"

"Sibbi asked the refugees living nearby. The ones that *would* talk to him all told him exactly what I told you. Geri said messengers had been to the capital to let me know. There are Croian citizens spitting at me because I've done nothing and let Satra take more land."

"We must drive them out," Agrim said, pointing south.

"No one wants to do that worse than me," I said. "But I don't trust even a single general will follow my orders. I can't fight a war with your company and five hundred Varian soldiers."

"If we do nothing, Satra gains more ground. They'll push through the Scar and come for the capital."

I nodded. "Sounds like you have a good grasp of what's at stake. Before I decide to torture Vegar, I'm open to suggestions on how to get the truth. I have to know why the messages didn't reach me and why Wary wore Satran armor. If we have traitors, they must be exposed and crushed."

"My men and I, we're not...Sire, we aren't spies. We don't do that kind of work."

I nodded. "I know, and I'm not asking you to, but someone has to know the truth. Someone took those messages. Someone provided the Satran armor and set the ambush. The list of people who want me dead is longer than I care to think about, but I'd bet their names are on that list."

"I'll think on this as we ride back to the capital, Sire."

I nodded. "Speaking of which, I'm ready to go. When we get back, we'll talk this over with Roi."

"Sounds like a good idea," he said.

The guards sat on their horses when we returned to the stable. Svan had Wary's body secured behind his saddle.

Mounting Andale, I groaned when the muscles in my chest aggravated my shoulder. The ride back to my quarters was a constant exercise in ignoring throbbing pain.

· · · ● · ● · · · ·

"Svan, put Wary's body in the compound courtyard, then take my horse to the stable and see he's fed and groomed. Agrim, keep two guards stationed at my door along with four at the gate at all times. Make sure your company knows someone ambushed us in the Scar, and it wouldn't hurt for them to suspect anyone in Vegar's company."

"I'll return for the meeting we spoke about after I talk with my men," he said.

I nodded, and replied, "Return as soon as you can."

Roi stopped mid-stride when I opened the door.

"Can't a king stay out all night without having someone send a search party?" I asked.

He glared at me, then softened his expression. "What are you wearing?"

"Long story. Have a seat while I change into a shirt that isn't made from thorny vines. I'll let you know what's going on while we wait for Agrim to return."

Removing my hammer sling with one hand was an awkward challenge. I tossed the shirt on the floor and pulled on a simple, woven, cotton one. Moving my left arm brought unwelcome agony, but the soft cotton felt like silk against my scraped skin.

Roi had a cup of water waiting for me at the table. I took a drink and explained how well the meeting went with Nikulas. His expression changed from a slight grin to a scowl as I told him about the ambush and running to The Trader's Cup for help.

"I'll speak with Geri about his behavior," he said.

"Don't be so quick to blame him before you hear the rest," I said, and continued explaining what we'd discovered.

His face went from red to pale as he listened. "We won't know if it's really Satra unless we send someone to those farms."

"But anyone we send risks capture or worse," I said.

He nodded as someone knocked on the door.

"I'll get it," he said.

Roi returned with Captain Agrim and offered him some water as he sat.

"I'm interested in your thoughts, Agrim," I said.

He shrugged. "I think we're still missing too much information."

Roi nodded with me.

He sighed. "A lot of truth died with Wary. It doesn't matter what your title is, Sire, a Croian tried to kill you. Worse, it was one of our warriors. Someone else has to know something."

"Are you certain all the Satran here at Eirickson's invitation were killed?" I asked.

"As certain as I can be," Agrim said, shrugging.

"So, you still could have Satran conspirators in hiding," Roi said.

"Obviously, we have some kind of hidden conspiracy," I said. "What we need is a way to find it."

"On your word, I'm ready to take Vegar into custody. This attack is exactly what I'd expect from him," Agrim said.

"Svan seems to agree with you," I said. "The problem is, the only evidence we have is a dead Croian warrior in Satran armor. Vegar could claim Wary hid his true loyalty." I rubbed my forehead before pointing at Agrim. "Who gains if General Hallfrid loses his power?"

"Agnor's his right hand and seems content to serve in that capacity. Commanders Haldan, Af'nid, Kolben, and Velief all follow Agnor's lead. All of them are too clever to get caught up in a weakly rooted scheme. If one or more are involved, ripping out the weeds will be difficult."

I stroked my beard. "Who will report Wary missing?"

"One of Vegar's company will tell Vegar. A search will start, and Vegar will report Wary has abandoned his company to Agnor, who will, most likely, tell Hallfrid immediately. Hallfrid should get word to you, but I wouldn't expect him to tell you in a timely manner...if ever," Agrim said. "But people saw Wary strapped across Svan's horse."

I shook my head. "I doubt anyone got a good enough look to recognize him. People saw a dead Satran brought in by one of my guards."

"So we wait for...what?" Agrim asked.

Roi snapped his fingers. "We don't wait. There are actions we can take. The Satran armor can serve a purpose. Take the armor, bury Wary, and wait for someone to mention his disappearance. They might lead to something useful, but we have a way to gather information now. Which of your guard is closest to his build?"

I squinted at Roi. "What do you have in mind?"

"You want to know what's going on in the south of Nikulas' skati, send a Satran soldier to look around," he said, smiling.

"Good idea," Agrim said. "Let me think. A few of my men might be close enough. I'll remove the armor to give me a better idea of the fit. Who's burying the body?"

"I'll do it," Roi said.

"That's a start," I said. "I have some business to attend to. That attack put me about a day behind. Agrim, have Sigric come here this afternoon. If I'm not back, he's to wait for me."

"As you wish," he replied.

"What are you going to do?" Roi asked.

"Tindra owes me a letter. I wanted to get it on the road to Varia yesterday evening. That reminds me, Agrim. I'll need a messenger too. He's to wait with Sigric."

"I'll handpick someone, Sire."

"Things may get worse soon," I said. "Who's guarding my door this morning?"

"Ingo and Lopt," Agrim answered.

"Thank you. I like to know who I'm walking with. Let's get this plan underway. There's a lot to do, and the sooner it's done, the better."

They nodded and left my quarters.

As bad as things are now, I have to believe we'll end up with a better Croy.

Chapter 17

Putting the sling back on to carry my hammer was an exercise in frustration. I ended up laying it on the bed, laying on top of the sling, and fumbling with the buckles until I had it in place. Despite the fact I couldn't fight, I wasn't leaving the compound looking defenseless. With my hammer in place, I grabbed the cloak I bought for Tindra and headed for the door. The guards bowed as I walked out.

"Where to?" one of them asked.

I looked at him. Loose curls of silver-gray hair flowed down the side of his head, leaving the top of his scalp empty and smooth. His blue eyes and unwrinkled face, combined with the fact his sandy-colored mustache hadn't turned gray to match his hair, told me he was younger than he looked. The lean muscle on his arms looked like a young man's also.

"You are?" I asked.

"Lopt, Sire. Proud to be of service," he answered, with a smile.

Turning to my other companion, I said, "That means you are Ingo."

He bowed low, causing his long, black braid to fall along his side. When he looked at me, I noted he had gray eyes, similar to Tundal's, but fair skin. *Probably not Satran.* Tall and thin, he reminded me of the running messengers used by the Varian military.

"Well met," I said. "I need to buy some meat from a local butcher. From there, I'm meeting a friend at Abi's house."

"You're safe with us," Lopt said.

The smiles and greetings as I entered the market square were a welcome change.

"I don't expect trouble but wait outside and keep your eyes open," I said, when we reached the butcher's shop.

"Back again?" Grith asked, when I entered. "Should I reserve a spot for the king?"

Several of his customers bowed when he called me king.

I chuckled and shook my head. "Just picking up some breakfast for a friend. What do you have?"

"Pork strips, fresh from the iron," he said. "How much do you want?"

Tapping my knuckle against my lips, I contemplated how much meat Abi would tolerate against how much meat Tindra would eat. "How much can I get for a silver single?"

"Enough to feed the three of you," he said.

"Give me half that amount, and you can have the coin," I said.

He shook his head and smiled while wrapping the sizzling meat. "Thank you, my lord," he said, bowing when I took the bundle.

"It's my pleasure," I said.

• • • • • • • • • •

"I may be a while. You don't have to stand at the door but keep the house in view."

"Abi doesn't eat meat," Ingo said.

"No, but her guest does," I said, and knocked on the door.

"What's that smell?" Abi asked, after opening the door.

"Freshly cooked pork for Tindra."

She curled her lip and let me in. "Good timing. She's in the garden ignoring breakfast."

"Does she have the letter I asked for?"

Abi nodded. "I helped her write it yesterday. Are you really sending the Thanes to an outcast home in Varia?"

I nodded. "You can't tell anyone, but I'm casting Boril and Porsey out of Croy because they're causing me trouble. Their families can help those people. Poetic in a way."

She walked with me to the garden. "Your secret's safe. You expect them to go along with it?"

"I'm making it sound like an honor. They aren't below deception, so why should I be? At least this deception is helping the country."

"Best of luck, Sire. Before you go in...what happened to your arm?"

"Caught an arrow in my shoulder yesterday."

She nodded. "Want me to look at it?"

"Before I leave, maybe. A herbalist sewed the wounds shut last night."

"Then you were probably well cared for," she said, and walked toward a different part of the house.

I walked into the garden to find Tindra in the same place I'd seen her last.

Her eyes brightened a little when she saw me, and her nostrils flared as I got close. "Meat," she said.

I smiled. "Good morning to you too."

"How much longer am I staying here?" she asked.

I put the wrapped meat in front of her. "From what I understand, you can leave whenever you think you're strong enough."

She opened the cloth, inhaled deeply, and growled before stuffing a piece of pork into her mouth.

"I brought you a gift," I said, placing the cloak on the table in front of me.

She smiled, kept chewing, and slid a folded piece of parchment toward me.

"The letter?" I asked.

She nodded and swallowed. "Exactly what you asked for, along with an assurance I'm alive and, mostly, well."

"Do you think your father will agree to hold them?"

"As long as they don't cause him any more trouble than Stina did."

"She lived there as punishment. They'll think it's an important assignment. I'll talk it up to be a significant honor. Do you want to know what I brought?"

She nodded before taking another bite of pork.

I held up the cloak. "I found someone who makes water-repelling cloaks. I bought one for myself and thought you'd like one."

She stopped chewing, and an expression moved across her face that I didn't recognize. Not joy or sadness, more like fear or anger. She swallowed. "Do you know where my sword is?"

"I have it. Made sure to get it out of the old council building before Halmar and I leveled it. Why?"

"I can't stay here if I'm going to get better, and I'm not going out unarmed."

"What brought this on?"

"You, that cloak. I know why you brought it."

"I told you. I thought you would like it."

She shook her head. "You wanted to remind me of what I used to be. That cloak represents the last time I *did* something besides feel sorry for myself. It worked."

I blinked and rubbed my forehead. "That's not why I bought it for you. I'm not trying to remind you of anything. Besides, you wanted out of the spion business...remember?"

"Hard to be much further out and still be breathing," she said. "I can be out but still be useful. That's what you're after, isn't it?"

I stared at her, slack-jawed. "I'm not after anything. This is a friendly gesture, nothing more. I don't have hidden motives with you. I'm not—"

She interrupted me by tossing a pork strip at my left shoulder.

Without thinking, I lifted my left hand to catch it, and the pain caused me to draw a sharp breath.

"You need me out there. Did you think I didn't notice you're hurt? What happened?"

I gave her a quick rundown of the ambush.

She ate and nodded as I talked, then took a long drink from the nearby pitcher. "What are you going to do about it?"

"Roi and the captain of my guard are working on the problem right now. We're putting plans in motion and gathering information. One thing we're not doing is acting just to act."

"Cautious and smart," she said. "Bring me my sword; I'm at your disposal."

"You've never been at my disposal. I don't treat people like that."

She shook her right arm at me. "I lost my hand for you. I killed my king's youngest daughter for you. I nearly died lying on a cold stone floor because I chose your side. You don't need to manipulate me with gifts—just tell me you need me. You know what I'm willing to do."

I rubbed my forehead. *At least she's getting her fire back.* "I didn't ask you to do any of those things. Stina attacked me, and you reacted, same as you would have for anyone else. It didn't matter that it was me getting cut or her doing the cutting. You saw a threat, and instincts kicked in. I could use your insight but not if you're still healing."

She tapped the stump of her arm on the table. "Wound's closed, stitches taken out weeks ago. I'm healed. Bring me my sword."

"I have some business to attend to. Roi and I will come back with lunch. I think you should talk to him before doing something you might regret."

"Don't forget my sword," she said, before biting into another pork strip.

I found Abi arranging containers and cleaning in her herb storage room. "I have a feeling Tindra's leaving today."

"Oh," she said. "Why?"

I shrugged. "I gave her a gift, and she yelled at me. Accused me of trying to remind her of being uninjured. I thought she would appreciate a nice cloak...how silly of me."

Abi frowned. "She hasn't said much to me about how she really feels. She's thanked me for the treatment and complained about the food, but she doesn't share much else."

"I think it's safe to say her past has given her trust issues," I said, with a weak smile. "Roi and I will come by later, and she'll probably leave with us. Thank you, again, for everything you've done. If you need anything, just ask."

"Thank you, my lord. You are too kind," she said, and curtseyed.

I nodded and left.

Ingo and Lopt hurried to my side about two steps from the house.

"Where to now, Sire?" Lopt asked.

"Back to my quarters," I said, leading them home at a hurried pace. Although I hadn't run since I last trained with the Varian guard, I felt proud to stay ahead of my guards. *Either I'm still in good shape, or they need to train more.*

"Stay here," I said. "I have something to take care of inside. I suspect when we leave, Roi and I will get lunch. You're welcome to eat with us."

"We're at your command, Sire," Ingo said, as both bowed.

Chapter 18

I walked inside to a full table with Roi, Sigric, and another man I didn't recognize waiting for me.

Sigric stood and bowed when he saw me. The other man jumped out of his chair and dropped to one knee. Roi nodded.

"Who's this?" I asked.

Sigric cleared his throat, "Svani, Sire, your messenger."

He stood a full head taller than me with long arms and legs, a runner's body.

"Good," I said, handing him the folded parchment. "I need to get this to Mikael, owner of the House of Daufi in the Varian capital. Make sure it goes directly to him and offer to wait for his answer. Don't be rude, I am asking for a favor, but impress upon him time is important. Also, if you must wait, enjoy your time there. You'd search far and wide to find nicer people."

"Yes, Sire," he said, head bowed. "I have my fastest horse prepared."

"Travel safe and swift," I said.

"Thank you, m'lord."

I waited for the door to close, before continuing, "Sigric, did your captain mention why I asked for you?"

"No, Sire," he said. "I figure it is related to the ambush, somehow. I swear on my life I had nothing to do with it."

I chuckled. "Sit. I didn't suspect you but, perhaps, you might have some insight into Vegar's activities."

He nodded. "Yes, I told you about the market square."

I shook my head. "Several people ambushed us. Someone put an arrow in my shoulder and two in Bior. Someone wearing Satran armor gave chase when we fled for safety. That someone is now dead."

"I don't understand," he said. "It sounds like you expect a confession."

I tapped my finger on my lips for a moment. "The dead man wearing Satran armor belonged to Vegar's company. Does anyone come to mind?"

Sigric's eyes opened wide, and his jaw dropped. The longer he stared at me, the more glassy his eyes became.

"I think you broke him," Roi said.

I snapped my fingers in front of his face. "Sigric, are you still with me?"

He blinked, shook his head, and stared at me a moment longer. "Sorry, Sire. I'm not sure I heard you correctly. Did you say one of Vegar's men, dressed in Satran armor, chased you?"

"Yes."

He shook his head again. "All the warriors knew General Hallfrid would kill you for what you did to him. Of course, none of us had any idea he would do something underhanded. Where would he get Satran armor?"

"Forget about the armor, for now," I said. "I've been told Hallfrid likes to humiliate people out in the open," I said. "Do you think he would set an ambush?"

Sigric shrugged. "Anything is possible, but he's always attacked in the open before."

"Perhaps the general thought an ambush would throw off suspicion," Roi commented.

"I doubt it," Sigric said. "He wants to be seen taking down opponents. That's why everyone fears him; he's not scared of anything...except you, Sire."

"Then Vegar set the trap?" I asked.

"Sergeant Vegar's a bully, chooses targets too weak to fight back, but Commander Agnor...he'd have no problem setting an ambush, especially if he thought it would gain favor from General Hallfrid."

"I need proof," I said. "Find out who planned the attack and who gave the order."

"Would be nice to know how they found out your travel plans," Roi added.

I waved my hand at him. "Enough people saw me leaving. We weren't being overly cautious. Someone could have easily followed us until we turned north and ridden back with plenty of time to place the archers in the Scar."

He nodded.

"The next part of this puzzle is worse. Satran soldiers, or someone acting like Satran soldiers, have taken farms in the southern part of the eastern skati. Considering some of our warriors dressed in Satran armor, am I looking for a rebellion inside our army?"

"I haven't heard word of a rebellion," Sigric said. "Pardon my asking, Sire, but who wore the armor?"

"Wary. What do you know of him?"

Sigric smiled. "He's an archer, but not one of Vegar's best. He's also sneaky and ambitious."

"Glad you didn't say he was smart. Any other sneaky, ambitious archers in your old company?" I asked.

He shook his head. "None like him, but the archers all tended to stick together. You don't know how many were involved?"

"No," I said. "We never saw them. If Wary hadn't tried chasing four people at once, we'd know nothing."

"I'm sorry, Sire," he said, shrugging his shoulders. "I don't know what else to tell you."

"Keep your eyes and ears open, but don't draw suspicion and don't say anything. Very few people know Wary's dead. We hope to use that to our advantage."

"I know nothing," he said, with a smile.

"Good. You're dismissed. Find Captain Agrim and see if he has anything for you to do."

He stood and bowed. "Yes, m'lord."

Rubbing my forehead, I waited until the door closed. "I can't fix problems fast enough," I said, with a sigh.

"What else is wrong?" Roi asked.

"Tindra."

"She seemed fine when we spoke."

I nodded. "She seemed fine when I took her breakfast before I gave her the cloak."

"She didn't like the cloak?"

"I thought it might bring some cheer. Instead, she seemed to get...I don't know. Angry or afraid or...something. She accused me of trying to manipulate her before she noticed my arm. I told her what happened, and she demanded I bring her sword. Said she would leave Abi's to help me but she wasn't going out unarmed. I know you want to keep what you told her between the two of you, but I'd appreciate some help."

"Did you talk to Abi?"

I nodded. "She says the wound has healed, but Tindra doesn't talk to her much. Never says anything about losing her hand."

"I won't violate her trust, not that she trusts me much anyway. I'm comfortable saying she's afraid...afraid she can't take care of herself anymore. I'd guess knowing someone tried to kill you reminded her of Stina's attack and everything that happened after. Here's a question for you: if she leaves Abi's house, where is she staying?"

I shrugged. "A room here, I guess. Speaking of which, housing for the guard."

"Don't change the subject. Is it a good idea for her to stay here?"

"Maybe. Kurt's coming. He wants to visit her. I don't want to take him to Abi's. Maybe Tindra will feel safer here, behind the wall."

He nodded. "I can see some sense in your thoughts. That might be good for her. Are you going to offer or wait for her to ask?"

I shrugged. "What difference does it make?"

"If you offer, it puts you over her. If she asks and you give in, she exercises some power. It might make her feel more able."

"I'll wait for her to ask for her own good. If she doesn't, I'll offer," I said.

"Sounds like a plan. Go get her sword. We can talk about the guard housing on the way."

"With two of my guards present?" I asked.

"You don't want them to know about where they'll live?" he asked, with a smirk.

"Good point. No reason to keep it a secret," I said, and left to get Tindra's sword.

"A bit early for lunch, isn't it, Sire?" Lopt asked, as I stepped outside.

I nodded. "We'll eat after I'm done at Abi's."

"Who's the blade for?" Ingo asked.

"A friend," I said. "Roi, about the guard's quarters."

"Captain Agrim and I talked it over. He's in no hurry to build anything. His men can stay where they are now, and if Porsey and Boril are leaving for Varia, his men would convert those homes into barracks. If that's not an option, we agreed to find a suitable location, near the compound, to house your guard."

Pointing to the guards walking with us, I said, "This isn't going to happen tomorrow. Your captain will let you know when it's time to move."

"Understood, m'lord," Lopt said.

We arrived at Abi's house and told the guards to stay close by, like before, while Roi and I talked to Tindra.

They nodded and took their positions a few paces away.

Abi opened the door and welcomed us into her home. "She's in her room."

I nodded. "Lead the way."

When we arrived at the door, Abi moved to open it.

I stopped her. "I'll knock. Let her decide if she wants us to come in."

The herbalist looked at me before moving to the side.

I knocked on the door.

"Who's there?" Tindra asked.

"Fitzeirick and Roi," I said.

"Did you bring it?"

"Yes," I said.

"Come in."

We stepped into a cozy room, similar to the guest rooms at House of Daufi, except with wooden fixtures and furnishings.

Tindra sat in a chair with the cloak draped over the back, wearing a simple, long-sleeve, tan, woven dress, and leather thong shoes.

"Are you sure you want to leave?"

She nodded. "It's time, and you need me."

I shook my head, but before I could say anything, Roi sat across from her.

"Like I said before, you're here to heal both your arm and your mind. Loss isn't easy. I didn't lose a hand, but I lost a family. Can't say I understand what it means to lose a hand, but don't risk yourself because you think Fitzeirick needs you."

"I'm not happy here. All I do is sit in the garden or sit in this room. I don't want to be a burden on Abi; she doesn't deserve that. I've been scared to leave, knowing Sabast could come after me, but I can't get over the fear by staying here. It's time to go." She stood. "Clip the scabbard to my belt on my right hip, please, Fitzeirick."

Once the sword hung in place, she reached for it, slid the blade partially from the scabbard, and nodded as she slid it back in.

"That's going to take some practice," she said, before fumbling her way into the cloak.

"Need me to carry anything?" I asked.

"No," she said. "Anifas took the armor. Didn't have anything else of value with me."

"Off to lunch it is," I said. "I hope you don't mind if a couple of guardsmen join us."

She shook her head. "Most kings don't eat with their guards."

I grinned. "I'm not most kings."

Roi chuckled.

Despite telling her about the guards, Tindra jumped when they approached a few paces from Abi's house.

"Nothing to worry about," I said. "This is Ingo and Lopt, my guard detail. Ingo, Lopt, this is Tindra, a friend of mine."

They bobbed their heads.

"Correct me if I'm wrong," Lopt said. "You were part of the attack."

She looked at him for a moment before nodding.

"She's allowed to come and go from the compound as she pleases," I said. "Pass the word around."

"Of course, Sire," Ingo said.

"Then we're off to lunch. Follow me."

Tindra looked winded by the time we reached Grith's shop.

"You sure you're ready to be out like this?"

She nodded. "I've done more sitting than walking for nearly two months. I'll live."

Chapter 19

I smiled at her, and said, "Grith, what's for lunch?"

"Broiled rabbit sandwiches and pear cider."

Out of the corner of my eye, I noticed Tindra lick her lips.

"One for each of us," I said.

"Two for me," Tindra added. "I need to get my strength back."

"You heard her," I said, and chuckled.

He sat plates and mugs along the counter and filled them with sandwiches and a pale-yellow liquid.

"How much?" I asked,

"A silver double for the food and a silver single for the drink."

I pulled a gold double out of my purse and tossed it to him. "Keep the rest."

He smiled. "If the other vendors hear about this, people are going to start accusing you of bribing me."

"Who knows," I said, shrugging. "There may come a day I can't afford to pay you so well."

He shook his head, and said, "That would be a sad day," before serving more customers.

I bit into the sandwich. The firm, bland bread held shredded rabbit meat. The sharp cider made up for the simple bread.

The guards seemed eager to eat and finished their meal first. "We'll wait for you outside," Ingo said.

Roi and I tried to pace ourselves, so Tindra wasn't the last one eating.

She tore into the first sandwich like a starving animal then took her time eating the second. After finishing her cider, she asked, "Where to now?"

"That depends on how you feel and what you'd like to do," I said.

"I feel better with some real food in my stomach. Would you show me where you're living?"

I nodded, and we left the butcher shop. Ingo and Lopt fell into step beside us, and we cut a wide swath through the crowd before turning toward home.

"What is this place?" she asked, when the walls came into view.

"The Thanes' compound. Each man on the council has a house. I'm living in the one belonging to the Thane I killed," I said.

"You don't have a castle?" she asked.

"Haven't even thought about building one...too many other things to take care of. We can talk inside."

She nodded while looking around. I couldn't tell if she was taking in the sights or not, but she didn't move with her typical wariness.

We stopped at the gate, and I introduced Tindra to the men there, telling them she could move about freely.

Roi tapped me on the shoulder. "You and Tindra catch up. I have some things I need to see to. I'll be back when I'm done."

"Anything I can help with?" I asked.

He shook his head. "Getting ready to send for my family."

I nodded and led Tindra inside.

Ingo and Lopt took their positions near my door as we entered the building.

Tindra looked around after I closed the door. "I wasn't sure what to expect, but bare stone walls and simple wooden furniture wasn't it."

"I threw out the Thane's extravagant furnishings. I'm not planning to live here forever but didn't want a constant reminder of what I fought to remove."

"Understandable," she said, sitting at the table. "What's the situation?"

I told her about the fight with Hallfrid, all the corruption I'd uncovered, my successful meeting with Nikulas, the activity in the southern end of the eastern skati, and the Croian warrior in Satran armor.

She whistled and shook her head. "You've been a busy man. Making enemies and some friends and getting deeper and deeper into trouble. I'm not in good enough shape to be much help now, but give me some time. I need to learn how to fight left-handed."

"I've seen you wield two swords; it shouldn't be that hard."

She chuckled. "You never noticed I always lead with my right?"

"Guess not. I was too busy dodging to pick up details like that."

She smiled. "You learned enough to win."

"We got lucky," I said. "Any other time, I'm not sure we'd have made it inside the building."

"Ambushes are typically successful, especially when no one expects an attack." She pointed to my shoulder. "You're going to need to work those muscles after the stitches are out. We can help each other. There's plenty of room in the courtyard."

"We'll see," I said. "Don't forget, Kurt's coming, and he wants to see you. What do you need to get ready for that?"

She frowned. "Clothes—I'm not much for dresses. A place to stay. But I have no coin. I'd have to find someone I trust to bring my cache from home. Is Varian coin good here?"

"I'm sure it's good around Nikulas' hall, but I haven't seen any in the capital. I'll gladly cover your expenses; Eirickson left behind a fortune. What did you have in mind?"

"You know what I wear. Another set of silks would be nice too, but I doubt I'll find any here, and a set of leather armor. I have a feeling I'm going to need it after all the trouble you've caused."

I shook my head and grinned. "You don't have to get involved. You wanted out, stay out."

"I thought about it," she said, eyes shifting to the end of her arm as her shoulders slumped. "Sitting in the garden at Abi's while she took the stitches out of my arm. It gave me something to distract from the irritation of the thread sliding through my skin. What would I do? Make a home somewhere, have a couple of kids to raise, cooking and cleaning? I never aspired to that. I always wanted action, adventure. I thrive when my heart is pounding. I have to be involved in something."

"I know I can't stop you, and I could use more friends," I said. "Also, I'd rather have you on my side. I know who to ask about clothes and leather."

"Can I stay here until I can find a place of my own?" she asked.

"Of course. I have plenty of room. Roi's staying here for now, but I don't think that will be the case much longer. Will it bother you if my guard ends up living in the compound?"

"No problem, as long as they stay out of my way."

"I can make sure of that."

She closed her eyes. "Do you know why Kurt wants to see me?"

I shrugged. "He didn't give me any specifics. Perhaps because you're a friend and he's concerned about you?"

She shook her head. "Kurt doesn't have friends; he has resources."

"Do you want me here when you talk with him?"

Her eyes flew open, and she stared at me long enough that I began to feel uncomfortable.

"Did I say something wrong?" I asked.

"No, I...I'm worried. What if he's coming to take me to Sabast?"

"I won't let him."

She pointed at me. "You won't jeopardize your alliance with Varia to save me."

"Kurt doesn't waste resources, does he?" I asked. "Ander won't let our agreement fail either. If Croy can't stop Satra, Varia falls next."

"With an injured wife and a dead daughter on his mind, Ander may not be thinking about what's best for Varia."

"You did what you had to...kept me safe," I said. "I'll do no less for you."

She nodded. "I believe you."

"Good. Ready to see someone about new clothes?"

Her face brightened. "Sounds like something I could enjoy."

"In that case, I know a good place to start."

Chapter 20

We walked out to find two new guards near the door.

"Where are Ingo and Lopt?" I asked.

"Serg...umm...Captain sent us to relieve them, Sire. I'm Ivar, that's Erland."

"Well met, this is Tindra."

They nodded to her. "Lopt told us she was staying here," Erland said.

"Keep spreading the word," I said, nodding.

I led the group to Fastan's shop in the nearby market square. "I brought you a customer," I said, as Tindra and I walked inside.

She looked up from her loom and smiled. "What can I do for you?"

"Shirts and pants?" Tindra asked.

"I sew shirts and dresses—don't have enough time for pants too. How about we go in back, and I measure you?"

Tindra nodded and followed her through a doorway.

I stepped back out and motioned to Ivar.

"Yes, Sire?"

"Where does my guard eat in the evening?"

"Those of us not on duty get food from the mess and eat in our barracks. Other companies won't let us eat in peace now that we aren't under Commander Ottar."

"Good to know," I said. "Get word to your captain to have two extra plates ready. Tindra and I will dine with you. When we leave here, we're going to another shop across the way. You don't have to say at my side, just keep me in sight."

"As you wish, Sire."

I smiled and walked back inside.

"...three long sleeve and three short sleeve, one each in black, red, and natural, is that right?" Fastan asked.

"Yes," Tindra said.

"I'm sorry I don't have any silk. I could ask around." Fastan said.

"Don't go out of your way," Tindra said. "It's more of a want than a need."

"How much do I owe you?" I asked.

Both women flinched and turned toward me.

"I'm sorry, m'lord," Fastan said. "I didn't see you there."

I chuckled. "No need to apologize. How much?"

"For you? Three silver singles."

"That's better than fair. Will you take a gold double?"

"Only if you take a silver single in change," the weaver said.

"I'd rather you keep it. Grith doesn't mind a little extra," I said.

"I'm not Grith," she said, putting her hands on her hips.

"Give Tindra the silver," I said, and handed her a coin.

Fastan slipped it into a pocket in her dress and gave Tindra a silver single. "They should be ready in three days."

"No hurry," Tindra said. "But I am looking forward to getting out of this dress."

"Don't get your hopes up," I said. "Thorgault may take longer to make pants if he can make them at all."

"If he can't, you'll find someone who can."

I nodded. "Let's go talk to him."

The tanner's shop smelled the same but looked a little cleaner, more organized. As before, he worked at stirring something.

"Thorgault," I said. "I'm back, and I brought a customer."

He looked up as I spoke and nodded. "That the lady ya bought tha cloak for?"

"The same," I said. "This is Tindra, a good friend."

He bowed to her. "The pleasure's mine, m'lady. What canna do fur ya?"

"I need pants," she said. "Can you make split goat hide?"

The tanner raised his eyebrows. "Lady's got expensive taste. I can, but it's work."

"I can pay for your work," I said.

"If you're payin', I'm workin'," he said, with a smile.

Tindra nodded. "Six pairs of split goat hide, dyed black."

"How 'bout from black goats?" he asked.

"As long as they match," she replied. "Can you add a scabbard strap on the right hip?"

"If ya have yur weapon wit ya."

"I do," she said. "Finally, how are you at making armor?"

"Ya want that split too?"

"No, I need fighting armor. Make it black too," she said.

"I can make something nice fur ya," he said.

Tindra nodded and smiled. "One special request: it must move with ease. I'm not big enough to trade blows. I have to be able to dodge."

"No problem, but it'll take time."

"I'll try to stay out of trouble until it's ready," she said, and chuckled.

"Not ta be improper, but I gotta measure ya."

She looked at me and winked. "No problem for me. Should I undress here?"

I sighed. *She must be feeling better.*

"Got nothin' ta cover ya with," Thorgault said.

She pulled off her cloak and handed it to me before struggling to unbuckle her belt and giving it and the scabbard to Thorgault.

He looked her weapon over as she shed the dress.

I sucked in a breath. It seemed like long ago, the first time I'd seen her undressed. The familiar scars were still there, but she'd lost weight, and I couldn't stop staring at the heavily scarred end of her right arm.

"I don't like the way it looks either," she said, with a frown. "But what choice do I have?"

"If ya don't mind me askin', what happened?" the tanner asked.

"My last armor didn't let me move fast enough."

"Oh," he said, then went to work measuring her with a rope and a stick, making notes as he went.

By the time he finished, Tindra had a bit of a blush over most of her body.

"Embarrassed?" I asked, as she slid the dress back on.

"Not as such," she said, with a grin. "But between the seamstress and... It's been months since I've been touched so much. Would you help me with the belt and cloak?"

I nodded and helped her finish dressing.

"When will her order be ready, and how much do I owe you?" I asked.

The tanner rubbed the back of his neck while looking over his notes. "Six days, five if I'm lucky, for tha pants. Armor'll take at least a month, say six weeks. How's three gold doubles for the pants and ten gold doubles for the armor sound?"

Tindra looked at me, eyes wide.

"What if she doesn't like something you make?"

"I'll make it right, no cost."

"Fair deal," I said, nodding before handing him the coins.

"'Preciate the business, m'lord."

"If I like your work, I'll send more your way," I said.

"Get ready ta line 'em up," he said, with a smile.

Chapter 21

When we walked out of the shop, a few people stared at Tindra.

"Looks like you made an impression," I whispered.

She shook her head and muttered, "Croians."

I chuckled and asked, "Anyplace else you want to go?"

She shook her head. "I'm feeling a bit winded. Could we go back to your home so I can rest?"

"Of course," I said, as the guards took their places next to us.

Getting close to the compound, I turned to Ivar. "Go find your captain. Tell him about tonight's meal and ask him to see me when he can."

"Yes, Sire," he said, and headed toward the barracks.

"What about tonight's meal?" Tindra asked.

"It's a surprise," I said, with a grin.

The guards at the gate bowed as we passed, and Erland walked to a shaded spot near my door.

"My room's at the end of the hall," I said. "Roi is using the last room on the right. You're welcome to the room on the left."

"Thank you," she said. "Will you take the cloak and my belt off? I'm going to lay down and rest for a little while."

"Glad to help," I said, handing her the belt and cloak back.

After her door closed, I took a seat at the table. *There's much to do and not much time to prepare. If Kurt and Aerison aren't here tomorrow, they'll arrive the next day...bringing news, maybe more problems. I hope to hear from Mikael soon. If Tindra's father agrees to hold Porsey and Boril in Daufi, I have to convince them to leave. Roi's preparing for Grima and Einns to join him. I won't have his complete attention afterward. The generals and Satra and Wary and... Maybe being king and doing away with the council was the wrong idea. How does Ander keep track of everything demanding his attention? Ah, his country isn't on the verge of tearing itself apart while preparing to fight off another nation.*

I put my head in my hands and breathed, trying to clear my thoughts and focus on something. I jumped when someone knocked on the door. "Who's there?"

"Captain Agrim, Sire. You sent for me."

"Oh, oh yes...of course. Come in."

"What do you need?" he asked, stepping inside.

"Sit," I said. "I wanted to know if you had talked to Kodren about using the Satran armor."

He shook his head. "The more I think about it, the less I like the idea. What will my men think of me if he never comes back?"

"I understand your concern, but we need information," I said. "If nothing else, we must know if Satra has taken land in Nikulas' skati. I can't make an informed decision without sending someone to find out."

"What difference does it make? Are you going to let Croians in disguise hold the farms?"

I shook my head. "If it *is* Croians, I don't have to take on the whole nation of Satra right away. I simply send enough warriors to kill the rebels."

"Makes sense," Agrim said. "Is that all?"

"Has anyone heard anything useful? Anyone looking for Wary?"

"No reports so far."

I nodded. "I'm expecting five hundred Varian soldiers in the next day or two. Figure out how we're going to house them."

"With Elias and his company?"

"There isn't enough room on those grounds," I said.

"Right...we'll need someplace bigger. How will we feed five hundred more men?"

I pointed at him. "I made your company my guard and left you in charge because you've been loyal to me and proven yourself intelligent and resourceful. Don't disappoint me."

He looked away from me. "Of course, Sire. Anything else?"

"Trust me, there's always something else. For now, find someplace to house those soldiers and arrange for some stonesyths and woodsyths to put up decent, temporary housing."

"Yes, Sire," he said, and left.

"That's how he does it," I said aloud.

"How who does what?" Tindra asked, from behind me.

I whipped my head around, pulling some muscles in my shoulder, and groaned.

"Shoulder?" she asked.

I nodded. "I'd been trying to figure out how Ander gets everything done. After meeting with Agrim, I realized he uses everyone around him to take care of what he can't attend to himself."

"You're just now figuring it out?" she asked, scratching her head.

"Agrim's one of the few people following my orders right now."

She frowned. "That must change, or Satra's going to tear your country apart once they decide they're ready."

"I know," I said. "I'm making moves as quickly as I think I can get away with them. Getting rid of Porsey and Boril without shedding more blood should be a big help. If I can find a way to pin the situation in the east on General Hallfrid, I can charge him with treason and get rid of him without much backlash. That could help my relationship with the other generals."

"And if you can't prove his involvement?"

I shrugged. "I'm not sure. Someone knows something. I can't believe Wary's the only Croian involved. I suspect all the ambushers were warriors in disguise but no one's talking."

Tindra closed her eyes and tapped her fingers on the table for a moment. "Who's missing?"

"What do you mean?" I asked.

She looked at me. "No one's talking, but is anyone other than Wary missing?"

I shrugged. "How would I know? It's not like I recognize every warrior."

"Order a head count," she said. "Have your generals account for every man under their control."

I chuckled. "The same generals who won't follow my orders? Hallfrid would probably give fake counts and try to make me look foolish when I didn't know the difference."

"Your only other option is to have patience," she said, and pointed at me. "No conspiracy stays secret forever."

"Like the war council?" I asked, raising my eyebrow.

"Ander knew about them and allowed it to exist until he needed something, or they caused problems. If they were well established here, you could use them for some of your dirty work. They worked well enough to fool Crum."

"Don't give them too much credit," I said. "He was desperate to find me or what happened to me. Running from Eirickson after he stumbled into that meeting made his situation even worse."

"Crum discovering the meeting proves my point. No conspiracy stays hidden forever," she said, looking smug.

"Once I can move my arm again, I'm going to wipe that look off your face," I said, and stuck my tongue out at her.

"You're welcome to try," she said. "But if you come at me with that thing sticking out, you might lose it. Hard to rule when you can't talk."

"You do know most rulers wouldn't allow open threats to go unpunished."

"But you are not most rulers."

I sighed. "You're right. I'm not. Most rulers would have executed Hallfrid."

"Because you didn't, you're a better man, but don't let people take advantage of your compassion," she said. "Otherwise, it becomes a weakness."

"And kings can't be weak."

"At least not when their subjects can see them. You can't be strong all the time."

"For the foreseeable future, being weak is a luxury I can't afford."

"You have to let your guard down sometime. If we're still friends, you can be weak in front of me. I won't tell anyone."

"We are, and thank you."

"Before you break into tears, are you going to tell me where we're eating dinner?"

"You surprised me with a meal. Maybe I'm repaying the favor," I said, grinning.

"Hmmmmm," she purred. "I could use a nice steak."

"I doubt it's steak, and I didn't say it would be a nice meal. Regardless it *is* a surprise."

"If there's no meat, we aren't friends anymore," she said, crossing her arms.

"Where would you live if you ended our friendship? A king can't have strangers living in his quarters, especially a strange Varian woman. Think of the rumors."

She flashed a predatory smile and cocked her head to the side. "Unlike most Croians, I don't mind rumors. Give me half a chance, and I'll use rumors to my advantage."

"I know all about you and rumors," I said, shaking my head. "Let's make our way to where we're eating tonight. Even if we're early, we can make conversation with the men we're joining."

She squinted her eyes. "Is this anything like your idea for us to live with the Varian guard?"

Taking a moment to study my fingernails, I quietly said, "Maybe."

"What made you think this was a good idea?"

"I need to spend time with the men I trust to protect me."

"Why am I going?"

"Because you need to be around people. Plus, you may spend some time training with them. Don't you want to know who you're beating on?"

"You've got a point there. I'll make the best of it," she said, then laughed. "Should I wear my sword? Remember the last time we went out for the evening?"

I nodded. "How could I forget? We'll have guards with us this time, so I doubt anyone will attack us. Still, if it makes you feel better, wear it."

She left the table and came back with her belt and sword. "Help me put it on, please."

After getting her belt buckled and sword settled in place, we left for the barracks.

Chapter 22

Ivar and Erland stood nearby and joined us as we walked to the gate.

"Where to now, Sire?" Ivar asked.

"Your barracks," I said.

"Dinner is still a while from now, m'lord," Erland said.

"Is there a problem if I arrive early?"

"Of course not, Sire," Ivar said. "You're welcome to visit any time."

"Good to know," I said, as we passed the gate.

Erland stopped us at the barrack's door. "Let me go in first. I'll announce you and make sure no one's going to embarrass Lady Tindra."

She snickered. "I'm difficult to embarrass."

"In that case, I'll make sure no one's going to embarrass themselves," he said.

I nodded.

He stepped inside, and called out, "King Fitzeirick and Lady Tindra have arrived."

Ivar bobbed his head, and said, "Please go in, Sire."

The beds had been stacked and pushed to the far end of the simple, stone building to make room for enough tables for twenty, or so, men.

"Where would you like to sit, Sire?" Erland asked.

I chuckled. "My back to the wall, away from the door. I'm carrying my hammer out of habit right now, but I'm in no shape to fight. If someone gets stupid and attacks while we're eating, I want as many of you between me and them as possible."

Several men laughed before moving so I could sit at the far table. Tindra followed and sat to my right.

Svan sat to my left, hawkish eyes lingering on Tindra. "Who did you bring, Sire?"

"I'm Tindra," she said, reaching across me to offer her hand.

He smiled, took her hand, and looked her in the eyes while brushing his lips across her knuckles. "Well met. I'm Svan. It's rare to have such beauty visit our humble quarters."

Tindra didn't pull her hand back and met his stare. "I question the wisdom of anyone who flirts with a woman accompanying the king."

He sputtered and looked away, smile vanishing. "I—I meant nothing...it's...simply—"

"You should meet Anifas," I said, interrupting his attempted apology.

"A Varian boy in a man's body," Tindra said. "He's much less elegant in expressing admiration than you, Svan."

"His attention did come in handy," I said.

She nodded. "Saved my life, most likely."

Agrim entered carrying a stack of bowls, leading several men carrying pots.

"What's for dinner, captain?" I called out.

He looked at me, eyes wide. "Sire. I'm sorry, I didn't know you were here yet."

"No need to apologize. What's for dinner?"

"Chicken and rabbit stew."

The men cheered.

"Does every warrior eat this well?" I asked.

"No, Sire," he said. "They're just glad to know the time spent hunting rabbit has been rewarded."

"Hunting?" I asked. "Croian warriors shouldn't have to hunt to eat. Is this Hallfrid's doing?"

"You misunderstand, Sire. My men receive better treatment from the cooks when we supply meat for them. It breaks up the boredom of cooking the same thing every evening. If we could've found a couple of deer, we'd have steak."

I nodded. "Good to know. Carry on."

"Sigric, Sibbi, make yourselves useful. Two kegs of apple ale and mugs for everyone," Agrim ordered.

They rushed out of the building.

Bowls were quickly handed out. Tindra and I were served first. Agrim took the last seat at my table.

While stirring the stew, I breathed in the steam rising from the bowl. It carried a faint peppery edge to the smell soon overpowered by cabbage. I slurped a spoonful and found it tasted much better than I expected and made an excellent meal compared to what I'd eaten with the Varian guard. To my surprise, Tindra smiled as she took the spoon from her mouth.

"Perhaps I should eat with my guards more often," I said.

A round of laughter greeted Sigric and Sibbi when they entered with our drink. Mugs were filled and passed around the room with practiced ease.

The sweet ale made an interesting contrast to the stew. It wouldn't have been my first choice, but it beat a glass of water.

"If it's not out of line," Agrim said. "May I ask why you wanted to eat with us?"

I nodded and swallowed a sip of ale. "Contrary to the claims of some generals and commanders, I am not a bloodthirsty tyrant. Let me start by saying everyone in here has my permission to speak freely this evening. I want you all to know I appreciate what you are doing for me. You're taking grief from the other companies, but that won't last forever. I also want to show you I *am* approachable. I'm certain you've all heard terrible things about me and my plans for Croy. The rumors and accusations will likely get worse before they go away, but I *am* Croian, born and raised. I'm not turning Croy over to Varia or into Varia. Everyone understand?"

The men replied, "Aye," in unison.

"That's why I'm here tonight, to show you who your king is. Now, someone pick a topic to lighten the mood."

"How'd you get the scar on your scalp?" Bior asked, from a nearby table.

I smiled, took another drink, and said, "I'm not sure you'd believe me if I told you."

"I watched your shoulder get stitched closed in Geri's stable. You took it like someone familiar with pain. I'll take you at your word," he said, grinning.

"Might make a good impression on the rest of us," Svan said. "As long as it wasn't something silly."

I looked at him. "Silly? Not by a long shot, though you'll likely laugh at one point."

Turning to the rest of the room, I told the tale. "Crum and I left Croy with the girl who turned out to be Princess Jesca of Varia. We traveled at night, working our way north through the central forest. A couple of hours before sunrise, we bedded down in a secluded clearing but accidentally caught the attention of four Satran soldiers. Crum hit one in the arm with an arrow—"

"Ouch," Bior blurted out.

I nodded. "The next entered the clearing right on top of me, and the fight was on. I took a few kicks to the ribs before I shattered his leg. Falling, he thrust his sword toward me and sliced my scalp but good. I killed him and took the fight to the others. Crum's arrows dropped the second soldier, and I pounded the third when..." I paused and rubbed the back of my head. "Get ready to laugh. Princess Jesca of Varia clubbed me in the back of the head with a large branch."

Roaring laughter filled the hall, before Agrim asked, "Why did she do that?"

I smiled. "I asked her the same thing when I woke. She meant to knock the last soldier down before he reached me. Even with her terrible aim, her attack stopped him in his tracks. Crum finished him with another arrow. Understand, being branded hurt like I'd never been hurt before, but that Varian herbalist stitching my scalp closed was torture. I'll never forget what it feels like to have a needle scrape against my skull."

Several men groaned before they applauded. I felt my cheeks warm with a blush crossing my face.

"How about you, Lady Tindra?" Svan asked, after everyone quieted. "Any war stories?"

She cocked her head and smiled. "Still more subtle than Anifas. I didn't live the sheltered life of a king, so I've been in several fights. One of which would embarrass your ruler, so I won't tell that story."

"Aww," someone shouted from near the door.

She shook her head. "Let it be enough to say he claims I cheated."

She waited for my guard to stop pleading with her to tell that story.

"Considering he wants you to know what kind of man he is, I think it would be better to tell you about fighting at his side," she said. "Not the fight you're thinking of...I'd rather not talk about what happened in there. Instead, this is a fight outside a bar in the" she paused and raised her eyebrows, "more...adventurous part of the Varian capital. We'd been out, together, that evening—"

Someone whistled.

"Nothing like that, mostly," she said, smiling, "I'd planned this outing so we'd be seen together and make an impression on certain people, but that detail isn't important to the story. We ran into some ill-mannered individuals who didn't know when to leave well enough alone. I tried to keep the peace, suggested they go their way and we'd go ours, but their runt leader had a different idea. I put out all the street torches in sight and killed two while the runt ran for his life and hid in an alley. Your king found him and crushed his chest. I never had a habit of carrying trophies with me, or I'd show you the ear I took from one of them."

I expected more applause, but silence hung in the room.

Svan looked a little pale when he spoke, "You cut off someone's ear?"

She looked him in the eyes and nodded. "Without going into another story, the thug had been rude and uncooperative, once, when I asked him for a favor. Because of his behavior, he owed me his ear."

"Wow!" someone exclaimed. "Cold-blooded woman."

Tindra looked around with a predatory grin. "Don't forget it."

I lifted my mug. "Drink! No need to be so serious this evening. Who else has a story?"

Someone on the far end of the room began a tale I couldn't hear. After a few spoons of stew, I got Agrim's attention. "Could I trouble to you have breakfast brought to my quarters in the morning?"

"Of course, Sire. I'll see to it personally. For how many?"

"I don't know what Roi's plans are, so enough to feed three, to be safe," I said. "Wait, four. If you're bringing the food, eat with us, and you can tell me where we are on our projects."

He nodded and turned his attention back to the storyteller.

I drained my mug while the story played out. After clapping with everyone else, I looked at Tindra. "You ready to call it an evening?"

She took a drink and nodded.

It didn't take long for everyone to notice I was standing. "Men, I enjoyed dining with you and hope you enjoyed my company. It's time for me to head to my quarters. Something tells me tomorrow will be another busy day."

Svan stood. "I'll see you make it safely. Sigric, come with us."

I shook hands with several men on the way out of the barracks. Others smiled at me and nodded as we passed. *Feels good to know I'm gaining their respect.*

Chapter 23

"I'd say you made an impression," Tindra commented, once we were outside.

"As did you, m'lady," Svan said.

Sigric sighed and shook his head. "Fighting men respect those who can hold their own. They like knowing their leaders are battle-tested."

"Then why am I not getting the respect of the rest of the guard?"

"From what you've told me, you already know the answer," Tindra said.

I nodded. "Hallfrid."

"Glad you said it and not me," Svan commented. "I do have a question, Sire. How did you two kill three people in the dark?"

"A smart fighter doesn't share all his secrets," I said, with a big grin. "Especially one that saved his life many times over."

"Understood," Svan said. "You didn't want to run from the Scar, did you, Sire?"

"Want to? No. But I didn't see another sensible option. Two archers against an unknown number, even ignoring the fact we couldn't see them, is a lost battle. Don't mistake a wise retreat for cowardice. Stupid, brave warriors end up dead. Wise, brave warriors live to continue the fight later."

"Especially when protecting their king," Tindra added.

"I didn't mean to imply you were cowardly, m'lord."

"The thought never crossed my mind," I said. "No worries."

"Thank you, Sire."

When we reached my quarters, I put my hand on Svan's shoulder. "I want you to know I meant what I said at dinner. I appreciate what you, what all of Captain Agrim's company does for me. It's an important service to our country."

He bowed to me. "My honor to serve."

I turned to Sigric and placed my hand on his shoulder. "The same to you, even more so. You put yourself at risk telling me about Vegar's crimes. I appreciate your trust. I hope your new assignment is an adequate reward."

He bowed. "I didn't expect a reward, Sire. Only to be spared any punishment coming to Vegar's company."

"The truth should always be rewarded. To do any less is to encourage lies. Good evening."

"Sleep well, Sire," they replied.

I saluted them and followed Tindra inside.

"Take off my belt and sword, please. I'll leave it hanging on a chair," she said, as we reached the table.

I did as she asked. "I hope Svan didn't bother you too much."

She looked at me and shook her head. "Felt nice, in a way, to know I can still get men's attention. Anifas took it too far, too quick...not that he ever had a chance."

"Doubt he'll pursue you like Anifas did," I said, smiling. "Sleep well."

"It's nice to go to bed with a belly full of meat and ale. Thank you."

I made it to my room, undressed, and fell asleep not long after laying down.

* * *

Roi's voice woke me, "Agrim's here with boiled grains, roast goat, and milk."

I yawned. "Wasn't sure you were coming back here."

"I'll move out when my family arrives. Wasn't sure if any of our old safe houses were still around, but I found one, not too far from here either."

"Good to know," I said. "I'll be out after I'm dressed."

Tindra beat me to the table, probably because she didn't have to find something to wear. She swallowed, and said, "Agrim found someone who made spiced boiled grains."

I looked at him. "Looking for another promotion?"

His eyes opened wide. "No, Sire. I—"

I held up my hand. "Relax, it was a joke. Thank you."

Roi chuckled. "He still hasn't figured out your sense of humor?"

Agrim shrugged. "Jarl Eirickson didn't seem to have a sense of humor."

"As I've told you many times, I'm not him," I said, pointing at him. "Mention his name again, and you might find yourself demoted."

"Sorry, Sire."

"Forgiven," I said. "Any progress on housing for the Varian soldiers?"

"Slow going," he said, frowning. "I hope to find something suitable today."

I nodded. "Frustrating when people don't cooperate, isn't it? How about picking lieutenants? Any ideas?"

"I haven't had much time to focus on it," he said, still frowning. "Svan is a good candidate; men tend to follow his lead. Picking a second is taking time."

"Understand, this is your decision. You know your company better than I, but I can suggest a couple, based on what I've seen."

"Of course, Sire. I'd value your input."

"Take a close look at Sigric. If you don't want to consider him because of how new he is to your unit, Sibbi might be a good choice," I said.

"Sigric? Are you suggesting him simply because he gained your favor?"

"Gaining my favor does not cloud my judgment. You gained my favor, and I haven't regretted the decision to trust you with important tasks."

"And I don't want to let you down. I ask, not to question your judgment but because I'm not sure how my men would respond to orders from a newcomer."

I nodded. "Certainly something you should consider. Any insight you'd like to share, Roi?"

My mentor looked at me with a questioning expression. "I don't know his men well enough to have an opinion. Besides, Captain Agrim doesn't know me well enough to trust my judgment."

I nodded. "Valid points. Agrim, use your best judgment."

"Thank you, Sire. I know it's an important decision so I don't want to rush. You will know soon after I have made my choices."

"Lastly, have you talked to Kodren? Knowing what's going on with those farms is crucial to how I start the push east."

He shook his head. "Not yet. I will today. If he accepts the assignment, he'll leave after sunset."

"Confidence is key," Tindra said.

Agrim looked at her. "What do you mean?"

She smiled. "If you've never been trained to infiltrate, going in with confidence is crucial to success. People tend to overlook anyone who looks like they belong where they are. If your man looks nervous, uncomfortable, no one will believe he belongs there. I've done plenty of work where I didn't belong. I'd be happy to help him develop a believable story, as long as he's smart enough to remember it."

"I appreciate the offer," Agrim said. "If he's willing to try, I'll send him to find you."

"Anything I can do to help," she said.

Agrim nodded to her. "If you'll excuse me, Sire, I have things that need my attention."

"Something just came to mind," I said. "Considering the fact messengers bringing news of Satran activity never made it to me, send two guards to each entry into the capital. I don't want Aerison and his men held or refused entry because some general or commander thinks they have a better idea of what's good for Croy."

"Good idea, m'lord. I'll send men right away."

I nodded. "Thank you for your time and bringing breakfast. You're free to go."

He bowed and left.

"I also have some details left to attend to," Roi said.

"Anything I can help with?" I asked.

"You have enough to take care of," he said. "With luck, I'll see you for lunch."

"I hope everything goes well."

"As do I," Tindra said, before turning to me. "Plans for today?"

I shook my head. "Seems like I'm waiting for...everything. Answers to letters, men to arrive, someone to get caught messing up, and crucial information to be gathered. I guess I should meet with Porsey and Boril to present their new assignment."

"I'll help with that if you think I can."

"I appreciate your eagerness, but I think I'd better do this alone. They already dislike me. Involving a Varian isn't going to improve the situation."

"I understand," she said. "Perhaps I'll go exploring."

I sighed. "Stay out of trouble."

"I'll do my best," she said, smiling.

"Would you like me to put your belt on for you?"

"I think going out armed and alone might attract the kind of attention that leads to trouble. I'm not ready to take care of myself in that situation yet."

I nodded. "Probably wise. I can send a guard to escort you."

She shook her head. "I know how to blend in. Don't worry about me."

I shrugged. "As you wish."

She laughed and headed for the door.

I finished the cup of milk and cleaned the table before walking to Porsey's quarters.

Otkel and Skegg stood at attention when I walked out. "Relax. I'm not leaving the grounds."

I knocked on Porsey's door.

A servant I didn't recognize answered.

"Tell Porsey King Fitzeirick wants to meet with him in the king's quarters. Be quick. I'm going to summon Boril now."

The servant glared at me before nodding and closing the door.

I expected the same treatment at Boril's. Instead, he answered the door.

"Yes?"

"I have something to discuss with you and Porsey. Do you need time to prepare before coming to my quarters?"

"No, I can leave now," he said.

As we crossed the courtyard, Porsey emerged from his home and hurried to join us. "What's wrong?" he asked.

"Patience," I said. "I'll explain once we're seated at my table."

I instructed my guards to make sure we weren't interrupted before we walked inside. The former Thanes sat near each other, opposite me.

"I called you here this morning to discuss an opportunity to leave your quarters and better serve Croy."

"You're lifting our confinement?" Porsey asked.

"Not inside Croy, no," I said. "I understand there's concern among our military that I'm going to surrender Croy to Varia or turn our country into a copy of theirs. Despite repeated attempts to make them understand that isn't the case, most of the generals resist my leadership, one openly. I'm sure you've heard the stories of how I handle rebellious uprisings. Trust me, they're true. However, I don't want my rule defined by bloodshed."

"It started bloody enough," Porsey said.

"Because I had no other choice," I replied. "Still, I have a mutually beneficial proposal. You two get a change of scenery, along with the opportunity to participate in diplomacy, and I get confirmation that Varia's not our enemy and is, in fact, our ally."

"You trust us to help you?" Boril asked.

I nodded. "I'm extending a tremendous amount of trust. You will operate well away from my oversight and influence."

"Sounds too good to be true," Porsey said. "How do we know you aren't going to kill us?"

"You should have died the day I killed Eirickson. Roald convinced me otherwise. Killing you now doesn't benefit me and could make matters worse. Again, I'm doing everything I can to avoid unnecessary bloodshed."

"What do you propose?" Boril asked.

"I'll start by saying you don't have to decide immediately. Groundwork is in progress, agreements are being worked out. I recently appointed Nikulas as ambassador to Varia, but I need more resources stationed in the Varian capital. I propose you two travel to their capital as diplomatic representatives on a long-term investigation. You will look into the relationship between Croy and Varia, make sure it is beneficial to us. I expect accurate, honest reports of your findings as often as you care to send them. The longer you stay, the stronger your influence upon the relationship becomes."

Now, I'll give them what they really want.

"Given enough time, you two might convince Varia I'm not the right ruler and get their assistance in replacing me. I trust that won't happen, but it is possible."

"I don't understand why you want *us* to do this," Boril said.

"It's a public show of my respect and trust. I'm giving you the opportunity for power and influence in the future of two countries. This is vastly more power than you had serving under my half-brother. Would he give you the chance to challenge him?"

Porsey rubbed his chin. "We would travel alone?"

I shook my head. "Details are still being worked out to arrange security and appropriate accommodations. I'd prefer you to travel with your entire house, family, servants, and anyone else you'd like to take along. You'll be out of the country for some time. Best you be surrounded by people you already depend on."

Porsey nodded. "How would we get there?"

"There are Varian wagons in Nikulas' hall that are due to return. Around thirty Varian capital guardsmen are ready to go home with the caravan. Either you ride in those wagons, or we add wagons of our own."

"We're supposed to trust Varians?" Boril asked.

I nodded. "This is a diplomatic mission to a friendly ally. They'll treat you with the respect you're due."

"This seems sudden after keeping us confined for weeks on end," Boril said. "You'll forgive me if I seem suspicious."

"I'd expect no less. If you weren't, you wouldn't be wise enough to do what Croy needs."

"What of Roald?" Porsey asked.

"He provides valuable advice to me."

Porsey thrust his finger toward Roald's house. "You mean he tells you what you want to hear."

"Quite the opposite. He recently advised me to let you go," I said, crossing my arms. "His age is a bit of a concern too. The last thing we need is one of our people dying in Varia. That would leave them open to suspicion and could damage the beneficial relationship we're trying to foster."

He pursed his lips and stared at me for a moment. "Obviously, we can't decide without talking to our families. How soon do you need an answer?"

"I am waiting on a response from the capital now. I expect it soon, but I don't know exactly when. Say two days, or do you need longer?"

"Two days should be long enough," Boril said.

"What if one or both of us declines the assignment?" Porsey asked.

I shrugged. "Then you stay, and I find others who appreciate the opportunity. They get the glory, and you stay confined longer."

He nodded. "Two days is acceptable."

"Please, take my offer seriously. This is a great opportunity for you. You are free to return home."

They left without saying another word.

I rubbed my forehead and sighed. *Another meeting to settle nothing. I'm getting good at those.*

Frantic pounding on the door got my attention. I hurried to the door and yanked it open.

Sibbi had his fist raised, about to swing again. "The Varians are here."

"Where?" I asked, looking over his shoulder.

"Outside the south gate."

"Did anyone refuse them entry?" I asked.

"No, Sire. I asked their leader to wait so I could get you. Thought it would look better if they entered with you in the lead."

I pursed my lips for a moment, then nodded. "Good thinking. Let's go. No sense in keeping them waiting."

Chapter 24

We arrived at the gate to find Sigric talking to Lieutenant Aerison while four warriors I didn't recognize did their best to look like they weren't going to let the Varians enter.

"Lieutenant Aerison!" I shouted. "It's good to see you well. I trust you had a safe journey."

"No one would be stupid enough to attack five hundred Varian soldiers," he said, smiling. "I bring news from the capital, but it's best discussed in private."

I cocked my head to the side for a second. "That doesn't sound good."

His expression didn't change. "Kurt asked me to tell you he's meeting with Sabast before coming here. Expect him the day after tomorrow at the latest." He looked at the four warriors and shrugged. "Guess you have to invite us in?"

"It would be for the best. After you're settled, we'll talk," I said, before turning to the stubborn men. "Make way."

All four glared at me before moving to the side.

Turning back to Aerison, I said, "I hate to say it, but we don't have a barracks for you yet."

"No problem," he said. "Expected we might have to make do for a while. We have wagons and tents."

"Thank you for understanding. Do you mind following me?"

"On foot?" he asked. "Take my horse; I'll ride on the lead wagon."

"How about I ride on the wagon? I'm not in the best shape to mount a horse," I said.

He raised his eyebrows.

"Ambushed in the Scar. Took an arrow in the shoulder before we escaped. Still hurts when I move wrong."

"That would do it," he said, before turning to wave the nearest wagon forward.

I nodded. "Thank you."

"Where are you going, Sire?" Sigric asked, when the wagon stopped.

Agrim hasn't picked a place...great. "Umm...we'll go...where Eirickson's home stood."

Sibbi laughed.

After one awkward attempt to climb onto the wagon without aggravating my shoulder, I settled on the seat and yelled, "On me!"

I guided the driver on the most direct path possible, but we still wound through a good portion of the capital. Shocked stares met the parade, along with insults and a few cheers.

At least no one attacked.

I stopped at the edge of the open space where my half-brother's personal hall once stood. Dismounting, I waved Sigric to me. "Let Agrim know the Varians are here. Tell him I said to gather the generals and commanders in their meeting room after lunch. Sibbi, when Lieutenant Aerison is done and his men settled in, bring him to my quarters."

They bowed and promised to carry out my orders.

Otkel and Skegg escorted me home.

Before I opened the door, I turned to them. "If I give you a couple of gold doubles, could you get me some decent ale?"

Otkel laughed.

"Anything specific in mind?" Skegg asked.

"Something old friends would share if they hadn't seen each other in a while."

"Might I suggest an exceptionally good mead?"

I tapped my finger on my chin for a moment. "Use your best judgment."

"You won't be disappointed, Sire."

I went inside and sat at the table to wait. Sitting alone, self-doubt forced its way into my thoughts. As a skald, it didn't seem like I spent so much time waiting for someone or something. *Maybe I took the simpler life as a regional leader for granted. Could it be I'm not the right person to rule Croy?*

The door opened, and Tindra stepped inside. "What's bothering you?" she asked.

"Frustration, self-doubt. Do I want to know why your hair's wet?"

"I know a little bit about self-doubt. It will tear you apart if you let it," she said, sitting across from me. "I found a bath." She shook her head. "Croians...you're all wound too tight."

I nodded. "Aerison's here with his men."

She glanced back at the door. "Where's Kurt?"

"Meeting with Sabast. Should be here in the next day or two. I won't let him hurt you."

"With your injury, you couldn't stop him," she said, shivering. "And I'm in no condition to fight."

I grinned. "Svan would gladly stand guard over you, especially if you asked nicely."

She glared at me, and the candle behind her lit.

My grin turned into a toothy smile. "Don't lie; you like the attention."

The candle flame flickered then went out. "I'm willing to play the game when I'm in the mood. Lately, I haven't been."

"Your...display at the tanner's shop, and you're not in the mood?"

She shrugged. "Should I have waited for someone to build a room?"

"Would it help if I told you I still liked what I saw?"

Her eyes lit up. "What about who you saw?"

I shrugged. "I think she's a work in progress."

She crossed her arms and looked away before the flame appeared again. "Have you—"

A knock on the door interrupted her question.

"Who's there?" I called out.

"Skegg, Sire. I have your mead."

"Mead?" Tindra asked. "Planning to drown your self-doubt?"

"No. I'm meeting with Aerison and thought he might like a drink," I said. "Bring it in."

He entered with a barrel, placing it on the floor near the table. "The finest crabapple mead you'll find, brewed by my brother."

"Your brother?" I raised my eyebrows. "Please pass on my thanks, Skegg."

"He hopes you enjoy it, Sire."

"Care to sample it with me?" I asked Tindra, after he left.

"I thought it was for you and Aerison."

"What kind of host doesn't make sure the drink is good before it's served?"

Tindra laughed. "I'll agree to sample it with you if you explain how you expect to get it on the table so we can get our mugs under the tap."

"Oh," I said. "I doubt I can lift it without hurting my shoulder."

"You don't want to tear those stitches out."

I sighed. "Then we wait for Aerison."

"Or you ask Skegg to put it on the table."

Someone knocked twice on the door then it swung open. Skegg stuck his head inside, and said, "Pardon the intrusion, Sire. Varian Lieutenant Aerison is here as you requested."

I smiled and stood. "Yes, let him in."

Chapter 25

Aerison walked to the table as the door closed.

"Perfect timing," I said. "If you wouldn't mind putting that barrel on the table, we can share some mead. It's said to be the finest in the capital."

"Hard to turn down such a tempting offer for a little physical labor. All things considered, I could use a drink anyway."

I went for mugs while he moved the barrel.

Aerison looked at Tindra as the golden liquid flowed out of the tap and a slightly sweet smell filled the room. "I'd heard you were still here. How are you doing?"

She lifted her right arm. "Well as can be expected, I suppose."

Once the mugs were filled, I returned to my seat. "You said you had news."

The tart, crabapple flavor tempered the usual over-sweet honey taste of mead, making a smooth, refreshing drink.

He nodded and smacked his lips after taking a drink. "I did. Tart over sweet seems appropriate, given the situation."

"I can tell something's bothering you, lieutenant," Tindra said. "What's wrong?"

He looked into his mug and sighed. "Queen Ines did not recover."

Tindra drew a sharp breath.

"You're certain?" I asked.

He nodded. "We left the day of her funeral."

"Poor Ander," Tindra said. "What's he going to do?"

"He's making moves to step down." Aerison swallowed another drink. "Princess Jesca became the face of her family. King Ander refused to leave his wife as she faded. With Crum's help, Jesca hosted well-wishers and let everyone know how her parents were faring. I don't think she could've handled the pressure without your friend's constant support."

He took another long drink. "With Jesca as the last of Ander's family line, she takes the throne. Most people were beyond happy to have her back, but things are happening too fast."

"Does this mean—" Tindra started to ask.

"Rushed wedding plans are underway as we speak. Crum will be King of Varia soon," he said. "No offense meant when I say this, but...I can't believe a Croian will sit as Varia's king."

I whistled and shook my head. "None taken—I know him better than anyone. He's a good man, but I don't know if he's ready to be king of anything."

"Fitzeirick, this is good for you...for Croy," Tindra said. "He knows what's at stake. There's no way he won't give his full support to defeating Satra."

"It may not be so easy," Aerison said. "Several powerful families are weighing their options. There could be a civil war."

I took a long drink and stroked my beard. "No nation can survive a war on two fronts. Why did Ander let you leave with five hundred men?"

"Kurt's agents have reported Satran movement through the central forest for nearly a week. My king insisted we support you. Also, we're untouched if war breaks out inside our borders; we can return fresh and keep order."

Tindra shuddered. "Eirickson's still at work, even in death."

I put my hand on her shoulder. "As I've told several people, things will get better."

"How?" she asked, pushing my hand away. "My people are preparing to fight each other. Varians will spill Varian blood on Varian soil, and he's behind all of it."

"Give Crum a chance," I said.

"Listen to him," Aerison said. "Nothing has happened yet."

She nodded before leaving the table.

Aerison and I drank together in silence until we refilled our mugs.

"Your men are settled?"

He nodded. "Tents are raised, meals are cooking."

"Speaking of which, it will be lunchtime soon. What do you want?"

He shrugged. "I've never had Croian food. What's good?"

"It's all fairly bland compared to Varian cooking. Excuse me a moment."

I went outside. "Skegg, another favor."

"Of course, Sire. What do you need?"

"Lunch. Here's a couple more gold doubles. Try to find something spicy for our guest."

"I won't disappoint you, m'lord," he said, smiling.

"You haven't so far," I said. "Just come in when you return—no need to knock."

He nodded and headed for the gate.

Aerison refilled his mug as I returned.

"Sent the same man who brought this mead to get food," I said.

He smiled. "Good choice. Anything I need to how about what's going on here?"

"I have about thirty loyal guards, Elias' men, and now you and your five hundred. The rest of the warriors aren't following my orders; their commanders tell them they don't have to. I plan to call a meeting with the generals and commanders this afternoon to introduce you. You'll get a firsthand look at what I'm talking about. Especially from Hallfrid."

"Sounds like a demotion or dismissal is in order. Humiliate him in front of his men."

"I've created enough animosity in the way I've handled uprisings, so I'm trying to cut back on the bloodshed. The first time Hallfrid openly challenged me, I broke his leg. Some say he may never walk again without crutches. If anything, he has more support now."

Aerison whistled. "That's hard to believe."

"Also, the ambush may have been Croians disguised as Satrans. We captured one of my warriors wearing our enemy's armor."

His eyes opened wide. "What did he have to say?"

"Don't know. He died before we could question him."

"What about his superiors?"

I shook my head. "Can't prove they knew about his involvement. I've got people looking for information. So far, no one's asking where the man is. Kurt's agents may be reporting the movement of Croians dressed like Satran soldiers."

"I don't envy you."

"Sometimes I feel the same way," I said, and laughed.

Skegg walked in carrying a bundle and a clay pot. The smell of pepper and meat followed.

"What did you bring us?" I asked.

"Peppered deer steak and steamed potatoes, Sire."

"If it tastes as good as it smells, I'd say you did a fine job," Aerison said.

"Another sibling?" I asked.

"No, Sire, just a place I know of."

"Leave it on the table," I said, standing. "I'll serve it after I see if Tindra wants to join us."

"Sit," Tindra said, from the hall, "I gathered plates, forks, and knives when I heard the door open."

She must have smelled the pepper and followed her nose.

I nodded and returned to my seat.

The smell intensified when we opened the bundle. "I need to tell them to find Varian food more often."

Tindra placed the plates and utensils gently on the table before handing them out.

I loaded each plate with a steak and poured some potatoes out for myself.

Tindra stabbed her fork into the meat, then looked at the knife and growled, "I'm a grown woman, and I can't cut my steak."

Aerison looked away.

"Do you mind if I help?" I asked.

"I do," she said, "but I want to eat. Go ahead."

I made quick work of cutting her steak into bite-sized pieces. "Do you want some potatoes?"

"I think the steak will fill me up, thank you."

I turned to Aerison. "Take as much as you'd like."

He nodded, and we set about enjoying our meal.

I noticed Aerison made it a point to not look at Tindra as we ate.

He finished first and said, "I best be getting back to my men. When should I come for the meeting?"

"I'll send one of my guards for you."

He nodded as he stood. "Thank you for the meal and the mead. Until I see you again."

"Thank you for coming," I said. "Especially in light of recent events."

"I think I made him uncomfortable," Tindra said, shortly after the door closed.

"Wasn't sure how to react myself."

"Sorry," she said, looking down. "It's so frustrating when I find something else I can't do one-handed."

"I'd say I understand, but I don't. All I can offer is help and hope that you find a way to overcome at least some of the obstacles."

"I almost feel like a child learning to care for herself, except I have no one to guide me."

"Roi's seen many things; maybe he can help."

She nodded and put another piece of steak in her mouth.

I swallowed another mouthful of mead, and said, "My shoulder's bothering me. I'm going to rest before I have to introduce Aerison to the generals and deal with their resistance to the idea of Varian soldiers working with us."

"I'll make sure no one disturbs you unless it's important."

"I don't plan to sleep. I'd hate to keep the generals waiting," I said, with a toothy smile.

"Yes, that would be terrible," she said, with a laugh.

Chapter 26

"Fitzeirick," someone said softly, as a hand brushed across my forehead. "Two people are here to see you."

I opened my eyes and yawned.

Tindra stood next to my bed.

"So much for not going to sleep," I said. "What's wrong?"

"Sigric's here. Some of the warriors are trying to cause trouble with Aerison's men. Also, Boril's demanding to see you."

I groaned. "Why can't people act like adults? Might be best for you to stay out of sight. I'm sure Boril doesn't want witnesses for whatever he's going to say."

"Understood."

Sigric paced near the door while Boril sat at the table, looking annoyed.

"Sigric, you first," I said.

"Sorry for bothering you, Sire. Agrim insisted I come to tell you. Several men under Kolben and Af'nid's commands are trying to provoke fights with the Varians. Aerison has managed to keep his men under control, but I'm afraid it won't last much longer."

I sighed. "Gather as many guards as you can; put them between the two groups. If my warriors can't act honorably toward our guests, lock them in a cell. Tell your captain I said to round up the generals and commanders now. I wanted them to meet Aerison, but I'm not inviting him into a wolf's den, and this behavior must be addressed immediately."

"You're probably right, Sire. I'll tell Captain Agrim."

I waited until he left before addressing Boril, "What's on your mind?"

"Your offer."

I raised my eyebrows.

"I'll take it. I'll go to Varia."

"The agreement isn't in stone yet, but how many are going with you?"

"Just me," he said.

"What of your wife, children...servants?"

"My wife left when you dismantled the council. Took my sons and went back to her family. I dismissed my servants soon after. I can take care of myself."

I nodded. "I'm sorry to hear you've lost your family."

"I don't need your sympathy."

"Where does Porsey stand?" I asked.

He shrugged. "Haven't talked with him."

"I'd prefer to send both of you. Two experienced diplomats are harder to deceive than a man alone, far from home."

"It seems you have some sense," he said. "I'll talk to him."

"Thank you," I said.

Boril nodded and left.

I combed my fingers through my hair and sighed. *Now I need to tell one set of misbehaving children to make the children under their command behave.*

"At least one's leaving," Tindra said.

"True, but now most of my guard's tied up keeping a fight from breaking out. I wanted them at the meeting, in case someone got stupid and attacked Aerison. I don't know where Roi is, so I won't have him. You won't be much help...no offense."

"I have a firm grasp of the truth," she said. "But you could have been a little nicer when you said it."

"Sorry," I said. "I'm frustrated."

She smiled. "Just keep in mind who's the root cause."

I nodded. "Most likely Hallfrid."

"Take your frustration out on him."

"Given half a chance, I will," I said. "Guess I'll strap on my hammer and head to the meeting."

"This will continue until you do what you must to stop it," she said, as I left.

I felt tempted to cause small tremors in the ground as I stomped my way to the meeting room. *I can't take my frustration out on innocents.*

I wasn't surprised to be the first one in the room and watched the door for who would be the first to suffer my wrath.

Agrim led a parade into the room; all five generals followed him, with commanders trailing behind. Svan herded them from the rear, and Sibbi stood guard at the door.

"Captain, at my right."

Agrim bowed and sat.

I looked from one man to the next on the opposite side of the room and noticed two empty chairs.

"Who's missing?"

"We couldn't find Agnor or Haldan, Sire," Agrim said.

Two of Hallfrid's men. I glared at the senior general. "I ordered *everyone's* attendance. This insubordination is wearing thin. Where are they?"

He met my stare, defiance clear in his expression. "On patrol."

My vision narrowed until all I saw was Hallfrid. "Where? I gave no order for patrols."

"They are training recruits near the central forest."

I thrust my finger toward him, my heart pounding in my chest.

The door opened, and Sibbi shouted, "Halt!"

Everyone turned to see who entered.

"Let me through!" a young man shouted. "Geri sent me from The Trader's Cup. He said I had to get word to the king, to stop for no one."

I stood. "Let him in."

A slender, young man hurried to me and dropped to a knee. "I beg pardon for interrupting your meeting, my lord. Authune and I were hunting near the central forest. We saw Satran invaders, a hundred or more, moving north along the edge of the woods."

"Your name?" I asked.

"Cael, Sire."

"Cael, look at me."

When he raised his head and locked his hazel eyes on mine, his lip quivered.

"Is it possible you mistook Croian warriors as our enemy?"

"No, Sire. We saw Satran armor."

"You swear on your life you saw Satran soldiers," I said.

His body shook, but he did not look away. "My family barely escaped their advance into the south of Skald Nikulas's skati. I'll never forget what they look like."

"Lies!" Hallfrid shouted. "There are no Satran left west of the central forest, Fitzeirick. You had them killed."

I turned back to the general and dug my fingers into the table. *I hope this works.*

Using my talent, I focused my voice into the table. The words boomed, "Arrest General Hallfrid and Commanders Af'nid, Kolben, and Velief! They do not leave this room as free men!"

Gasps filled the room, but no one moved except Hallfrid.

He leveraged himself to his feet and bellowed, "This is an outrage! You have no grounds."

"I accuse you and all of your commanders of treason."

"Treason?" he screamed. "You are the only man in this room guilty of treason, and you call yourself our king."

Still grasping the table, I tried to send my voice again, "Sit. Down. Now."

The words rang from the stone around us.

He flinched and fell into his chair, his hands moving to cover his ears.

"You can leave here still breathing, or the floor can soak up your blood. The choice is yours. Either way, I have more important matters to attend to. All Croians in this room who care to save the lives of their countrymen, stand. Now."

Generals Jomar, Heming, and Gudmann stood along with all the commanders except those under Hallfrid.

General Nothri crossed his arms and remained in his seat. "I refuse to follow a branded traitor. You'll have to arrest me too."

I noticed his commanders stood.

"General Nothri, it seems your men don't agree with you. I charge you with willful and gross insubordination as well as willfully and knowingly supporting accused traitors. You will be imprisoned and share their fate after this matter is investigated."

"My men will not stand for this!" Hallfrid screamed, spit flying from his mouth.

"Then they will die." I pointed to General Jomar. "Have your commanders arrest these four and lock them away. Understand, if even one escapes on the way to imprisonment, your men will be considered party to the treason."

No one moved.

"General Jomar," I said. "Are you with me or against me?"

He shivered. "With you, Ja—Sire. But I can't ask my men to risk their freedom. Remove the risk of punishment, and I will give the order."

"Is no one in this room capable of following simple orders?" I asked.

General Gudmann cleared his throat. "Commanders...I mean *all* commanders standing with us, arrest the traitors, and see they are secured in cells. So commands our king."

At least Gudmann understands it's time for action. If they won't listen to me, they will follow his orders. Maybe this is the path to cooperation.

Men rushed to surround the accused. Af'nid and Velief tried to fight their way out but were soon beaten unconscious. Several men sythed bindings from stone and forced the accused from the room.

"Thank you, General Gudmann. Now, we have a hostile force moving north. I suspect they mean to take Nikulas's holdings. You each have one hundred warriors under you, and five hundred Varian soldiers arrived earlier today. I think it would be unwise to send all eight hundred and leave the capital defenseless. Jomar and Heming, round up as many of your men as you can and ride, with all possible speed, to defend

Nikulas. I will ask Aerison to send half his men to support you. Svan, once the commanders under Generals Jomar and Heming have done their duty, tell them to coordinate with the commanders formerly under Nothri to get them under different generals. General Gudmann, have your men round up everyone under General Hallfrid, especially those harassing our Varian guests. The men who want to cooperate will remain warriors and free men. Those who do not...prison or executed on the spot. I leave it to the judgment of your men."

The generals hurried from the room without a word.

"What of me, m'lord?" Cael asked.

"Go back to Geri. Tell him warriors are on the move. Keep everyone inside until he receives word its safe."

"Thank you, m'lord."

"Captain Agrim, come with me."

"Yes, Sire."

I walked toward the door. "Sibbi, run ahead of us and tell the guards with Aerison help is coming."

"As fast as I can, Sire."

"Has Kodren left yet?" I asked Agrim.

"No, Sire," he replied. "He and I agreed it would be best to leave after dark."

"Find him and call it off; I don't want him mistaken for a Satran."

"Immediately, Sire."

Chapter 27

The longer I walked, the more activity I saw. Warriors rushed around, strapping on armor and weapons.

Aerison stood next to Sibbi when I reached the Varian campground.

"You only want half of us?" Aerison asked.

"Half going north, immediately. Prepare the other half to move at dawn. They are to head south after they exit the Scar. If they find anyone but farmers, they cut down anyone armed and seize the land. I want your men to search for signs of Satran presence, but they are under strict orders to not harm innocents nor let them come to harm during any fighting."

"I'll keep my best men back until dawn."

I nodded.

"Sire," Sibbi said. "Did you tell the generals about this plan?"

"And risk letting Hallfrid know?"

He nodded. "Understood, but there could be Croian warriors there."

"If they are posing as Satran, they deserve what happens."

He nodded again.

"Lieutenant, your men will stay in the south until told otherwise, but I want a report as soon as the area is secured. It is of utmost importance I'm told of any evidence of Satran activity there, especially if they find Croians with Satran armor."

"It will be done. Whatever they find, you will know as soon as possible."

"Sibbi, you are at the lieutenant's disposal until Agrim or I tell you otherwise."

"Yes, Sire."

"Aerison, tell your men I appreciate their effort. Remind them there are Varians living in Nikulas's lands; they will be saving their countrymen along with mine."

"They shouldn't need the extra motivation, but it couldn't hurt," he said.

I put my hand on his shoulder. "Travel safe and swift. I look forward to victory on both fronts."

He nodded.

"Sibbi, I'm going to my quarters. Spread the word in case someone needs me."

"Yes, Sire."

I dodged packs of warriors on horseback while making my way home. Roi stood near the gate, talking to the guards posted there.

"What's going on?" he asked, when I got close.

"Things are going to get better," I said.

"Looks like we're going to war," Hedin said.

"Word came a large number of Satran soldiers were moving north through the central forest. I've sent men to protect Nikulas."

"And the guard?" Erland asked. "Are we going to fight?"

"The guard stays, along with General Gudmann's men. I won't leave the capital unguarded, in case this is a diversion."

"Smart," Roi said. "Must have had a good teacher."

I laughed. "Yes, I did. I'm going inside; you're welcome to join me."

"I came to talk to you anyway," he said.

I didn't see Tindra when we got inside.

Pointing to the barrel on the table, I said, "Care for some mead?"

"Why not? We can drink to my new home."

I coughed. "It's settled?"

He nodded. "Where I've been all day. It's not far from here. I'll be easily available. I *am* the king's right hand, after all."

"I hope you haven't sent for Grima and Einns. It's not safe to travel right now."

"Seems cleaning kept me from sending the messenger into the middle of a fight. I can wait a little longer. What did I miss in the meeting? How did you get the generals to cooperate?"

"I charged Hallfrid and his commanders with treason."

"Without evidence?"

"Sometimes things happen at the right time," I said, and explained the events as they unfolded.

"I can't believe Hallfrid planned to capture Nikulas's hall," Roi said.

"Maybe he sent a force to convince Nikulas to take his side. Regardless, he committed treason. Hopefully, I'll have more evidence before sundown tomorrow."

"What happens tomorrow?"

I told him about the orders I gave Aerison.

"Clever, no way anyone expects that move."

"Glad you agree," I said. "If they find Satran armor, I'll need to find an executioner."

Roi nodded. "You can't get their blood directly on your hands."

I pointed to my shoulder. "I'm in no shape anyway."

He chuckled and filled his mug again.

"What's so funny?" Tindra asked, from the hall.

"Join us," I said. "You're missing all the good news."

She cocked her head, eyebrows raised. "Good news? Hasn't been much of that lately. Pour me a mug and fill me in."

Roi set a mug of mead on the table for her while I explained what had happened.

"Oh," I said. "I forgot to tell you, I'm closer to figuring out how to send my voice through stone. I did it again, on purpose this time."

Roi smiled. "Still learning. That's a good sign."

"What about hearing?" Tindra asked.

"I haven't tried, but I think it's possible. What's your opinion, Roi?"

He looked at me. "What do you mean, hearing?"

"I can feel pressure against stone and push my voice out through stone, which makes me wonder if a stonesyth could hear sound through stone."

He pursed his lips and tapped his chin with a finger before shrugging. "I didn't know anyone could send their voice through stone. You've done it twice, but only because you saw someone else do it. I suppose hearing through stone is possible, but I can't imagine how it would work."

"Would come in handy for a spion," Tindra said.

Roi chuckled. "True. Listening without being in the room keeps you out of harm's way."

"Exactly," she said.

"Back to the task at hand," I said. "I finally have more things going my way than against me. I need to plan for what's next."

"It's dangerous to assume victory before it happens," Roi said. "I'd advise caution until you know the outcome of the battle at Nikulas's hall...if there is one. You don't know, for certain, that's where they were going. What if they're moving into Varia?"

"Seems like an unnecessary risk," Tindra said. "March past someplace Croy can send warriors from, constantly harassing their movement and blocking a retreat. It wouldn't make any sense for Satra to open a second front so far from support."

I nodded. "If they were going to push into Varia, why not through the eastern pass? Much easier travel and closer to the territory they control."

"Good points, but nothing about the past year is something I'd consider sensible," Roi said. "Take that into consideration, and you have to give some weight to the possibility they aren't attacking Nikulas. You're still waiting on useful information."

I smiled and lifted my mug. "To useful information."

"Aye," they said, in unison.

Tindra drained her mug and looked at me. "What happens if you lose and Nikulas's holdings are captured?"

"How many Varian agents live in and around his hall?"

She shrugged. "I don't know an exact number."

"Fifty? Twenty?" I asked. "It must be more than ten."

"I would guess between twenty and fifty. Why?"

"I'm sending roughly two hundred Croian warriors and two hundred fifty Varian soldiers against a force of around one hundred. The agents will defend themselves and those around them and keep Nikulas safe. Whoever is attacking isn't expecting their resistance. Kurt's there with Sabast and Halmar. I don't know about Kurt, but the other two know how to fight. Even if the attackers number two hundred, I have more than double that number on our side. Our victory is almost certain, but I wonder how many attackers will survive to be questioned."

"In a typical situation, I would agree," Roi said. "However, you forgot the possible deception. If those are Croian warriors in Satran armor, they can simply remove their armor and blend in with their countrymen, lying in wait to attack from the inside."

"I have to trust the people who live there to notice and take action," I said.

Roi nodded. "You're probably right, but temper your confidence."

"I'm more concerned with what the other half of the Varian force will face in the south. There lies the unknown factor. Something's happened there, the refugees at Geri's didn't move north for no reason, and I'm not sure what I want them to find. If Satrans have settled there, we free the land and prepare to push east as soon as possible. If disguised Croians have pushed out their own countrymen, executions start before we make final preparations to push east."

"Imprisoning your main detractors spurred the rest of your military leaders to action," Tindra said. "I'd say executions are in order regardless."

"They die in due time," I said.

Someone pounded on the door.

Roi hurried to open it, knife in hand.

Sibbi all but fell into the room. "Sire, you're needed. Aerison's hurt. We took him to Abi."

Chapter 28

I closed my eyes and shook my head. "What happened?"

"Sergeant Vestin and Skard, a warrior in his company, snuck past our line and attacked him."

"Arrest them," I growled.

"They're dead," he said.

"Good. Roi, I assume you're coming with me." I looked at Tindra. "You?"

"I doubt you'll need me."

"True, but Aerison might like to see a friendly Varian face," I said.

"He has men with him," Sibbi said.

"I'll stay to tell anyone looking for you where you are," she said.

"Understood. Let's go."

People crowded the road leading to the herbalist's home. Sibbi did his best to clear a path. I pushed my talent into the ground and shouted, "Make way for King Fitzeirick!"

Between the odd vibrations beneath their feet and my voice coming from everywhere, the crowd split.

"Impressive," Roi said.

"Still figuring it out," I replied. "But it's getting easier."

We arrived at Abi's and faced a wall of Varian soldiers standing guard. To a man, they looked ready for a fight.

"I'm sorry this happened," I said, to the man in front of the door.

"He trusted you," he growled, through clenched teeth.

"I know, I know," I said, raising my hands. "This won't go unpunished, but I'd like to see him now."

He said, "Only you may enter," before moving to the side.

I nodded. "Roi, Sibbi, find out where the uncooperative warriors were taken. We'll meet in my quarters."

"I hope all is as well as can be," Roi said, before turning to leave.

Another Varian soldier blocked the way out of the entry. A vein pulsed on his sweaty forehead.

"I'm King Fitzeirick, here to see Lieutenant Aerison," I said.

He nodded stiffly. "Sergeant Aksel, Aerison's left hand. This is a mess we didn't need."

"I'll do what I can to make it right," I said.

"You may not be able to," he said, crossing his arms. "This is a volunteer force. A good number are questioning why they should stay."

I nodded. "If you think it would help, I'd be glad to meet with them. Our futures could depend on their efforts tomorrow."

"I'll send someone to talk to them now," he said. "I can't promise anything."

"Understood," I replied. "Where's Aerison?"

"Hallway to the right, third door on the right."

I put my hand on his shoulder. "Abi's the best we have. He's in good hands."

"That's what Sibbi said."

"Where will you be?" I asked.

"I'll wait for you at the entrance."

I nodded and went to see my friend. Thought I wanted to barge into the room, I wasn't sure what was happening inside, so I knocked.

Abi answered, "One moment, I'm almost done."

Soon she came out, hands and apron covered in blood. "Sorry, Sire," she said, eyes wide open, "I didn't know it was you."

"No need to apologize. I'm sure you had your hands full," I said. "How bad is it?"

"He bled heavily before they got him here, but I think he'll live," she said. "His left arm is broken along with some ribs, but that's the least of my concern." She shivered. "Back of both thighs were sliced, deeply. I'm not sure he'll ever walk well. If the muscles don't heal right, he may never walk again at all."

I sighed and shook my head. "Can I see him?"

"He's asleep and needs to rest. I'll ask one of the men watching him to find you when he wakes."

I nodded. "I don't want to cause him more trouble. That will be fine. Thank you again." Reaching into my purse, I grabbed a handful of coins. "I'll leave five gold doubles in the kitchen on my way out to pay for his care."

She gasped. "Sire, that's—"

"Not nearly what your service is worth."

She blushed. "Thank you for the kind words, m'lord."

"You've earned them twice. I hate to rush off, but I have a mess to clean up."

"Of course, m'lord. I wish you success."

I hurried to the kitchen and left the coins behind a jar before finding Aksel outside.

"What do you think?" he asked.

"Abi's confident he'll live. I trust her judgment."

He closed his eyes and sighed. "It looked bad."

"From what she told me, it sounded bad. What happened?"

"I wasn't far from Aerison, relaying orders for the morning, when two of your men rushed him. One attacker hit the lieutenant's arm with a hammer and knocked him off balance. The second gashed the back of Aerison's legs and pushed him to the ground. A couple of archers preparing their gear for the morning downed the second man—Vestin, one of your guards called him—before he could do anything else. The other kicked Aerison in the chest and tried to run."

The vein throbbed faster, and his face grew redder as he spoke.

My stomach twisted into a knot as he described the incident.

After wiping sweat from his brow, Aksel growled, "He didn't get far."

"They did this without my knowledge," I said.

"I know. Aerison told Espen and me you had powerful men working against you. We'd made plans to prevent an ambush after moonrise. No one expected an overt attack during the day."

"What do I need to know about the men I'll be speaking with?" I asked.

He steepled his fingers in front of his chest. "They are proud veterans, doing what they thought would help defend their homeland. Seeing their commander bloodied by men who were supposed to be allies...they don't take betrayal well."

"You understand what's at stake, right?" I asked. "The men going south tomorrow could set our beginning strategy when we push through the central forest."

He nodded. "We talked about it before he sent Espen and half our soldiers out earlier today. Aerison told us you trusted the Varian soldiers more than your own. That won't win a war."

"I know," I said. "But information gathered by your men should help me win back the loyalty of most of my warriors. The rest will be imprisoned or dead."

"Wait in my tent. I'll bring some men to talk to you."

The tent seemed spacious until Aksel and seven other men crowded it.

I bowed low before looking each man in the eye. "I'm King Fitzeirick—"

"We know who you are," a burly, red-headed man with a scarred left cheek said gruffly. "Why should we stay, supporting you, after your men tried to kill our lieutenant?"

I took a deep breath and held it for a moment before speaking. "Lieutenant Aerison is a good man; he helped train me when I needed it. I have a tremendous amount of respect for him, and I feel terrible that he's hurt. Injury during combat is one thing but being cut down by treacherous cowards is—it's terrible. I wanted to say that before anything else, so you know I appreciate and look up to him. I won't beg you to stay, but the reason you volunteered to come all this way is the same reason you should remain here and see the battle through to the end. Satra is as big a threat as they've ever been."

I paused and met their eyes again. "What I tell you next must stay secret, for now. I need every man to give me their word."

Several of the soldiers looked at each other before each man nodded.

"On our honor," Aksel said.

"Some of my people have kept information from reaching me, information about possible Satran activity closer than ever before. I suspect a fair number of my military leaders are involved in a treasonous conspiracy. When you go south tomorrow morning, the most important part of your mission is discovering the truth. Aerison knew this. Aksel knows. Now you do too. My leaders will no longer hide information, waiting for the opportunity to use it against me. If you find what I expect, men will pay with their lives. I will need royal executioners. Volunteers will be looked upon with favor. Stay, and you will have an opportunity for revenge."

The burly man stepped toward me. "What are we looking for?"

"If you find the Satran have taken that land, kill them all and take it back. If you find Croians in Satran armor, cut them down, take the land, and bring me evidence. If you find innocent Croians living peacefully, secure them and tell me."

"Which do you want us to find?" he asked.

"Erlin," Aksel barked. "Enough questions."

I bobbed my head to the sergeant. "He needs more information to make up his mind. I know how that feels. Erlin, I want you to find the truth, nothing more. Stay, bring me the truth, and get your revenge. Otherwise, leave. Go back to Varia and hope this war doesn't come to your door. You aren't mine to command. I cannot order you to stay and won't ask you to leave. I truly hope to see you again. If I don't, I'll know you chose to leave. I won't think less of you for it; every man has a limit of what they're willing to take. Seeing supposed allies attack your leader—that's plenty of reason to go if you ask me."

"It is a shame your men don't follow you," Erlin said. "If staying is what it takes for my axe to spill blood for my lieutenant, I do it gladly." He turned to his fellow soldiers. "What say you?"

The six men bowed.

"All I ask is you spill no innocent blood," I said.

"I will see they behave with honor," Aksel said.

"Thank you," I said. "I'll be in my quarters. Any of my guards know how to find me if you need me."

Each man offered me his hand as I walked by.

I shook each one on my way out.

Chapter 29

I noticed Porsey talking with the guards as I approached the compound. "A word," he said, when I got close.

"Of course," I said. "We can talk inside."

"Would you care for some mead?" I asked, before sitting.

"No. This won't take long. Boril told me he talked to you; said he'd decided to take your offer."

I nodded.

"You don't really expect me to work for you if I go, do you?"

"I expect you to work for Croy."

"Even if I believe working for Croy means someone else should lead?"

"In the Varian capital, you're far from my oversight or influence. I went there and returned to overthrow my corrupt half-brother." I shrugged. "Who's to say you can't make history repeat?"

"I can't decide if you're too confident for your own good or the best liar I've ever seen."

I looked at him.

"Fine. I'll go, only because I think it's the easiest way for me to get you exiled or executed."

"If you truly believe that's in our country's best interest, I wish you all the success," I said, smiling. "Are you going alone?"

"No. Unlike Boril's wife, mine is loyal. I trust servants will be provided due to my standing as a diplomat."

"Like I told Boril, negotiations are ongoing. I am doing everything I can to ensure you receive accommodations fitting your status."

"At least you have *some* sense of propriety."

With a nod, I offered him my hand. "Thank you for putting Croy's needs above your own."

Porsey stood and turned for the door.

"You should have plenty of time to pack. The fighting near Nikulas' keep may delay messengers, but it shouldn't be more than a day or two."

"Fighting?" he asked, turning to face me again.

"The guards didn't tell you? Someone spotted a large Satran force moving north and alerted us. I sent warriors to keep them from taking Nikulas' holdings."

"Interesting," he said, tapping his chin with a finger. "With Hallfrid at the lead, a victory is assured."

I laughed. "Hallfrid's been imprisoned for treason."

He glared at me, and said, "All the more reason to see your head roll," before storming out of my home.

"And there goes problem number two," Tindra said, through a smirk as she entered. "He really has it out for you."

"I didn't realize you were listening," I said.

She shrugged. "Old habits."

I nodded. "I'd love to see the look on his face when he figures out he's traded one prison for another."

"Especially if he finds out it's a Croian on the throne," she said, and laughed.

"I didn't think you'd be happy with Crum in charge of Varia."

"It's good for you and should strengthen the relationship between the two nations. Over time, after Satra is eliminated, they may join. There's already enough Varians living in your nation to question why you don't work toward being one big country."

"I can't propose anything like that until long after I've gained everyone's trust, and Crum's going to have a hard enough time keeping power for a while."

Roi walked in without knocking. "I sent Sibbi back to the Varian camp after we found the detained warriors. There's about fifty held in a makeshift jail, not far from where the traitors are imprisoned."

"And you're sure they're secure?"

"Every man watching them swore to me they'd kill anyone who tried escaping," he said.

"Good enough for now," I said. "There's more good news. Porsey has agreed to go to Varia."

"That *is* good."

I smiled. "He told me he plans to work against me there...wants to see my head roll."

Roi laughed. "It's good to have a goal. How's Aerison?"

I frowned. "Not good. Broken arm and ribs, but that's the least of his problems. Vestin cut the back of both thighs, deep. Abi's not sure he'll ever walk again."

Tindra drew a hissing breath.

Roi blinked a couple of times before slamming his fist onto the table. "Did you talk to him?"

I shook my head. "He's sleeping. Abi said she'd send for me when he's awake. I had to talk to some of the Varian soldiers to keep them from leaving. I think I have my executioners."

"You'll have to talk to the generals first, make sure they don't have a problem with Varians killing their peers," Roi said.

"Some of those soldiers are out for blood. One way or another, they're going to get it. I'd rather they do it under my control than take matters into their own hands."

"They deserve some blood for what's happened," Tindra said.

"True, but Roi has a point. I'll talk with the generals first to make sure I don't cause more trouble."

"Good luck. Until they thought Croian lives were at risk, their loyalty to Hallfrid ran deep," Roi said.

"More fear than loyalty, I suspect."

"You'd better hope you're right," Tindra said. "If they decide to unite against the executions, they could do Porsey's job for him."

"And doom two countries," I said.

"You know that. I doubt they do," Roi said.

"They can go along with my plan, or they can dirty their hands. Either way, if I can prove Hallfrid is a traitor, he dies."

"What if you can't prove anything?" Tindra asked. "Hallfrid doesn't strike me as someone stupid."

"Weren't you the one saying no conspiracy stays hidden forever?" I asked.

She raised her hand. "Only trying to point out a possible outcome. Will you release him?"

"I'll change the charge to willful, gross insubordination. I'd have to release his commanders, but he'd stay locked up."

"And the warriors you have detained, what are you going to do with them?" Roi asked.

"My guard gave an order; they ignored it. Willful insubordination. Keep them detained a while." I pointed at him. "Before you ask, Nothri stays locked up for the same reason."

He nodded.

"I don't know about you two, but I'm getting hungry. Anyone want to go to Grith's with me for dinner?"

"I'll come. I can talk to Fastan and Thorgault to see how my new clothes are coming," Tindra said.

"You two go. I need to move some things to my new home."

· · · ● · ● · · ·

The market square wasn't as busy as I expected.

"Grith, where's everyone?" I asked.

"Warriors on the move, people tend to stay home."

I nodded. "Trouble around Nikulas' hall."

"Satra?" he asked.

"According to the initial report. I'll know more after the warriors return."

"Hope our men win."

I smiled. "They will. What's for dinner?"

"Deer stew."

"Sounds good, two bowls. What's to drink?"

"For my favorite customer, I have a beer that complements the stew well. Or you can have some water."

"I'll try the beer," I said.

"Water for me, please," Tindra said.

Tindra wolfed down her meal like a starving animal. "I'm going to check on my orders."

Trying to relax, I took my time. The dark stew wasn't spicy like the deer steak I'd eaten for lunch, but it tasted better than a bland chicken dish. The beer was more bitter than I preferred, but after drinking sweet mead all day, anything would be bitter.

I left a gold double on the counter when I finished.

Grith saw it and nodded. "Have a good evening, Sire."

I returned the nod and left to find Tindra walking out of the tanner's shop. "I don't see any new clothes."

She chuckled. "A couple of short sleeve shirts are ready, but without pants, they don't do me much good. Thorgault's having trouble finding enough black goat skins to split. He showed me some of the armor, and I like what he's doing."

"As long as you're pleased when it's done," I said. "I'm heading home in case someone's looking for me."

"Sounds good."

Chapter 30

The guards bowed as we approached the gate.

"Any news?" I asked.

"All's quiet, Sire."

I nodded, and we walked to my quarters.

"When do you think Kurt will get here?" Tindra asked, sitting at the table.

I shrugged. "No doubt the fighting will delay him. If I had to guess, no earlier than tomorrow morning."

She pursed her lips for a moment then said, "We should probably sleep now. Tomorrow could be busy."

"I'm afraid you're right," I said. "Sleep well."

I woke to a dark room. Dressing, I walked outside. The sky was brightening in the east.

When I turned to walk back inside, someone called from behind me.

"Sire, there's a Varian soldier here. He said you wanted to know when Aerison woke."

I nodded. "Tell him I'll be there shortly."

I walked back inside, went to Tindra's room, and softly called her name.

She blinked a couple of times and looked around the room.

"What?" she mumbled.

"Aerison's awake. I'm going to see him now. Want to come with me?"

She yawned and stretched. "I know how much I appreciated visitors while I recovered. Let's go."

I counted eight Varian soldiers keeping watch near the Abi's door. When we got close, one of them opened the door for us.

"The herbalist is resting," he said.

I nodded, and we quietly walked to Aerison's room.

A Varian near the door let us in.

Aerison sat in the bed, back against the wall and legs out in front of him.

He gave me a weak smile and waved his hand toward two chairs near the bed. "Have a seat."

"How are you doing?" I asked.

"Alive. Heard you talked to my men, convinced them to stay."

"I simply told them the truth and left the decision to them," I said.

"Aerison, you're hurt—" Tindra said.

"Tell me something I don't know," he said, and grimaced.

"You didn't let me finish. Don't worry about your men; focus on your recovery. I know all too well; it helps to talk. We came to visit you so you can lean on your friends. How are you really doing?"

He frowned and hung his head. "I hurt. Every breath is painful."

I nodded and tapped my chest. "Broken ribs will do that to you."

"My legs don't work right. Your herbalist said I may not walk again."

"I've sliced a few legs to keep prisoners from running," Tindra said. "If the cut didn't go to the bone, the leg may mend over time. Don't give up on yourself." She lifted her right arm. "I know how easy it is to accept defeat. Find someone who won't let you."

He glanced at his splinted arm.

"It'll heal soon enough," I said. "Around the time the ribs quit bothering you, I'd guess."

"Abi told me you spent weeks here, Tindra. Is that right?" he asked.

She nodded.

"Is it true she doesn't eat meat?"

She laughed. "It's true, and everything is bland compared to what you're used to eating."

"All the more reason to recover quickly," he said.

"I'll have one of my guards show your men a good butcher shop not far from here. It's not Varian cooking, but it's better than nothing but leaves and vegetables," I said, smiling.

"Take that offer—trust me," Tindra said.

He nodded. "Any word on the battle?"

"Nothing yet," I said. "I'd be surprised to hear anything before midday."

"True, and if the fighting continues..."

I nodded. "They won't send messengers until it's safe to spare the men."

"Trust Aksel to do what's needed today. Espen's my right hand only because he's served longer. Aksel is easily his equal."

"He seemed like a good man," I said. "Any orders I need to take to him?"

"I've sent word to him."

I nodded. "I know you need rest. Your men are in good hands. I won't bother you unless it's necessary."

"Thank you."

"If you need to talk, send for me," Tindra said.

"I may take that offer in a few days."

We left, staying quiet until getting outside.

"I hope he doesn't defeat himself," Tindra said.

"I know. Had he been injured in battle, it would be an honor but taken out of the fight by treachery...it's an insult."

"I'll keep in touch with him, help keep his fire up."

"Good idea, but don't let yourself get down in the process."

"I won't," she said, smiling at me, "I've got things to keep me busy now."

A blond-haired man, dressed in Varian leather armor, holding the reins of a horse, stood in front of the gate to the courtyard. My guard blocked his way.

Tindra stopped mid-stride. "That's Kurt."

"In armor?" I asked. "More likely, it's a messenger letting me know Aksel and his men have left."

"I'm telling you, that *is* Kurt, and we don't have any weapons."

"Even if you're right," I said, "my guard won't let anything happen."

She whipped her head left and right. "Where's Sabast?"

"Kurt knows better than to bring him here without my permission."

"If he grabs me, is your shoulder good enough to fight him while I escape?"

"Tindra, he's not going to grab you. Prey gets preyed upon, remember. You're not prey so stop acting like it," I said firmly.

"A vulnerable predator isn't much better than prey."

"I'll keep you safe. Just don't do something stupid," I said.

"Like get close to Kurt?"

"Like run," I said.

"Fine but keep yourself between him and me."

"I'll make sure nothing happens to you," I said.

We walked toward the compound, Tindra slower than usual, and I called out to the guard when we got close.

Kurt turned and waved.

"See," I said. "Friendly."

"Or a trap," she whispered.

I sighed and offered him my hand.

He bowed before shaking it. "King Fitzeirick, good to see you."

"And you," I replied.

"Tindra," he said. "You look...well, terrible. You're white as cotton. Are you well?"

"I've been better," she mumbled.

"We visited Lieutenant Aerison this morning," I said. "He was badly injured yesterday. Tindra's upset."

Kurt nodded. "Where can we talk?"

"Have you eaten?" I asked.

Tindra kicked my foot.

"Before the fighting started yesterday evening."

I turned to the guards. "One of you see his horse is taken care of and bring some breakfast to my quarters."

"At once, Sire."

"Let's talk while we wait," I said. "Come with me."

Tindra moved to stay out of his reach while we crossed the courtyard. She stopped at the door until Kurt, and I entered. Once inside, she sat in the chair closest to the door.

"How did you get here?" I asked.

"Sabast—"

"Where is he?" Tindra shouted.

Kurt blinked several times. "Near Nikulas, where I left him. What's *wrong* with you?"

Her face turned dark red, sparks filled her eyes, and every candle in sight burst into flame.

Could he have asked a worse question?

Waving her right arm, she said, "What's wrong with me? Your boy cut off my hand and tried to kill me. How do I know you're not here to take me to him, or King Ander, or finish the job yourself? Avenging his daughter's murder would buy a lifetime of favor from him."

"I told you, Ander said he understood what happened," I said.

"Ander is a different man now," Kurt said. "He's—"

"Sent you to get his revenge," Tindra said.

This is getting nowhere.

"Stop it!" I yelled. "I've already lost one fiancée because I wasn't there to defend her; I'm not going to lose another. If Ander or Sabast wants my wife-to-be dead, they have to go through me."

Tindra gasped then covered her face with her hand. "*Why* did you tell him that?"

Chapter 31

"I hadn't heard. Seems congratulations are in order," Kurt said, eyebrows raised, as an uneasy smile parted his lips.

I need to convince him and tell the truth. I shrugged. "Recent decision, so we hadn't told anyone. Much like Varia needs a king, Croy needs a queen."

Tindra's jaw dropped, and she stomped to her room.

Not the reaction I expected. Didn't mean to spring this on her but I thought she would go along. Isn't this what she wanted? Maybe she's more serious about leaving her old life behind than I realized.

He coughed.

"I must say I'm surprised...never thought you two felt that way toward each other. I guess that makes the gift Per sent even more special."

I squinted. "Per sent a gift?"

"My wagon's still in Nikulas' stable. Halmar's bringing it when it's safe. Per heard about Tindra's injury and made her something. Also, I have some weapons for you and an idea to pitch, but I want to tell you the bad news first."

"I've had more good news than bad over the past day or so," I said, shrugging. "Guess I'm due a balance. What's wrong?"

"Like I said, Ander's changing. I'm sure Aerison told you he's stepping down."

I nodded.

"What the lieutenant doesn't know is Ander's not leaving the game entirely. He's acting as the liaison between us and Crum's court."

"Why is that bad news?"

"He doesn't fully trust Jesca's ability to rule."

"She seemed better by leaps and bounds when I last saw her," I said. "Has something happened?"

"No, she's fine...especially with Crum at her side."

"I'm still not hearing any bad news," I said, shrugging.

Kurt nodded. "With Ander out of the public's eye, most of the resources meant to support your war have to stay in Varia to keep the crown on Crum's head until enough people see him as a suitable ruler. You and I both know what a civil war in Varia would mean. We can't let it happen."

I shook my head. "Like Tindra said, even dead, Eirickson's still causing trouble." I sighed. "If we can't outright defeat Satra alone, we'll fight to hold them back until Varia can send more troops."

"Do you want me to handle the two men you're sending to Daufi?"

I raised my eyebrows. "You know about them?"

"Why are you surprised?"

"I guess I shouldn't be," I said. "Keep an eye on them, intercept any communications they send out. Otherwise, don't worry about them unless they step outside the walls. Then they are yours to deal with appropriately."

"You don't want your troublemakers here making trouble there, got it."

A knock at the door interrupted the meeting.

"Who's there?" I asked.

"Breakfast, Sire. Boiled grains and milk."

"Come in."

Two guards entered and placed a stone pot and pitcher on the table.

"Thank you. We'll serve ourselves. Please, take this barrel away."

They bowed, hefted the barrel, and hurried out.

"We do need to address Sabast," I said, going to get bowls.

He glanced toward the hall. "He's not a problem. Are you going to get Tindra?"

"She won't eat while she's upset. I'll see she gets breakfast after you leave. Regarding Sabast...you weren't there," I said. "If not for Anifas, he would've killed her."

"He wasn't thinking straight. None of us knew Stina sought him out more often than not when she went out on the town. He thought they would marry, sooner or later, and he'd be on his way to the throne someday. Hearing her voice froze him in place until Tindra struck. I'm sure you can relate. You're the kind of man who reacts harshly to someone hurting those you care about."

Another layer to Eirickson's plotting. What other surprises wait to be uncovered?

I nodded. "Considering the situation, I understand what Sabast felt in the moment, but I don't believe my temper burns quite as hot."

Kurt chewed his lip for a moment. "So...she's settling down...with...you." One eyebrow rose when he looked me in the eye. "Tell me the truth. You two are engaged?"

I met his gaze. "There hasn't been an announcement. She's been busy recovering, and I've been busy making messes. No time to spread the word, so you're the first to hear it. I'd appreciate it if you keep it to yourself for now."

He nodded. "Discretion. No problem."

"And about the weapons in your wagon..."

"It'll be easier to show you when they get here. If it's not too much to ask, could I visit Aerison after we eat? Ander wanted me to pass on some information."

I nodded. "I'll have a guard escort you to the herbalist's house. Where are you staying while you're in town?"

"With my fellow Varians, assuming they have room."

"They're in tents; we haven't had a chance to build more barracks," I said.

"As long as I'm out of the weather," he said, turning his focus to eating.

After his second serving, Kurt patted his stomach.

"I'd heard Croian cooking was bland, but that wasn't too bad...warm and filling at least. Who can get me to Aerison?"

"Before you go, I wanted to tell you Nikulas will be our ambassador to Varia. I guess he'll act as the liaison between me and your people."

"Good to know," Kurt said. "Crum should be happy to see another Croian in the castle from time to time."

I nodded and walked him to the door. "Ingo, this is Kurt, a friend of mine from Varia. He would like to visit with Lieutenant Aerison. Escort him to Abi's house."

He nodded. "Of course, Sire."

I closed the door, and called out, "Tindra. He's gone."

She came to the table, still red in the face, and tapped her foot on the floor.

"We're getting married?" she asked.

"I thought you *wanted* to marry me."

"I did." She chewed her lip for a moment. "I do. But..."

"But what?"

She slopped two helpings of grains into a bowl.

"I don't want you to marry me simply because Croy needs a queen."

"I told you I'd keep you safe."

She shook her head. "That's no reason to get married."

"Remind me," I said, looking at the ceiling while stroking my beard. "Who said 'people get married for worse reasons'? Why, I believe, and correct me if I'm wrong..." I fixed my gaze on her. "It was you."

"Things were different then," she said, lifting her right arm. "We complemented each other. Together, we could've been greater than either of us were apart."

I chuckled. "Sure, things were different then; they weren't as difficult. But I know you're still capable of doing whatever's needed. Quit hiding behind your injury." I felt a chill in the room. Pointing at her, I added, "And stop lashing out with your talent like a child. If you keep that up, I'm going to spend my fortune buying candles."

"Fine," she barked, and stuck her tongue out at me as the candles went dark. "If we're getting married, I want your sword."

I cocked my head and smiled. "Traditionally, at least in Croy, the new bride gets the husband's sword often. Especially the first night."

"I meant your family sword," she said, grinning. "You will present it to me officially. Our children will be added to it when they are born."

A shiver ran down my spine. "Children? I mean...I don't have my family sword. I gave it to Geri to settle my debt, and now he hates me."

She shrugged. "Not my problem. Get it back, or Kurt will figure out you lied to him and let it be known that King Fitzeirick is not true to his word. I bet that would make more messes than you have now."

"You wouldn't dare spread such a rumor."

She smiled the predatory smile that fit her typical attitude. Unfortunately, it looked good on her. "*I* wouldn't have to."

"I'll figure something out."

"I'm sure you will. One question. What do I call you now?"

I squinted. "What do you mean?"

"A nickname. What do I use? After we're officially engaged, I mean."

"I have more important things to worry about."

"More important than what your wife will call you for the rest of your life? I mean...the obvious ones—love, honey, lord...but everyone calls you lord, dear. But people expect me to be clever, inventive, so I can't use those. I'm open to suggestions."

I sighed. "I'm sure you'll come up with something. I'm going to see if the rest of the Varian soldiers left this morning."

I opened the door, and a fist struck me in the chest. Pain flared in my shoulder as I pushed the dark-haired attacker away. Stumbling back from the door, I called for my guards to subdue him.

Tindra rushed to my side.

Chapter 32

The guards standing nearby looked at me. One of them chuckled. "Sire, it's Sigbrand, reporting from the battle."

Looking at the lanky man sprawled on the ground, the familiar heat of embarrassment crept across my face.

I offered my hand. "I'm sorry. I thought you were attacking me."

He refused my aid and pushed himself to his feet before bowing.

"My deepest apologies, my lord. I didn't mean to strike you. I meant to knock on the door, not expecting it to open."

Tindra laughed and stepped back.

I chuckled and shook my head. "Maybe, someday, I'll feel secure enough in my capital that I won't assume everyone is attacking me. What news do you bring?"

"General Heming sent me as we chased the retreating soldiers south," he said, and bowed again. "We arrived to find the bulk of the force outside of the hall. I don't think they expected much resistance from inside. Forcing them to fight on two fronts cost the Satran force many men."

"You're positive they were Satran?"

"Yes, Sire. Everyone I saw was."

"Our losses?"

"I don't think anyone died. Didn't see anyone fall that didn't get up. We dropped twenty Satran, maybe more, from what I saw. Shortly after sunset, most of the fighting concentrated inside the walls. A new skirmish broke out after dawn when the force went into retreat. General Heming ordered every able fighter to chase them back into the forest and make sure they know not to come back."

I nodded. "What about the Varian soldiers?"

"They don't fight the same way we do, but they held their own. I'd fight with them at my side again."

"I appreciate a warrior's perspective. Thank you. You are dismissed."

He bowed again. "My pleasure, Sire."

• • • • ● • ● • • •

I left for the Varian camp and found it empty.

"They left at sunrise," Sigric said. "Fairly impressive sight, if I say so."

"Thank you."

"It is my duty, m'lord," he said.

I decided to let Aerison know his men were on the move, so I walked to Abi's. A Varian soldier walked out carrying a pot and some bowls as I reached the house.

"Is the lieutenant awake?" I asked.

He nodded. "Breakfast is being taken to him now."

"Thank you," I said, and made my way to his room.

I knocked on the door and stepped back.

Abi looked out, "Yes? Oh...Sire. What can I do for you?"

"I'd like to talk to Aerison."

"Of course," she said, "I'm done in here for now anyway," and walked toward the kitchen.

Stepping into the room, I raised my voice a little, "Lieutenant Aerison, I can't believe you're not up and around. You've had a whole *day* to recover."

He looked at me, swallowed, and chuckled. "I've got many more days of recovery before I'm out of this bed on my own. I know my men left this morning."

I nodded. "But you don't know the men sent north did themselves proud."

"As expected, didn't need you to tell me."

I smiled. "I haven't received a full report from my generals, but their messenger brought news of success. Few injuries and no losses on our side, enough enemy fell to drive them back through the forest. Once I have the report from your men going south, we'll form a battle plan."

"You can't hold a meeting with all your men in here," he said. "Include Espen and Aksel; they'll help in my absence."

"Your insight will be missed."

He sighed. "You know where to find me."

I frowned. "I'm sorry you're hurt."

"It's not your fault, and I know you'll see it doesn't go unpunished."

I nodded. "Kurt came to see you?"

"He did," Aerison said. "The situation in Varia is not good right now, but my king made his decision, and I'm loyal."

"Crum has your support?"

He shook his head. "The throne has my support, so long as the man sitting on it doesn't order me to kill countrymen. Truth be told, many question Jesca's choices, but I think she's got better sense than Stina."

"Despite everything she's been through, she's got a good heart."

"Jesca did everything she could to come home; Stina abandoned her country to marry the man plotting to conquer us. That's all I need to know."

"Good point," I said. "I have some business to attend to. If you need me, send someone to find me. Also, when you get ready for some meat, have one of your men ask my guard to take them to a butcher named Grith."

"Thank you for the recommendation. I'm doing my best to follow the herbalist's advice for now."

I nodded and smiled. "Tindra made it about six weeks before screaming for meat."

"Sounds like a typical Varian."

"She's many things," I said, "but I'm not sure typical is one of them."

Aerison started to laugh then groaned as he clutched his ribs.

"I know how bad that feels," I said. "Sorry, I didn't mean to cause you undue pain. I'll leave you to eat and rest."

He nodded, face white.

I didn't see Abi on the way out and nodded to the Varia guards watching her house as I walked out the door.

Stopping at the gate to the compound, I asked the guards if they had seen Roald.

"I haven't seen him around for a few days," one of them said. The other three nodded or grunted their agreement.

"Thank you. I'll check on him."

I hurried to his quarters, knocked on the door, and received no answer. Knocking harder, I yelled his name without a response. The door didn't move when I leaned against it.

Bolted. I hate to barge in, but something's not right.

Pushing my talent into the wall, I forced the bolt strap out of the stone.

The unmistakable smell of death tainted the air when I pushed the door open.

I called out for him again.

Silence.

The stench grew stronger as I stepped inside. A brief glance showed all the candles were unlit.

I backed out, and yelled to the guards near my door, "Get Tindra and come here!"

She ran from the house, the guards hardly able to keep pace with her.

"What's wrong?"

"I think Roald's dead, and you're probably better able to tell if someone killed him."

She put her fist on her hip and cocked her head. "What's that supposed to mean?"

"Of the two of us, which is more likely to recognize an assassination?"

The guards looked from me to her.

"True," she said, nodding. "Where is he?"

I shrugged. "Didn't see him in the sitting room or at the table."

"His quarters are the same as yours?" she asked.

"As far as I know."

"If you suspect an unnatural death, I suggest the guards stay outside while we search the house," she said. "Never know who's watching, and it could be a trap."

"Good plan. Let's go," I said, and took a deep breath.

We found the meeting room empty. Nothing seemed out of place.

A quick check of both guest bedrooms showed them to be dusty from disuse.

I walked to the room at the end of the hall and knocked. The latch rattled on the other side, but Roald didn't make a sound.

"Door's secured. I'm guessing an assassin wouldn't lock himself inside."

"A stonesyth could've gone out through the wall," Tindra said.

I nodded and sythed the bolt strap from the stone wall. It fell to the floor with a clank.

"Roald," I said, while pushing the door open a crack.

The horrible smell grew stronger.

"I think we found him."

Tindra coughed and followed me into the room.

Roald lay on his side, facing away from the door. His hands rested under his head.

"Check him for wounds," I said, after a heavy sigh. "I'll let the guards know we need a grave."

After sending one guard to find a couple of stonesyths and the other to tell Agrim I wanted him to oversee the burial, I looked for anyone paying attention to Roald's quarters.

"Looks like he died in his sleep," Tindra said, after walking outside. "Poisons cause discomfort before they kill. Typically stomach cramps, so the victim dies bent over or clutching at their stomach. I found no wounds, and he had a calm look on his face."

I nodded. "Thank you. Good to know he wasn't killed."

"Do you want me with you when you tell his family?" she asked.

"As far as I know, he's the last. His wife died years ago. If he had children, I never met them."

Agrim led four men into the courtyard and bowed when he got close. "At your service, Sire."

"Thank you," I said. "Bury him in the courtyard. I'll let his peers know he's gone."

"Of course, Sire," he said, before assigning tasks to his men.

"I'll go with you," Tindra said. "I should meet the people you're sending to live with my family."

"Of course. Boril has become more friendly. Porsey is still looking for a way to pay me back for disgracing him."

She nodded and walked next to me to Porsey's quarters. I knocked, and he soon opened the door.

"What are you doing here?" he asked.

"I wanted to let you know Roald's dead. We found him in bed. Best I can tell, he died in his sleep," I said.

"Why should I care?"

I raised my eyebrows. "He sat on the council with you. Surely you had a friendship."

"He *wasn't* my friend," Porsey said. "The old man supported you. That makes him a traitor to his country."

"Roald's the reason I spared your life," I said, pointing at him.

He glared at me. "It would have been better for both of us if you'd have killed me like you killed Auti. Roald told you to keep us alive just to humiliate us."

"He asked for mercy on your behalf because he believed I was a better man than my half-brother."

Porsey clenched his jaw. "He saved me for his own gain, not because he cared about my life. I have packing to finish."

Before I could say anything, he closed the door.

"Sounds to me like you should have killed him," Tindra said.

I shook my head. "Roald was right to stop me."

"You do understand Porsey isn't looking to disgrace you," Tindra said. "He wants you dead."

"I'm aware," I said, nodding. "One reason I took away his influence as best I could. Still, I believe he's the one who instigated the resistance among the military leaders. It took Croian lives being threatened to get most of them on my side."

"But they wouldn't come to your aid before?"

"Eirickson," I said, raising my hand to knock on Boril's door.

He didn't answer.

Boril better not be dead too. I knocked harder and called his name.

The door swung open, and Boril looked at me wide-eyed. "What's wrong?"

"Sorry, I'd come to tell you Roald's dead. When you didn't answer right away, I feared the worst."

"I wasn't expecting anyone," he said. "Saw no reason to hurry to the door." His chin quivered as his eyes looked to the ground. "Roald was a good man, fair, sensible. He tried to guide me when I joined the council." He shook his head. "So many times, he cautioned against blindly siding with the jarl, but I knew what Eirickson expected of me."

Pointing over my shoulder, I said, "My men are giving him a burial in the courtyard. You're welcome to say some words."

He raised his gaze but didn't look me in the face. "No. It wouldn't be right. I'm not the man I should have been. Not the man Croy needed...it seems."

I put my hand on his shoulder. "That doesn't mean you can't voice respect for a fallen friend."

He gave me a weak smile and nodded. "Maybe later. After I've had a chance to gather my thoughts."

"As you think best," I said.

He bowed and closed the door.

"How did he ever get a leadership position?" Tindra asked. "A cold man wouldn't follow someone that spineless to a fire."

"I think that's why Eirickson wanted him. It's easy to get your way when everyone agrees with you."

Chapter 33

Before we reached the funeral, a guard yelled for me at the gate, "There's a wagon here! The driver's looking for Kurt."

Tindra moved behind me. "It's Sabast."

"You don't know that," I said. "But go back inside if it makes you feel safer."

She answered by running back to my quarters while I hurried to the gate.

"Hello," Halmar mumbled.

I smiled. Of all the men the war council sent with me, I liked the big stonesyth best. *He's a man of few words who gets things done.* "Well met. I believe Kurt's at the Varian camp." I glanced at a nearby guard. "One of you go get him. Halmar, come with me, visit with Tindra while we wait."

The wagon creaked as the big man hopped to the ground, and we walked to my quarters together.

Opening the door, I called out, "Tindra, Halmar's here."

"Alone?" she yelled, from her room.

"Yes."

He looked at me.

"She's afraid of Sabast."

He shrugged. "No worry."

She ran out and hugged him. "Nice to see a friendly face."

His dark brown eyes lit up, and he chuckled. "Same. Sorry about the hand."

"When's Sabast coming?" she asked.

"Don't know," he said. "Don't worry."

"How can you tell me to not worry?"

"Kurt said hands off."

"See," I said. "Kurt's taking care of you."

She shook her head. "I don't trust Sabast."

"You're safe," Halmar said.

"Tindra, listen to him. What's in the wagon?"

"Wait for Kurt."

I nodded and pointed to the table. "We can sit and catch up. How have you been?"

"Good," he said, while sitting. "You?"

"I've been busy. Seems like I make more problems than I solve," I said. "I trust the Croians have treated you well."

He nodded. "Not home, though."

"Not home yet," Tindra said. "Or have you changed your mind?"

"Not sure," he said.

She nodded.

"I thought you wanted to be Sabast's right-hand man," I said.

"Maybe not."

"It sounded like a good opportunity for you," Tindra said. "I don't mean to pry, but what's bothering you?"

A knock on the door broke the conversation.

"Come in," I said.

Kurt walked in. "Halmar, I trust the trip was smooth."

He nodded.

"Tindra, Per sent something for you if you'd like to join us," Kurt said.

"Is this a trick?" she asked.

Kurt growled and threw his hands in the air. "For the last time, no, it's not a trick. No one is coming for you. You are safe—from me, from Sabast, from anyone you think might be out to get you. Even if I hadn't ordered Sabast to leave you alone, he's not going to cross your fiancé."

"Fiancé?" Halmar asked.

She groaned and put her hand over her eyes.

"I asked him to keep it quiet," I said. "Tindra and I are getting married."

"Oh," he said. "Good."

Kurt cleared his throat. "Now, please come with me to the wagon. I'm sure you're going to want this."

She kept Halmar between her and Kurt as we walked to the wagon.

Kurt lifted the seat and pulled out a dark sack.

"You may need some help getting it on and adjusted the first time, and be careful taking it out; I'm sure it's sharp."

"What?" she asked, taking the sack. "It's a blade?"

Kurt nodded. "Of a sort, yes."

Carefully, she reached inside and pulled out a leaf-bladed, short sword with a long, leather cup on the end.

"Put your arm in the leather and buckle it down tight," Kurt said.

"A little help," Tindra said, offering me the cup.

I held it open for her.

She shoved her arm in, and I cinched the straps tightly into the buckles.

"Step back," she said, before taking a few tentative swings ending with a respectable thrust. Her face glowed as a wide smile spread across her lips.

"Looks good on you," I said.

She nodded. "It's going to take some getting used to."

"I meant the smile," I said, and winked.

She blushed and looked away.

"What about a scabbard?" I asked.

"He didn't have time to make one before I left," Kurt said.

"No problem," I said. "I know a good tanner. I'm sure he can make something that'll work."

"How long until your shoulder heals?" Tindra asked.

"A few days, and I'll get Abi to take out the stitches. I'll see how bad it is then. Why?"

"I need to practice," she said.

"Not before we get a sturdy cover for that thing. I don't want to lose a finger or worse, just so you can practice."

Kurt laughed, then asked, "Fitzeirick, ready to see something you've never seen before?"

"Sounds interesting," I said.

We followed him to the back of the wagon, and Kurt brought out a strange, T-shaped thing.

"What's that?" I asked.

"We call it a crossbow."

"Doesn't look like any bow I've ever seen," I said.

He put one end to his shoulder. "It goes across your body instead of vertical like a normal bow."

"Why make a new bow?" I asked.

He offered it to me. "It's easier to aim and has more force. Doesn't take as much practice either. Put the end against your shoulder and point the front at your target."

I did as he instructed. It felt strange but not as awkward as aiming a bow.

"There's no arrow."

He nodded, grabbed a quiver from the back of the wagon, and led us to a spot several paces from a large tree in the courtyard.

"It takes a stonesyth to draw the string."

"I'll try," I said, "but I'm not back to full strength yet."

"Give it to Halmar; he's been practicing anyway."

I handed the crossbow to Halmar and watched.

He pulled some strength from the ground before drawing the string. It caught on a small metal rod standing above the surface of the wooden body.

"You put the arrow in the channel in the wood, aim by putting the tip of the arrow on your target, and fire by squeezing the metal piece underneath," Kurt said.

The crossbow twanged loudly, and the arrow buried itself almost halfway into the tree.

"How long will the string stay drawn?" I asked.

"Until you release it," Kurt said.

"Can Halmar draw it and hand it to me?"

Kurt nodded.

Halmar sythed some strength again, caught the string, and handed me the weapon.

"Point it toward the tree," Kurt said, as he placed the arrow on the crossbow, "then squeeze."

The bow pushed against my shoulder for a split second before the arrow flew toward the tree, striking lower and to the right of Halmar's shot. I lowered the crossbow and let out a whoop of cheer. "It *is* easier to aim. I want one for every man in my army."

"Slow down." Kurt patted me on the back. "I only have ten with me. There's a downside too. A good archer can fire three or four arrows in the time it takes to ready and fire the crossbow."

I squinted at him. "That's a pretty big downside."

Kurt smiled. "Every weapon has good and bad points. A regular bow's performance varies with the strength of the archer. If you can draw a crossbow, no shield or armor will stop the arrow. Shooting an unarmored man, the arrow won't stop and is still a danger to the men behind him. It can fell a horse and injure someone hiding behind it. As you saw, anyone can aim it accurately with little practice. Also, the arrows are all the same length where traditional bows require arrows made for each archer."

"But this won't replace a skilled archer on the battlefield," Tindra said.

"No," Kurt said, "but it *will* give non-archers the chance to hit from afar, once or twice, before charging into battle. We believe we can make these bigger, mount them in wagons or on ships, and send arrows made from small trees across the battlefield or into walls and gates."

"I'd like to see one that big," I said.

"It's being worked on now," Kurt said, "but no promises.

"Any other surprises?" I asked.

"We're working on another idea, but I need you to show me something first," he said.

"What?" I asked.

"I understand there's a beach at the end of the mountain chain that splits your two territories. From what I've heard, before the Carved Scar, people regularly used the beach to get past the mountains. We have an idea for boats, troop transports, but I'd like to see the beach to get an idea of what we're dealing with if we try to go to sea."

"Not sure who told you about them, but they left out an important detail. Croians made the Carved Scar because so many people died when the sea got rough and smashed the barges to splinters on the end of the mountains," I said.

"These won't be barges," Kurt said. "If you don't want to take me, I understand, but being able to move companies of men from here to the Satran shores could make a big difference in battles."

I nodded. "No doubt you don't understand what I mean without seeing for yourself. I need to talk to Roi, but we can go first thing in the morning."

"Understood," he said. "Where do you want the crossbows?"

"Take them to the Varian camp. Train them on use, maintenance, and how to make arrows. If there are any woodsyths good enough, see if they can make more."

Kurt nodded. "Halmar, coming with me?"

He answered by climbing on the wagon.

"Tindra, it's good to see you happy. Be careful with that blade of yours," Kurt said, before snapping the reins.

"I think we should go see Thorgault about a scabbard," I said, before turning to the guards. "One of you find Roi. I need to speak with him after I get back."

"Of course, Sire."

"I can check on my clothes," Tindra said.

"And we get some lunch."

She offered me her hand. "At your side, husband-to-be."

"I thought you wanted to be discreet," I said.

She shrugged and grinned. "Seems word's spreading on its own."

I chuckled and nodded before taking her hand and heading to the tanner's shop.

Chapter 34

Tindra, walking with the sword strapped to her arm, got many curious looks as we made our way to Thorgault's.

"How's business?" I asked, as we stepped inside.

"Busy, m'lord. What canna do fur ya?"

"I've brought more work," Tindra said. "And I need you to make a change to my armor."

"I see," he said, pointing to the blade. "Where'd ya get that from?"

"A friend from Varia sent it. I need a cover, preferably one I can secure with some ties."

"What color cover?"

"Black."

"Mind it dyed?"

"As long as it works," she said.

"Ya want the cuff inside or outside tha sleeve of yur armor?"

"Inside, please. I think it will be more secure that way," she said. "And how are my orders coming along?"

Thorgault wiped his forehead. "Armor's near done. Was near done. Still gettin' leather ta split for pants. I should have enough scraps to cover tha blade. Can ya leave it?"

"As long as I can get it back after I eat," she said.

"See me after ya eat."

She nodded, unbuckled the cup before slipping it off her arm, and handed it to the tanner.

Tindra nodded, and we walked to Grith's.

"Well met, butcher," I said, as we walked in. "What's for lunch?"

Grith bowed when he heard my voice. "Roast pork today. I'll throw in the ale for free."

"Two pork sandwiches, but I'll pass on the ale. Water for me."

"I'll take the ale," Tindra said.

"Two sandwiches, ale, and water. I'll take a silver single, not a copper more," he said, serving us sandwiches piled high with chunks of pork.

I didn't argue and placed the coin on the counter before taking a bite. The meal was Grith's usual, good and filling. Tindra finished before me and left for the tanner's shop.

"...think you could make something like that?" Tindra asked Thorgault, as I walked up minutes later.

He nodded while rubbing his chin. "Tha leather's easy. Got enough dyed black to make tha cuff. Hafta get wit a smith fur tha fork."

"What are you two talking about?" I asked.

She turned to me. "I had an idea while eating. Per made this for a blade; why can't one be made for a fork so I can feed myself?"

"Sounds like a good idea," I said. "How much?"

Thorgault scratched his head for a moment. "Gold double oughta cover it. Gotta give the smith his share."

I handed him the coin. "The sooner it's made, the better. How's the cover for the blade?"

Tindra said, "Looks good to me," and handed me her short sword, covered in black leather.

I looked it over and admired the craftsmanship. He'd added a couple of loops to the leather cuff so the scabbard could be secured in place.

"Keep the cover on, and you won't hurt yourself," I said, smiling.

She stuck her tongue out and took the weapon from me. "This way, I can practice and not hurt whoever I'm training with."

"That too," I chuckled.

"Sire!" someone yelled, behind me.

I turned to see Sigric, red-faced and breathing heavy, pushing his way through the crowd.

"What's wrong?"

"Generals Jomar and Heming have returned. They're waiting at your quarters."

"Thank you for finding me," I said. "Tindra, coming?"

"I want to talk to Thorgault about my idea."

I nodded and jogged to the compound.

"They're waiting at your door," Ingo said.

Continuing my pace, I greeted the generals and invited them inside. Once we were seated, Heming spoke, "We arrived before too many civilians got hurt, but the Satran had breached Nikulas' southern gate. His men kept them busy until we overwhelmed the force. We asked the Varian soldiers to stay behind, watching for anyone hiding, and hounded the retreating Satran. They turned southeast, but we stayed on their tail, archers forcing them to keep running until we chanced being ambushed in the forest."

"You're sure they were Satran?" I asked.

"No doubt," Jomar said.

"No Croians or Varians in their ranks?" I asked.

"None that I saw," Jomar replied.

"Can't say I saw anything but Satran men fall, Sire," Heming added.

"And they headed southeast through the central forest, not directly south?" I asked.

"Correct," Heming said. "Why do you ask?"

"I have reports of people in the southern part of the eastern skati driven from their homes by Satran soldiers. If that is the case, why didn't the attacking force flee south?"

"Who told you Satra had taken land there?" Jomar asked.

"Someone I trust," I said. "And I've seen the refugees myself. Did either of you know?"

"Of course not," Heming said.

"No, I did not," Jomar added.

"Yet my source said they sent several messengers. Who would keep such information from me?"

Jomar looked at Heming and nodded. "Hallfrid," they said together.

"Either of you heard of a warrior named Wary?" I asked.

Jomar scratched his head for a moment. "Can't say the name's familiar."

Hemming nodded, though. "Overheard Commander Agnor telling Hallfrid he'd given Wary leave to see to family in the south of the eastern skati. Why?"

"Wary's dead," I said. "He took part in the ambush that injured Bior and me."

"Who else was involved?" Heming asked.

"I don't know. We caught Wary only because he gave chase when we ran."

"Seems risky. Why didn't Agrim's men recognize him?" Jomar asked.

I frowned. "He wore Satran armor."

The color drained from both men's faces.

"Now you understand why I'm asking if the attackers went south or not."

Jomar nodded.

Heming stared at me for a moment. "What are you doing about the claim of attacks in the south?"

"I sent the other half of Aerison's men to investigate. They have nothing to gain by deceiving me."

"Do you think the attack on Nikulas' holdings is related?" Heming asked.

"I don't know enough to say with any confidence. I aggressively went after all known Satran and their sympathizers after killing Eirickson. It's possible my actions foiled enough of their plans to make the Satran leaders take that long to reorganize. It's also possible your peer collaborated with Satra all along, waiting for a chance to kill me and take leadership of the country for himself. Did you see any evidence of Agnor, Haldan, or any of the men under their command while chasing the Satran?"

"I didn't, m'lord," Heming said.

"Nor did I," Jomar added.

I shook my head. "We have at least sixty warriors, supposedly on training patrol near the central forest, and no one saw them?"

Both generals shook their heads.

I crossed my arms. "Where are they?"

"Perhaps they patrolled to the south," Jomar said, pointing.

"Where other Satran actions pushed Croians out of their homes," I said.

Hemming rubbed his hands together. "Maybe they were ambushed by Satran soldiers in the south."

"With no word? Not even one man making it back to find help?" I asked, shaking my head. "We'll know for certain when the Varians return."

"And then what?" Heming asked.

"Depends on what they have to say," I said. "See to your men and await further orders. Let them know the fight may begin soon. Make sure they're ready."

The generals stood.

"One more thing," I said, standing to look them in the eyes. "If I can prove Hallfrid and his men are working with Satra, heads will roll. Between you two and General Gudmann, select a few executioners." I paused, pressing my lips together. "If you can't, I'm sure some of Aerison's men would be glad to pay Hallfrid and his fellow traitors back for their lieutenant's pain and suffering."

They looked at each other.

Hemming nodded. "I can assure you Varian involvement won't be necessary. We'll take care of our own mess, even if I have to do it myself."

I offered him my hand. "I appreciate your commitment."

He shook it, and they both bowed before leaving.

I returned to my seat to consider what I would do if Aksel brought back news of Croians posing as Satrans.

The door opened. Tindra walked in ahead of Roi.

"A lanky runner came through the gate behind us. Said his name is Svani, and he's back from the Varian capital," Roi said.

"Let him in," I said. *I hope he brought good news.*

The messenger handed me a sealed letter. "From Mikael himself, m'lord."

I took it from him. "Thank you, Svani. Your service is appreciated. You're dismissed."

"Glad to be of service, Sire," he said, and bowed before leaving.

"Would you like to read it?" I asked, offering Tindra the letter. "Don't know if there might be something personal in it."

"Doubtful. Father knows the difference between business and family."

I read the letter quickly. "He has concerns about them escaping, but I've talked to Kurt about that. His people will deal with them."

Tindra smiled and nodded. "Sounds like everything is in place then."

"Good," I said, and turned to Roi. "I have some errands for the king's right-hand man. Tomorrow morning, I'm traveling south, to the beach, with Kurt. You're in charge should something happen while I'm gone. Please locate enough wagons to move Porsey, his family and belongings, and Boril with his belongings to the House of Daufi. I plan to give Roald's quarters to Agrim, and his company can turn the other two quarters into their new barracks. Round up enough stonesyths and woodsyths to build housing for the Varian soldiers where they have tents now. Do you know when Grima and Einns will arrive?"

He smiled wide. "They're a couple of days away."

I nodded. "When I get back tomorrow, go to The Trader's Cup and wait for them. While you're there, get my sword from Geri. I still owe him for helping me after I escaped the tunnel. Whatever he asks, pay it."

He looked sideways at me. "Why do you need it?"

"I plan to marry one day, and my fiancée demanded I give her my sword."

"Why would she—" Roi's eyes opened wide. "You found Aesa and didn't tell me? Where is she? I take it she's well."

Tindra glared at me. "You haven't told him?"

"No, I haven't." I stood, went to him, and put my hand on his shoulder. "Roi, Satra captured Aesa. One of their generals took her as a trophy. She killed herself."

His mouth opened and closed several times. "How do you know?"

"Stina died wearing Aesa's necklace. Before I killed Eirickson, he told me how he got it...and what happened."

"That's...terrible. I'm so sorry. You should've told me sooner." He shivered and some color left his face. "Who's your promised now? Anyone I know?"

Tindra stepped away from Roi after I nodded toward her.

Chapter 35

"You're marrying *her*?" Roi shouted, face changing from pale to red.

"A spur of the moment decision, but a sensible one...for several reasons," I said.

"Sensible?" he echoed, voice still raised. "You're trying to rule this country. Have you given any thought to how your people are going to feel about having a Varian queen?"

"She's attractive and graceful and knows her way around a royal court. All good assets of a queen," I said. "I figure our people will accept her about as well as the Varian people accept a Croian king."

"Ugh," Roi groaned. "Don't remind me he's going to rule Varia—and don't change the subject. This is a bad idea."

Tindra closed her eyes and shook her head.

"Why? She almost died defending me. Is that not proof of her loyalty?"

She turned toward the door. "I'm going to leave you two alone to sort this out."

Roi shook his head and the floor quivered. "A leader should be able to take criticism."

Several candles flared as she looked over her shoulder at him.

"I can take anything you throw at me, but that isn't going to help you two settle this."

"She's right," I said. "Let her go. Maybe then we can discuss this calmly and keep you from damaging my house."

Roi crossed his arms and the floor stopped shaking.

I waited for the door to close before continuing. "I've known you my whole life, and I value your judgment, but Tindra's been at my side more than you or Crum since I arrived in Varia. She did more to get me in position to kill Eirickson than anyone else."

"She beat you unconscious and tied you up," he said. "Or have you forgotten that minor detail? I'd say saving Jesca and returning her home did more to put you where you are."

"She helped with that too. Regardless, it doesn't matter now," I said. "I told Kurt we were engaged to save her from Sabast. And I could do worse."

He shook his head. "I'm not sure how."

"You don't get to question this," I said, pointing at him. "You abandoned me to save Grima. I saw how happy you were and forgave you, released you from your oath instead of demanding you stay at my side."

"Grima didn't deserve what happened to her. Tindra's a manipulator and a deceiver and a schemer," he said, pounding on the table. "Or have you forgotten that too?"

"She and I came to an understanding months ago. She's been nothing but honest with me since. You counseled her at Abi's, tried to help her deal with her loss. I don't understand why you're upset."

He took a deep breath and rubbed his temples for a moment. "I'm upset because I'm your friend and mentor, and I think you're making a bad choice. Advising her is one thing. Supporting a marriage I don't agree with is entirely different."

"I made the decision, told Kurt, and now I have to follow through or look untrustworthy. I need Varia's support, and you know it. A stain on my reputation will be more damaging to Croy's future than having a Varian queen. You don't have to agree with me; just get my sword. Geri's more likely to give it to you than even listen to my request."

He threw his hands in the air. "Fine, but I get to say 'I told you so' when this goes bad."

I nodded. "But first, you have to stand at my side during the ceremony."

He shook his head. "I have much to do before I can go to Geri's. I'll see you when I have your sword." The door slammed shut behind him.

I sat, staring at the door, unsure how I should feel.

I didn't expect him to be enthusiastic, but I never thought he would be against the idea.

The door opened. Tindra sat next to me and took my hand. "That went well."

I looked at her and tried to smile.

"You don't have to marry me," she said.

"I want to. Otherwise, I wouldn't have said anything to Kurt."

"You sure you didn't do that out of pity for me?"

"I've never pitied you. And before you ask, it's not from some sense of obligation either."

"And Roi disapproves because he thinks I've taken Aesa's place?" she asked.

I shook my head. "You can't take her place. I'll always miss her."

She nodded. "I understand."

"It's because of what you were, what you did before. I doubt Crum would approve either."

"Crum's views will change soon enough. A crown is easy to pick up but hard to wear."

That made me smile. "Why didn't you tell me that before I decided I should be king?"

"I thought you already knew."

I nodded and chuckled. "I thought I did too."

Squeezing my hand, she said, "I'm serious. You don't have to marry me if it's going to cause so much trouble."

"He'll see," I said, squeezing back. "You're not the person you were."

"Are you saying you like who you see now?" she asked, with a crooked grin.

"I better understand who I see. You're becoming a better person."

"But I've lost my confidence. That's not an improvement."

"You'll get it back over time. You don't have to marry me either, you know. Tell Kurt you changed your mind," I said.

"And look like I backed out of a commitment? I wouldn't damage my reputation like that," she said.

"Then we get married," I said.

"When?"

I scratched my head. "I have to clean up some of these messes first."

"Not any time soon then," she said, with a smile.

"The last time I planned a wedding, I ended up branded and in a dungeon."

She nodded. "I'm going to bathe. Care to join me?"

"No," I said, "I have other things to attend to. Maybe next time."

"Guess I should start getting used to the life of a queen now," she said, chuckling as she left.

I should find Agrim and tell him to move.

I called to Ingo when I got close to the gate.

"Yes, Sire."

"I'm planning to ride south in the morning, have someone make sure my horse is ready."

"Of course, Sire. I'll see to it myself."

"Thank you," I said. "Do you know where Captain Agrim is?"

"Check our barracks," he said. "If he's not there, someone will know where he is."

"Thank you."

I found some of Agrim's men training outside. "Where's Captain Agrim?"

"Inside, playing cards last I saw, m'lord," one said, before dodging a charge.

I nodded, walked inside, and found him seated, back to the door, at a small table with two other men.

"Wasting time with games?" I asked gruffly.

He turned so quickly he fell out of his chair. Jumping to his feet, he bowed and stuttered an apology.

I laughed. "Calm down, it's fine. We all need to relax sometime. I've brought some news, but it means work for you and a few of your men."

"Whatever you need, Sire," he said.

"I'm sure you heard Roald died recently."

He nodded.

Putting my hand on his shoulder, I smiled. "You get his quarters."

He looked at me, slack-jawed.

"There's a catch. You have to go through his belongings. Keep anything you want. Bag up the rest; I'll send them to Varia with Porsey and Boril."

"How soon should I start?" he asked.

"The sooner, the better. I suspect we'll send the former Thanes north in a few days. Once they're gone, your men can convert their quarters into barracks."

He turned to the table. "You heard King Fitzeirick. Round up everyone not busy, and let's get to work."

"I appreciate your sense of urgency," I said.

"Thank you, Sire," he said, and rushed past me.

I took my time strolling back to my quarters. As I walked, Crum's advice about smiling and waving to show people you were friendly came to mind. I waved to a few people glancing toward me. A few sneered or frowned, but most smiled and waved back. *I'll take what I can get.*

I arrived at the gate in time to watch Tindra, wet hair shining in the sun, walk across the courtyard. She showed a little of the grace and confidence I'd seen after we first met.

"I hope I'm not out of line for asking," Svan said, "but does she know you look at her like that?"

"She wants me to look at her like that," I said. "For a long time, I wouldn't let myself, but she's different now."

"I've heard she's dangerous."

I looked at him. "From who?"

"A couple of the men in the first company of Varian soldiers that arrived after you killed Eirickson," he said. "They said she's tougher than she looks and has more blood on her hands than most soldiers."

"They weren't wrong."

"Is that why you keep her close?"

"Not exactly." I chuckled. "She knocked me out the first time we met."

He laughed. "I've felt that way toward a couple of women in my life."

I shook my head. "You misunderstand. She knocked me unconscious."

"Oh," he said. "So, you're keeping an enemy close?"

"She wasn't really my enemy then, though I didn't know it at the time. She certainly isn't now."

"It is true she killed that Varian princess?"

I nodded. "She did it protecting me. Stina tried to gut me like a lamb. Tindra struck without hesitation."

He whistled, long and low. "Sounds like someone you want on your side."

I nodded. "I'd rather have her at my side than facing me. I've never met someone so focused on doing their job. She knows how good she is and isn't someone to be taken lightly...doesn't fight fair either."

"Firesyth?"

"You can't tell by the way she carries herself?" I asked.

"Didn't want to assume," he said. "You know what they say about firesyth women, especially Varian firesyth women."

I looked at him. "My mother was a Varian firesyth."

"Oh," he coughed. "My lord, I meant no offense."

"I'll let it go. This time."

"Thank you, Sire," he said, with a quick bow.

I hid my smile until he couldn't see my face.

Chapter 36

Tindra set her cup down as I walked in. "What are you smiling about?"

I shook my head. "Nothing of any importance. Did you cause another commotion at the bath?"

A crooked grin appeared on her face. "You'd know if you would've gone with me."

"I take that to mean you did," I said. "I'm thinking about having Abi look at the stitches in my shoulder. Come with me to check on Aerison."

"Sure. I can try to cheer him up the way Roi did for me."

"After what Roi said about you, I thought you'd be mad at him."

She shrugged. "He gave you his opinion. I even agree with some of what he said."

I rubbed my forehead. "Then why did you leave?"

"You two need to work it out between you. I didn't want Roi thinking I'm pressuring you."

"You could have stayed to support me," I said, as I opened the door. "Make sure you say hello to Svan as we pass the gate."

She scrunched her face. "Why?"

"Trust me," I said.

"Does it have anything to do with the smile on your face when you walked in?"

Stepping outside, I said, "Maybe, maybe not. Perhaps I just want to make sure you're being polite to my guard. They'll be living in the compound soon."

She closed the door and hurried to catch up to me.

Crossing her arms, she said, "I am always polite."

I shrugged. "Fine, suit yourself."

The guards greeted me and bowed as we passed.

Tindra said, "Hello, Svan. How are you?"

"F-Fine Lady Tindra. You look...uhh...like you are having a...umm...nice day."

She lifted her right arm and smiled. "I've had much worse."

He pursed his lips and nodded.

"See you later, Svan," I said, choking back a laugh.

"Yes, Sire," he said, and bowed.

Tindra kept giving me sideways glances until she thought we were far enough away that Svan couldn't hear her. "What was that about?"

"Politeness and manners," I said. "That's all you need to know."

"If you won't tell me, I'll ask Svan."

"Doubt he'll say much," I said, smiling.

She stuck out her bottom lip. "Normally, I'm the one keeping secrets. Not sure I like knowing someone's hiding something from me."

"That reminds me of what Crum said before he found out Mam was Jesca," I said, and laughed.

She punched my arm. "I told you to not compare me to him."

I stuck my tongue out at her. "You two are more alike than either will admit."

"Humph," she grunted. "Maybe I shouldn't marry you."

"All you have to do is tell Kurt you changed your mind. Once I've settled my score with Satra, I'm sure beautiful Croian maidens will throw themselves at my feet."

"You certainly have all the qualities of a king, especially the overly high opinion of yourself," she said.

"I have good days and bad," I said, laughing again.

"And one day, I'll be able to tell the difference."

Only two guards stood outside Abi's house.

"How's Lieutenant Aerison?" I asked.

"He seemed to be in a fair mood during lunch," one said.

"Good to hear," I said. "Thank you."

Abi opened the door soon after I knocked. "King Fitzeirick. I wasn't expecting you today."

"When were you expecting me?"

One of the Varians snickered.

"Well...I'm not sure, but not today."

"May we come in?" I asked.

"Of course, Sire."

"Hello, Abi," Tindra said.

"Tindra, nice to see you," she replied. "You're looking well."

"I'm feeling better," Tindra said. "Is Lieutenant Aerison awake?"

"He was when I took the empty tray from his room a while ago."

"I'll see if he wants company," Tindra said, and left us in the entryway.

"Abi," I said, "I'd like you to look at my shoulder and see if the stitches can come out."

"Let's go to the garden so I can see them in natural light," she said. "But if they aren't itching, they probably aren't ready."

I followed her to a small table, away from the center of her garden, sitting in a patch of sunlight.

"Take off your shirt and sit on the table," she said.

As soon as I sat, she ran her fingers across the wound on my chest. "Doesn't feel warm, nothing leaking. That's a good sign. Now for the back."

I fought the urge to giggle as her light touches tickled my skin.

"Looks about the same. I'd like for them to stay in a couple more days, but if you insist, I can take them out."

"Please," I said. "If I get busy over the next few days, I may not have time to see you."

She nodded, and said, "Wait here," before hurrying back inside and returning carrying a small, cloth pouch.

She set the pouch on the table, removed a small metal pot, and took off the lid.

The smell of spiced rotten fruit wrinkled my nose.

"Since you insist on having these out early, I'll put this paste on your wounds."

"What's it for?"

"Keeps it from getting fevered," she said, as she took a small knife from the pouch.

After nodding at her explanation, I braced myself for the cold touch of steel against my skin and the strange ticklish scratching of thread sliding through my flesh.

Cutting the threads in my chest didn't bother me, but I flinched when the cold metal slipped across the wound in my back.

"Hold still," she said. "I could have cut you."

"Sorry."

"Almost done," she said, while continuing to pull thread out of the back of my shoulder. "There, all out. This ointment will sting a little."

At first, the cold, slimy goo ran a shiver across my chest. Tensing my muscles like that made my shoulder complain a moment before the sting hit me. Gritting my teeth against the sharp pain, I nodded. Then the burn set in.

"Is it supposed to feel hot?"

"Oh," she said. "Is it burning?"

"Yes," I hissed.

"Perhaps I used too much pepper in this batch. Shouldn't matter, though. Let me finish, and I'll wrap a bandage to keep it from sticking to your shirt. Leave the bandage on overnight."

"When will the burn stop?" I asked.

She shrugged. "If it's still burning after dinner, come back."

"I've had worse," I said, before my back joined in the minor torture. "Varian herbalists make hot treatments the way Varian cooks make spicy food."

Abi sucked in a sharp breath as she pulled some bandage cloth from a pocket in her apron. "That sounds unpleasant."

"It is."

She quickly wrapped my shoulder.

"All done. Don't use your left arm too much until your shoulder stops feeling tender. If you open the wound, it will take longer to heal."

"Thank you," I said. "What do I owe you?"

"Nothing...and don't argue. I won't accept payment for such trivial work."

I smiled. "I don't expect charity. A king should pay his way."

"It's not charity," she said. "I'd do the same for anyone."

"If you insist. I'll stop by Aerison's room. Tindra and I can see ourselves out."

She curtsied, walked to some nearby plants, and plucked some leaves.

I heard Tindra talking as I got close to Aerison's room. "...on your feet again before you know it, but don't rush, or you'll make it worse."

I paused outside the door, not wanting to interrupt their conversation.

"I know you're right. Abi said the same thing earlier today. It's just...what good is a leader who can't get out of bed without help? I feel useless."

She sighed. "What good is a grown woman who can't cut her own food? At least you'll walk again, given time. I'll never get my hand back. Once you're on your feet, you can lead just as effectively as before."

"You could've lost more than your hand. You served Varia's interests and did right by Fitzeirick. Any soldier would wear that wound with pride."

"I wasn't a soldier."

"Could've fooled me."

My face grew warm as I realized my politeness had turned into eavesdropping. I cleared my throat before stepping into the room.

"How are you today?"

"Same as yesterday," he answered gruffly, before smiling. "Still alive, so there's hope. Heard anything from my men?"

I shook my head. "No word from the south yet."

"They're all good men," he said. "They'll send a messenger as soon as they can spare one."

"I know. I'm getting impatient. The attack on Nikulas unified most of my leaders; I'd like to take advantage of their cooperation and start pushing east."

"You're new to this," he said. "Don't get in a hurry."

"Listen to him," Tindra added. "Remember what happened last time you rushed into a bad situation?"

I chuckled. "At least there's no one to brand me."

"That's one way to look at it," she said.

"Tindra," I said, "my shoulder's tender. I'm going to my quarters to rest."

"I'm going to talk with Aerison a little longer. I know how much better a little company can make you feel."

"Of course," I said, and left for my quarters.

Chapter 37

Agrim's men crowded the normally quiet courtyard, working to clear Roald's quarters and move their captain's few belongings into his new home.

Sibbi ran to me. "Sire, we stuffed all Roald's clothes in sacks, but where should we put them?"

"Store them with Agrim until Porsey and Boril leave for Varia. I'm giving the clothes to the house they're staying with."

He bowed and hurried back into the building.

I nodded to the guards at my door and made my way to bed. I didn't expect to sleep with the throbbing and burning in my shoulder, but I needed to rest.

· · · ● ● · ● · · ·

Someone took my hand and sat on the bed.

"Are you not well?" Tindra asked.

I yawned and shook my head. "Just tired."

"It's nearly moonrise. Did you want to sleep through dinner?"

"No. I didn't expect to sleep at all. At least the stuff Abi put on my shoulder quit burning."

"Good." She squeezed my hand. "Rest a little longer. I'll send one of the guards to get food."

I grabbed a couple of coins from my purse.

She nodded and took them.

My hand missed the warmth of being held. *I could get used to that.* A tear welled in the corner of my eye. Blinking it away, a steady flow started, and I shivered before sobbing.

Tindra stopped at the doorway and looked back. "What's wrong?"

I sat up and shrugged as a frown twisted my lips downward.

A candle flickered to life as she got close to the bed. "Aesa?" she asked.

My chest tightened when she said the name. I nodded.

"You never mourned her or your mother," she said, and wiped my cheek.

"There's always too much at stake...couldn't afford the distraction." I covered my face with my hands.

"Go ahead, let yourself feel the loss."

I pulled her to me, pressing my face against her stomach, and let down my guard. Memories of Aesa, the first time I saw her, our first kiss, how it felt when she became my promised, the last time I saw her alive. Everything that once brought me joy turned to sadness flooding my thoughts. My chest ached. Breaths came in short gulps. My body shook. I released all the sorrow I'd pushed away.

She stroked my hair and encouraged me to let it all go. "You're not using me to replace her. I won't let you. You know that, right?"

I nodded.

"Good. Don't feel bad that you still love Aesa. You're a good man, better than most, for holding out hope for so long. Neither of you got what you deserved."

I shivered one more time before relaxing my hold on Tindra.

"Before this madness started, I gave you my word, told you I'd be here for you. Nothing's changed."

"I—I don't know what came over me," I said. "Telling Roi about Aesa's fate wasn't easy, but I thought I had accepted the loss. You holding my hand felt...nice. Maybe right. When you walked away, something inside crumbled. I couldn't help myself."

She ran a finger along the scar on my scalp.

"I didn't let myself grieve the loss of my hand for a while. You never saw it because I thought you needed me to be strong. Abi saw my frustration and sadness...she saw my fear. I tried to hide it from Roi, but I could tell he saw it when he told me I had to accept the loss before I could get better and move forward with my life. Have you talked to him about Aesa and your mother?"

I frowned and shook my head. "He knew about my mother's death before I did."

"It might do you both some good, and it couldn't hurt to make sure he knows I'm not Aesa's replacement."

I wiped my hand down my face. "As if I didn't have enough weighing on my thoughts."

She chuckled. "Did you think being king would be easy? Get yourself together. I'll send someone for dinner before we starve."

One corner of my mouth turned up into a half-smile, and I lay down after she left.

Talking to Roi is a good idea. He seemed to help Tindra deal with her loss. He and I have been through too much to not be able to talk openly and come to an understanding. Closing my eyes, I took deep breaths to calm myself and pluck out the troubling thoughts trying to take root in my mind.

"I'm putting food on the table. Come eat when you're ready," Tindra shouted, pulling me out of my thoughts.

Feeling energy from the solid strength of the stone floor under my bare feet lifted my mood as I walked to the table. The smell of rabbit and potato filled the air.

"How is it?"

"Surprisingly good for Croian food. I'm starting to miss Varian spices, though. Maybe it's time you hired a cook?"

Shredded rabbit filled the split potato. I took a bite and agreed with her opinion. "I'll hire Einns as soon as I have a castle and Grima will let me."

"She seems reluctant to let him branch out on his own, but he's a good choice."

"Can't blame a mother for looking after her child, wanting him to be the best he can be," I said, before taking another bite.

Tindra swallowed and nodded. "True. My parents always supported me. Speaking of parents and kids and such...do you feel like talking about us?"

My fork paused on the way to my mouth, and I raised an eyebrow. "We'll marry when the time is right, have kids, and grow old together."

She laughed, loud and long, right arm clutching her chest before taking a breath and pointing her fork at me. "You—You think it will be that simple? Us, you and me...a half-Croian, half-Varian king with a traitor's brand will just marry the one-handed, Varian, ex-spion, have kids, and grow old?"

"Assuming I rid us of the threat from Satra, yes."

She scoffed. "For a year, you've fought to survive, focused on nothing but destroying your half-brother to save two nations, and now you plan to sit back and let life happen?"

"No," I said. "I'm building trust and putting the right people in place to help me keep control of Croy while preparing to destroy Satra. I'm not stone-headed enough to think I can do this on my own."

"I'm not trying to argue with you, but throwing coin around is not how you build trust. Believe me, I know what a handful of gold will buy."

I tapped my finger on the table.

"Eirickson let his men take advantage of merchants and ruled through fear. I'm paying them to show I'm better than he was. They spread the word, tell others I'm more than fair and loyal, then our lives are easier. Not at first, of course, but once the war is won, things will be better for everyone. Ander lived an easy life for many years, did he not?"

She chuckled. "Not for quite some time after losing southern Varia to Eirick. The country was far from calm then. Plus, he married a respected woman of high birth. I can't imagine how things would have turned out had his wife been Croian. Have you given any thought to how much trouble our union is going to cause?"

I nodded. "Of course, but I trust you can convince them I made the right choice. And I'll be retaking the far east and turning south. Taking land instead of losing it. That will please my people."

"Thank you for appreciating my abilities, but it's going to take more than good looks and a quick wit to win over an entire country. I won't be the only Varian gaining power as the war progresses. In order to accomplish your goals, you'll be indebted to Kurt and his men. Are you willing to let them help you keep what you take?"

I frowned. "I haven't decided."

"Kurt thinks you have, and he's keeping the crown on Crum's head to show you how much he can help."

"What do you mean?" I asked.

"It's obvious, and I know him. It's how Kurt works. His group keeps your best friend in power in their country, which is not without risk—someone could make a power grab and start a civil war. But having Crum depend on the war council and Ander whispering in his ear makes the crown more friendly to them. Helping you gain the throne here gets them a foothold in Croy. If you manage to wipe out Satra, their focus shifts to other business opportunities—"

"And everyone suffers for their benefit," I said, cutting her off.

She glared at me. "They are not bad people because they live by different rules than you."

"So, you agree with people operating outside the law?"

A candle near her flared as she raised her voice, "I've lived most of my life in the gray areas of the law, often sanctioned by my king. More often than not, Varia has benefited from the actions of the council—including helping you." She paused, looked away from me, and turned back with a strange grin. "How did you get me off-topic? I didn't want to talk about politics; I wanted to talk about us."

I smiled and stuck my tongue out at her. "You directed the conversation, not me."

Pressing her lips together, she shook her head before shaking her finger at me and smiling back. "Just like a royal, twisting words to make it sound like someone else's fault."

I shrugged, smiled wider, and took her hand. "I am what I am. You knew this when you swore to help me. I'm starting to think you find me irresistible."

She squeezed my hand and raised her eyebrows. "Irresistible? Really? What would make you think such a thing?"

A loud knock interrupted the conversation.

"Who's there?" I shouted.

"Svan, Sire. A Varian messenger has word from the south."

Tindra nodded when I looked at her. "Let him in!"

A tall, lean Varian stepped in the door, bowing when he reached the table. His leather showed signs of battle, blood-caked around a couple of larger slits.

"Are you hurt?" I asked.

"I'll live," he said. "Sergeant Aksel sent me with word of the fighting. Your men invited us in and kept us off our guard until we were set upon by Satran soldiers."

I squinted. "My men?"

"A Croian warrior named Agnor greeted us. Had his right hand, Vegar, escort us through the settlement."

I growled, and the building shook.

Tindra laced her fingers through mine. "Focus your anger in the right direction."

Closing my eyes, I took several deep breaths before looking at the messenger. "How bad is it?"

"Another is getting word to Sergeant Espen to lead the rest of us in support. Sergeant Aksel asks you to send at least one hundred trusted men as soon as possible. He doesn't want the innocents to think we're invading."

"Svan!" I yelled.

He rushed into the house. "Yes, Sire."

"Send someone to the southern gate. The remaining Varian soldiers are leaving soon. Make sure they get through without delay. Find General Gudmann and bring him to me with all haste."

He bowed and ran out.

I turned back to the messenger. "Tell Sergeant Espen a Croian force won't be far behind him."

"Gladly, King Fitzeirick."

"Travel safe and swift," I said. "And thank you for your service."

He grimaced while bowing before leaving.

"I hope my generals found some executioners," I muttered.

"It's as bad as you feared," Tindra said.

"Worse. I knew Hallfrid hated me but never believed he'd actively conspire with Satra. He's no better than Eirickson."

"Now you know, and you're prepared to do something about it."

I nodded. "But I have to kill seasoned commanders and generals. Not an ideal way to go into battle."

She squeezed my hand. "You've been successful with far less."

I rubbed her right arm. "Not without cost."

"True," she said, "but I lived, thanks to you."

"Don't forget, Anifas kept Sabast off you."

"And he's been properly thanked."

I cocked my head sideways but didn't ask.

"Kurt's going to be here in the morning. I'm riding south with him for a few hours. I promise I'll spend time with you, discussing us, soon."

She nodded. "I'll hold you to it."

Chapter 38

A knock on the door ended our conversation.

"Come in," I called out.

Svan entered ahead of General Gudmann.

"You sent for me?" Gudmann asked.

I nodded. "Gather all the men under your command and leave for the southern region of the eastern skati as quickly as possible."

"May I ask what we're getting into?"

"A messenger brought word from the Varian force sent to investigate the rumors of Satran soldiers in the area. Agnor and Vegar greeted them before leading them into a trap. Hallfrid's men were supporting Satra soldiers—"

"To the fire with him and all his men," he said, through clenched teeth.

"On that, we agree," I said. "The other Varian soldiers are already moving to support their countrymen. Sergeant Aksel asked for a Croian force to come and keep the few innocents still there calm. I don't need more Varian blood spilled, and I don't want good Croian citizens believing the Varians are invading."

"Of course," he said, as he turned away. Opening the door, he paused and turned back. "Sire, about Satra...Eirickson and Hallfrid both swore we were safe."

"You spent too much time listening to lies. What happened in my skati should have convinced everyone of the truth," I said.

He nodded and left.

"Svan, tell Generals Jomar and Heming I'll need those executioners we talked about soon. They have until I return tomorrow, or I'll let the Varians have Hallfrid and the rest of the traitors."

He shivered. "It's that bad?"

"Worse."

He bowed. "I'll make sure they understand."

"One more thing, barring another emergency, I'm not to be disturbed until Kurt arrives tomorrow."

"As you wish, Sire," he said, and left.

I turned to Tindra. "Glad I could enjoy my meal before getting news I didn't want to hear. I think I'm ready to call it a night...join me?"

Her eyes shot open. "Are we going to—"

"Sleep. We're going to sleep."

"Oh," she said, and drooped her shoulders. "Why do you want me to sleep with you?"

I gave her a sad smile. "I don't want to be alone tonight. Roi's moved out, and you're much cuter than him. Besides, our engagement was unplanned. Why should our first night together be any different?"

"Doesn't this go against your Croian customs?"

I shrugged. "Ordinarily, it would, but now you're my promised, and in this case, there's no one to offend. My parents are dead, yours are far away."

"What they don't know won't hurt them? That's part of your society?"

"Not normally, but...gray area?"

She laughed. "They wouldn't mind anyway. If you need me to stay with you tonight, I'm all too happy to oblige."

I stood and pulled her into a hug.

"I thought you only wanted to sleep."

I nodded.

"Keep this up, and I'm not going to let you sleep," she said, with a sly grin. "At least for a little while."

"Behave yourself, or I'll be fine sleeping alone."

She stuck her bottom lip out in a mock pout but nodded.

"I don't have any clothes to sleep in. I learned the hard way it's too easy to get tangled in dresses. Are you sure this won't be a problem?"

"No," I said, winking at her. "I'll undress too...so you feel more comfortable."

Tindra smiled when I took her hand and led her to my bedroom.

She raised an eyebrow as her dress hit the floor. "And we're just going to sleep?"

I finished undressing and nodded.

"You still look good," she said, after settling in the bed.

"Thanks. So do you," I replied, crawling under the blanket. "Would you mind putting the candles out?"

With a nod, the room went dark. Having Tindra's warm body curled up next to me felt better than when she held my hand. I waited for her breathing to slow before falling asleep.

I woke alone. While pulling on fresh clothes, I heard the door close. Hurrying down the hall, I found Tindra putting a basket in the middle of the table.

"Breakfast," she said. "I figured you and Kurt would want to eat before you left."

The smell of warm bread filled the air. "What did you get?"

"Sweet rolls and a skin full of apple juice."

I licked my lips. "Sounds good. Hope he gets here soon."

She smiled. "It's not quite first light, but I don't expect he'll make you wait long. I know you want to wait until we have time to talk, but I need to say something about last night."

I held my hand out for her. "Of course. What's on your mind?

"I enjoyed being next to you...feeling wanted. It's nice to know you still find me attractive," she said, lacing her fingers in mine.

I kissed the back of her hand. "I never denied a physical attraction to you, even told you before I liked what I saw."

A knock on the door interrupted the moment.

"Who's there?" Tindra asked.

"Kurt."

"Come in," she said.

He entered wearing a black, leather outfit that reminded me of my night out with Tindra. His sword hung on his right side.

Never noticed he's left-handed.

"Come. Have breakfast with us," she said, sweeping her arm toward the table.

He grunted. "I expected to eat something hard and cold on the way south. A hot breakfast is an appreciated surprise."

"I'm still learning how to treat guests. It hasn't been a high priority all things considered," I said.

"Every ruler has his own style. Don't try to copy Ander, though you could have a worse example. I will say I'm curious how Crum will run his court," he said, sitting.

"He knows how to entertain," I said.

"But does he know how to host?" Tindra asked, as she handed Kurt a roll. "Jesca doesn't have the experience I do; she won't be much help."

Kurt nodded as he chewed. "King Ander's servants aren't all leaving. Those who stay behind will make sure everything goes smoothly."

"With any luck, they'll keep him from making a complete fool of himself," Tindra said, after handing me my food.

"Are you sure you don't want my help?" I asked.

"I can take care of our guests," she replied, bringing three cups to the table and filling them before sitting.

"Speaking of servants," Kurt said. "Any plans to recruit?"

I shook my head. "I've got too many problems to worry about. I'll find people once things have calmed."

He smiled and looked at Tindra. "Seems your queen-to-be doesn't mind doing the job."

She returned his smile, and her eyes flashed. "I do what's necessary. You, of all people, should know."

"That you do," he said.

After swallowing my last bite, I drained my cup and excused myself to put on my hammer. Kurt stood near the door when I returned.

Tindra blocked me as I passed the table. "A kiss for a safe journey?"

I smiled and leaned toward her.

She turned my head slightly and kissed my cheek.

I turned back to her, and she planted her lips firmly against mine.

"And one to remember me by."

Kurt chuckled.

"Are you expecting something to happen while I'm gone?" I asked her.

She shrugged. "With you, anything is possible."

Kurt's chuckle turned into a full laugh before he followed me outside.

"Meet you at the southern gate," he said, mounting his horse.

I hurried to the stable and met Lopt, walking my horse out to me.

He bowed. "Good morning, Sire."

I took the reins. "Thank you for getting him ready."

"My pleasure. Travel safe."

My injury reminded me it wasn't fully healed when I pulled myself onto Andale. Fortunately, the horse moved smoothly, so I wouldn't be uncomfortable for the entire ride.

"What's the best route to the beach?" Kurt asked, when I arrived at the gate.

"Follow the mountains, keeping them to our left."

"Easy enough," he said.

I nodded and heeled Andale into a trot.

We rode side by side, watching for any surprises waiting in the shadows lingering before the sun rose over the peaks.

Chapter 39

"She's a good actress," he said. "But you probably already know that."

I cocked my head. "What do you mean?"

"Tindra. She plays the part of bride-to-be well."

"What makes you say she's acting?"

"It's what she does," Kurt said. "She plays the part needed to take advantage of the situation. She said it herself before we left: she does what's necessary."

I shook my head. "She's not acting. We *will* marry, and she'll be queen of Croy."

"When?"

"When the time's right."

"So, she won't commit. Typical Tindra. Anyone can buy her loyalty, but no one will ever earn it."

"She showed the depth of her commitment when she risked her life to protect me," I said, poking my finger at my chest. "*I'm* the one who won't set a date. There's too much going on now to organize a wedding."

"I see," he said, and looked away.

"Speaking of loyalty. Why is the war council backing Crum as king?"

"That's not a simple question to answer," he said, still turned away.

"We've got time."

Nodding, he turned to me. "Jesca won't let him leave her side. We believe it's best for Varia to have Ander's blood sit on the throne."

"Why not one of your men?"

"You ask as if you don't know we operate in the shadows," he said.

"I know you do, but this would be the war council's chance to run Varia in your favor."

"We already do," he said, smiling. "Ander works with us. He has Jesca's heart and ear. Crum bows to her requests because she has his heart. Their children will grow up Varian, influenced by us...keeping things the way we want them."

"Crum's not stupid," I said, folding my arms across my chest.

"That's what we're hoping. He seems smart enough to know why he'll stay in power. Why do you keep insisting we are evil?"

"You operate outside of the law. You were plotting to...I don't know what you were plotting, but it never seemed like anything good."

"We work to keep Varia stable and whole. Our way sheds less blood and wastes fewer resources than a civil war," he said. "How can you question our motives when *we* put you in the position to kill the biggest threat to your country, your people? Are you telling me Croy isn't better off with you in charge?"

"Not yet...but it's going to get better."

"And we can help it improve, once things are settled back home."

"If you're not ready to provide more assistance now, why are you here?"

"Getting the lay of the land and seeing what resources we'll have to work with. Do your people have any experience navigating water?"

My brow furrowed on its own. "Not that I know of. Why?"

"We can make seaworthy boats big enough to transport fifty or sixty men across water faster than they can march on land. Does that sound like an advantage when invading Satra?"

I didn't answer right away, choosing instead to imagine what he'd described. *Moving two companies at a time from Croy into Satra faster than they could march there.* "How quickly could they leave?"

"Almost as fast as you can get them loaded. If we know where the Satran forces are, a company or two could ambush and retreat before they get trapped. Plan out an attack right, and as long as everyone does their job, you can attack the flanks of Satran forces from the shore."

I smiled. "I like the way you think. How soon could you start making these new boats?"

"As soon as we know Varia is stable."

I nodded and pointed to clouds gathering in the distance. "Looks like we might be riding in the rain before the journey's over."

"From what I know, you've been through worse," he said, through a smirk.

"All I'll say is Sabast may have exaggerated."

"Halmar told the same story."

"You can trust him," I said, and chuckled.

"I know," Kurt replied. "That's why we offered him the job of Sabast's right hand."

"You don't trust Sabast?"

He shrugged. "I take him at his word, but he's young and lacks...focus, at times. He benefits from having an older, wiser—at the risk of sounding insulting—more stone-headed second-in-command to keep him on track."

"In my experience, firesyths can be temperamental," I said. "Remember, I was raised by one and engaged to two."

"Yet you grew into the man you are under the guidance of a stonesyth."

My eyes opened wide. "You know about Roi?"

He smiled a predator's smile. "We make it a point to know about the people we associate with. Especially when their friends are stalking someone in Varia."

I took a deep breath and considered the implications of Kurt's statement.

"Then you know about Olver and Grima and—"

"Her boy, Einns if I recall. Yes. Would you like to know who his father is?"

I licked my lips as the burning grew more intense. *Does Roi care?* Weighing my options, I chewed on my lip for a moment before making a decision.

"No. It's none of my business. I'm sure Grima will tell him when she thinks the time is right."

He nodded. "Not all men would be willing to pass on such an opportunity. Information has value."

"I don't hold things over my friend's heads."

He shrugged. "Some people say loyalty is to be admired, but blind loyalty can be costly. Are you willing to pay the price of being loyal to your friends if—when—it comes time to settle a debt?"

Pulling the reins, I stopped Andale.

"I know you're not threatening me because I don't take threats lightly. It's just me and you out here, and if only one of us returns...their story is the truth."

He turned and raised his hands. "I'm not threatening anyone, and certainly not the King of Croy. Only wondering what the future holds for our nations. Politics does strange things to friends, strains some loyalties while strengthening others."

"It seems to me you know something you're not sharing," I said, heeling Andale back into motion.

The predator's smile returned. "I know many, many things I'm not sharing. Plans, moves, possible moves and eventualities. Remember, information has value. That's one of the things that makes Tindra worth every copper."

"And what would it cost me to know what you know?"

"Likely a higher price than you're willing to pay," he said, the toothy smile growing wider. "Of course, payment isn't always made with coins. Depending on how things play out, you may be paying in loyalty."

I scoffed. "You don't know what I'm willing to pay."

A cool breeze hit us head-on. No doubt we were riding into a storm.

He shook his head. "Perhaps we should change the subject. What are your plans to push Satra out of twice-conquered lands?"

"Nothing solid, yet. Anything I told you could change after consulting with my generals and the Varian sergeants."

"Sound thinking," he said, with a nod. "Looking forward to personally repaying Satra for killing your people?"

A few small raindrops sprinkled from the sky.

I shook my head. "I'm in no shape to fight, and it doesn't make sense to risk getting hurt. I have a country to lead."

"I know you well enough. You're blooded and have a taste for fighting. I also don't believe you'll trust your generals to retake your homeland without your direct oversight."

"They're starting to come around to my way of thinking."

The wind blew harder as larger drops fell more frequently.

"I'd heard you were busy getting things under control."

"Some people don't know when to take advantage of opportunities, and others wanted to stir unrest. Neither situation worked toward my best interest."

He nodded and pointed toward the edge of the sky. "If we hurry, it looks like we can ride through this weather."

I followed his finger to a hint of blue past the mass of clouds and heeled Andale to a fast canter.

Chapter 40

Riding through a sparse stand of trees, warm sunlight and the sound of waves crashing on the shore greeted us.

A few men stood in knee-deep water, casting nets.

"Here it is," I said, squeezing some water from my hair.

"And it's never used except for net fishing?" Kurt asked.

"Before they made the Carved Scar, everyone traveled on simple barges across calm water. Few braved the sea when it grew rough, and many families had stories of unexpected storms smashing barges into the end of the mountain range, killing everyone on them. With the scar making it easier to pass through the mountains, the beach is all but abandoned."

"Given such a history, I can see how your people don't have much experience on the water. We'll need to change that for this idea to work. Are you afraid of the water?"

After a quick shake of my head, I said, "No. I can swim."

"Good," he said, and got his horse walking. "I want to get closer and see what the view looks like."

Andale balked at getting his legs wet, but Kurt's horse took to the water like he belonged there.

Kurt pointed to the east. "Any idea how far Satra is from here?" "If I had to guess...two and a half days ride in good weather."

He smiled. "I'd guess fifty strong men could get a boat there in half that, maybe less."

"What about their supplies?"

"That includes food, water, armor, and weapons," he said.

"But not horses?"

He chuckled. "No. Our experience says horses don't care to travel on boats. Either take the enemy's horses or push forward on foot."

I pressed my lips together and nodded, considering the possibilities.

"What keeps the Satran from capturing the boats and using them against me?"

"Ideally, when the fighting's over, there's no Satran alive to worry about, but you and I both know things don't often work so well. In favorable conditions, the boats can leave the shore with as few as nine men. Either leave a few men behind to get the boat away from the shore or one to burn it before it's taken."

"Trapping the men in enemy lands."

"If the Satran are threatening to take the boats, odds are your men aren't alive anyway," he said, frowning.

"You make a good point," I said. "What else do you need to see?"

"It is possible to follow the shore to the other side of the mountains?" he asked.

"When the water's no deeper than this, yes. Why?"

He shrugged. "Getting the lay of the land, looking at possible defensive positions if Satra surprises us."

"I'm preparing to push Satra out of all Croian territory."

"Yet you have no idea what's waiting on the other side of your central forest...do you?"

I crossed my arms. "Not yet. Scouts will go out soon."

He nodded. "How often do you eat fish?"

My brow furrowed as I searched my memory. "I can't remember the last time I had any."

"And your warriors?"

"Maybe those from this part of Croy...I don't know," I said.

"Along with faster transport, this water can help feed your men as long as they're willing to eat fish," he said, looking toward some fishermen not far away. "Let's see what they're catching."

I followed him out of the water.

"Well met," Kurt said, as we dismounted. "Is the fishing good here?"

"You have the look of a Varian," the man said, as he pulled in his net. "You plan to take our sea like you will our land?"

Kurt glared at him for a moment, then smiled. "Quite the opposite. I'm working with your king to get your land back."

The fisher chuckled. "Am I supposed to believe an obvious lie? Jarl Eirickson said the Varians aren't to be trusted."

I cleared my throat and stepped toward him, hand out. "Well met. I'm King Fitzeirick."

He barked a cackling laugh. "And I'm a Thane. You two best be going."

Withdrawing my offered hand, I bobbed my head. "It's my fault you don't know me. I haven't had a chance to visit this part of Croy."

His hand moved to a long knife at his waist. "I'm warning you, I *will* defend myself...gut a man as well as a fish."

Stepping back, I raised my hands. "We mean you no harm." I turned to Kurt. "Best we go, no sense in aggravating a man making his living."

"You have a point," Kurt said. "One more question. How much do you sell your catch for?"

"Won't sell to a Varian for any amount."

Kurt nodded once.

We got back into our saddles and headed north.

After passing through the trees, Kurt glanced over his shoulder.

"You have a problem. Maybe bigger than you realize."

I frowned and nodded.

"How do you plan to fight effectively if your people don't know who you are?"

"My influence is starting to spread in the capital. Word will reach here."

"Considering his attitude, if you wait for word to reach here, you'll be fighting a war on two fronts. My advice: send a few trustworthy men here as soon as possible to gather support."

"And I thought things were about to get better," I muttered, shaking my head.

"What?"

"You're right," I said. "I'll find some men to send this way. I'm guessing Ander never had this problem."

"No, but he's facing a bigger challenge now. While everyone is pleased having Jesca as queen, Ander's pushing the court to support Crum as king."

"Can't say I envy him leading that charge."

He chuckled. "It's a good thing most Varians still respect Ander. Otherwise, I'm not sure he could sway enough people to avoid a power struggle."

"I'm learning about power struggles myself. If you're in the capital over the next few days, you can watch the executions."

"You can't kill your way to respect."

I nodded. "Never wanted to, but some people can't deal with change."

"Especially sudden, unexpected changes."

Nodding again, I added, "I'm sure Tindra and I will eat lunch shortly after I get back. You're welcome to join us."

He shook his head. "After I see you safely back, I'm returning to Varia."

"Before you rush back, see if Elias and his men are ready to go. You could accompany the two former Thanes on their way to House of Daufi."

"There *is* safety in numbers...and I suppose, you'd like me to watch your people—make sure they reach their intended destination."

"It would go a long way toward solving some of my power struggle problems."

He smiled. "I'm nothing, if not helpful."

"And I try to be appreciative by offering you a meal."

"If I'm going to wait, I might as well take you up on the offer."

Chapter 41

When we reached the gate to my compound, the guards stood inside watching something. Before I could ask, I heard a familiar fighting yell—Tindra.

Using Andale's size, I forced my way through the crowd inside the gate as the clack of wood smacking against wood filled the air.

Dressed in a long-sleeved black shirt and black pants, with the cover over her short sword and her scabbarded sword in her left hand, she faced Svan, wielding a wooden practice sword. They circled each other, looking for an opening. Tindra lunged toward him, sweeping her sword low.

He jumped over her blade, slashing downward.

She blocked his swing with the leather-covered, short blade and sliced her scabbard upward, hitting him in the right thigh.

A guard standing near me held his hand out toward Ingo. "Pay up."

I tapped the guard on the shoulder. "What's going on?"

He pocketed some coins and looked at me. "Oh...Sire. I didn't know it was you."

I nodded and asked again.

"Don't know exactly how it started," he said, "but they've been going at each other long enough we've started betting. I'm up six to three."

I shook my head and smiled.

"She's looking tired," Kurt said behind me.

I looked back at Tindra. She breathed hard and sweat dripped from her chin.

"Out of shape. Six weeks of doing nothing will do that to you," I said, before leaning to dismount Andale. *I'd best put a stop to this before she hurts herself.*

Before I could get my foot free from the stirrup, Tindra screamed and charged Svan. He dodged, and she ran into a couple of the men standing in a circle around the two 'combatants.' She spun on one foot and scowled at him as he backed away, holding his sword in low guard. I recognized the predatory smile as Tindra's lips parted.

He better watch her closely, or he'll end up on the ground.

She held both blades at her sides, points trailing behind her, and stalked Svan.

To his credit, he kept moving, trying to get her to show her hand. But despite his attempts to throw her off, he wasn't ready for her feign. When he brought his sword up to block, Tindra attacked.

Svan ducked a wild, high swing of her short sword and rolled to the left. Spinning around to face her, he swung as she turned and struck the cuff covering her wrist. Her eyes flew wide open, all the color drained from her face, and the noise coming from her didn't sound human. Falling to the ground, she dropped her sword and rolled into a ball, clutching her right arm against her chest.

Svan stood, frozen in place, with a look of complete shock.

I jumped from my horse and ran to her. She flinched when I touched her and shrieked again.

I looked over my shoulder. "Someone get Abi. Svan, help me get her inside."

"Yes—Yes, S—Sire," he stammered.

She thrashed, fighting us as we carried her to bed.

After placing her on the bed, he turned away from me.

"Sire, I resign as a member of your guard. I'll wait for word of my reassignment in the barracks."

Tindra returned to her balled-up state as soon as we released her.

"No need to resign," I replied. "Unless you intended to harm her."

He hung his head.

I sighed. "Wait in my meeting room. We'll talk there."

"Shhh," I hissed softly, turning my attention to my fiancée, and stroked her hair. "You're safe. I'll make sure no one hurts you."

She made a strange whining sound and moved her head away from my touch.

"Abi's coming," I said. "She'll make sure you're not hurt."

I sat on the bed, staying close until Abi walked in.

"What happened?" she asked.

"She took a blow near her wrist and"—I waved my hand toward the ball on the bed—"did this."

Abi nodded. "It might be best if you let me work alone."

"I'll be in my meeting room," I said, pointing down the hall.

I walked into the meeting room to find Svan, eyes closed, on his knees.

"Take a chair," I said.

He didn't move.

I cleared my throat. "Take. A. Chair."

He nodded and groped blindly for a chair.

"Stop being stone-headed. Open your eyes, sit, and let's talk."

He moved to the nearest chair without looking at me.

"I know she's your promised, the queen-to-be. I didn't want to spar with her, but she insisted."

"Wait...how do you know she's— Never mind, not important right now," I said. "Start from the beginning."

He nodded, eyes still cast down. "After you left, she sent for me...asked me to go with her to the market. We stopped by the tanner first, and he had pants for her. She seemed thrilled. After dropping them in my arms, she hurried to the tailor's shop and returned with shirts. I gladly carried the load. We practically jogged back here. She told me to get a practice sword and meet outside after she changed clothes. I thought she planned to work on her form or something. Instead, she charged like she'd gone wild."

"She prefers surprise attacks." I rubbed my chin. "I wonder why she didn't wait for me to get back."

Svan looked at me, brow furrowed. "Excuse me?"

"She's been anxious to get back in shape. I guess the new clothes lit the fire in her, and she had to try them out."

"And now I've hurt her," he said, frowning.

"You did nothing wrong. I suspect you opened a wound that's far from closed—"

"I don't understand."

"She lost that hand to a sword not long ago."

"The day you killed Eirickson?"

I nodded.

"I'd heard stories but..."

"*You* did nothing wrong. Tindra should've waited for me to get back. I can't fault her for being excited, anxious to test herself..." I shook my head. "What's done is done. Take your sword; I have a job for you."

He nodded. "As you wish, Sire."

"Find Sergeant Elias and tell him Kurt will be traveling with his men back to Varia. Make sure Roi has wagons ready for Boril and Porsey and his family. I want them loaded and ready to leave with the Varians."

"Of course, my lord."

"If Kurt is still outside, send him to my table and have someone see to my horse."

He bowed. "With all haste, Sire."

I sighed and rested my head in my hands for a moment before leaving the meeting room. Kurt wasn't at the table, so I assumed he'd gone to take care of his business.

Abi stepped out of my bedroom as I looked down the hallway and hurried to me.

"I gave her something to help her rest. She'll likely sleep until sunset."

"How bad is she hurt?"

"Once I got that blade off her arm, there's barely a red mark. I doubt it will bruise."

"Going by her screams, I feared it might be much worse."

She shook her head. "She hides it well, but that part of her arm is still tender. And...I think the blow reminded her of that day."

"I agree. What can I do to help?"

The herbalist shrugged. "I can help wounds heal, but I know nothing about calming her mind."

"Short of helping her sleep, you mean."

She smiled weakly. "Yes...but it isn't *really* helping her."

"I'll talk with her," I said.

She nodded and left.

What am I going to do with Tindra? I can't stop her from deceiving herself.

My stomach growled, reminding me I hadn't eaten lunch. I didn't want to eat alone, so I knocked on Agrim's door.

He didn't answer immediately but opened the door before I knocked again and blinked when he saw me.

"I didn't mean to make you wait, Sire."

"No worry," I said. "Are you settling in?"

"Getting there. What can I do for you?"

"I haven't had lunch yet and don't want to—"

"I saw what happened. Please accept my apology on behalf of Svan. He—"

"Stop," I said. "I've already talked with him, and there's nothing to apologize for. Come with me to lunch. Let's talk."

Chapter 42

Agrim seemed unusually nervous as we made our way to Grith's shop.

"King Fitzeirick and the captain of his guard...two of my favorite customers," the butcher said, as we stepped inside. "Two bowls of goat stew?"

"And some ale," I said.

He smiled, and said, "Have a seat."

"About Svan," Agrim said, as we sat.

I glared at him and threw my hands up. "I *said* he did nothing wrong. Why does no one listen to me?"

"Sorry, Sire," he replied, looking down.

"That's not why I asked you to eat with me. Wanted to let you know things are going to be busy soon, and your men need to be extra mindful of what's going on."

Grith placed our food and drink on the bar.

I nodded and handed him a gold double.

"More than enough, Sire," he said.

I nodded. "Use the rest for someone else's meal."

He smiled and went back to work.

"My men are always at their best," Agrim said.

"I don't doubt your men or their ability, but I expect new...unrest in the coming days. It could get bad."

"What do I need to know?"

"Porsey and Boril should leave town in the next day or two; Svan is finding out for certain. The Varian soldiers found the rest of Hallfrid's men, the ones on training patrol, conspiring with Satran soldiers in the southeast. Executions of all charged with treason will begin soon after our new diplomats are outside the capital. I want at least two of my guard at every gate. No one leaves the capital without my seal until the following morning. The rest will be at the execution, watching for troublemakers. Make sure everyone understands I expect something to happen within days of Hallfrid losing his head."

"More uprisings?"

I shrugged. "I thought we'd removed the Satran from our land before the Varian report. Now, I don't know what to expect, but I want you and your men prepared. It could get bloody again."

He sighed and shook his head. "I'd hoped those times were behind us."

"It's not what I want to do; it's what must be done. Croy can't move forward until we remove the disloyal."

"Sounds ugly when you say it that way."

"I'm learning being king isn't always pretty. By the way, Svan said he knew of my engagement to Tindra. Do you know who told him?"

"I heard it from the Varian soldiers keeping watch at Abi's. Congratulations, Sire," he said, smiling and offering his hand.

Kurt said something to someone. Returning his smile, I shook his hand. "Thank you."

"Since we're discussing executions, I'm guessing you aren't planning to wed soon."

"Good guess. Those details will wait until things settle."

"Wait too long, and we'll be at war. Not a good time to marry."

I nodded and washed down the last of my stew with half a cup of ale. "Finish your lunch. I should get back to look in on Tindra."

He nodded, slurped down the stew, and belched.

Grith chuckled as we left.

· · · ● · ● · ● · · ·

"I hope she recovers," Agrim said, as we parted ways at the gate.

"Thank you," I replied, and hurried to my quarters.

She lay on the bed, uncurled but still asleep, and didn't move when I sat near her. I brushed my hand through her hair, and she murmured something.

"What?" I asked softly.

She didn't respond.

I ran my hand through her hair again.

"Don't wanna be here," she said quietly. "Wanna go home."

My hand froze, and the shiver down my back ended as a knot in my stomach.

Kurt's words echoed in my head. "She's a good actress, plays her part well."

Maybe she's been playing me all this time. Is that why telling him we'd marry upset her? I shook my head and left the room.

Sitting at the table, I let myself think out loud. "She risked her life for me. She's been honest with me. How do I —"

A hard knock on the door interrupted my one-sided conversation.

I'll have to figure this out later.

"Who's there?"

"Svan, Sire!" he yelled, through the door.

"Come in."

He entered red-faced and breathing hard.

"What's wrong?"

"I've done what you asked and wanted to report as quickly as possible."

"I know you take your duty seriously. No reason to strain yourself."

"As you say, my lord. After what happened, I—"

"Stop," I said harshly and pointed to the chair across from me. "Sit. Do you and Captain Agrim happen to be related?"

Svan sat, looked at me, and scratched his head. "No, why do you ask?"

"Because neither of you listens to me, I thought maybe deafness ran in the family. For the third and final time...you did *nothing* wrong. As a matter of fact, you went beyond your duty when you carried the clothes for Tindra. She may be my promised, but she holds no authority over you. You could have refused her request."

He shook his head. "Not to argue with you, Sire, but if she has your heart, she has my respect. I did nothing more for her than I would have for my mother or sister."

I smiled. "If only more men acted like you."

"The good ones do, my lord."

"I know, from personal experience, that some good men do not...but that's getting further off subject. What do you have to report?"

"Sergeant Elias expects to leave once the sun tops the mountains tomorrow. Roi arranged for four wagons; they'll be waiting outside the compound in the morning."

I smiled. "Good. Please let Captain Agrim know about the plan and tell him I said executions will start tomorrow afternoon. Visit Porsey and Boril. Tell them they leave early tomorrow. At first light, you will bring them breakfast, then gather three men to load their belongings in the wagons. The four of you will escort the caravan outside the wall. After they leave, report back to Agrim for further orders. Expect to be busy over the next few days."

He stood, bowed, and said, "With all haste, Sire."

I followed him to the door and told Sigric to find Generals Jomar and Heming for me. I went back and checked on Tindra. *Still sleeping.*

Pouring a cup of water, I sat at the table, and my stomach burned at the thought of spilling so much blood tomorrow afternoon.

It's necessary.

The water wet my throat but didn't quench the uncomfortable fire in my gut. Resting my head on the smooth stone table, I took slow, deep breaths to calm my nerves.

None of this is what I wanted, least of all ordering the death of so many warriors.

I sat there, with my eyes closed and breathing, and nearly fell asleep. Ordinarily, the knock on my door would have aggravated me, this time, one thought came to mind.

Give the order and get this messy business over with.

"Come in!" I yelled.

Sigric entered and held the door for the two generals.

I stood and shook their hands before asking them to sit.

"I'm sure you know why you're here," I said. "The time has come. Do you have executioners selected?"

General Heming looked at Jomar.

"All ten of our commanders volunteered," Jomar said.

"I'll admit I'm surprised," I said.

Heming nodded. "After a bit of debate, Svert convinced the others it would be the most honorable way for the accused to die."

They don't deserve honor. Clenching my jaw, I stared at them until the flash of anger passed. "The executions will happen tomorrow after lunch."

"My only argument is you're killing experienced leaders and twenty-one warriors while preparing for war," Jomar said.

"But I can't fight a war using leaders and men ready to aid the enemy," I said.

"I know," Jomar replied. "That's the only reason I've agreed to support you."

"Where will they die?" Heming asked, before I could say anything else.

"Outside the prison," I said.

"In the open?" Jomar asked.

"I have no intention of announcing the event, but I won't keep people from watching traitors die," I said.

"Understood," Heming said. "Do you need anything else?"

Before I could answer, Jomar cleared his throat. "You do know there will be consequences for this, don't you?"

I nodded. "Plans are in place to deal with any uprisings."

"The same way you dealt with opposition before?" Jomar asked.

I nodded again.

"You can't kill your way to respect," Heming said.

Closing my eyes, I took a deep breath. "I know. Believe me...I know. If I had another option, I'd gladly take it. I can't rule, can't make Croy better, and continually deal with hostile people, including my military leaders, working against me. Croy can't be stable with high-ranking officials supporting an enemy prepared to tear the country apart."

"When does it end?" Jomar asked.

Looking him straight in the eye, I said, "When the last Satran stops breathing."

He stared at me for several heartbeats. "You're serious. You won't be satisfied with getting the far eastern skati back. You want them all dead."

"I've never been more serious."

"That's going to take men," Heming said. "Lots of men."

"Carts don't pull horses," I said. "Let's not get ahead of ourselves. We haven't even started taking back the territory Eirickson gave them. We can take advantage of the resources there to supply our efforts and open the eastern passage so Varia can move men and supplies through. At least those are my initial ideas. I'm sure it will take several meetings to make a solid battle plan. For now, let's get rid of our immediate problem."

"As you say," Jomar said.

"Tell your men to be ready. This will be messy, but the sooner it's over, the sooner we move forward."

"Of course, Sire," Heming said, as they left the table.

Chapter 43

A noise from the bedroom caught my attention. I hurried to check on Tindra.

"Where—" She coughed. "Where am I?"

"In our bed," I said.

"Oh," she replied, after clearing her throat. "I'm home."

The hair on my arms stood. "What? I'm not sure I heard you."

She looked around. "Sorry. My throat's a little scratchy. I said I'm home."

I put my hand over hers. "Where you want to be?"

She squinted at me and nodded. "Would you bring me some water?"

I smiled. "Of course."

The candles were lit when I came back.

"I hope you didn't punish Svan too harshly. It wasn't his fault," Tindra said, after taking a long drink.

"I know. I don't blame him. Even praised him for helping you carry your new clothes. You, on the other hand, knew better than to spar with him."

"It felt so good to be out of that dress, I felt like the old me...thought I was ready."

"Obviously, you're not."

She looked away from me.

"I could have used you at my side earlier," I said.

"What did I miss?" she mumbled.

"Executions will happen tomorrow. I ended up having a heated discussion with two of my generals. Your presence might have helped."

"Sorry," she said softly.

"Did Svan mention he knew about our engagement?"

"No, why?" Her head turned quickly, and she looked at me, eyes wide open. "How does he know?"

"He's not the only one," I said. "Best guess is Kurt mentioned it to some of the Varian soldiers. Rumors spread through tight-knit groups faster than fire through straw."

"Is this a problem?"

I shrugged. "Not for me, but I thought you should know...spare you the surprise of someone asking. Did you know Kurt saw you go down?"

Her face lost a little color. "Oh...no. He did?"

I nodded. "Is that a problem?"

"It's rarely a good thing to let a predator see you as vulnerable. Thank you for telling me."

"You're safe. He knows I'm not weak," I said, holding my hand out for her.

She took it. "Did you two fight?"

I shook my head. "On the way to the shore, we had...an aggressive difference of opinion on a few topics."

"What topics?"

"Nothing of any consequence," I said, with a shrug. "Would you do something for me?"

She squeezed my hand as her face brightened. "Anything."

"Look me in the eye and tell me something that may or may not be true."

She squinted. "Why do you want me to lie to you?"

"I didn't say you had to lie. You can tell me a truth I don't know."

She pulled her hand from mine, rubbed her ear, and looked away for a few heartbeats. Staring into my eyes again, she said, "I fell deeply in love the moment I saw you."

I smiled. "Too easy. I know that's a lie."

After chewing her lip a moment, she smiled back. "I don't regret losing my hand defending you."

I shook my head. "You're not even trying to deceive me."

She glared at me. "Is this some test? I haven't lied to you in months—do you believe that?"

"I do."

Her eyes stayed locked on mine as a hint of fire flared in them. "Let me guess. The discussion leading to your aggressive difference of opinion centered on my ability to deceive."

I shivered. "He thinks you're acting, playing the part of my promised and queen-to-be. He said you're doing what you have to do to gather power, and you don't really want to marry me."

A candle flared. "And you believed him?"

Pulling her to me, I kissed the top of her head. "I'm sorry. Kurt got to me. There's so much going wrong, and I need something to go right. Things will get better after tomorrow."

She pressed her head against my chest and sighed. "You keep saying things will get better; it's starting to sound like you're trying to convince yourself."

I chuckled. "If I don't already believe I can make Croy better, how can I succeed?"

I felt her nod. "That's why people follow you. Because you believe in yourself."

"Not everyone. If they did, I wouldn't have so many bodies to bury tomorrow afternoon."

"True. Perhaps I overestimated your ability to lead."

Before I could say anything, she laughed and, after a moment, I joined her.

"Sorry," she said, after catching her breath. "The conversation grew too serious for me."

"Thank you. Are you hungry?"

"My stomach tells me I slept through lunch."

I pulled her to her feet and looked into her eyes. "We'll just have to eat dinner early then. But maybe we could try somewhere other than Grith's."

Pulling on her boots, she looked at me. "Where are we going?"

"That's the problem. Grith's is the only place I know of."

She stood and placed her hand on my cheek. "Ask one of your guards. Surely one of them knows where to get a meal."

"Good idea," I said. "By the way, you look great in the new clothes."

Smiling, she nodded. "Thank you, but you know I make everything I wear look good."

I chuckled. "There's the Tindra I know and love. So humble."

She slapped my arm. "How about you show me how much you love me? Find me some food."

Leading her to the door, I held it for her, and we walked to the gate together.

"Erland," I said, as we passed through. "Where's a good place to get an early dinner?"

"With good drink," Tindra added.

"It's a bit of a walk, but The Sneaky Bear tavern should offer what you're after. Skald Nikulas makes it a point to eat there at least once when he comes to the capital."

Tindra cleared her throat. "Fitzeirick, remember what happened last time we went out for an evening on the town?"

I smirked and nodded. "Drinking and a dance."

She laughed. "I know you didn't drink enough to forget the fight afterward."

"If I may, Sire," Erland said. "It's not right for you and Lady Tindra to argue in public."

Smiling at him, I said, "We didn't argue. We ran into some thugs and had to defend ourselves."

"Oh," he replied. "You won't have such problems at the Bear."

"Lead the way," I said.

He led us to a part of the capital I'd never visited. I tried to avoid attention, but many people bowed as we passed. *At least no one's scowling or attacking me.* We stopped in front of a sizable wooden building with a large, detailed, wooden statue of a bear standing watch by the door.

"Wait here, m'lord," Erland said. "I'll announce you."

I grabbed his shoulder. "Is that necessary?"

Tindra squeezed my hand. "Have you forgotten our visit to The Stag pub?"

Though memorable, the evening hadn't crossed my mind recently. "Of course, I remember."

She smiled. "I suspect this place has more in common with The Stag than with Tyres' Fool."

"So, there won't be a dance performance?" I asked, then chuckled.

Erland's confusion grew as we spoke. "Sire, I'm sorry, but there's no dancing here. It's not that kind of place. I can take you someplace else where you can dance."

Shaking my head, I said, "If you've never been to the Varian capital, you won't understand. We had no plans for this evening, but dancing isn't necessary. Please, announce us."

Chapter 44

Erland bowed, then hurried to the door. He pulled it open and spoke loudly, "King Fitzeirick escorting his promised, Lady Tindra of Varia."

Tindra leaned into me. "At this rate, everyone's going to know about our engagement before the day's over."

"And I thought Kurt could keep a secret," I said.

"When it serves his purpose," she replied. "We'll probably never know what he got in return for talking."

"Doesn't matter," I said. "All of Croy will know once we're married."

As we stepped through the door, a well-groomed man wearing a white shirt and black pants hurried toward us. His pace slowed as he got close. He stopped an arm's length away and ran his hands down his shirt, smoothing it, before bowing. His blue eyes locked onto mine as he spoke, "It is our honor to have the king visit our pub. I am Kalfken."

"Well met," I replied. "Are you the owner?"

He shook his head. "No, Sire. I manage it for the family."

"Anyone I might know?" I asked.

"Have you met Elder Thane Roald's grandchildren?"

"I didn't know he had children much less grandchildren," I said.

Kalfken nodded. "His son started the pub after he married. Kisping and his wife, Ingrid, put everything into making this place a success. Tore and Tola carry on the business in the family name."

"Where are they?" I asked. "With Roald's passing, I'd like to give the family my condolences in person."

He nodded. "They don't live in the capital. Moved to Nikulas' holdings years ago. Word came from Boril. I think he fancied Tola at one point. I dispatched a messenger as soon as I found out."

"I'll write them a letter," I said. "I respected Roald."

Tindra squeezed my hand.

"My promised and I would like to eat. Is it too early for dinner?"

Kalfken raised his eyebrows. "I'm not sure the kitchen is ready to serve customers just now, but I will check once you are seated. Would you prefer to dine in the great room? Or perhaps you'd like a quiet meal in a private room upstairs?"

I looked around the room. The Sneaky Bear reminded me of Geri's inn. Not far inside the door, stairs led left and right, but the great room in front of us drew my attention. Tables of various lengths, seemingly strewn randomly through the room, made the pub feel inviting like an old friend's home.

Tindra cleared her throat and nodded toward a small table near the center of the room. Candlelight from several hanging fixtures overlapped, putting it in a pool of light.

"There," she whispered.

I considered her suggestion for a moment, then chuckled, remembering her flair for the dramatic.

"The little table, where we can be seen."

"Of course, Sire," he said. "Follow me."

Kalfken clapped his hands twice after we took our seats. "Katla, Vallen," he called out. "My lord, lady, our two best servants will see your needs are met."

I thanked him as he turned to walk toward the back of the building. Then two women, dressed in flowing, light-brown gowns, rushed to the table and curtsied.

"Our cook said the stew isn't ready yet," one said. "Might I suggest drinks before your meal?"

I shrugged and looked at Tindra.

She smiled. "Better to have something in my stomach while we wait."

I nodded and turned to the ladies. "What would you recommend?"

"We have fresh casks of drakas, sweet with a hint of spice."

"What's drakas?" I asked, brow furrowed.

"A mead with some of the water removed. It comes from a brewer in Nikulas' holding."

I raised my eyebrows. "Sounds interesting." Turning to Tindra, I asked, "Care to try it?"

"I'm game," Tindra said, nodding.

"Bring us each a mug," I said, with a smile.

They returned quickly. One carried two mugs, which she placed in front of us, and the other carried a large, glass pitcher full of a dark, golden liquid.

"Kalfken suggested we offer you a pitcher," she said.

"We don't have to drink it if we don't like it?" Tindra asked.

"Of course not, my lady."

I nodded. "No harm then. Leave it."

She smiled and set the pitcher on the table. "I'll make sure you get the first bowls of stew when it's ready."

I lifted the heavy mug, nodded to Tindra, and took a drink. A thick, sweet liquid flowed across my tongue. When I took a breath, the slightly spicy burn appeared. Far from unpleasant, like peppers, it encouraged me to take another drink.

Tindra pursed her lips for a moment. "Excellent flavor."

We talked about what happened earlier and drank as a few groups entered the pub. When we finished the pitcher, one of the ladies brought another and told us, "Dinner is almost ready. The cook's preparing one of his specialties, sweet and savory boar stew. It uses mead as part of the base."

"Sounds..." I paused, trying to find the right word. "Wonderful."

For some reason, Tindra laughed, quietly at first but soon grew louder. Despite not knowing why, I joined her. We managed to get ourselves back under control as a small group of well-dressed men entered the pub and sat not far from us.

Several more people were seated by the time we'd emptied the second pitcher. The weight of their stares made part of me uncomfortable while another part welcomed the attention.

"A third?" I asked Tindra, louder than I'd intended.

She shrugged and gave me a crooked grin. "Why not?"

I nodded and raised the empty pitcher.

One of the servant ladies came to the table. "Your stew will be ready soon. Would you rather I bring more then?"

I looked at her, staring at her light-brown eyes, and wondered why she would ask such a question. *I'm the king. I get what I want.* "Bring more drakas now."

She curtsied and took the empty pitcher. "As you wish, Sire."

"That's better," I mumbled.

Tindra smiled and reached for my hand. "Your people are still getting used to the idea of having a king."

After considering what she said, I nodded and returned her smile. "I rid them of the cowardly dictator hiding behind the useless Council of Thanes. Everyone should be happy." Standing and lifting my arms over my head, I shouted, "Where are the smiles? And let's hear some laughter! We should all celebrate the better Croy that's coming."

Tindra stood next to me and shouted, "Here, here!"

A few patrons raised their cups, echoing Tindra's statement of support. Most frowned and looked away.

Kalfken appeared at my side. "Sire, most people come to this pub because it tends to be quiet...relaxing. While I admire your call for bettering our nation, I believe you're making some of our patrons uncomfortable."

I turned to him and put my hand on his shoulder before looking around the room again. "Sorry, sorry. I got carried away with my... What's the word?"

Our host cocked his head and shrugged. "Enthusiasm, Sire?"

Patting his shoulder roughly, I smiled and nodded. "Yes, thank you. My enthusiasm for my country and improving life for my people. Please excuse my...outburst."

A few raised their cups, most ignored me.

"Please, Sire, return to your seat," he said.

"Yes, of course," I said, and flopped into the seat.

"I'll see you're served soon," he said, before hurrying away from the table.

"He seems nice," I said, turning to Tindra.

"He does. I like this place."

"I hope the food's good—the drink is excellent. I'd like to have some more," I said.

"You should get more."

"When I see one of the ladies, I will."

"But don't make a scene," Tindra said, patting my hand. "No reason to bother these nice people while they wait for their meal."

"Right," I said. "I did that before, and Kalfken asked me not to. I'm king, but that doesn't mean I should be impolite."

She nodded. "Manners are important."

People turned away from me as I looked around the room, searching for our servers. Somehow, they made it to our table without me seeing them move through the room.

One placed two bowls on the table. "M'lord, lady," she said, while handing us spoons. "Your stew is ready. The cook insisted I wait until you taste it."

I stirred the dark, brown liquid. Chunks of potato and carrot moved behind the spoon. The unmistakable smell of cooked pork filled my nose, chased by the combined scents of honey, salt, and a hint of pepper. I scooped up a piece of meat and took a bite. Tender and well-seasoned—possibly the best pork I'd ever eaten.

"This is amazing. My compliments to the cook," I said. "Can we get another pitcher to go with it?"

While I asked, the second server placed another pitcher on the table.

"I'll let Joen know you enjoyed his work."

Pouring another mug each for Tindra and me, I watched as she took her first bite. "I'd swear this came from Varia," she said.

I nodded, and we devoured the meal, pausing only to drink more drakas.

One of the serving ladies returned to take the empty dishes off the table as the other put a plate piled high with small, tan-colored balls in front of us. "It's Joen's new treat. He calls them mead milk puffs and wanted you to be the first to try them."

I was surprised by how light the ball felt when I picked it up. After studying it a moment, I placed the whole thing in my mouth. It practically melted as I bit into it, filling my mouth with a buttery, sweet honey taste.

"What is this?"

"I don't know how he makes them."

Turning to Tindra, I smiled at the look on her face.

"Joen's my new favorite cook," I said.

Tindra nodded. "What a wonderful dessert. They don't have these in Varia."

The server curtsied. "He'll be pleased to hear the praise. Kalfken asked to speak to you before you leave."

I smiled at her. "He's welcome to join us."

She smiled and left the table.

Half the puffs were gone when Kalfken approached.

"It sounds like you enjoyed yourself, my lord."

I nodded until I could swallow another treat. "Everything exceeded all expectations."

"Here, here," Tindra said, raising a puff over her head before putting it in her mouth. Several people near us snickered.

"Considering your standing and high praise, I've decided to extend you the same generosity Jarl Eirickson enjoyed and give you—"

I growled and stood. The room spun a little, forcing me to grab the table or risk falling while I fought to keep my balance.

"You would watch your tongue and not insult me so. I'll not have my name associated with the man who let our enemy settle in our lands. He committed the highest treason, and I made sure he paid the price."

The host bowed low. "Please, my lord, accept my deepest apology—I meant no offense. What can I do to please you? Name it."

Pulling my purse from my belt, I handed it to him. "Take this as payment. Both for our meal and as an apology for my earlier behavior."

He sucked in a loud breath. "Sire, no. I couldn't accept such a payment from our king."

"Nonsense," I spat. "A king must pay his way. It's only right."

He shivered before smiling. "Only if you insist, Sire."

"I do."

He nodded. "Let me help you to the door. It's the least I could do in light of your generosity."

"My promised and I have made it through far worse than walking out of a pub," I said, and turned to leave. The room moved again, and I fell back into the chair.

"Perhaps we should take his offer," Tindra said.

Pursing my lips, I scratched my head while considering whether her suggestion made sense. Before I made much progress, Erland stood beside me.

"Let's get you to your quarters, m'lord," he said. "Maybe I should help you to bed?"

I held out my hand. "Good idea. I am feeling a bit...sleepy."

Grasping my forearm, he hauled me out of the chair and let me lean against his shoulder while he helped Tindra to her feet. "Did he cause any problems I should know about?" Erland asked Kalfken.

"Nothing that can't be forgiven."

"In that case," he said, "we bid you good evening."

"King Fitzeirick is welcome back. Anytime," Kalfken said, as we stumbled out of the pub into the dimming twilight.

Erland grunted a couple of times when I leaned heavily on him.

We drew looks, some smiles, and several frowns as he all but carried me back to my quarters. At the gate, the men posted there ran out to help us to my door.

Once we made it inside, I said, "We can make it to the bed from here."

Erland waited for the rest to leave before asking, "Are you sure, Sire?"

"Yes, Erland," Tindra said. "We're sure."

I think he smiled when he said, "Understood," and left, closing the door behind him.

Tindra hugged me tightly, and said, "Bed me."

Chapter 45

"Have a little patience; we'll get there."

"And when we do, don't fall asleep."

Halfway down the hall, I finally understood what she meant. "You want me to—"

"Bed me, take me...whatever you want to call it. Make me yours."

"Are you sure?"

"Never been more sure."

"I'm...it's...maybe." I couldn't find the words.

"Stop thinking and act. Our engagement was spur of the moment; our first time in bed together wasn't planned...why not do this on impulse? You need it, maybe more than I do, and we both want it."

"This seems like—"

She grabbed my beard and pulled my face to hers. "Stop talking," she said, before pressing her lips against mine.

The kiss seemed to last forever as we stumbled and bumped our way to the bed. She moved away, and I fought to stand as the room tilted. My fingers fumbled with buttons and ties as I struggled to undress.

Tindra laughed. "Relax. There's no hurry. We've got all night."

After a deep breath, I focused on getting my clothes off and soon, we lay down together.

I lay still for a moment, hoping the room would stop spinning every time I opened my eyes.

Tindra snuggled up to my side and caressed my cheek, her fingers gently brushing over the upside-down T-shaped scar on my cheek while kissing the side of my neck.

"I'm ready when you are."

Her warm body and soft lips soon distracted me from my drunken dizziness. After pushing her onto her back, I held myself over her, afraid my weight would be too much for her smaller frame.

She pulled me into a short kiss, then said, "Don't worry. I'm stronger than I look."

I nodded and slid into her.

Her eyes flew open, and she smiled the brightest smile I'd ever seen.

We made love. It was wonderful and awkward and over too soon.

"I'm...I'm sorry," I said, as I tried to move off her.

She held me in place. "Sorry for what?"

"I'm not at my best. That...wasn't what it should have been."

She smiled. "It's been a long time for you, right?"

I looked away from her and nodded.

"Plus, the first time is always awkward, and...you have nothing to be sorry for."

"Thank you," I said. "I'm glad you understand."

"You're welcome. I enjoyed it, and I know you did...what else could one ask for?"

"Sleep?"

She nodded. "Lay down and hold me. We'll fall asleep together."

I did as she asked and fell asleep cuddling with my future wife.

• • • ● • ● • ● • •

Loud, pounding footsteps echoing down the hall woke me. My eyes didn't want to open until I brushed chunks of grit out of their corners. Tindra lay still on my chest, her legs straddling one of my thighs.

Her name crackled from my dry throat, across my parched lips.

Lifting her head, she looked at me and blinked several times.

"Someone's here," I said, after clearing my throat.

As we untangled ourselves from each other, Roi called out, "Fitzeirick, are you awake?"

I froze and stared at Tindra.

She met my gaze with a smile. "He'll find out sooner or later. Don't tell me you regret last night."

"No, I don't, but it almost feels like it happened to someone else."

"Is Tindra with you?" Roi asked, from the door.

"Yes," I replied. "We'll be out in a minute. Would you have some water ready for us?"

"Sure."

"He doesn't sound happy," she said, as she dressed.

I shuffled down the hall, trying to ignore my headache.

Tindra followed, humming a tune sounding too cheery for how I felt.

"You look terrible," he said, when we reached the table.

I took a cup from the table and swallowed the water in one gulp. My tongue felt coated in wet wool.

Handing the cup to Tindra, I said, "More, please."

She curtseyed, leaning a little to her right. "Yes, your highness."

Roi looked from her to me. "Do I want to know?"

I shook my head. "Doubt you do. I take it Grima and Einns made it safely."

"They're getting settled into our home now. Did you know the Thanes, well...Porsey, is refusing to leave until he talks to you?"

Tindra handed me a full cup. "Is it past first light?"

"Well past."

I groaned, emptied the cup, and headed for the door.

From my door, I saw Kurt waiting outside the gate to the compound.

My head pounded as I made my way across the courtyard.

"Heard you had an...interesting evening," he said, as I got close. "Interesting enough to delay our journey, it seems."

I shaded my eyes from the stabbing sunlight. "My apologies. I overslept."

"Too much drink will do that," he replied. "Will you talk to your man so we can be on our way? Elias and his soldiers are anxious to get home."

"Please let the sergeant know I am deeply sorry," I said. "Where's Porsey?"

"Next to the last wagon."

The pounding worsened as I walked, and I suspected I'd need to pull some energy from the ground to make it back to my quarters. Stopping at the wagon, I looked at Porsey. "What can I do for you?"

"Nothing," he spat. "I wanted to get one last look at you, to fix the image of your branded face in my mind. Seeing you in such poor condition serves to strengthen my resolve. I will work against you at every opportunity. You will curse the day you sent me to Varia."

I rubbed my forehead, trying to hide my disdain for his petty outburst.

Of all the selfish—No, don't play into his hand. Just get him out of the capital. Smooth his feathers and set him on his way. The world tilted a little when I bowed. "Porsey, I admire your dedication. All I ask is you do what you think is best for Croy."

"Did everyone see," he crowed. "The king bowed to *me*. He knows I'm his better."

"Do not mistake respect for subjugation," I said. "Travel safe and swift."

"I'll see you regret ever returning to the capital," Porsey said, as the wagons lurched forward.

I watched until they were out of sight before dragging myself back to my quarters.

Stopping at the door, I looked at one of the guards, and said, "Go get Abi, I have a pounding headache."

I got inside and flopped into a chair at the table. Tindra was nowhere to be seen.

"Tindra tells me there are executions scheduled later today," Roi said.

I groaned, rested my head on the table, and closed my eyes.

"I'll take that as a yes," he said. "You planning to attend?"

I nodded, rubbing my cheek on the cool stone. "I sent someone for Abi to see if she can help with this headache. Where's Tindra?"

"She went back to bed."

I grunted.

"Should I ask why you two are in such bad condition?"

"Erland took us to a pub," I said. "They serve evil mead."

"Is that why you slept with her?"

"Wasn't our first night together."

"Are you—"

"Same as you and Grima. Don't lecture me."

He chuckled. "Fair enough. When's the wedding?"

"When's *your* wedding?"

"We'll discuss it when you're thinking clearly."

I sighed. "And my family sword? Did you get it from Geri?"

"I did," he said. "You'll get it when you are *thinking clearly*."

Someone knocked on the door, interrupting me before I decided to yell at Roi.

"I hope that's Abi," I groaned.

"I hope she has something to fix you," he said. "Don't get up."

"Where is—Oh, he looks terrible," the herbalist said. "What happened?"

"Going by what he said, evil mead."

"He drank too much?"

"Yes," I grunted.

"I need a cup of water," she said.

"Here," Roi said.

Abi took the cup and emptied a pouch of powder into it. "Sit up and drink this ... all of it."

I forced my head from the table and took the offered cup. The cool liquid smelled like tree bark and tasted like limestone dust.

I've had worse.

"You need some broth," she said.

"I'll send a guard for some," Roi said, before heading for the door.

"Check on Tindra, in the bedroom," I said, laying my head back on the table.

"Same problem?" she asked.

I nodded and closed my eyes.

"Were you expecting a messenger from Varia?" Roi asked.

"Umm...not that I recall."

"One arrived as I sent someone for broth," he said. "Should I let him in?"

"Sure," I said, lifting my head and wiping my eyes. "Maybe it's good news."

The messenger followed Roi to the table, bowed low, and offered me a sealed parchment. "King Fitzeirick, it is my honor to bring word of the royal wedding and give you an official invitation."

This better not be a joke. I took the parchment, verified it carried the Varian royal seal, and opened it.

To the honorable King Fitzeirick of Croy,

You are formally invited to celebrate the union of Crown Princess Jesca of Varia to Crum of Croy. The ceremony will begin midday, following the next full moon. Feasts and five days of celebration to begin immediately after their union is complete.

At the bottom of the page, Crum scrawled a note to me.

You still owe me three obsidian arrowheads.

I laughed. "Crum still wants those arrowheads."

"You have to admire his persistence," Roi said.

"If I had the time and could safely find the spot, I'd go syth that old mountain lion carcass from the ground and give him back the arrowheads he wasted trying to kill it."

Roi smiled and nodded. "I'd give anything to see the look on his face if you managed to pull that off."

"It would serve him right, but Satra controls the central forest now. No way for me to even start looking. You know, I haven't paid much attention lately; when *is* the next full moon?"

"About three weeks," Roi said.

"But I can't be in Varia that soon. Not with a war to plan."

"Crum will never forgive you if you miss his wedding," he said.

I rubbed my forehead and muttered, "Why now?"

He chuckled. "You knew this was coming."

I glared at him. "I'll write him a letter, explaining my absence. He'll be king soon. He has to understand my obligation."

"It's the least you can do," he said.

Pointing to the messenger, I said, "Wait here," and stumbled to my meeting room.

Chapter 46

Grabbing some parchment, a quill, and a jar of ink, which I almost spilled, I sat down and scratched out a short note.

Dear Crum and Jesca,

I cannot put into words how happy I am to hear of your wedding announcement and receive the invitation. Without a doubt, the celebration will be talked about for years to come. Unfortunately, due to obligations I am sure you are aware of, I will not be able to attend. Know you have my full blessing and support, and I look forward to the day I can see your faces again. Crum, I will get the arrowheads to you as soon as I have some obsidian in my possession.

I grabbed my seal and headed back to the dining table for some wax. After sealing the message, I gave it to the messenger. "This is for Crum."

He took it and bowed. "I will get it to him with all haste."

"Thank you," I said. "Travel swift and safe."

"Abi left while you were away," Roi said. "I guess she made Tindra drink the same thing she gave you. Good thing I told the guard to bring enough broth for two."

"Thank you. Guess I'll pay Abi later," I said, patting my coin purse...or where I expected it to be.

Looking around the room, I mumbled, "Where is it?"

"Where's what?" Roi asked.

"My purse."

"I didn't notice it on you when you came out," he said. "Maybe you left it in your room."

"I don't remember taking it off before bed," I said. Turning toward my room, a memory worked its way through the fog in my head. *Oh, no.* "I gave it to the host at The Sneaky Bear."

Roi shook his head. "How much did you drink?"

I looked at him and shrugged. "Don't remember exactly. We shared three or four."

"Three or four cups shouldn't have affected you this much."

I looked away. "Three or four pitchers."

"Ohhh," he said, and laughed. "That's a different story. Any idea how much coin you had?"

"At least twenty gold doubles worth."

He laughed again. "Guess you made them very happy."

I nodded and flopped back into the chair.

"Is she worth it?" he asked, after a moment of silence.

"Is who worth what?"

"Tindra," he said. "Is she worth all the trouble that comes with her?"

"This isn't her fault. We went someplace new for a meal, and the mead tasted amazing. Plus—"

A knock on the door interrupted me.

"I hope that's your broth," Roi said, as he stood to see who had knocked.

"Grith sent fresh, hot, pork broth," Hedin said, placing a large, stone pot on the table. My stomach knotted. "Why did it have to be pork broth?"

Roi looked at me. "You've always liked pork."

"We had boar stew for dinner."

Roi chuckled as he got bowls and spoons and placed them on the table. "I'm going to see if my family needs anything." As he turned, the chuckle turned into a belly laugh before he walked outside.

Hedin's mouth hung open as he looked from the door to me.

"You may go."

"I hope you feel better soon, Sire," he said, and walked out the door.

Afraid to lift the lid on the pot and fill the room with the smell of cooked pork, I shuffled down the hall to get Tindra.

Not going to suffer alone.

"We have some broth," I said, opening the door. "Abi said it would help us feel better."

"Her tonic helped a little."

"True. My head isn't throbbing quite as bad."

"Tell me the broth didn't come from the pub, and I'll have some," Tindra said, sitting up in the bed.

"It came from Grith's."

Her lips moved into a weak smile. "How's it taste?"

"Don't know," I said, trying to keep my expression neutral. "Wanted to share it."

She nodded. "How nice. I appreciate the thought."

We slowly made our way back to the table, and I lifted the lid.

Tindra sniffed at the steam then fanned her hand in front of her nose. "Ugh. That smells like pork."

"Because it is."

She growled, "Why didn't you tell me?"

I grinned. "You didn't ask."

"I bet you just didn't want to be miserable alone."

"True, but we need something in our stomach. Trust me, I don't like the idea any more than you."

"It won't kill us," she said, nudging her bowl toward the pot. "I hope."

I nodded and poured her bowl full of steaming, smelly broth.

She picked up her spoon, then looked from the bowl to me.

"You too. I'm not suffering alone."

I poured a serving for myself, wrinkled my nose at the smell, and swallowed a spoonful. Ordinarily, it wouldn't have tasted bad, but the flavor brought back memories of the previous night, and my head throbbed again.

Tindra finished hers before I'd eaten half of mine. "It's not trying to come back up," she said. "I'll take some more."

After refilling her bowl, I swallowed a spoonful of my cooling meal. Deciding the broth tasted a little better warm, I added some to my bowl and ate faster.

Tindra finished her serving and pushed the bowl away. "Finish yours. We have to get ready."

"Ready for what?"

"The executions," she said. "Or have you forgotten?"

"Not forgotten, exactly. More like I'm distracted at the moment."

"Better get focused. Not attending the execution will cause you more harm than the executions themselves. Trust me: it's one thing to kill them, but people will consider your absence insulting or a sign you are too weak to deal with the problem."

I nodded. "What does one wear to an execution?"

"Dress like you're ready to fight because you might have to."

I sighed. "I know. But I don't want you fighting if this goes bad."

"I won't go unarmed," she said. "It would give the appearance I don't support you."

"If trouble breaks out, stay behind me and cover my back," I said, shaking my finger at her.

"Yes, my lord," she said, with a slight smile.

Abi's treatment must be working. I feel good enough to put up with Tindra's sense of humor.

Unfortunately, I hadn't had time to put together much of a royal wardrobe. I chose a clean pair of woven pants and a matching shirt.

"You need to talk to Fastan and Thorgault about some clothes," Tindra said. "Speaking of which, I wonder if he's done with my armor and the fork."

"Assuming we're not fighting for our lives, we'll stop by his shop after the executions are finished."

She finished dressing in all black and nodded. "Would you mind fixing my sword in place?"

After putting my hammer across my back, I leaned down to attach the scabbard to her belt, and she stole a quick kiss.

"What was that for?" I asked.

"Because I felt like it," she replied, grinning. "You might as well get used to it."

"That may take time," I said, then kissed her back. "And practice."

"I'd tell you to practice all you want," she said, "but we have someplace to be."

Generals Heming and Gudmann were talking with the guards when I opened the door.

"Well met, generals," I said.

Both looked my way and nodded. Gudmann stepped toward me. "We wanted to talk to you before this afternoon's activity starts. Your men told us you were feeling poorly."

"Nothing that won't pass," I said, shrugging. "Come in."

I led them to the meeting room. "Sit. What's on your mind?"

Tindra sat to my right and took my hand in hers.

Gudmann said, "I'm not sure she should be in here."

"There's nothing you'll say she hasn't heard before," I said, squeezing her hand. "I wouldn't swear to it, but I'd guess she's been party to more executions than the three of us combined."

She nodded. "As long as you count assassinations as executions."

Gudmann raised his eyebrows and looked toward Heming.

"Can you swear this is the last time we'll be ordered to kill Croians?" Heming asked.

I looked him in the eyes. "It's my deepest desire. What's about to happen troubles me more than you know. I hope you two agree that Hallfrid's actions, his treachery, leaves me no other option."

Heming nodded. "That's the sole reason we agreed to help. We've talked to our commanders and asked them to secure support for you, for your rule. If we have to spill any more Croian blood, yours may run with it."

"I don't take threats lightly, General. Choose your words carefully."

He nodded. "I meant no offense, Sire. My statement is a warning. There are rumblings of unease among our warriors. Such feelings are a fertile ground for ill will and discord, which could lead to a bloody revolt if left unchecked."

"Soon, they can release their anger and frustration on the Satran people," I said. "It's my hope the land they took doesn't see another drop of Croian blood. I want my old skati's soil to be red with the blood of those barbarians."

"So, you give your word, you risk your honor, that our warriors will not be ordered to kill another Croian after today?" Gudmann pressed.

I frowned. "I can't make that promise. If more uprisings happen, your men may be called on to end them." Heming shook his head. "Would assurance we will deal with any further unrest be enough for you to give us your word?"

"I have a company of men working to rip these rebels from the ground, stem and root. You may have more men, but they have other responsibilities," I said. "I wonder, what makes you think you'll know about further problems before I find them?"

Gudmann put his hand on Heming's shoulder. "Tell him."

"Hallfrid encouraged several uprisings. We thought hatred drove him to work against you; we didn't know his efforts helped Satra. While there may still be some loyal to Hallfrid, we're confident we can sway them."

"I appreciate your honesty," I said. "Captain Agrim and my guard are tasked with securing the area and ending any uprisings occurring today. I'm willing to let your men keep the peace, but if you cannot, more bloodshed may be necessary, and I expect our warriors to follow orders." I let go of Tindra's hand to offer my hand to Heming. "That's the best I can do."

Hemming looked at Gudmann before gripping my hand firmly. "Not an ideal arrangement, but you have our support."

"Have your men make final preparations," I said. "I'll be at the prison shortly."

"We'll be ready when you arrive," Gudmann said, standing.

Tindra and I walked them to the door, then went to find Agrim.

Chapter 47

We hurried to the barracks and stopped Agrim as he walked out.

"Everything ready?" I asked.

He nodded.

"Good," I said. "After today, have Generals Gudmann or Heming assist in dealing with any uprisings."

He squinted. "Why?"

"The generals think they can change people's minds without more bloodshed after Hallfrid's gone. I promised them I'd put an end to Croians killing fellow countrymen."

"I hope they're right."

I nodded. "Also, tomorrow, have your men work on converting Porsey's and Boril's homes into barracks. I want the guards moved in as soon as possible."

He smiled. "As you say."

"You're free to go; pass the word."

He bowed and hurried away.

"To the prison?" Tindra asked.

"As long as no one else comes up demanding my attention," I said, taking her hand and heading for the prison.

The bleak, stone facade stood as a foreboding presence as we approached the base of the mountain containing Croy's prison. Even though the sun shined brightly, a dim gloom seemed to gather around us as we got closer. My footsteps slowed as I fought back memories of dark tunnels. I'd never been given a tour, but somehow, the cells could hold anyone, regardless of their talent or how powerful they were.

The tunnels had a fault. Maybe this place does too.

"Much more imposing than anything I've seen in Varia," Tindra said.

I drew some strength from the ground and knocked hard on the metal-bound wooden door.

A slender metal panel slid, revealing a pair of eyes. "Who knocks?"

"King Fitzeirick and Queen-to-be Tindra, here for the execution," I said.

"Sire, General Gudmann has the prison on lockdown until preparations are complete."

I pressed my lips together and nodded. "Probably for the best. We'll wait for him outside."

"As you wish, my lord," he replied, and slid the panel back in place.

Tindra squeezed my hand. "Are you sure we should wait alone, out in the open?"

Pulling a crude bench from the stone below the surface, I sat and pushed my talent out to make sure no one approached undetected. "Guardsmen will be here soon enough, and it's not like someone can sneak up on us here."

She looked around again, shrugged, and joined me on the bench. After a moment, she pressed herself against my side.

"Relax," I said, rubbing my thumb on the back of her hand. "Agrim and four others are not far away."

"How do you know it's Agrim?"

"I'd recognize his walk anywhere. I could probably pick him out of a moving crowd with my eyes closed."

"Have I ever told you how much I envy you for knowing that trick?"

"Not that I recall," I said. "There are some firesyth tricks I'd like to be able to do...like lighting a candle or lamp from across the room."

"They are handy," she said. "Guess it's easy to take one's talent for granted."

Squeezing her hand, I said, "True."

The captain of my guard walked into view ahead of his men. He noticed me, waved, and walked faster. "Sire," he called out, as he got close. "I didn't expect you to arrive before me. Sorry I didn't have waiting to greet you."

"You were following my orders. No harm done."

He nodded and turned to his men. "Engli, Orn, double-check the wall. Vald, make sure everything else is ready."

Without a word, the men went about their tasks.

"Agrim, why do you have two of your stonesyths here instead of working on barracks?" I asked, watching Engli and Orn inspecting the chest-high wall not far from the path.

"Those two do good work," he said, smiling, "but aren't among my most powerful."

"I look forward to seeing what your best do with those buildings," I said.

"It can't be too nice, or other companies will be jealous," Agrim said.

"The chopping blocks are in place and firmly planted, Captain," Vald said, from inside the wall.

I noticed several men, at least a dozen, walking heavily toward us as Agrim nodded.

"Agrim, someone's coming," I said.

He glanced at me with a questioning look, then barked, "Positions," as he drew his sword and dagger.

The two stonesyths rushed to my flanks, axes at the ready, as Vald hurried to join Agrim, swords in hand.

A moment before the group came into view, I stood and wrapped my hand around the grip on my hammer. *My injured shoulder won't let me do much fighting, but my men need to see I stand with them.* The sound of Tindra's sword sliding out of its scabbard made me step forward. "Remember to stay behind me," I whispered.

Generals Gudmann and Heming walked at the front of two lines of men carrying large axes over their shoulders.

Gudmann stopped when he saw our state of readiness. "Not the welcome I'd expected," he called out.

"Stand down!" Agrim yelled.

Heming laughed and motioned for the men to move again.

I hurried to greet them.

Gudmann nodded at me. "How'd you know we were coming?"

"A trick I picked up some time ago," I said. "Never know when someone might try to sneak up on you."

"True," he said, and looked toward the walled-off area. "Everything's in order?"

"It is," I said.

"Agrim," he called out. "When do you expect the rest of your company?"

"Soon," he replied.

Gudmann nodded. "I'll bring out the first group of prisoners once they arrive and secure the area. Heming, get the men in place." He turned back to me. "Where are we burying the bodies?"

"Any reason the walled area can't be their grave?"

He nodded again. "As you wish, m'lord."

The commanders took their places next to the blocks. Some took a few swings with their axe while others paced; a few sat on their block and rested their chin on their axe handles.

In groups of two or three, my guardsmen arrived and checked with Agrim before standing watch where he directed.

Before the last of them moved into position, a few citizens walked up.

I stood, but Agrim waved at me to sit. "I'll deal with them," he said.

"They are welcome to watch."

He nodded before walking to the small group.

"General Gudmann, I believe we are ready to begin," I said.

"Will you allow any last words?" he asked.

"They may spend the end of their life wasting their breath if they desire," I said.

Agrim returned as Gudmann knocked on the prison door. "The men have agreed to stand and observe. They understand any attempt to stop the executions or other misconduct will not be allowed."

"Thank you," I said. "I would have—"

"*King* Fitzeirick! False ruler of Croy!" Hallfrid yelled, interrupting me. "You aren't man enough to face me. Using others to do your dirty work. I call for *your* head!"

Chapter 48

I looked at the disgraced man, hands and feet in metal shackles. Some part of me pitied him, being prodded forward at spear point.

He drew a deep breath, and yelled, "Our nation will suffer under your rule! Mark my words! You *will* regret ever returning!"

General Gudmann took him by the neck and forced him to his knees behind Commander Ottar's block. "Shut up and die with at least a little dignity, traitor," Gudmann said, shoving Hallfrid forward.

Ottar swung his axe as soon as Hallfrid's head hit the wood.

Having never witnessed a beheading before, I wasn't sure what to expect. The axe struck the wooden block with a loud 'thunk.' Hallfrid's head rolled to a stop, facing me, mouth moving as if he were still trying to speak.

A queasy feeling moved from my stomach up my throat, carrying a sickening bitterness to my mouth.

"You don't look well," Tindra whispered, as I looked away.

"I didn't think it would be this hard to watch," I replied quietly.

I looked back in time to see General Nothri kneel and put his head on a block. "Death is better than living under a traitor's rule!" he yelled, before the axe fell.

I turned to the small crowd. Most of them looked away as more men were marched from the prison. One or two glared at me. A few watched the axes fall with expressions of disbelief.

"Watching those you condemned is the honorable thing to do," she said, under her breath.

I squeezed her hand, and whispered, "I'm not sure I can."

"Don't show your regret here," she replied quietly.

I nodded and willed myself to watch men die.

The last of the condemned marched out, their footsteps making a sickening sound as they stepped onto the blood-soaked ground around the chopping blocks.

Bitterness filled my mouth when the axes fell again.

"See to the bodies," Agrim ordered.

I felt energy flow through the ground as the stonesyths opened up a mass grave and pulled strength to move the bodies.

Eventually, I went numb to everything except the pungent, coppery odor filling my nose and the thunk of axes hitting wood echoing in my ears. I jumped when General Gudmann stood in front of me, and said, "It's done, Sire."

Drawing a deep breath, I stood, blinking several times before he came into focus.

"You and your men...thank you for your," I paused, unsure of what the right words were, "service. Take a couple of days to recover."

He bowed. "I'll tell them. Remember your promise."

Putting my hand on his shoulder, I nodded. "Of course. Captain Agrim knows. He'll spread the word through his company."

"Good," he replied.

"No doubt we'd all like to avoid this...business...in the future."

"Costly lesson," Gudmann said. "Even if it was necessary."

"I agree."

The general walked away without a reply. Looking around, I saw the few citizens who were there to watch had left at some point. *Can't blame them. I'd have done the same thing if I could've.*

I turned to Tindra. "I'm not sure I can eat anything this evening."

She nodded. "We witnessed a lot of death. No one should feel right after seeing that."

"I need to lay down."

"Home and to bed, it is," she said.

We walked to Agrim. "I'm not expecting trouble but an escort back to my quarters would make me feel better."

"Of course, Sire," he said. "Svan, Ingo, Lopt, Kodren, Engli, Orn, see King Fitzeirick and Lady Tindra home safe."

We attracted a lot of attention but had no problem making our way through crowds and arrived without incident.

"Ingo and I will stand watch at your door this evening, Sire," Svan said.

"Thank you," I said, nodding.

Tindra led me straight to the bedroom. We undressed, and she pulled herself against me and quickly fell asleep. Unfortunately, the sounds and sights and smells from the executions troubled my mind. Tossing and turning did little to clear my thoughts. Sleep didn't come until much later. Even then, good rest evaded me, hiding in dreams of my own head across a wooden block.

· · · · ● · ● · · ·

The smell of warm bread and cooked meat woke me. I gently moved Tindra's arm off my chest, scooted out of bed, and quietly pulled on some clothes.

"Heard you had a rough afternoon...skipped dinner," Roi said, as I came down the hall. "Thought you'd like some breakfast but given how you look..." He shrugged. "Maybe I was wrong. Are you well?"

"Didn't get much sleep." I shuddered. "Yesterday *was* some ugly business."

"Executions usually are."

"Why didn't my adviser give me that insight beforehand?"

"Some lessons are better learned through firsthand experience. I'm guessing you won't be as willing to order mass executions in the future."

I took a bite from one of the rolls, chewed quickly, and swallowed. "It's not like I haven't spilled blood before, plenty of it by now. But always to defend myself, or Crum, or Jesca...or save Croy."

"Didn't the executions save Croy too? Hallfrid and his allies were working with our enemy."

"True, but I could have killed Hallfrid when he challenged my rule before. I hurt him, sure, but... Wasn't sparing his life then a mercy?"

"I would think so," Roi said.

"And my mercy led to having others bloody their hands on my behalf," I said, running my hand through my tangled hair before taking another bite.

"Ordering a traitor's death is part of the responsibility of ruling," Roi said, frowning. "Perhaps some tea would lighten your mood. Abi said it would help settle your stomach."

I nodded, took the cup, and washed down the warm bread. "Thank you. I think a change of subject would do me more good. How's your family?"

"Settled in."

The bedroom door creaked open.

"Roi brought us breakfast," I said.

Tindra's pace quickened, and she thanked Roi as she sat and made a sandwich with a roll and some strips of rabbit.

He put a cup of tea in front of her.

She nodded and took a sip.

"Fitzeirick, any plans for the rest of the day?" he asked.

I swallowed the last of my roll. "I need to get some clothes made; my wardrobe is nearly empty."

"You're preparing to start a war, and clothes are a concern?" he asked.

"A king should have clothes for every occasion," Tindra said.

"I also need a new coin purse, and I have no armor."

"Are you planning to participate in the battle?" Roi asked.

I shrugged. "I never expected to be branded or sitting as king of Croy."

"I suppose you have a good point," he said. "I need some of your time...alone."

Tindra washed down the last of her sandwich. "I'll go visit with Aerison now if you'd like."

"Good idea. Wouldn't be a bad idea for me to talk to him too. I'll find you at Abi's after Roi and I are done."

She grabbed a couple of pieces of rabbit and left.

"May I speak freely?" Roi asked.

"Of course. Why would my mentor think otherwise?"

"Because it seems to me that you're making bad decisions lately."

"I thought we were through talking about yesterday. I had enough evidence to prove Hallfrid and many of his men were committing treason. The generals are on my side now because I took care of the problem."

"You sure it's not because you took care of *their* problem?"

I shook my head. "I spoke with them before going to the prison. They supported Hallfrid until I proved he'd sided with Satra and drove Croians from their homes. I also promised I would not order them to spill more Croian blood."

"At least you're on the right track there," he said. "I'm hearing Hallfrid made himself a thorn in the side of many people. Now, on the subject of marriage—"

"It's going to happen," I said. "I'll lose credibility with too many people if I back out."

"Not your marriage," he said. "I'll address that lapse in judgment next. On the subject of *my* marriage...Grima would prefer to have no ceremony at all. If we come to you with our vows, would you witness our commitment?"

My heart sped up, and my eyes opened wide as happiness for my mentor filled my chest. "Of course. I'd be glad to," I said, smiling at him. "Just so you know, Kurt offered to tell me Einns' father's name. I turned him down."

"Thank you," he said, nodding. "Grima and I have never discussed it. Honestly, I don't care. It's not important. He's a good boy. That's all I need to know."

"Then the matter's settled."

"Exactly," he said, then frowned. "On the subject of *your* wedding, though...I don't agree with your decision." He held up his hand when I opened my mouth. "I know I can't stop you, but I'll do my best to discourage it."

Rubbing my forehead, I sighed. "She protected me, like she swore to Crum she would, so I'm protecting her."

"That's no reason to marry her."

I shrugged. "People have married for worse reasons."

He scoffed. "Following other bad examples is rarely the right course of action."

"Why are you so dead set against this?"

"Because of what Tindra is, how she works. She's not a good person. You deserve better."

"She's changing. I didn't like what she was, but she's working on being better," I said. "She was there for me when you and Crum let me go into battle alone. She lost a hand defending me. Self-sacrifice wasn't part of her nature before she swore to assist me. She promised to give her life for me if that's what it took for me to control Croy."

"Didn't think I'd change your mind but wanted to voice my opinion anyway. I'd best get going. Einns wanted some items from the market to get cooking again," he said, expression unchanged.

"Roi, watch her and think about what I said. I'm not asking you to change your opinion blindly, and you don't have to be her friend."

He pressed his lips together and nodded. "Send for me when the strategy meetings begin."

"Having you at my side will be helpful," I said, offering him my hand.

He stood, took my hand, and pulled me out of my chair into a tight hug. "I'm glad you're alive."

I clapped him on the back and let go so he could go about his business. After strapping on the sling and setting my hammer in place across my back, I started for Abi's house.

Chapter 49

I'd passed the same unremarkable alleyway several times walking from my home to Abi's. This time, I heard an odd hissing sound as I approached. Stopping to look, I heard it again before a bony, light-skinned hand beckoned to me from the shadow of a chimney.

"Show yourself," I said, reaching for my hammer.

"Too dangerous," came the quiet reply.

"Yet I can't say *I* feel safe walking into an alley to talk to a stranger."

"You will come to no harm. I swear."

Looking around for obvious threats before moving, I stepped toward the alley, stopping just outside while pushing my talent into the ground. A single, lightweight person stood behind the chimney.

"Who are you?" I asked.

"No one of consequence. A servant, if you will. Come closer, please."

"Why?"

"There are those who want to thank you for your service yesterday. I bear a token of their gratitude."

"They are welcome to visit me. Perhaps over dinner."

"They prefer to remain anonymous."

"Not interested," I said, stepping back. "I'm familiar with groups who think it best to operate in the shadows. I don't need more of that kind of headache."

"Accepting their gift comes with no obligation. Refusing could be taken as an insult."

"Your masters must think I'm stone-headed if they expect me to believe a gift comes with no obligation. Tell them I respectfully decline...until they're willing to meet face to face."

As I took another step, the servant spoke louder, "Wait. You can use all the support you can get."

I stopped. "And I'm gathering support by the day."

"Some say you're trying to buy support, considering how much coin you're throwing around. Maybe this token is a repayment of your...kindness."

"Slide it toward me and don't move until I'm gone," I said. "Otherwise, I'm going about my business."

The thin hand placed a black, leather scabbard, about the length of my forearm, with a plain, brown, leather-wrapped handle sticking out on the ground and shoved it toward me. It slid to a stop just inside the alley.

"If you move, I'll consider it an attack and will defend myself," I said.

"We mean you no harm."

I looked around one more time before cautiously stepping closer and grabbing the weapon.

The stranger stood still as a statue until I walked far enough away that I quit tracking them.

Curiosity led me to examine the gift. A thick-spined knife, sharpened on one edge. I slid it back in the scabbard and tucked it into my belt before continuing to Abi's house.

One Varian soldier stood guard at the door, and he let me inside. Glancing around as I made my way to Aerison's room, I didn't see Abi.

Probably in her garden.

The door to his room stood open. I found him alone, sitting on his bed.

"Well met, Lieutenant," I said, stepping into the room.

"I wasn't expecting a visit from royalty," he replied, smiling. "Have a seat."

"Where's Tindra?"

"She went to refill the water pitcher."

I nodded. "How are you?"

"Abi says the wounds on my legs are closing well. The stitches are starting to itch. Hope she takes them out soon."

I grimaced and ran a finger along the scar on my scalp. "That is uncomfortable. Are you walking yet?"

Frowning, he shook his head. "Not without help. Abi says she'll have crutches ready after the stitches come out."

"Look at *me*," I said. "You can't keep a determined man down."

He chuckled.

"Speaking of determined...should I send someone to check on your soldiers before I start making battle plans? None of them have returned, and I'd like them to participate."

"I have no report either," he said. "Probably a good idea to send a messenger."

"Everything sounded good before I sent more men to the southeast. I assumed they're working with my warriors to secure the area, but I've been too busy to think much about it."

"So I've heard."

Tindra walked in, holding the pitcher close to her body, supporting it with her right arm. "When did you get here?"

"Not long ago," I said.

"Did you have a productive meeting with your adviser?" she asked, while filling a cup.

I shrugged. "We spoke."

She frowned and put her hand on her hip. "I don't want to come between—"

"This isn't Aerison's concern," I said, interrupting her. "We can talk about it later."

She nodded before sitting in a chair near the nightstand. "You're right. We'll talk later."

"Aerison, how do you recommend I use your soldiers?"

He looked toward the ceiling and rubbed his chin for a while.

Tindra moved her chair next to me, took my hand, and smiled when I looked at her.

"As tempting as it sounds, don't try to combine my forces with yours," Aerison said. "Place them on your flanks; use their mobility to your advantage."

Closing my eyes, I ran my fingers through my beard while considering his advice. "I'll talk it over with my generals. They may not trust Varians to keep them safe."

He laughed. "If they don't trust us, we might as well go home."

Smiling, I nodded. "I know, and we need the men."

"So I've been told," he said, shaking his head.

Looking at Tindra, I asked, "You told him?"

She nodded. "He needs to know how things are going in case his men come to him with problems."

"True," I said. "But next time, let me know before you let anyone know about our situation."

"Of course," she said, squeezing my hand.

"Lieutenant, any insight into how I should plan for the upcoming battles?" I asked.

He looked me in the eye. "What do you know about the enemy and their preparations? Where are they camped?

"Little to nothing beyond they are somewhere to the east of us," I said.

"Make scouting your top priority. Going into battle knowing nothing is like fighting blindfolded. Not a good chance for success," he said.

"True," I replied, nodding. "Any other wisdom to share? I'll take every pebble I can get."

"My service as a soldier had just started when Eirick took the conquered land from us. Most of my lessons then were on how to avoid getting killed."

"Kurt left for home at a bad time," Tindra said. "The war council has some excellent tacticians."

"Doubt I can wait for him to return. Hopefully, my generals know how Eirick conquered that territory so easily," I said.

"Everyone in Varia knows that," Aerison said, smiling. "He caught us by surprise. I doubt the Satra will be so complacent. You've made your intentions clear."

"That I have," I said. "I'm sorry I have to go, but I have other matters that require my attention. I hope you mend quickly. You'd be a welcome asset on the battlefield."

"Thank you," he said. "I'd like nothing more than to be on my horse with my soldiers."

"Sooner than you know," Tindra said. "With any luck."

"May your dealings go in your favor," he said, as we stood to leave.

I reached toward the front door, and it moved away from my hand.

"Make way!" someone yelled from outside.

Chapter 50

Tindra and I pressed ourselves against the wall as two warriors rushed through the door, carrying someone.

"Find Abi," I said, to Tindra, as I followed the group.

They laid someone on the bed and looked back at me. "Sorry, Sire," one said. "He collapsed at the eastern gate. We think he's Varian, but he's cut up good."

"Let me see," I said, pushing past them.

To someone who didn't know him well, the swollen shut right eye and gashed left cheek might have kept them from identifying him. I had no doubt it was Kurt.

I turned to my men. "Did he say anything before he fell?"

"I think he said Satra has returned."

I sat on the bed and rested my head in my hands. "Tindra's looking for Abi. Help her."

They didn't make it through the door before Abi entered. "What happened?"

"He was hurt during a Satran raid," I said.

"Who is it?" Tindra asked.

"Kurt," I said, hurrying to her side.

"Are you sure?"

"See for yourself," I said, sweeping my arm toward the bed.

"No!" Abi barked. "Everyone out until I can look him over."

I pulled Tindra out of the room. "Let her work. We'll talk to him when he's awake. I need my generals now."

"I'm staying in case she needs help."

"I thought you were scared of Kurt."

"He can't do anything to me in his condition. Plus, he—" She broke off in a sob.

"He what?"

She shook her head and pushed me away, tears continuing to flow.

I nodded, then reached for her hand. "Do what you can to help. I'll find you later."

She nodded and walked back into the room.

I found my men outside, talking to the Varian soldier.

"You two, find General Gudmann and Heming. Tell them to report to the meeting room in my quarters immediately."

"Of course, Sire," they said, and ran away.

Grabbing the Varian's arm, I said, "I'm not sure what happened, but the fact he's alone could mean the Satran have spilled Varian blood."

"I understand," he said, expression growing angry.

"You'll get your chance," I said. "Maybe soon."

"I'll await new orders from my commanders."

I nodded and jogged back to my quarters.

Agrim pushed the door to his quarters open when I entered the courtyard.

I called out and waved him over.

"Yes, Sire?"

"I have reason to believe the Satran are gathering to attack Nikulas' holdings again. Send a messenger to General Jomar telling him to return with half his men along with the Varian soldiers."

"You're sure they're attacking again?"

"I think it's better to be safe than sorry."

"Should we send someone to warn Nikulas?"

"The attack will reach his hall before anyone leaving the capitol would."

"Understood. I'll send a rider on our fastest horse."

"When you're done, find Roi and bring lunch to my quarters—enough to feed at least five."

"Yes, Sire."

I grabbed a cup of water and headed to the meeting room, wanting to enjoy a little peace before the madness began.

I'd barely had a chance to catch my breath before the generals rushed into the room and sat across from me.

"What's going on?" Gudmann asked.

"I think it best to wait until everyone shows up," I said. "Don't want to repeat myself."

"How long will that take?" Heming asked.

"Captain Agrim usually completes his assignments quickly."

"Speaking of Agrim," Heming said. "You took him from Ottar's group and never gave the commander a replacement."

"As far as I'm concerned," I said, "that's between General Jomar and Commander Ottar to decide. I have no business telling them who they should promote."

"Jarl Eirickson insisted on having an active role with such matters," Gudmann said.

I sucked in a deep breath and held it to the count of ten. "I'm tired of people mistaking me for my half-brother, General. I am *not* Eirickson and *will* not continue his ways."

"My apologies, Sire," Gudmann said.

I nodded to him. "Don't do it again."

"Yes, m'lord."

"And make it clear to everyone else," I said.

"Of course, Sire."

Agrim and Roi entered together, carrying our meal.

"Pass the food around," I said, before they sat, "and we can begin. I have good reason to believe the Satran are on their way to attack Nikulas' holdings again."

"Why now?" Heming asked. "And why there?"

"Controlling the area gives them an open path between Croy and Varia," Roi said. "Also, having Nikulas' hall and the surrounding area provides them a place to stage attacks deeper into Croy."

"I agree," Gudmann said. "We have warriors ready to send into battle but no idea how many Satran are on the move. What if this is a diversion to draw our forces away from the capital?"

"Agrim, are the messengers on their way?"

"If they haven't left yet, they'll leave soon."

"Good," I said. "I ordered Jomar to send half his men back here and asked for the Varian soldiers to return as well. Jomar's men will help secure the capital. The soldiers will leave for Nikulas' holdings after a night's rest."

"You should have sent the Varian's directly north," Heming said.

"I considered it but delaying them behind our forces puts them fresh, covering our backs, and ready to stop any Satran push south...assuming our warriors fail."

"It's a gamble," Roi said.

"Before we get too far into this, do either of you know how Eirick drove Varia from their land?"

Heming shook his head.

"I was a footman then," Gudmann said. "We fought on the move, cutting down one Varian before moving on to the next. If you didn't kill him, the warrior behind you did...or the one behind him. Like wolves chasing deer, hounding them, we struck and kept moving to keep them confused and unable to catch their breath."

"I'm not sure that strategy will work against Satra," Agrim said. "Every Satran we've faced in the uprisings fought to his last breath, a danger until he couldn't move."

"Good to know," I said. "Last time we routed the Satran force and let them retreat. This time, we cut them down. Not a single one escapes."

"How far do we chase them?" Gudmann asked.

"Not a single one escapes," I said, tapping my finger on the table to emphasize each word.

"I advise caution," Roi said.

"Why?" I asked. "You know how I feel about Satra; I want them all gone, ground to dust."

"The exact reason you should be cautious," he replied.

We jumped when the front door slammed into the wall. Everyone drew weapons when the meeting room door swung open.

Tindra entered the room and drew a sharp breath.

"I thought you were helping Abi," I said.

Her eyes snapped from the swords to mine. "Kurt's awake, and you need to talk to him. *Now*."

"Tindra," Roi said, "we're trying to plan a course of action and get warriors on the move as quickly as possible. The king doesn't have time for this interruption."

"Boril's dead, so is Porsey's family. Porsey went with the Satran," she said. "You *need* to talk to Kurt."

"You mean they killed them and captured Porsey?" I asked.

She sighed. "Listen to me. Kurt said Porsey *went* with them. You need to hear what he saw."

I looked across the table. "Gudmann, Heming, get your men ready to move. Agrim, put the guards on alert. Roi, you're coming with me to talk to Kurt."

The generals and Agrim bowed and hurried out of the room.

Chapter 51

"What aren't you telling us?" Roi asked, as we walked to the door.

"I'm not going to put words in his mouth," she said.

"Fitzeirick, how trustworthy is this man?" Roi asked.

"He's been good to his word so far," I said.

"Kurt's many things, but a liar isn't one of them...and I know liars," she said.

"Of course you do. You lie for a living."

"Not now," I growled, hoping my tone made it clear to drop the subject.

As we got close to Kurt's room, the air filled with the smell of mint and garlic. Inside the room, the smell grew stronger. Abi sat next to the bed, feeding Kurt spoonfuls of some concoction.

He saw me and tried to sit up.

"Lie still," Abi said firmly.

"I have to tell Fitzeirick," he said, a breathy weakness in his voice.

She looked over her shoulder and her eyes opened wide when she noticed us. "Sorry, Sire. Didn't hear you come in."

"No worries," I said. "I need to hear what he has to say."

"As long as he lies still," she said.

"I'll make sure of it," I said.

She nodded and left the room.

I looked him over as I took her seat. Abi had applied some kind of paste to the cut on his cheek but swelling kept his eye shut.

"What happened?"

"I'll call it an ambush, but truthfully, it was probably bad luck. The fifty or so Satran soldiers looked surprised when they ran into us. Of course, we weren't expecting to cross them either, so both sides were unprepared. They won because of numbers."

"Tindra said Porsey went with them," I said.

"He did. The stone-headed, no-good, gutter rat offered to tell them everything about you and your plans if they spared his life. Of course, he didn't bother to say a word until after the other Croians were hacked and bleeding to death."

"He let them kill his family?" Roi asked.

"Didn't raise his voice to save them," Kurt said.

"Boril, too?" I asked.

He chuckled then coughed and groaned. "Porsey looked the Satran in the eye and told them he served as your chief adviser."

"That's a lie," Tindra said.

"To the fire with him," Roi muttered.

"How about the Varian soldiers? Did they cover your escape?" I asked.

"No. Outnumbered, our escort fell quickly. Maybe I lived because I didn't put up a fight. I acted like a simple trader, riding with the group for safety. They beat me, tied me up, and meant to take me back to the main force somewhere in the forest. Guess they intended to make me a slave. After getting my hands loose, I waited until they were listening to Porsey brag instead of watching me. I'd like to say I slipped away, but they noticed before I made it too far. Good thing I know how to hide."

"Any idea how many Satran are in the forest?" Roi asked.

"Never saw them."

"And you're sure they were headed toward Nikulas' holdings?" I asked.

"As sure as I *can* be."

"You're going to move forces on this information?" Roi asked.

"I am," I said, "and I want Porsey dead on sight."

"How much does he know?" Tindra asked.

"He claimed to know everything about the new king and his plans," Kurt said.

"And everyone in this room knows that's an outright lie," I said. "He knows the size of our army and that the Varian soldiers are here. Satran will be aware of the support I'm getting from the north. He knows Nikulas is our ambassador to Varia."

"What else?" Roi asked.

"Considering how well he lied," Kurt said, "I'd suspect he's a spion. Regardless, he'll tell them anything to save his own skin."

"Calling that weasel a spion insults the profession," Tindra said.

"Never thought you'd be easily offended," Roi said.

"I don't appreciate disrespect," she said.

"Noted."

"I've asked nicely," I said. "If you two insist on going at each other, can you wait until the enemy isn't preparing to pounce?"

"Don't get mad at me for defending myself," Tindra said.

I sighed. "I'm not mad at anyone. I'm simply saying there's a time and a place...and this isn't it."

"Noted," Roi said, and left the room.

I sighed again. "He's got the right idea. We should leave and let you rest."

"Make them pay," he said, before we left.

We caught up to Roi not far from Abi's.

"What do you think?" I asked.

"I think you're about to break your promise to Gudmann and Heming."

"I'll make sure they understand Porsey willingly joined the Satran. He's a traitor," I said.

"Like Hallfrid, Nothri, and the rest?"

"Worse," I said.

"You'd better let them know now," Tindra said. "I need to talk to Thorgault, tell him to start gathering leather for you."

"Thank you," I said, and turned to Roi. "Coming to the barracks with me?"

"Wouldn't be much of an adviser if I didn't."

Stopping at the first warrior we saw, I asked him where the generals were.

"General Heming's at the stable. Last I saw General Gudmann, he was going over wagon loading with the quartermasters."

I thanked him, and said, "Roi, go tell Heming we're coming to him."

He nodded and hurried toward the stables.

Walking through an ever-thickening crowd of warriors, I arrived at the building where their supplies were stored. General Gudmann stood outside, barking orders.

"General," I called out, waving to him when he looked my way.

He grabbed a passing warrior, pointed toward a stack of sacks, and told him to load them in the wagons before coming to me.

"My lord, how's the Varian?"

"Abi's taking care of him. He'll live. He gave me some bad news though."

"Worse than another Satran attack?"

I nodded. "In my opinion, yes. Come with me to the stable so we can discuss the situation with Heming."

"Give me a moment," he said, and turned back to the storehouse. "Commander Alrik, I'm being called away. Make sure these supplies are loaded with all haste."

"Aye," someone yelled from inside.

Roi and Heming stood outside the stables, waiting for us.

"What's going on, Sire?" Heming asked.

I took a deep breath and frowned. "Porsey's forcing me to break my promise to you."

"Why?" Gudmann asked.

"According to Kurt, Porsey led the Satran to believe Boril was my most trusted adviser. They killed the poor man when he couldn't tell them anything."

"Oh," Heming said.

"It's worse," I continued. "He let them kill his family before claiming to be a high-ranking Croian with information about me and our plans. He traded lies to save his own life."

"And you trust the Varian is telling the truth?" Gudmann asked.

"Kurt may have questionable morals, but I've never caught him lying to me," I said. "I believe the story."

Gudmann turned to Roi. "You heard the same thing?"

Roi nodded.

"And you believe him?" Heming asked.

"It didn't *sound* like a lie," Roi said.

"When we find him, he's a dead man," Gudmann said. "Your promise doesn't cover deserters."

Heming nodded as Gudmann spoke, adding his consent with an "aye."

"I'm glad you understand," I said. "I don't want to go into this war with my generals doubting my ability to keep my word."

"Being upfront about the problem at hand helps," Gudmann said. "Any idea what Porsey might tell them?"

"Considering how he lied about Boril, anything he thinks will keep him alive," I said. "The most damaging thing he can tell them is that we're getting support from Varia. If that information gets back to whoever is in charge of Satra, they could decide to attack Varia through the eastern passage. Varia's got enough trouble right now. An unexpected attack could be devastating."

"Nothing we can do about that," Heming said. "Anything else?"

"Kurt not making it back to Varia is not good for us either," I said.

"Why not?" Gudmann asked. "Who is he anyway?"

"He passes as a tradesman...which he is, of a sort," I said. "He's connected to a sizable group of powerful people. They've offered to assist us in destroying Satra, but their help comes with a cost. We get aid, and they get to set up shops in Croy while I ignore any criminal activity they're involved in. Varia's on the brink of a civil war; Kurt's people are doing what they can to keep it from happening. Until that situation is stable, we aren't getting much of anything from them."

"Are you willing to pay that price?" Heming asked.

"I haven't decided," I said, "but they think I am."

"Tindra's a bad influence on you," Roi said. "Deceptions start to feel like betrayal after a while. I've dealt with people like Kurt before. They don't appreciate betrayal."

"I'm doing what I must to make Croy better," I replied. "We can argue morality later."

Roi shrugged. "Simply doing my job as mentor and adviser."

"Noted," I said, with a grin.

"What do you want us to do?" Gudmann asked.

"What you're already planning to do: defend Nikulas' holdings and kill Satrans. Don't send anyone hunting for Porsey, but if you see him, he dies."

"Understood, Sire," he said. "We'll leave in the morning."

"You're free to go," I said.

They nodded. Heming headed back into the stables, shouting orders to the stable keeps and horsemen. Gudmann turned and jogged toward the barracks.

"What are we going to do?" Roi asked.

"I need to talk to you about something in private."

"No place more private than your quarters, unless Tindra's there," he said.

"I wouldn't mind her insight on this too."

Chapter 52

I slid the scabbard from my belt and laid the covered knife on the table. "What do you make of this?"

"Looks like a long knife or a short sword," he said, glancing at it. "I thought you favored your hammer."

"I do. This is a gift."

"Nice of her to give you a weapon you don't want."

"You know who gave it to me?"

"Of course. Tindra."

I shook my head.

"I'll play along," he said, brow furrowed. "Who gave it do you?"

"A servant."

"You don't have any servants."

Crossing my arms, I said, "Never said I did."

"This game's no fun," he said. "Whose servant then?"

I shrugged. "That's the best part...I don't know."

Looking back at the blade on the table, Roi closed his eyes and scratched his head. "A servant, someone's servant, gave you this, but you don't know who or why?"

"I think I know why," I said. "Someone, or some group, is pleased Hallfrid is dead."

"Why not present it to you in person?"

"According to the servant, they want to remain anonymous."

"Should I ask what the servant looked like?"

I shook my head. "They hid in a shadow only exposing a pale, skinny arm."

He pointed to the knife. "May I?"

I nodded. "Of course."

Lifting it, he looked over the scabbard for a while before wrapping his hand around the handle and pulling the blade out. After a detailed study of the blade and handle, he said, "No markings anywhere, but it's obviously well made."

"Perhaps Kurt's group has competition in Croy," I said.

"If there's a secret group operating in the capital, I've never heard as much as a rumor," he said, still examining the blade. "If you suspect something like that, why did you take it?"

"The servant said it would be seen as an insult if I refused, and they know I need all the support I could get."

"They have a point," he said. "What did you promise them in return?"

"According to the servant, it came with no obligation. Simply a token of gratitude."

"You want me to look into it?"

"Not hard enough to give anyone reason to suspect you are. But keep an eye out for pale, boney servants."

"Understood," he said, sliding the blade back into the scabbard. "If you don't need anything else, I should get back home."

"Speaking of your home," I said. "Are you planning to invite me over sometime? I'd like to see Grima and Einns again."

"You don't need an invitation," he said. "You're always welcome in my home."

"Then why haven't you told me where it is?"

"Oh, I... This safe house has been kept secret for so long, I didn't think to tell you where it was."

"Then how did my guards know where to find you?"

He chuckled. "Some of them helped me move a few things into it."

"So...where is it?"

"Not far past the stables. It looks like a cobbler's workshop, but it's never open for business. I'm thinking about opening the front up as a seamstress shop, if Grima wants to work."

"What about a bakery for Einns?" I asked.

He shook his head. "He needs to work in a bigger kitchen, learn more before going it alone."

"I made an impression at The Sneaky Bear," I said, smiling. "Want me to see if they can give him a job?"

"I don't want him working as a favor. I want him to earn his position."

"Very well," I said. "But the offer stands."

"Thank you, and drop by...now that you know where we are."

I nodded. "As soon as I can. Tell them I said hello."

He nodded on his way out.

Tindra stepped in before Roi could close the door.

"Look at what I have," she said, holding up a cuff resembling the one Per sent her.

"Thorgault finished your fork?" I asked.

Her face lit up when she smiled. "Yes, and it fits perfectly. Can't wait to try it out."

"How's the progress on your armor?"

"He's still working on it," she said, smile fading.

"We'll go eat dinner soon," I said, and pointed at the knife on the table. "Right now, I've got something I want you to look at."

She picked it up and looked at me. "For me?"

"No. Someone gave it to me."

Holding the scabbard against her body with her right arm, she drew the knife. "Nice gift," she said. "Peace offering from Roi?"

I shook my head and told her the story as she examined the knife closely.

"Someone likes you," she said. "This couldn't have been cheap. It rivals anything I've seen from Per's shop. The balance is perfect, the edge flawless. Anyone who knows how to fight with a seax will be jealous."

"What did you call it?"

"Seax," she said. "Fairly common design in Varia. Haven't seen any in Croy, but I haven't gone shopping for a blade either. I assumed there were some around."

"Do you think you could find out who made it?"

"If you want, but consider your benefactors didn't come to you openly. They want to remain hidden for a reason."

"Should I tell Kurt?"

Tindra chewed her bottom lip for a moment. "The war council doesn't have an established presence in Croy yet and are focused on keeping Varia stable. I'd say don't mention it; he's got enough to worry about. Once he has people in place, they can fight it out with your mystery admirers."

"What if I don't let them operate in Croy?"

She shook her head. "Kurt's been good to you and done everything he can to support you. Crossing him would only make your life more difficult in the future. Plus, you know what to expect from his group, and you know nothing about this servant's masters. What makes you think they're better than the war council?"

I shrugged. "I don't like any of this secret 'group in the shadows' business, regardless of where it comes from."

"Sunlight hates shadow but shadows continue to exist. Kurt and the council are many things, but they aren't outright evil. Criminals, certainly, but not without honor. They are good to their word. Can you trust this unknown group?"

"Trust them? Honor them? I don't *want* either group in Croy."

She smiled. "Yet you have both. One's here, apparently well established, and you know nothing about them. The other you invited. You know they have rules, and you know what they want. If you ask me, I say let Sabast and Halmar do your dirty work when the time comes."

"What if I suspect your advice is biased because of how much money you've made working for the war council?"

She chuckled. "Still suspicious? Good. But I work for no one but you now. Remember, I *am* your promised, so what benefits you is best for me. Varia has benefited from the war council's presence; no reason to believe Croy would be any different...especially after you destroy Satra. Though I do wonder why you're worried about this now. It seems you have more pressing matters demanding your attention."

"I'm sending most of my army to fight against our enemy and protect my people," I said. "I have no way to directly influence the battle. Trying to figure out who this group is and what to do about them is something I can do."

"I see your point. Neither of us have bathed lately. How about cleaning up before we eat?"

I nodded and smiled. "Sounds good. Let's grab some fresh clothes."

"Carry the seax along with your hammer; it's probably best if you make a habit of wearing it."

"Why?" I asked. "I don't have much use for it and no training to speak of."

"If I gave someone a gift like that, I'd want to see them carrying it. Never know who's watching when we're out."

I sighed. "As much as I don't want to admit it, you're right."

We walked past The Sneaky Bear on the way to the bathhouse.

"We're *not* going there to eat," I commented, as we passed.

"Not anytime soon," Tindra said.

Chapter 53

The warmer air inside the bathing house carried the fragrant smell of flowers. Tension left my shoulders with every breath.

Although there weren't many people soaking, a few noticed me and pointed.

"Feels good to just stand here and breathe," Tindra said.

"It does," I said, looking around the room. "Wonder how it's done."

"Some herbalist concoction boiling over the fires warming the water, I'd guess," Tindra said. "Find a crate for our clothes, and let's get in."

After putting our clean clothes away, we undressed and waded into the large, warm pool.

Doing my best to ignore the stares and hushed whispers, I sat on a ledge trying to let the warm water and floral air take my worries away while cleaning myself.

"Even the soap smells good," Tindra said. "I'll scrub your back."

Though she could only use one hand, she did a thorough, and pleasant, job of washing and massaging my back.

I glanced over my shoulder. "Your turn."

While washing her back, I looked over her scars again and ran my finger across the stab wound that made her giggle.

"Stop it," she said. "Giggling's bad for my reputation."

"You have no reputation in Croy," I said, rubbing soap across her skin.

"Do you want people calling me Croy's giggling queen?"

"Other than not being very regal, what would be bad about that?" I asked. "My people might enjoy a happy queen."

"You just said it—it's not regal."

"And you, the cunning cutthroat for the Varian crown, are the living example of regal," I said.

"I *can* be."

"I think that remains to be seen," I said, lathering the soap in my hands before running my fingers through her hair.

"Massage my scalp, and I might forget your insult."

I shrugged and rubbed my fingers hard against her skin. If my presence in the bathhouse didn't attract enough attention, Tindra's moans had all eyes on us.

"I think you're enjoying this a little too much," I whispered. "People are staring."

"Let them," she said. "I'm done." With a shudder, she dropped below the water.

She surfaced, shook her head, and slicked back her short hair.

"I'm ready to eat."

"Me too," I said, "but we have to take our dirty clothes back home first."

She nodded. "Wouldn't do for the king of Croy to carry his laundry to dinner."

Leaving the pool, I noticed Tindra took longer steps adding an exaggerated sway to her hips.

"Keep that up and you'll get a reputation in Croy," I said quietly, as we dressed.

"Happy queen. Fun queen. What's the difference?" she said, grinning.

"What happened to regal?"

"Fun *and* regal...why not? I've never shied away from a challenge."

I chuckled and shook my head. "Let's eat at Grith's so I can talk to Thorgault about armor and pick up a new coin purse."

"Sounds good," she said. "Home isn't too far out of our way."

Grith's was full when we arrived.

"Get dinner while I visit the tanner. We'll eat at home."

She curtsied. "As you say, my lord."

I raised an eyebrow.

"Regal," she said, smiling.

I shook my head and walked across the square to the tanner's shop. "Well met, Thorgault."

Turning from his work, he smiled when he saw me. "Well met, Sire. What can I do fur ya?"

"First, you can sell me a coin purse," I said. "Seems I left mine in a pub."

"Happens ta da best of us," he said, with a chuckle. "Lemme find tha box."

After searching through several wooden containers, he asked, "Color?"

"Black or brown would be fine. I don't need anything special."

He reached into the crate, pulled a couple of pouches out, and showed them to me. The brown one looked nicer, with a polished, silver buckle to hold it closed but I chose the simple, drawstring, black pouch.

"One of my more popular items," he said. "Take a copper double for it."

"Will a silver single do?"

"Same thing," he said, taking the coin. "Anythin' else?"

"War's coming, I want a good suit of armor."

"Plannin' ta fight?"

"Never know what the future holds. I want to be prepared."

"Assume ya want it black, like her's," he said, pointing.

I turned to see Tindra walking toward us, carrying a basket.

"I'd like something more suited for forest and plains fighting, browns and greens."

"Sure," he said. "Need ta measure ya."

Looking around, I said, "I'm not sure Croy's ready for its king to undress in a market square."

"Hate ta say it, Sire, but that's tha best way ta make sur it fits right," he said.

I sighed and pulled the seax from my belt, dropping it.

"Plan ta carry tha blade on tha battlefield?"

"Not sure," I said. "It's a recent addition to my wardrobe. I *will* wear my hammer."

"Figured as much, but ya already have a holder for it," he said. "Tell me if I'm outta line fur askin', but may I see da knife?"

"I see no harm."

I undressed while he inspected the scabbard. "Not one of mine, but quality work. Excellent stitchin'. Who'd ya get it from?"

"It was a gift."

He nodded and pulled the knife. After a long whistle, he said, "Some men would kill fur a blade this nice."

"I'd like to find out who made it; they deserve recognition for doing good work."

"Can't think of a smith in tha capital who makes a blade wit this shape. Maybe in Nikulas' holdings?"

I shrugged. "Suppose that's possible. Can we finish the measuring? I'm growing hungry smelling my dinner in the basket."

"Of course," he said, sliding the blade back into the scabbard and onto my belt. "Please accept my apology, m'lord. Don't mean ta keep ya from yur meal."

"It's easy for a tradesman to get distracted by quality work," I said, smiling. "I understand."

"I'll make the armor wit tha knife in mind, but ya don't have ta wear it if ya don't want."

"Perfect."

"Stand up straight wit your arms out to ya side."

As he worked, I felt myself blushing.

After measuring my leg, he asked, "New boots? Know a excellent cobbler."

"What I've got is fine for now, but you can send me his way after the armor's finished."

He nodded. "Done. Ya can get dressed. Next time I talk ta him, I'll tell him ta expect ya."

"Sounds good. How much do I owe you?"

"Depends," he said. "How much metal do you want in tha armor?"

"Metal?" I asked. "You use metal in your leather armor?"

"For battlefield use, yes," he said. "Sew in steel plates for tha chest and back, some for tha thighs and shins too...if ya want."

"He wants," Tindra said. "The king must be protected."

He looked past me to her. "Steel helmet?"

"Leather covered to keep it from shining," she said.

He nodded. "Ten gold doubles an' I'll make sure it's so comfortable ya could sleep in it, helmet and all"

"I don't have that much with me," I said.

"Won't start on it until I finish her armor...say two days. Pay when ya pick hers up."

Holding out my hand, I nodded. "Deal."

He shook it and smiled. "Ma pleasure, Sire."

"Pants," Tindra said.

"Oh, yes," I said. "I could use a few pairs of pants. Say, two brown, two tan, and two black."

He glanced at Tindra. "Please tell me ya don't want split goat too, Sire."

"Anything's fine as long as they're comfortable and durable," I said.

He nodded. "If ya don't mind dyed, I can get the black done faster."

"I don't mind," I said. "How much?"

"Nother gold double?"

Reaching into my pocket, I grabbed a coin and handed it to him.

"Thank ya, Sire."

"Interesting that you didn't gather a crowd," Tindra commented, as we left the market.

"Not my fault you're better looking than I am."

"But you are cute with an all-over blush."

I chuckled. "If you insist. Is that deer I smell?"

"Deer steaks and roast potatoes."

"Sounds great. Can't wait to eat."

Chapter 54

Once we got settled at the table, Tindra slid her new fork over her arm and buckled it in place. Stabbing the fork into the meat wasn't a problem for her but maneuvering it to her mouth while keeping the meat on it seemed challenging. At one point it seemed like she'd smeared more meat across her cheek and lips than she'd managed to get in her mouth...and that didn't count the times the meat fell off on the way.

"Take it slow," I said, after she let loose a particularly aggressive growl. "Getting frustrated isn't going to help."

"I know," she said, hanging her head. "I feel like a child...helpless."

"I learned, the hard way, the best way to overcome a bad situation is steady determination. I'd have never escaped without the determination to stay alive...and look at me now."

She chuckled. "King of a nation under attack."

"And I'm determined to correct that situation too."

Looking at the piece of meat on her fork, she said, "I won't let this defeat me."

I smiled. "You did say you never back down from a challenge."

"I did," she said, slowly moving the fork toward her mouth until the meat touched her tongue.

"Good job," I said. "Practice like that, you can only get better."

She nodded as she chewed.

I put my plate back in the basket. "Once you're finished, let's clean your face and go to bed. It's been a tiring day."

She swallowed. "Sounds like a plan."

I left the table and wet a small cloth to clean her face for her.

"Finished," she said, after placing her plate in the basket. She turned to me and I wiped her face while she removed her fork.

"You should clean that," I said.

"I will," she replied, "along with the rest of the utensils...but they can wait until morning. I'm ready for bed."

We walked together to the bedroom, undressed, and fell asleep against each other.

· · · ● ● ● ● · · ·

I woke before her and lay still for a moment, listening to her breathe, and enjoying the feeling of her warm body against mine. I flinched when the front door opened. Tindra mumbled something and rolled over.

I dressed quickly and went to see who'd entered my home.

Roi waved at me from the table as I walked down the hall, then I noticed Grima sitting next to him.

"Morning," I said quietly, as I sat. "Grima, it's good to see you again."

She smiled. "Glad to be here."

"Tindra's still asleep?" Roi asked.

I nodded.

He dropped a sheet of paper on the table. "Our marriage agreement. We'd like you to sign it."

I smiled and offered him my hand. "Of course. I'd like nothing more. Let me get a quill and ink."

He shook my hand and nodded.

I hurried to get the items I needed, returned, and signed the document making Roi and Grima husband and wife.

Grima blinked tears from her eyes. "Thank you, Fitzeirick. Einns is working on breakfast, and we'd love for you and Tindra to join us this morning."

I nodded. "Congratulations, and it's my pleasure. I'm happy for the both of you." I looked at Roi. "Are you sure you want Tindra at your house?"

"Not my idea," he said. "But I don't have to be her friend."

I pressed my lips together and nodded again. "I'll be over shortly, and I'll bring Tindra if she wants to come. She normally doesn't sleep this late; she may not be feeling well."

"We look forward to your visit, and tell Tindra I hope she's not getting sick," Grima said.

I smiled. "She's probably fine. We both had rough days yesterday."

"Roi seemed preoccupied yesterday too," Grima said.

"King Fitzeirick's kept me busy," he said, and chuckled.

"Satra's kept *us* busy," I said, "but this isn't the time to discuss such matters. Go home to your son, and enjoy the morning."

"We will," Roi said. "Thank you, again."

Grima hugged me and said her thanks before they left.

I walked back to the bedroom and found Tindra had rolled back over. Sitting on the bed, I touched her forehead. She didn't feel abnormally warm.

"Wake up," I said softly, "We've been invited to breakfast."

"Hmm," she groaned and mumbled something.

"Tindra," I said, a little louder, "Roi and Grima have invited us to eat with them this morning."

Her eyes fluttered open, and she gave me the half-smile of a waking child. "Good morning."

"I'm going to Roi and Grima's for breakfast. Einns is cooking, so it'll probably have some Varia flavor."

"Sounds wonderful," she said, carrying out the words as she stretched. "Let me get dressed."

"At least I can enjoy a quiet morning. I have a feeling today will turn stressful soon. Need to meet with my generals after we eat."

"Considering how things usually go," she said, after putting on a shirt, "you're probably right. Want me to go with you?"

"Unless you have something better to do."

"I could go looking for thin, pale servants."

"I'm not worried about my benefactors right now."

"If you want me by your side, I'm delighted to be there."

"You could practice acting regal," I said, and laughed.

"Maybe I will," she said, pulling on her boots.

I led her past the stable then followed my nose to the front of a building exactly as Roi described it, complete with a crooked, hanging, wooden sign showing a hammer pounding nails into the sole of a boot. The windows were shuttered and closed by latches that looked rusted in place.

"Are you sure Roi lives *here*? *This* is where he brought Grima and Einns?" Tindra asked.

"Fits the description," I said, and knocked on the door. "Guess we'll find out."

Roi answered and the smell of hot sweet bread spilled out.

Compared to the outside, the home was surprisingly nice inside, well furnished with several comfortable-looking, cloth chairs and an ornate, long, stone table near the left-hand wall.

Einns manned a fireplace and stove taking up most of the far, right-hand corner of the room. He turned and smiled when he saw us.

I waved to him.

"Where's Grima?" Tindra asked.

"Upstairs," Roi said.

Grima walked from the back of the building, wearing a white, long-sleeve, woven cotton dress. Nothing fancy but it looked pretty on her.

"I'm not one to wear dresses," Tindra said, "but that's beautiful. Did you make it?"

The dress billowed as she spun around and then curtsied. "I did. Glad you like it."

"I have spiced apple juice ready," Einns said.

"Everyone take a seat," Roi said. "I'll get it."

As we got settled, Roi carried a pitcher and cups to the table.

The seasoned juice reminded me of my mother and how she prepared it for me as a young boy.

"Reminds me of home," Tindra said.

"Not quite as spicy as they make it in Varia," Einns said, as he placed a platter of bread on the table.

"Dig in," Roi said, grabbing a thick roll.

I chose one and took a bite. The sweet outer crust covered a peppery-flavored, chewy middle. "Interesting taste," I said.

Einns nodded and swallowed. "I made them to complement the juice."

"Good choice," Tindra commented.

Einns sniffed at the air. "I think the honey-glazed pork strips are ready. Be right back."

Tindra and I looked at each other and frowned.

"What's wrong?" Grima asked.

"We had a...bad experience with honey and pork recently," I said.

Tindra nodded, pressing her right arm against her stomach. "Not my best morning."

"You're safe—there's no mead involved," Roi said, shaking his head.

"Did you get some bad mead?" Grima asked.

I frowned. "Too much good mead."

"Oh."

Roi chuckled.

The smell of warm honey and cooked pork reached the table before Einns.

My mouth watered, and my stomach churned. "I'd better eat another piece of bread before I try some of your honeyed pork."

"Me too," Tindra added.

"No hurry," Einns said. "Honestly, it might taste better after it's had a chance to cool."

Roi and Grima didn't wait; each of them stuffed a strip of meat into each other's mouths and sucked the flavor off their fingers.

Einns groaned and looked away. "They do that every time I make this."

Tindra chuckled.

"One day you'll find someone you want to do that with," I said to him.

"Not soon, I hope," Grima said, with a grin.

Roi shrugged and reached for another piece of meat.

I summoned up the courage to try a piece myself. After biting through the thin coat of honey, I found he'd used salt pork, so it wasn't as sweet as I'd feared.

"Tasty. The salt makes a big difference."

Einns shrugged. "Thank you. It's what I had on hand."

Tindra's hand flashed across the table, grabbing a piece. She hummed after biting into it.

"Not just the salt," Tindra said. "You added something else."

"My secret," Einns said, smiling.

"He won't tell me either," Grima said.

"Some secrets are worth keeping," Roi said, after taking a drink.

"Good to know we agree on something," Tindra said.

"Roi said you two plan to wed," Grima said. "Any idea when?"

I shook my head. "We haven't officially announced our engagement, but word seems to have traveled on its own. I'm too busy to plan a wedding now. We'll set a date when the time's right."

Grima nodded as I spoke, then smiled. "Tindra, I'd be glad to help with planning. Even if you're not sure when, it's better to have things planned ahead of time. Plus, with Roi spending so much time with Fitzeirick, we should get to know each other better."

"I—"

Tindra bumped me with her arm. "I'll get back to you," she said. "Like Fitzeirick said, we're in no hurry, and I'm not ready to set aside any time to start planning today...but thank you for offering."

"Of course," Grima said. "I'm here when you're ready."

"Speaking of which," I said. "Roi mentioned you might be interested in opening the front of the shop as a tailor. I know of a weaver and seamstress you might want to meet."

She nodded to me. "We talked about it, but I...we haven't decided if it's for the best. I certainly won't do anything until Einns finds work. Much like you two, I'm in no hurry."

I smiled. "I understand. If you decide you want to open a shop, let me know."

"You'll be the third, maybe fourth, to know...I promise," she said.

We carried on talking like old friends until my stomach felt like I couldn't eat another bite.

"Hate to leave such good company, and great cooking, but I should check in with my generals while I can still move. I'm afraid if I eat much more, you'll have to roll me around in a cart."

Einns laughed.

"I think I've had my fill too," Tindra said.

Grima stood with us as we left the table. "Thank you both for coming this morning. It meant a lot to us."

Roi walked us to the door and hugged me. "Thank you, for everything. I hope your plans work. I'm here when you need me."

"I'll do my best to leave you alone on your wedding day," I said, grinning. "I can't promise to give you a whole month of peace though."

He laughed. "I've had more peace since you sent for me than I expected."

I nodded. "Still, enjoy the time with your new wife while you can. I expect us to be busy once the fighting starts."

"As long as you listen to me," he said.

"I will," I said, "as long as you're making sense."

He chuckled and shooed us out the door. "See to your kingdom."

Chapter 55

As we got close to the compound, Tindra said, "I have things to take care of at home. Do you really need me?"

"You tend to notice things I don't, but I won't force you to be there. What else needs your attention?"

"You have no servants. Someone has to get the baskets back to Grith, and there's plenty of cleaning to be done."

"You've never seemed concerned about your living conditions before."

"That doesn't mean I thrive in filth," she said. "If I'm to be queen, I should have a clean home."

"If it bothers you so much, see to it," I said. "I'll be glad to help when I get back."

"Perhaps it's time to hire a few hands."

"Not at the moment," I said. "And don't go looking for any pale, thin servants either. I told you not to worry about that group."

"The thought never crossed my mind," she said, and turned toward home.

Stopping, I watched her walk away until she'd passed through the gate into the compound. *Hope she doesn't cause trouble. I have more important things to worry about right now.*

A parade of warriors marching blocked the way to the barracks. Several of them noticed me and nodded as they passed.

I continued on to the barracks once the supply wagons passed and found Bior standing watch.

"Good to see you up and around. How's the leg?"

"Still healing, m'lord, but I'm whole enough to do my duty."

"Take the time you need to recover."

"Aye, Sire. I'll be fine."

I pursed my lips for a moment. "If you insist. Have the generals left?"

He nodded. "Sorry, Sire. You missed them; they led the line away."

"Guess I took too long at breakfast," I muttered. "I'd hoped to say something to convince the men they were doing the right thing, to encourage them."

"General Heming whipped them into a frenzy. I suspect the Satra won't go after Nikulas again once those warriors run them off."

I smiled. "A favor?"

He nodded. "Of course, Sire."

"I'm heading home. Get word to the gates. Jomar is to go to his barracks and wait for me. I want to know as soon as he arrives. When the Varians arrive, send them to their camp and send a runner to let me know they're here."

"Consider it done," he said, bowing.

On the way home, my thoughts wandered. The war was beginning. Refugees living near The Trader's Cup could go home, and feel safe, but they didn't know yet. Roi's animosity toward Tindra... *He still has my family sword.*

Shaking my head to chase the stress away, I waved to the guards while passing through the gate. *Are they even necessary now?* I turned and walked to Agrim's quarters.

He answered, shortly after I knocked, "Yes, Sire?"

"May I come in?"

"You're always welcome here, my lord," he said, stepping aside. "Take a seat at the table. I can get you something to drink."

I looked around as I entered. Agrim left the structure the same as Roald had it, but the furnishings were much more modest. A simple, wood table sat where Roald's ornate marble and slate table had been. Plain, unpadded, wooden chairs surrounded it.

"No, I'm fine. Are your wages not enough to afford nicer accommodations?" I asked, sitting.

"I'm well paid, Sire," he said, sitting across from me, "but I grew up with furniture much like this. It keeps me grounded."

"Nothing wrong with remembering where you're from," I said. "What does your wife think?"

"I'm not married, Sire, unless you count my dedication to my country."

"As long as you're happy."

He nodded.

"I want your honest opinion, so speak freely. Do you think it's necessary to keep men posted at the gate now?"

He frowned. "Have they inconvenienced you?"

"No, not at all. Your men have been most helpful and appreciated. It's just...I wonder if they may be more useful elsewhere considering I've eliminated those working against me."

Rubbing his chin, he looked at me before glancing over his shoulder and turning back. "Only those we know about, Sire."

"True," I said, nodding. "Perhaps I'm being optimistic."

"I'll talk to the men, find out what they think. No doubt they see and hear much more than the two of us. Regardless, I'll keep two men posted near your quarters for your safety."

I smiled. "If nothing else, they deter unnecessary interruptions."

"Agreed," he said. "Is that all?"

I shook my head. "Have you selected lieutenants?"

"Although life has been busy since you asked, I spent as much time as possible considering my options and settled on Svan and Sibbi."

"Good choices, given what I know of them."

"Thank you, Sire. I'll pass along the compliment."

"My final question—and you need not answer immediately. Would you consider another promotion?"

He raised his eyebrows. "Dare I ask what you have in mind?"

"I'm down two generals and about a hundred and fifty warriors before the war starts. I expect to lose men in the fights to come. I need leaders, and I'd like you as one of them."

His jaw moved, but no sound came out.

I raised my hand. "Take time to consider the offer. Work out what you want to do with the compound guards first."

He stood and bowed. "Of course, Sire. Regardless of my decision, thank you for the consideration."

Standing, I offered him my hand. "I wouldn't ask if I didn't think you deserved the title and were able to deal with the responsibility."

Shaking it, he nodded. "Thank you."

I clapped him on the shoulder and went home.

Walking in the door, I didn't see Tindra. I called for her and received no answer.

Deciding she'd gone out, either returning things or causing trouble, I went to the meeting room and grabbed the seax. It balanced well in my hand as I drew it from the scabbard. Trying to remember some of my early training with a wooden sword, I made a few weak thrusts and followed up with awkward swipes. *I prefer my hammer.* Even then, I *could* use the seax with one hand while my hammer required two strong arms...something I wouldn't have until my left shoulder healed fully.

The door opened and someone walked in, whistling. Knife in hand, I stepped out of the room.

Tindra stopped, lips puckered, and cocked her head when she saw the blade.

"Oh, it's you," I said. "Hello."

She grinned. "It *is* me. Hello yourself."

"Where were you?"

Her grin turned into a toothy smile. "It's a surprise. Why are you wielding the seax?"

I shrugged. "Seeing what it felt like."

"And?"

"I like my hammer better."

"I can teach you how to use that blade effectively."

"I'm sure you could," I said, raising my eyebrows. "What's the surprise?"

She chuckled. "Don't change the subject and think I'm going to tell you."

"Why were you whistling?"

She tilted her head again. "I'm happy."

"Does your happiness have anything to do with the surprise?"

Shaking her head, she walked to me, pushed the blade to the side, and caressed my cheek. "Are you a child?"

"No," I blurted out. "Just curious since, as best I recall, I've never seen you happy."

She pulled her hand away and stood, looking at me. "Well...now you've had a glimpse. What's the rest of the day hold?"

I shrugged. "Meetings, once General Jomar and the Varia soldiers arrive."

Someone knocked on the door.

"Let them in and tell them I'll be a moment," I said.

Tindra whistled her tune again as she turned for the door.

I slid the knife back into its scabbard and hurried to find out who was here.

Sibbi stood just inside the door, talking quietly with Tindra.

I called to him and said, "Congratulations."

His brow furrowed. "For what, Sire?"

"Oh," I said. "You should talk to Captain Agrim as soon as you can."

"I will, m'lord, but I understood you wanted to know when General Jomar arrived."

"Is he at his barracks?"

"He said he'd wait for you there after taking care of his horse."

I nodded. "Then I'll give him a few minutes. You should find Svan. The two of you need to see your captain."

He bowed. "Now that I've done my duty, I'll do exactly that."

Tindra closed the door behind him. "He seems to be a good sort."

I nodded. "All of Agrim's men are. They were loyal to me from the start. Some of them helped save your life."

She frowned and looked at her right arm. "Thanks for reminding me."

Walking to her side, I pulled her into a tight hug. "I didn't mean to make you unhappy."

I felt her shaking as I held her. *Definitely didn't mean to make her cry.*

The laughter grew louder as she pushed away from me. Once she caught her breath, she said, "Sometimes you are simply too easy to fool."

I frowned at her. "That wasn't very nice."

"No," she said, still chuckling, "but it was funny. Go meet with your general. I'll have something ready for lunch when you get home."

"Make it a late lunch," I said, patting my stomach. "I still feel full from breakfast."

She nodded. "Einns cooks well for a boy his age."

I kissed her forehead and left for the barracks.

Chapter 56

Jomar paced as I walked in.

"Good to see you back safe," I said, offering my hand.

He nodded and shook it. "Thank you, Sire."

"I trust things are better in the southeast?"

"Much, though it wasn't until I spoke with the few citizens left there that I understood how bad it was before the Varians arrived. Then I had to convince our people we weren't supporting a Varian invasion. I left Commander Hallis in charge. He's from the area. They'll listen to him."

"Good thinking."

"Considering the circumstances, the Varians fought in self-defense."

I nodded. "I take it the soldiers made a good impression on you."

"They came out on top in an ambush, says something. Several of the witnesses said the Varians did their best to keep the innocent out of harm's way. Impressive discipline, m'lord."

"Would you trust them to have your flank or back?"

"Any time," he said, nodding.

"Good to hear because they're going to cover the back of most of our army soon."

"Sending my men back out, Sire?"

"No. You're here to help keep the capital secure. I want additional men at each gate. Rotate shifts to keep them rested," I said.

"Understood, but if you're not sending us, who will the Varians back?"

"Gudmann and Heming left this morning to drive another Satran attack away from Nikulas. As soon as the Varians arrive, I'll ask them to leave on minimal rest. They'll trail behind our thrust and, hopefully, catch the Satrans by surprise."

A smile spread across Jomar's face. "I like the way you think. I suspect they are up to the task."

"Good. Decide which of your men goes on watch first and get some rest. If this operation goes well, they'll be the first to scout into the central forest."

"Understood, Sire. It will be our honor."

"You have no idea how much it pleases me to hear you say that," I said, smiling.

Someone ran into the room.

I turned to see Ingo, red-faced, skid to a stop before running into me. "Sorry for interrupting, Sire," he said. "The Varians are here."

I nodded. "Thank you for your prompt report. Go tell Captain Agrim that General Jomar's men will bolster the guards at the gates."

He bowed. "With all haste."

Before he could turn, I added, "Try to avoid running your captain over when you deliver my message."

Jomar snickered behind me while Ingo nodded several times and left.

Men were still unloading carts when I arrived at the Varian camp.

"Where are your sergeants?" I asked a nearby soldier, after he'd dropped an armload of supplies.

"Check the center of camp, your majesty."

"Thank you," I said, with a quick nod, before jogging away. Dodging working soldiers, I found a square stone building and knocked on the door.

Espen opened it. "Yes...oh, King Fitzeirick. Please, come in."

I followed him to a large, ornate, wooden table with a map of Croy carved into the top. Pointing to it, I raised an eyebrow. "Something I should know about?"

"Lieutenant's idea," Aksel said. "Makes it easier to plan our moves."

Interesting idea. "I appreciate you returning so quickly. How are your men?"

"None seriously wounded," Espen said.

"Good to hear," I said. "I'm sorry things went the way they did."

"We weren't going in blind," Aksel said. "The whole situation didn't feel right when we got there. Your warriors were the only people outside; no one was working."

I nodded. "Good thing you noticed. Now, how much rest do your men need before they're ready to fight again?"

"We'd hoped for a few days," Espen said, looking at Aksel. "Why?"

"The Satran ambushed Sergeant Elias and his men before they reached Nikulas. Sorry to say your fellow soldiers died to superior numbers. We believe the Satran are attacking Nikulas' holdings again. I've sent as many warriors as I dare. I need you to protect my men from a rear assault and, hopefully, cut down any Satran soldiers heading this way or fleeing from the fight."

Aksel frowned, and his shoulders slumped.

Espen patted him on the back. "We'll leave by nightfall. Our wounded will stay behind. The rest will be glad to take the fight to those who spilled Varian blood. It's our turn to pay them back."

"Thank you again. I wish I didn't have to ask this of you and your soldiers," I said. "There's one thing you need to know. There may be a Croian, a man named Porsey, among the Satran."

"Say no more, your highness. We have men who specialize in rescues," Aksel said.

I shook my head. "I don't want him rescued."

Espen squinted.

"He isn't a hostage; he's a traitor."

"Understood," Espen said. "Anything else we need to tell our men?"

"Let them know I appreciate what they've done, and I'm sorry they can't have the rest they deserve."

"We'll do our lieutenant proud," Aksel said.

I nodded. "Of course. Travel swift and safe."

"Thank you," Espen said, as I turned to leave.

• • • • ● • ● • • •

Exiting the camp, I headed to Abi's to let Aerison know what I'd asked of his men.

The Varian guarding the door greeted me.

"Your fellow soldiers are back," I said, as he opened the door.

"I know," he replied, "but this is my assigned post."

I nodded. "You're doing a fine job."

He bowed. "Thank you."

"One thing before I go in," I said. "Where do you sleep?"

"Abi lets me sleep in the entry so I can continue guarding the door."

"Admirable dedication," I said. "I'll make sure Lieutenant Aerison knows."

"He does. I take him breakfast every morning."

I smiled. "Admirable indeed. I hope your day is uneventful."

"They have been, for the most part. Thank you."

I nodded to him and went inside.

Abi stepped out from her kitchen, carrying a tray with plates of food and a jug.

"Need a hand?" I asked.

She jumped, nearly dropping the tray. "Oh, my king. You startled me. Yes, some help would be appreciated. Who are you here to see?"

"Aerison."

"Take his salad to him, please?"

"Be glad to," I said, took a plate, and walked to his room.

He sat on the bed, legs dangling over the side.

"You look better than the last time I saw you," I said.

He looked at me and nodded. "Trying to stretch my legs a little, keep the muscles from locking up while I heal. That my lunch?"

I offered him the plate. "Salad, compliments of Abi."

He took it from me, grunted, and said, "I think she serves nothing but vegetables to motivate people to leave."

I chuckled. "Tindra all but frothed at the mouth for some meat after about six weeks of Abi's meals."

He stuffed a leaf of some kind into his mouth, chewed, and swallowed. "Don't get me wrong, she's one of the most caring people I've ever met...seems to be an excellent herbalist. Fruits and vegetables, as a change, isn't bad. I do miss meat, but I'm not craving it."

"From what I understand, she thinks it makes you healthier and helps the healing process," I said. "But I'm not here to discuss her cooking. Elias and his men stumbled into a Satran force advancing north. I hate to bring bad news, but they are all dead."

Setting the bowl in his lap, his shoulders slumped as he closed his eyes. "Hope they died fighting."

"From what I know, they did. Your sergeants agreed to have your soldiers on the move by nightfall to go back up my warriors."

"I expect they want Satran blood for killing Varians. Besides, a trained and disciplined soldier never questions reasonable orders from his commander...he does what's asked."

"Is it reasonable to send them without even one night's rest?"

"Did you ask for the impossible?" he asked, looking at me.

"No."

"Ask for more than you needed?"

I shook my head. "Of course not."

"Send them on a doomed mission?"

"Don't believe so," I said, chuckling. "I'm confident we can stop the attack or, worst case, retake Nikulas' holdings."

He shrugged. "Then Aksel and Espen had no reason to refuse your request."

"I appreciate their dedication and cooperation. You should be proud of them and all the men under your command."

He shook his head. "It's not a question of pride. It is duty, nothing more and nothing less. We don't act out of the need for praise. We do what is asked because it's necessary. If not for well-prepared armies, civilization could not exist."

I pressed my lips together for a moment, considering what he said. "That being the case...I still want to express my appreciation."

He nodded, chewed on another mouthful of salad, and lifted his legs.

"Planning to go somewhere?"

He smirked and swallowed. "No. Abi insists I move them, get exercise, when I can. The goal *is* to walk out of here...the sooner, the better."

"Given your conditioning, discipline, and determination, I have no doubt you will," I said, smiling. "Tindra is expecting to eat lunch with me sometime today. It's probably best I go."

"Tell her I said hello."

"Will do."

Chapter 57

There were still six men guarding the gate to the compound. I nodded as I passed. Reaching for the door to my quarters, Tindra called my name from behind.

I turned to see her entering the courtyard, carrying a basket.

"Lunch?" I asked, after hurrying toward her.

"Yes," she said, "though I'm surprised you made it here before me."

"Why?"

"From what I understand, you've been all over the capital this morning. The general's barracks, the Varian camp, and Abi's."

Looking sideways at her as I opened the door, I asked, "Have you been following me?"

"No," she said. "Why would I?"

"If you haven't, how do you know where I've been?"

She shrugged. "Old habits die hard."

"What, exactly, do you mean?"

"I have friends," she said. "Friends who watch out for my interests."

"Friends...or spies?"

"Friends. Don't you think I'd warn you if there were spies around? I haven't hidden anything from you since before we left Varia—"

"Except why you decided to attach yourself to Sergeant Elias," I said, interrupting her.

"I shouldn't have to explain self-preservation to you. Doesn't matter. The only thing I've kept from you since is the surprise I'm working on."

"Don't think you're going to distract me by mentioning your mysterious surprise. Who's watching me?"

"I told you, people I've made friends with. People smart enough to work for the future queen. And they aren't watching you, as such. Simply paying attention when they see you and—"

"Watching me."

She put the basket on the table. "This isn't worth arguing about. I'll explain while we eat."

I looked at her for a moment before sitting.

She sat across from me. "I worry. You've made some influential people uncomfortable, angry."

"Hallfrid and those working with him are gone."

"Poisonous weeds have deep roots. Cutting the stem doesn't always keep them from growing back."

"You're talking like a woodsyth."

"Blame all the time I spent at Abi's," she replied, smiling. "You knew Hallfrid presented a threat. What about hidden threats yet to reveal themselves?"

"I can take care of myself."

"Show me," she said. "Get your hammer and meet me in the courtyard."

I shook my head. "My shoulder isn't ready yet."

"Meaning you can't take care of yourself. Not right now. So, I've done what I can to keep you safe. Knowing where you are, or have been, is an additional benefit."

"I see," I said, taking her hand. "But if you aren't keeping secrets, why haven't you told me who these friends are? Who do you trust with my safety?"

"The same men you trust with your safety."

"What do you mean?"

"Your guard."

I blinked several times. "I still don't understand."

"I've taught a few of your guard some basics. Mostly how to follow someone without being noticed and pass along information by hiding it in plain sight."

"Does Agrim know you've co-opted some of his men?"

"Not if they use the lessons I've given them," she replied, chuckling. "Now, would you like to eat?"

I nodded. "This doesn't smell like it came from Grith's."

She smiled as her hand snaked into the basket. "Doubt he knows how to make spiced hen."

"Where did you get this?" I asked, after swallowing a bite of the tender meat.

"A small butcher I found while exploring the city. It's run by a man named Goran and his daughter Britt."

"Those sound like Varian names."

She nodded. "Moved here from Nikulas' holdings when Britt was a baby."

"And Britt's mother?"

"Died not long after giving birth."

"Oh."

"They seem to be doing fine. I enjoyed seeing some new Varian faces."

"Once the war is over, you can go back if you want," I said. "If you miss Varia, I mean."

"I wouldn't go so far to say I *miss* Varia. Some of the people, yes, but I'm satisfied...happy here. I do wonder how my parents will make the trip to attend our wedding."

"When the time comes, I'll send a wagon for them."

"Thank you."

Swallowing, I snapped my fingers. "That reminds me. You should write another letter, letting them know the people I sent aren't coming."

"I will, but it won't reach them anytime soon."

"Get it to a messenger once the way is safe."

"Or," she said, "send it with Kurt when he's well enough to travel."

"That is an option, assuming he decides to go back instead of staying behind to exact some personal revenge on Satra."

She shook her head. "He doesn't like getting his hands dirty anymore. I think he lost his taste for it once he figured out how to make more money having others do the messy jobs."

I squinted. "How does one make money paying others to work?"

"Remember, he doesn't have friends; he has resources. His coin comes from providing his resources to those willing, and able, to pay."

"Why wouldn't his resources deal directly with someone needing their services?"

"Some do," she said. "But working for Kurt has benefits—like staying alive for not crossing him. A resource that isn't working for him is considered to be working against him and gets disposed of."

"Because the war council takes care of its own problems."

"Exactly."

"So, if I decide to not let Sabast operate in Croy...I'm a problem."

"The war council is not above planning the death of a king, if one decides to believe rumors," she said, shrugging.

I ran my fingers through my hair. "Has anyone ever told you that you don't make life easy?"

"If they did, I didn't pay attention to them. What are you going to do about Kurt and Sabast? You don't want them in Croy, do you?"

"I didn't, until I found out about a group of Croians working in the shadows. Maybe having the two compete with each other will minimize the impact either has."

She nodded then tilted her head. "Or it could turn into a bloodbath. The war council doesn't allow direct competition, and all this time, Ander used them to his, and Varia's, benefit."

"While they schemed to overthrow him."

"Looking back, I think he knew and had a plan to deal with the problem if...when it presented itself."

"Maybe you *should* teach me how to use that knife," I said.

She smiled. "Gladly. If you're finished eating, we can start now."

"You've fed me well. Let's start."

"I'll meet you outside," she said, before leaving the table.

Chapter 58

Tindra walked out, carrying her sword in its scabbard, shortly after I did. "Lesson one: the difference between a sword and a seax. While I can stab with my sword, it's meant for slashing. The seax will do both equally well, plus you can chop nearly as well as with a small axe. There's a downside to its versatility, length. You have to work in close to strike effectively. Leave it covered and come at me."

I charged her, intent on stabbing her in the ribs.

She twirled her sword, knocking my blade to the side, and tapped me on the neck with hers. "Work your way in. Try again."

I shifted my weight forward, balancing on the balls of my feet, and shuffled toward her.

Tindra's eyes flicked from my seax to my face and back as she backed away from me, sword at the ready.

Lunging toward her, I thrust the blade then whipped it side to side.

She spun away and slapped my back with her scabbard. "That's not it either. You started well then turned into a charging bull. At least try to distract me. Dance your way closer to set up your strike."

Turning to face her, I noticed we'd attracted the attention of my guards. "I don't dance," I said. "I'm not built for dancing."

"You *can* dance," she replied. "I've made you dance before...and I'll do it again if you insist."

"You fought dirty. Don't deny it."

"Fighting fair's a good way to die," she said. "Trade with me. Use my sword like you would your hammer's handle."

Her sword felt like a feather compared to my heavy hammer, but I knew how to block and fight with it.

"When you're ready," I said.

She took on the predatory posture I'd seen many times as we trained. I also knew she could disguise her intentions well while stalking her target.

Holding the sword at the ready, I tried to predict where she'd attack and plan my defense.

Staying low, she held the seax close to her body, almost resting across her right hip, and moved so quickly, I couldn't react to her first attack. The knife sliced across my right leg, near the top of my knee. I took a swing at her. She ducked and rolled behind me.

Before I could turn, I felt the covered blade press into the small of my back. "Finished," she said.

I lowered the sword and shrugged. "I can't move like you. You have a firesyth's grace. I'm a stone block."

"Blades are weapons of finesse; treat them like an extension of your arm. Perhaps you can see what I mean with a demonstration," she said, and turned to look at the men watching. She pointed at one. "You. Come at me."

He shook his head. "Lady, it wouldn't be right."

"Your name?" I asked.

"Haf, Sire."

"Haf, I'll make you an offer. Two gold doubles if you can best her."

His eyes opened wide. "Truly a generous offer, Sire, but I'd rather not fight your promised."

"It's not a fight," I said. "It's training. A demonstration for my benefit if you will. Nothing more. No one's going to get hurt."

"With all respect, my king, I saw what happened when she faced Svan."

"I made a mistake and paid for it," Tindra said. "Won't happen again."

He pressed his lips together and unclipped his scabbard. Bringing his weapon to ready, he nodded to her.

She crouched, again taking the position she used against me.

His eyes darted back and forth, up and down.

He won't find an opening.

She circled, studying him.

Her feet shifted slightly, and she faked a thrust.

He twitched but didn't commit to her feign.

Smart.

With another fake attack, she reversed her direction and stepped closer.

Haf twisted to follow her, stumbling as his feet tangled when they crossed.

But clumsy.

She rolled, closing the distance between them as he tried to regain his balance, and stood, bringing the end of the covered seax to his throat.

"You move well," he said, with a slight bow.

"You don't," Tindra said. "Why didn't you step back when I moved toward you?"

"I didn't think you would reverse and close."

"Stay light on your feet and expect anything."

"With respect, my lady, I'm used to facing armored opponents. You move with ease compared to most fighting men."

"In other words, you've never faced a hidden threat?"

"I...I guess not, no."

"Do you know what I did before I helped King Fitzeirick overthrow your jarl?" she asked.

Haf glanced at the guards behind him. "Only from rumors."

Tindra laughed. "Oh, how I love rumors. The more outlandish, the better. Tell me what you've heard."

"I...I'm not comfortable saying such...things to a woman," he stammered.

"Let me guess," she said, turning to flash me a smile before continuing. "I'm King Ander's favored whore, sent away to keep his wife from finding out the truth."

His face went pale. Several others murmured and looked away.

"No? How about I'm a scout for the coming Varian invasion?"

Haf shook his head.

"Everyone here is so afraid of Varia, it blinds them to the real threat." Tindra swept the seax toward all the guards. "How many of you have heard I'm a Varian spy? That I work for King Ander, here to manipulate your new leader into doing his bidding?"

Three men nodded before Haf said, "That's the word around the capital."

"Rumors about me are so very entertaining. I haven't started one in a long time, so I wonder who's been telling tales."

"It's... That's just what we've heard, my lady," Haf said.

"Oh, I have no doubt you didn't start it because at least half of it is rooted in fact. Whoever's spreading those words knows me, or thinks they do. Yes, I *served* as a spion for Ander. Did business as a mercenary as well, but I gave it up and swore my life to your king. I do no one's bidding but his. Do you believe me?"

The men nodded.

"Good. In the future, please tell me if you hear any rumors concerning me."

They nodded again.

"Now, do any of you know what a spion does?"

"I believe we all do," Haf said. "They watch people the king suspects, gathering evidence to use against them."

"Another half-truth," she said. "I have done exactly that, though it bores me. I had much more fun extracting truth from prisoners and disposing of threats to my king. Do I look like an assassin to any of you?"

"No, my lady," one of the men behind Haf said.

"And that makes you a dead man, along with the king you're meant to guard. Every king has enemies, known and unknown. King Fitzeirick has done a decent job removing the known...so who is going to protect him from the unknown?"

"We will, Lady Tindra," Haf said.

"Yet, *you* don't think I'm an assassin. Which is exactly what an assassin wants—for you to overlook them." She turned to me. "I'll speak with Agrim about this. Your guards need more training. They need to be prepared to face unexpected threats." Tossing the seax to me, she headed toward Agrim's door. "If necessary, I'll offer to teach them all myself."

I nodded. "Men, thank you for your service. Please return to your posts."

They bowed and quietly went back to their duty.

I shook my head and went back to my quarters, hoping her enthusiasm for my protection didn't cause more trouble than it was worth. While putting our blades away, though, I decided she made a good point. If there *were* any assassins preparing to do me harm, my guards weren't ready for the worst. *I'll talk to Agrim when I get a chance.*

Chapter 59

My thoughts drifted to Crum. *He'll soon be King of Varia with the support of their former king and people working to keep the country stable. Yet I'll miss his wedding because I'm struggling to keep order in my home country. Amazing how much life changes in a year.*

The door opened, and Tindra walked in. "Agrim's agreed to talk to his company and is considering letting me train them on what to watch for."

"Good," I said. "That sounds good."

"Sounds like you have something on your mind. Want to talk about it?" she asked, taking a seat across from me.

"Nothing serious. Thinking about Crum and how much has changed for all of us this past year."

She sighed. "A lot has changed and a lot more will change, I'm afraid."

"What makes you say that?"

"At some point, you're going to feel the need to join the battle. I won't be any good to you on the battlefield, not with only one hand, so no one will have your back. If things go wrong out there, who runs Croy? Certainly not me."

"If you're queen, no one would expect you to step down."

She chuckled and shook her head. "If I were *Croian* and queen. Not one of your citizens will allow a Varian woman to rule. If you think otherwise, you're lying to yourself."

"I think it best to not get ahead of ourselves," I said, patting her hand. "How about we go clean up and take a walk before finding dinner somewhere?"

"Sounds like a great idea. I'll get fresh clothes. Maybe we can drop by to see Fastan before we eat."

I looked at her. "Didn't she finish your shirts?"

Tindra nodded. "I have her working on something else now."

"Oh. What?"

She smiled. "It's a surprise."

I sighed. "Another surprise?"

She shrugged, and said, "Or the same surprise...you never know," before chuckling as she left the table.

"Don't forget your fork," I called to her. "No telling what Grith's serving."

She hurried back, carrying our clothes. "Let's go."

I took my part of the load, and we made our way to the bathhouse, put our clothes in crates, and waded into the lukewarm water.

"This water's never hot enough. When you build a castle, the private bathing room will be built to my standards." Tindra said.

"Of course. Any other requests?"

"Nothing comes to mind at the moment," she said, handing me a bar of soap. "Wash my hair?"

"Gladly," I said, making a generous amount of lather in my hands and then working it into her hair.

She all but purred as I worked. "That feels wonderful. Let it sit and do my back."

"What if I make you giggle again?" I asked. "I'd *hate* to ruin your reputation."

"Maybe I've decided being known as the giggling queen of Croy isn't so bad."

"Are you sure you're the real Tindra?" I asked, while lathering my hands again. "Whistling, speaking with the captain of my guard about my safety, and now you don't mind giggling. I'm starting to suspect you're an impostor."

"Have you considered I'm changing, adapting to my new life?"

A shiver ran down her back as I rubbed my soapy hands on her skin. "Are you sure you're not simply playing a part?"

She turned around, grabbed my beard, and gently pulled my face to hers. "I am *not* playing a part. I *am* happy and starting to see the joy in settling down."

"I believe you," I said. "Don't be angry with me because I'm not comfortable with an unexpected change in you."

She sank under the water to rinse and surfaced behind me. "Hand me the soap."

As her slick hand rubbed my back, she said, "I've told you before not to try and figure me out. Whatever you decide will almost always be wrong. Expect the unexpected from me, and I'll keep your life interesting."

"My life has been more interesting than I expected lately; it doesn't need your help," I said, and laughed.

Scrubbing her fingers through my hair, she said, "This situation won't last forever. You'll win the war and eliminate Satra. What's next?"

"I'm not thinking about what's next," I said. "I need to focus on now."

"I'm not saying you should ignore what's coming, but don't concentrate on now so much that you lose sight of where to go after. You're a king now. Kings must have a vision for the future of their people, their country. Short-sighted rulers don't last long."

I chuckled. "I hope Crum doesn't learn that lesson the hard way."

"With Jesca at his side and Ander as his mentor, he'll do fine."

I ducked under to rinse and turned to face her when I surfaced. "As long as he keeps Kurt happy."

"Ander can keep the war council under control."

"He won't live forever."

"Neither will Kurt, and by the time both pass, everyone will be used to Jesca and Crum ruling. I believe the Varian people will be happy knowing they no longer have to worry about animosity from Croy. Both countries should prosper from a healthy, friendly relationship."

"True enough," I said. "At least after Satra is gone."

She nodded. "I think I'm as clean as I'm going to get. Ready to go?"

"Sure."

We dried, dressed, and left for Fastan's shop.

The weaver looked the same as usual, hard at work with sweat plastering her hair to her forehead.

"Well met, Fastan," Tindra said, to get her attention.

"One moment," she said, without looking up. "I have to finish this."

"Don't rush on our account," I said.

"But these are for you, Sire," she replied.

I furrowed my brow. "What's for me? I don't remember ordering anything from you."

"Surprise," Tindra said.

"What is she working on?"

"I decided you needed a few new shirts," Tindra said.

Before I could say anything, Fastan said, "Here, try this on." She held a long-sleeved, brown and gray shirt. "If this one fits, so will the other three."

I walked to her and took the shirt to look it over. The colors looked like shadows across dead leaves. "Cotton?" I asked.

"Yes, Sire. I dyed and wove it myself."

I pulled my shirt off and slipped the new one over my head. It fit a bit looser than I preferred but not as loose as most Varian clothes. "How did you know my size?"

Tindra chuckled. "I brought one of your old shirts for her to use as a pattern."

"I didn't know how well the shirt fit," Fastan said, "so I made these a bit bigger."

I nodded. "They'll be fine. Are all four this color?"

"No, Sire," she answered. "I made two brown and a black. Tindra asked me to make that one to match the armor Thorgault's making for you. I'm not sure it will match exactly though."

"It will do fine," I said, smiling. "How much do I owe you?"

"Nothing," Tindra said. "I paid her upfront."

I nodded. "Fastan, do you have a sack we could use to carry the shirts and our dirty clothes?"

"I'll find one."

While the weaver searched for a suitable sack, I leaned close to Tindra and whispered, "I appreciate you doing this, but why not just tell me? Why keep it a secret."

"Because I wanted to have some fun and surprise you," she said. "I thought everyone liked a nice surprise from time to time."

"I guess I've had too much to think about. Thank you."

She tugged my beard, pulling me into a kiss.

Fastan cleared her throat. "Sire, sorry for intruding, but I found a sack you can use."

I felt my cheeks warm as I stepped back from Tindra. "Thank—Thank you," I stammered, reaching for the coarsely woven sack.

As I stuffed the clothes inside, Tindra said, "I'm going to check on my armor."

I glanced back at Fastan. "Sorry about the..."

She smiled. "No worries; it was only a kiss. If I were you, I'd keep an eye on her before she orders something else from Thorgault."

I nodded, said, "Good idea," and tossed the sack of clothes over my shoulder before running to catch Tindra. By the time I'd crossed the market, she had black, leather leggings on before slithering into a matching top.

Her head popped out of the top carrying one of the biggest smiles I'd ever seen. Marching in place, she lifted her knees high while flexing her arms. "Needs a little breaking in, but I can move well. It's worth every copper."

Thorgault saw me and waved. "Ever seen 'er lookin' so happy?"

"Not in a long time," I replied, before admiring my promised. "I take it you're going to wear it the rest of the evening?"

"If I don't wear it, it won't get broken in."

"Sire, I'm startin' on yur suit soon as I get tha metal," Thorgault said.

"I'm in no hurry," I said. "Not sure I can wear armor until my shoulder finishes healing anyway."

He nodded. "Understood, but I wanna have it ready fur ya."

"I appreciate your dedication," I said, and turned back to Tindra. "Are we going to eat now or take a walk first?"

"We're here; let's eat."

I nodded and reached for her hand.

"Have a good evenin', Sire," Thorgault said, as we turned to leave.

"Good evening to you, too," I replied.

Chapter 60

We walked across the market square hand in hand. *I guess people are getting used to seeing us together. Almost no one pays us any attention anymore.*

Grith greeted us when we entered and complimented Tindra on her armor. "I'd watched Thorgault working on those pieces tirelessly. Wondered who they were for—didn't realize you were a fighter."

"She'll surprise you if you aren't careful," I said.

"You're only saying that because you've never bested me," she said, and chuckled.

"What's good this evening?" I asked, shaking my head.

"For my king and the queen-to-be, I have some tender roast goat, piled on salted flatbread, and fresh ale to drink."

"You made it just for us?" I asked, smiling.

"Well...no, but it seemed like a nice thing to say," he replied.

I nodded. "It was."

Tindra smirked and sat down. "We'll each take a plate and a mug."

"Yes, we will," I agreed, sitting next to her. "Looks like you can eat with a regular fork this evening," I said quietly.

"Or I can practice with my special fork."

Grinning, I said, "You could but, considering the mess you made last time, you might want to practice in private until you get better at using it."

She looked at me for a moment before nodding. "Good point."

Grith set plates, piled high with shredded pork, in front of us. "I'll bring your ale right away."

The lukewarm meat had good flavor but no real seasoning. *I miss Varian cooking.*

Tindra put some meat on a piece of flatbread and took a bite. "Oh, that's pretty good."

"And the ale complements the flavors well," I said. "But I'd still like some spice in the meat."

"Be careful," Tindra teased, grinning. "Your Varian heritage is showing."

"I'm not ashamed of who I am or where I come from. Besides, I think the brand on my face makes people more uncomfortable than the split in my family tree."

"You not being ashamed isn't the same as no one else caring."

I shrugged. "I'm king. What someone else cares about doesn't change that fact."

"No, but it could impact how cooperative they are when you deal with them."

"I suppose you have a point," I said, before taking another bite.

"When do the Varian soldiers leave?" she asked.

"Hopefully before sunset," I said. "Why?"

"If we eat quickly, we could walk to the south gate and see them off."

"Didn't know you'd like to watch them leave."

"It's not that I want to watch them leave," she said. "It's the impression you'll make being there. Think of it as a show of support."

"I hadn't considered how they'd take my presence at the gate. You're right; it's a good idea for me to be there. I didn't want to rush dinner, but maybe we should in this case."

Tindra answered by shoving meat and bread into her mouth, smiling as she chewed.

I followed her example, though with a little less food in each bite, and we quickly cleared our plates before finishing the mugs of ale.

"A good meal, as always Grith," I said, tossing him a gold double.

"And you're paying more than you should, as usual," he said, after catching the coin.

"Use the extra to feed someone less fortunate," I replied, as we left.

I chose a path to the gate which took us by my home to drop off the sack of clothes and Tindra's fork. Although we didn't arrive at the southern gate to see the beginning of the formation, we watched about three hundred men and their supply wagons leave. I made sure to smile and wish them swift and safe travels and returned every bow or salute I received.

Once the procession passed through the gate, Svan jogged over to us. "M'lord, I wasn't told you would be here."

"Last minute decision," I said.

He looked Tindra up and down. "You ready to join the fight?"

"No," she said. "New armor, trying to break it in."

He nodded. "Looks good on you."

She smiled. "I make everything I wear look good."

He pursed his lips for a moment before a quiet laugh escaped. "That you do, my lady."

I cleared my throat and frowned. "I don't believe it's good form for a lieutenant of the guard to flirt with the king's promised."

"Oh," he said. "I'm not...not flirting, Sire. Sorry if that's how it sounded, Lady Tindra. I spoke the truth as I see it. Nothing more, I...I promise."

I couldn't stop the frown from turning into a smile. "And she appreciates the compliment."

"Yes, I do," Tindra said, "but I believe it's time to head home. Are you ready, Fitzeirick?"

"Seems I've done my kingly duty this evening. Yes, we can go home."

Her quick pace made it hard to keep up with her.

"In a hurry?" I asked.

"Trying to stretch the leggings."

"By jogging?"

"Taking long strides."

"Guess I have a lot to learn about wearing new armor."

"Don't you remember how stiff the leather over laminar armor was? You know, the reason Sabast was able to cut my hand off," she said.

"I thought the linked metal plates made it so stiff."

"Partly, but most of it came from us not breaking it in," she said. "You'll see. Once this leather stretches, I'll almost be able to dance in this."

"I don't—"

She sighed. "I know...I've heard it before. You don't dance."

"Not what I was going to say. I don't need armor I can dance in."

"Because you don't dance."

"Yes, because I don't dance."

She laughed. "I need you to help me take this off."

"Be glad to," I said, smiling.

Once we made it to the bedroom, Tindra lifted her arms over her head and bent over. "Pull."

I grabbed the leather sleeves and tugged. The armor and her shirt came off together. "Guess I pulled too hard," I said.

She stood and raised her eyebrows. "I planned it that way. Undress and lay down while I get out of these leggings. I'm sure my pants will go with them."

"Why am I lying down?" I asked.

"Wearing that armor has put me in a mood. Do what I asked. I'm sure you'll enjoy it."

Smiling, I shrugged and followed her instructions.

As soon as she finished undressing, Tindra straddled my legs and caressed my thighs. "Good to get the blood flowing."

"Don't think I need much help with that," I quipped.

Sparks streaked across her eyes. Leaning forward, she kissed my chest before sliding forward, stopping with her legs across my hips. After rubbing back and forth a few times, she leaned forward and kissed me, hard, before lifting herself and then sinking down on top of me, joining us together. I locked eyes with her when she started moving again.

She said, "Put your hands on my breasts to help hold me up."

Happy to oblige, I squeezed them lightly.

Her sigh turned into a moan, and she sped up her pace.

Although not as awkward as our first time, it still ended too soon.

Tindra sythed all the candles out and lay against my chest, pressing her ear to my heart. "Getting better," she said.

"We'll practice more after the wedding."

"I hope to have it right by then."

"No need to rush," I said. "We should have plenty of time once things get better."

"I'll ponder the future in my dreams."

I kissed the top of her head and held her until her breathing slowed and grew shallow.

Thoughts about Satra's advance on Nikulas' hall kept me from falling asleep quickly. *Will my warriors arrive in time to save our people, or will they have to retake the city? Should I have sent the Varians on a counterattack to the central forest instead?* I did my best to push the questions out of my mind to get some sleep. *Whatever challenges await tomorrow are likely best faced after a good night's rest.*

Chapter 61

Unlike most mornings, I wasn't awoken by a knock on my door or hearing someone in my home. Instead, Tindra's stomach growled loud enough to rouse me...though she seemed to sleep through the noise. I gently rolled her off me, then made sure she was still breathing because that didn't wake her either.

After dressing quietly, I walked to the meeting room to contemplate what to do until I received a report from the second battle for Nikulas' holdings. Regardless of the outcome, I needed more men ready to fight, so recruiting would become a concern soon. I also needed someone to train those recruits. Agrim seemed reluctant to serve in that role. I'd need another general, maybe two, as well.

Tindra, she's changing, seemingly, for the better. Roi still has his doubts, but I see how she's different. And I need to get my sword from him. Another problem demanding my attention.

Sighing, I laid my forehead on the stone table. Finding comfort in the smooth, cool surface, I leaned farther forward and stretched my arms out to the side. Turning so my cheek rested on the table along with my arms and upper chest, I closed my eyes. My focus turned to the energy flowing through the stone. Pressing my will into it, I relaxed and pushed my stress through the floor into the ground. *I should do this more often.*

The tight binding of my talent to the stone beneath me made it easy to notice when Tindra's feet pressed against the floor. When she passed the door to the meeting room, I sythed a little piece of the floor to brush her foot as it raised to take another step.

She squealed.

I couldn't hold back my laugh.

The door creaked softly as she pushed it open. "That wasn't funny."

Pressing my lips together, I sat quietly for a moment more, waiting for the humor to fade.

"Yes, it was," I said, as my eyes opened to the sight of my promised standing naked in the doorway.

"It takes a lot to startle me. I don't like it when people get the drop on me."

Smiling as I sat up and pushed the chair back, I patted my leg. "Have a seat, and we'll talk about it."

She grinned and all but threw herself into my lap. Grabbing my ear, she whispered, "It was *not* funny. Not in the slightest."

"I knew where you were the moment your feet touched the floor. You were moving so fast, I thought you might walk all the way outside if I didn't slow you. I could have grabbed your ankles or let you sink into the floor."

"Neither of those would have been funny either," she said, releasing my ear to run her fingers through my beard.

"I couldn't let the first queen of Croy walk into the courtyard naked."

"You didn't *know* I was naked," she protested.

"Yes, I did. You didn't stand still long enough to get dressed."

"It's not fair you can tell what I'm doing from another room," she said, and gave me a quick kiss.

"Your father sees through stone."

"Because he couldn't get around without help otherwise. Your eyes work fine."

"Learning how to read pressure on the stone kept me alive in those tunnels. Odds are I'd be dead had I not figured it out."

"Do you ever wonder if this is worth all the loss you've suffered?"

"If I hadn't confronted the Council of Thanes and killed Eirickson?" I asked, then shrugged. "I'd have died fighting Satra. My mother and Aesa would still be dead. Maybe at my side but dead nonetheless. Roi and Crum would have died fighting at my side. My skati would still belong to Satra. Jesca would still be in the tunnels, and Sir might still be alive, but I wouldn't have met them. Eirickson and Satra would be preparing to invade Varia, eventually killing untold numbers of your countrymen."

"And you wouldn't have met me," she said. "When you put it that way..."

I hugged her tightly. "It was worth it. Go get dressed, and let's get some breakfast. You can take me to meet Goran."

She kissed me again and slid off my lap. "Be right back."

Pushing my talent back into the floor, I tracked her steps to the bedroom before reaching out farther and feeling the pressure of the two guards not far from my front door. When I felt Tindra leave the bedroom, I left to meet her in the hallway.

"After we eat," she said, "we're going to work on your shoulder."

"I'm not strong enough to swing my hammer yet."

She nodded. "Understood, but there are things you can do to help. Stretches and movements. If you let it sit for too long, it'll never get back to fighting condition."

"I've never tried stretching to help heal an injury," I said. "Worth it, I guess, as long as it doesn't hurt. Remember, I don't move as well as you...and I never will."

"I plan to do the work in my new armor, so I won't be moving very well either."

Nodding to the two guards as we walked past, I asked her, "Where is Goran's?"

"A ways past Roi's."

"Good," I said. "We can stop by on our way back. I need to talk to him."

Passing the gate, I noticed no guards stood nearby. *Guess Agrim made his decision and reassigned the men to more important tasks.*

"Will it be a long visit?"

"Depends," I said. "I have something I need to discuss with him."

"It's me, isn't it?"

"Partially," I said. "But I have other things that need his attention too."

"He thinks I'm bad for you...that you're making the wrong choice."

"He doesn't know you, not—"

"He doesn't want to know me," she replied, sparks flashing in her eyes.

"Calm yourself. No sense in burning a house to the ground. I'll let you in on a secret: he's treating you almost the same way he treated Crum when we were younger."

"Really?" she asked.

"I think he still expects nothing but trouble when Crum and I are together, but he's found some respect for my 'brother.' Truth be known, Roi and Crum are the closest thing to family I have left. Roi values family bonds."

"So, what should I do?"

"Be yourself—your true self," I said. "Show him you're trustworthy, in both actions and words. Let him see you the way I see you. A person changing, for the better."

"I'll keep that in mind."

Glancing at Roi's house as we passed, no one would mistake it for a shutdown shop anymore. Someone, most likely Grima, had cleaned the front and the windows, plus the smell of Einns' cooking hung in the air. I smiled, thinking Roi had the family he'd always wanted.

"I hope Goran's cooking tastes as good as Einns' smells," I commented.

"I bet they're similar," Tindra replied. "You'll find out soon enough."

Looking around, I noticed people watching us as we walked. Crum's advice about smiling to put people at ease came to mind. I added a wave and nod to my smile. A few smiled back but most kept a wary eye on us.

Tindra sniffed the air. "We're close. Can you smell the difference between his cooking and Einns'?"

I stopped, closed my eyes, and took a deep breath. "It smells about the same."

She grabbed my hand. "The longer you stand there, the longer it is before we eat."

I chuckled and walked alongside her as she guided me to Goran's eatery.

Chapter 62

Stepping in the door, the murmur of several conversations filled the room, and the air smelled of cooked pork and numerous spices. I noticed there were few empty tables and almost all the people eating had the somewhat teardrop-shaped faces and high cheekbones of the Varian.

Tindra led me to a short counter. "Goran. Brought you a new customer."

A squat man, not much taller than Tindra, came from the back. Sweat plastered brown hair to his inflamed skin. His gray eyes watered, and he blinked several times before wiping them with the back of his hand. "Tindra, I didn't expect you back so soon."

She chuckled. "Looks like you're standing too close to the fire."

He shook his head. "No, got distracted by something Britt's working on and let it get away from me."

"Be careful," I said. "From what I'm told, firesyths aren't fireproof."

Tindra squeezed my hand.

He nodded. "I know—learned the hard way. You must be King Fitzeirick."

"I am."

"Ordinarily, we enjoy sitting with everyone, but could we have some privacy today?" Tindra asked Goran quietly.

He sidestepped and looked past me. "Best I can do is a table in the corner."

"That will be fine," I said.

"Follow me."

He led us along the edge of the room to a small table.

"What's for breakfast?" I asked, sitting.

"Beaten eggs and cubed pork," Goran said.

"Never heard of beaten eggs," I said.

"We crack eggs in a bowl then mix them with seasonings and meat cut into cubes then dump the mixture into a hot pan, stirring the whole time. Fast, easy, and filling."

"Sounds interesting," Tindra said.

Goran nodded. "I'll have some out soon."

"Excuse me," an older-looking woman, sitting nearby said. "Are you Sar'sa's son?"

"Yes, ma'am. I am."

She smiled and held out her hand. "Thought you looked familiar. I'm Elibet. I'm sure you don't remember me. You were no more than knee-high when I moved here with my Croian husband."

"I don't remember you, sorry," I said, taking her hand. "Where's your husband?"

The corners of her mouth relaxed. "He passed, five years ago."

"Sorry for your loss," I said, patting her hand.

"No need to apologize; you didn't know. I don't mean to keep you from breakfast but seeing you reminded me of home."

I nodded and let go of her hand.

A young, blonde-haired, brown-eyed Varian girl approached. Like her father, her red face glistened with sweat. "Lady Tindra," she said, eyes wide.

"Britt," Tindra said. "This is King Fitzeirick."

Before I could say anything, the young girl let out a squeak.

Tindra poked me with her elbow. "Oh, I forgot...you have an admirer."

"Oh," I said. "How old are you?"

"Twelve."

"Going on twenty," Goran added, with a laugh, coming to bring us something to drink. "Cool apple juice. Britt, mind the fresh batch of eggs."

She nodded and hurried away.

"We need to bring Roi and his family sometime. Einns is about her age and loves to cook," I said.

"I'm not sure I need the trouble of a young boy in the kitchen," Goran said, grinning.

"He spent most of a year in Varia. His food would meet your approval," Tindra said.

"Not worried about his cooking," Goran said. "I'm worried about one of them chasing the other around the kitchen...or what might happen if they catch each other."

"I don't think he has an eye for girls just yet," I said.

Goran shrugged. "Bring them someday. What could it hurt?"

"Thank you," I said. "We don't mean to be a burden."

"No burden. I'm glad you're here. I've never served a king."

"I told you he likes Varian cooking. It's a safe bet we'll be back," Tindra said, taking a drink.

"I'll have a fresh batch of eggs ready soon."

"Sounds great," I said.

"My pleasure, Sire," he said, before walking away.

"You seemed surprised when we walked in," Tindra said.

"Never knew so many Varians stayed in this part of Croy after the war. It's obvious now that I spent too much time isolated in my skati when I was a skald. Things might be different if I would've come to the capital more often. For sure I'd have known more about my country—things I've only recently learned."

"Maybe, but how would your absence from the territory have been seen by your people? Would it have changed their opinion of you?"

I frowned. "Can't go back, so I'll never know."

"You'll never know what?" Britt asked, bouncing around the corner with a clay jug. "Can I fill your cups, Sire?"

I nodded. "Tindra and I were discussing how my past may have been different, had I made other choices," I said, as she poured our drinks with practiced ease.

"Is that why you have that brand? Because of choices you made?" she asked, smiling wide.

"I don't think—" Tindra started to say, but I held up my hand to stop her.

"She doesn't know, and I don't mind," I said. "I'm not ashamed of what I did; I'd do it all over again. Britt, I was branded a traitor for doing my best to protect my people—really everyone in Croy—from a Satran invasion. My half-brother didn't like how I expressed myself and disposed of me. In the end...he's dead, I'm king, and Croy will be better for it."

Britt's eyes opened wider as I explained my branding. Nibbling on her bottom lip, she gave me a quick nod and hurried back to the kitchen.

"I think you scared the poor thing," Tindra said.

I shrugged. "Didn't mean to."

"I hope my daughter didn't make a scene," Goran said, carrying a big plate piled high with fluffy, yellow food dotted with dark pink squares.

"Not at all," I said, "though I'm afraid I scared her. She asked how I got my brand, and I told her...without all the terrible details."

His brow furrowed as he placed the plate on the table. "What do you mean?" After I explained, he relaxed, and a grin turned his lips as he gave us forks. "Serves her right. Thank you for letting me know. Hope I'm not out of line thinking you two wouldn't mind sharing a plate."

"Not at all," I said.

"Enjoy your breakfast in peace."

I nodded.

Tindra said, "Thank you."

"You didn't bring your fork; good thing you don't need it," I said.

"Maybe I should get a pouch for it."

"Sounds like a good idea," I said, loading my fork.

"This is tasty," Tindra said. "Wonder why I never had it in Varia?"

"He got the idea from somewhere. Some Croian cooking uses eggs. Of course, I've never eaten a meal made mostly from eggs. I wouldn't want to eat it every day, but it's not bad."

"Agreed," Tindra said, before taking another bite.

Since we had no plans for the morning, we took our time working on the pile of food. From time to time, Goran checked on us but Britt never came back.

After one more swallow of juice, I patted my stomach, and said, "I'm done."

Tindra ate a little more before finishing the last of her juice. "Me too."

"I forgot to ask him what we owe," I said.

"I paid a gold single last time."

"I'll leave a gold double, seeing as I may have frightened his daughter."

"More than fair."

As we stood, Goran came around the corner. "Leaving?"

I nodded. "Full stomachs and I need to visit someone. I left a gold double on the table."

"That's too much, Sire. Give me a moment to get your change."

"Keep it. Like I tell Grith, use it to feed someone who can't afford it."

He bowed. "Thank you, Sire. You're welcome back any time. We're honored by your visit."

"Where's Britt?" Tindra asked.

"Sent her on some errands."

"I hope I didn't scare her too badly."

"She'll be fine," he said. "You know, there are many here who are happy to see a half-Varian leading the country. We hope you plan to repair the relationship between Croy and our homeland."

"How would they feel about a Croian sitting on the Varian throne?" I asked.

He gave me a questioning look. "I don't know. How would a Croian take power?"

"My best friend is marrying Princess Jesca soon," I said, smiling. "He'll rule at her side."

"That can't be," he said. "Princess Jesca is dead."

"I believed the same thing, but she's alive and well," Tindra said. "Fitzeirick rescued her when he escaped."

He stared at her, long enough for me to grow uncomfortable, then said, "You're telling the truth...I can see it in your eyes. King Ander's eldest is alive? Amazing. Wait, a marriage doesn't put them in power until Ander dies, though."

"He's stepping down," I said. "Croian agents, under orders from Eirickson, attacked the royal family. Crum, my best friend, did what he could to keep them safe. Ander was injured but not as badly as Queen Ines. When his wife passed, he decided to step down. Because of Crum's bravery, Ander agreed to let him marry Jesca. They will ascend to the throne soon after the wedding."

His shocked expression changed to one of happiness, and a smile appeared on his face. "And what of Princess Stina?"

Chapter 63

I pressed my lips together as Tindra looked away.

"She died in the fight between me and Eirickson."

Scratching his arm, the confused, questioning look returned. "Why was she in the Croian capital?"

"To marry Eirickson so he could claim control of Varia after his men killed the rest of her family. I tried to protect her, but in the confusion...her death was an accident. I'm sorry you're hearing about it this way. But Ander's legacy will live on in Jesca."

He blinked several times. "Stina came here to plot against her father?" He frowned before offering me his hand. "I can't imagine what would lead to such a situation. Thank you for telling me, Sire. As you can tell, we don't get any word on the happenings in Varia."

I shook his hand. "Like I said, I'm sorry to be the one bringing sad news, but things will be better in the future."

"Listening to you, I believe they will," he said, smiling again.

"I appreciate your trust," I said, and then led Tindra out of the eatery.

"Are we still stopping by Roi's on the way back?" she asked.

I nodded. "You don't have to stay."

"He'll never get to know me if I'm not around him."

"Very true," I said.

· · · · ● · ● · · ·

When Roi's house came into view, we saw Grima brushing white paint around the windows.

"Well met," I said.

She turned and smiled. "Hello, my king, Tindra. It's good to see you two again so soon."

"As much as I'm going to need Roi in the coming weeks, months, or longer, you're likely to be unhappy with me," I said.

"I could never be unhappy with you. You introduced me to the best man alive."

"I'm not so sure about that," Tindra quipped, squeezing my hand.

I chuckled. "Is he home?"

She nodded. "Getting dressed to run an errand. Should be out soon."

"I'll probably delay him a little while. We need to discuss something."

She opened the door. "Make yourself at home."

As we walked in, Tindra whispered, "Does she not realize her husband is your adviser, which makes her one of the most powerful women in Croy?"

"For all I know, she doesn't want to be involved in court matters," I said, taking a seat at the table.

"But she will be because of who she's married to."

I nodded. "Maybe you should talk to her about it sometime."

"I think you're right."

Roi's footsteps on the wooden stairs announced his presence as he descended from the room above. "Couldn't stay away more than a day?" he asked, smiling, when he saw us.

"Important business," I said. "And I wanted to let you know about a Varian eatery Tindra found, not far from here. The owner has a cute daughter, maybe a year or so older than Einns."

Roi laughed. "Are you trying to do Crum's job?"

"No, but it seemed like something you'd need to know before you went," I said.

"Speaking of Einns," Tindra said. "Where is he?"

"Shopping for ingredients," he replied, not looking at her. "What's on your mind?"

"With warriors going into battle, I need to make sure you're available to help me decide our next moves as we get reports."

He nodded. "Of course. As always, I'm at your beck and call."

"Good. Now, you do have my family sword...right?"

He hesitated. "Yes."

"It's time you give it to me."

"I don't think it is," he replied.

"It belongs to me.

"Yet you left it with Geri."

"To cover a debt I couldn't pay then."

"A debt you sent me to settle."

"That ceremonial sword holds my family's line. It belongs to me. You gain nothing by keeping it from me."

"Croy gains nothing by you rushing into a bad idea," he said.

"If I may," Tindra said. "What have I done to offend you? Perhaps something between us needs to be settled."

As he turned to her, the floor quivered.

"You've done the only thing you know how to do," he said. "You've lied and manipulated and all but tricked him into the idea of marriage. It's what you were hired to do. I've known your plan since the day after I met you."

The air around me cooled as Tindra drew in heat. "Fitzeirick made it clear he would *not* tolerate lies and manipulation from me. I was *not* hired to marry him. As a matter of fact, I didn't do what I was hired to do. At great personal risk, I took him to Ander instead of turning him over to the war council. Before then, I can't remember the last time I did what I thought was right instead of what I was paid to do.

"My connections and skills put him on the throne. He and I—we...worked together. We protected each other. To ensure Fitzeirick came out on top, I put him above everything, even my own country. I *could* have stabbed him in the back, literally. Then Sabast would have killed Eirickson, and Croy would be ruled by a puppet with Kurt holding the strings."

She put her right arm on the table and stared at Roi. "I lost a hand in service to Fitzeirick. What did you lose?"

He opened and closed his mouth several times before she stood and stomped out.

"I'm not asking. I'm telling you...give me my sword," I said. "I decided to marry her—on my own. She didn't trick me; she even protested."

"That's part of the trick. She plays the game well."

"I can tell I'm not going to change your mind," I said. "I don't need your approval, but I do need the sword, and I'm not leaving until I get it."

"Fine," he said, as he stood. Pointing at me, he continued, "I don't want to hear you complain when this goes bad for you, for the country you claim to care about. She's going to betray you. I'm not sure how, but she will."

"She already had her best chance to betray me, and she didn't. She could have stood by and let Stina open my gut, could've helped the princess kill me. Instead, Tindra chose me, and Croy, over her own king and killed his youngest daughter."

Roi turned and walked to a corner of the room. Pushing his hands into the stone floor, he raised a rectangular rock from the ground, brought it to the table, and dropped it. "It's in there."

As I reached for it, he asked, "Do you love her?"

"I'm better off with her at my side. I believe her skills and experience will serve the country well as the queen. Also, because it's the right thing to do."

"That's not a reason to marry someone."

Picking up the stone box, I said, "People marry for worse reasons all the time."

He didn't respond.

Before I turned to the door, I said, "I *will* need your wisdom as the war moves forward."

He nodded. "I'll always tell you what I think is the right thing to do."

"I ask for nothing more."

Grima approached as I closed the door. "Fitzeirick, what happened in there?"

"Roi and I had a difference of opinion."

"Which caused Tindra to leave in tears?"

I shrugged. "Difference of opinion."

"He doesn't like her, but I don't understand why."

"He thinks she's bad for me, going to betray me."

"Why?" she asked. "She's always been nice to me."

"He roots his opinion in what she used to be. In service to her king, country, and others, she lied, manipulated, and worse. After we met, she chose me over that life."

"And that makes her a bad person?"

"You remember I said Tindra told me someone sent her to marry me?"

Grima nodded.

"She lied. A secret group in Varia hired her to bring me to them. Instead, she brought me to King Ander and helped me defeat Eirickson. All Roi remembers is her lie. He suspects she's still plotting against me."

She gave me a weak smile. "I'll talk to him."

"Please...don't," I said. "I'd hate for my decisions to cause an argument between you two also."

"I appreciate your concern, but I can handle him."

I smiled and nodded. "I'm sure you can. Hope your painting goes well."

"Thank you. Hope the rest of your day does the same."

Chapter 64

By the time I made it home, my arms burned from carrying the rock holding my family sword.

Ingo opened the door for me.

I hefted the load to the meeting room and dropped it on the table.

Pushing my talent into the floor, I searched for Tindra and didn't find her. I sighed. *What is she doing now?*

Pressing my hands against the stone, I softened the top, reached inside, and lifted my family sword clean from the enclosure. *Looks like Geri took good care of it.*

I heard the front door open and looked out to see Tindra walk in carrying a black, leather pouch.

"For your fork?" I asked.

She nodded then frowned. "I'm sorry I let him get to me."

"It's fine. You told him the truth. Come in here."

"Speaking of the truth," she said, as she entered the room. "You lied to Goran about how Stina died."

"I wouldn't call it a lie. More like a simple explanation of a complex situation."

"You didn't tell him who killed her."

"Why make him think less of you because of what you did in the middle of a fight? You didn't kill her on purpose."

"You're right," she said, nodding. "But you lying to protect me took me by surprise."

I shrugged. "I told him what he needed to know and nothing more. You should know the difference."

"Fine," she said. "You didn't lie but you didn't tell the whole story either."

I took a breath. "We can stand here and debate the morality of what I said, or you can tell me why this sword is a necessary part of our engagement."

"I'm surprised he gave it to you," she said, smiling.

I shook my head. "He and I have too much history for a simple disagreement to crack our friendship."

She looked sideways at me. "Sounds like a shaky foundation for a friendship, if you ask me."

Grinning, I lifted the sheathed, ceremonial weapon. "Here it is."

She nodded. "My father's not here...and he's blind. Draw the sword and hold it where I can inspect it."

I pulled the sword quickly. Clearing the scabbard, it rang quietly until I laid the blunt tip across my hand.

"On one knee," Tindra said.

I knelt and bowed my head, holding the sword in the palm of my hands for her to look over.

A faint vibration spread through the ceremonial weapon as she ran her finger along my family line. "You are who you claim. Your family is as you say," she said. My hands rose, briefly, as she removed their load by lifting the sword. "King Fitzeirick of Croy, I will marry you."

I froze in place, my mind unexpectedly focused on the difference in how I proposed to Aesa and what had just happened. A simple promise exchanged between us, symbolized by clasping a necklace on her, seemed insignificant compared to subjugating myself before the woman I'd asked to marry.

"Everything all right?" Tindra asked, shocking me out of my thoughts.

"Sorry," I said. "I got, umm...distracted."

"Aesa?"

I nodded and looked down. "Sorry."

The sword clanked on the table, then Tindra ran her fingers through my hair. "I can't say I understand, because I've never had real feelings for anyone before, but I don't blame you."

"Thank you," I said. I stood and hugged her tightly. I couldn't find better words to express my appreciation for her understanding, so I stood there and held her.

Eventually, Tindra patted me on the back and said, "Let's work off some of that breakfast. Meet me outside."

"I'm in no condition to train against you," I said. "If anything, I need to rest my shoulder after carrying the stone box."

"I didn't say anything about sparring. You need to stretch."

I frowned but did as she asked. Grabbing the somewhat lighter block, I carried it outside and let it crumble to dust.

"How do you think the fighting's going?" Ingo asked.

"No way to know until someone returns with word, but our way, I hope."

"Waiting..." He nodded. "That's the frustrating part."

"Hard to argue with the truth," I said.

Tindra walked out wearing her armor. "Come with me."

"Have fun," Ingo said, chuckling as I followed Tindra to the middle of the courtyard.

"Stand facing me and do your best to follow my movements."

I nodded and took a breath.

Starting with her arms stiff at her side, she raised them to shoulder level, then made large circles by rotating her shoulders.

My left shoulder ached after the third circle, and I slowed.

Soon, she stopped, arms straight over her head, and bent to the right side before grabbing the back of her neck with her left hand.

As I moved, the muscles in my injured shoulder protested.

After a count of ten, she bent the other way.

Another count of ten, she straightened. "I can't do this exactly right, but clasp your hands over your head, arch your back, and pull your arms back as far as you can."

I followed her instructions and sucked in a breath as pain shot through my shoulder.

After two more arches, she started the pattern again with circles.

We kept at it until rivers of sweat ran down my forehead. Just before we stopped, the pain in my shoulder wasn't as sharp.

"Don't know about you, but I need to bathe. It would help to get some heat on your shoulder," Tindra said.

I looked at her and scratched my head. "How do you know about treating injuries?"

She smiled. "In my line of work, you have to learn how to take care of yourself."

I shrugged and went with her to get clean clothes, stopping for my family sword to put it away.

Having grabbed clean clothes, we left for the public bath, walking hand in hand.

"I miss my private bath," she said, as we entered the water.

"You'll have another, in due time."

We soaked in the warm water and cleaned each other.

"I'm ready for some lunch," I said.

"Wait. Let me work some heat into your shoulder."

"What are you going to do?"

"Don't trust me?"

"Yes, but a firesyth saying they're going to work heat into me sounds like a good way to get a new scar."

"I have more control than that. Turn around."

The water cooled as I turned, and then a feverish hand pressed firmly against my back.

"Ugh. This works better with two hands," she said. "Lean back. Let me support some of your weight."

I leaned against the warming hand, and she rubbed it across my shoulder, massaging the damaged muscle around the scar. The cooling water prickled my legs and stomach as heat spread into my upper back.

"Turn around."

I turned to a face of concentration. Sweat flowed down her forehead, some pooled in the corners of her closed eyes before running down her cheeks like tears.

"Lean against my hand again."

The water cooled further around us as Tindra drew warmth from it to push more heat into my body.

Shivers ran through my legs as the water became uncomfortably cold. "I hope you're nearly done."

"It's worse for me," she said, her jaw quivering. "I need to spend some time near a fire, and I'm starving."

"We'll go to Grith's."

She shivered the entire walk to the butcher's shop.

Chapter 65

Grith welcomed us as we stepped inside.

"Tindra needs to warm herself. Can she spend a few minutes near your cooking fire?" I asked.

"Of course, Sire."

She muttered, "Thanks," and hurried to the back of the shop.

"Is she ill?"

I shook my head. "We were bathing. She took warmth from the water and worked it into my shoulder, trying to help me recover. The water got too cold. Uncomfortable for me, but it hit her hard."

He raised his eyebrows and nodded. "That would do it."

"What's for lunch?"

"Rabbit stew."

"Sounds good. Two bowls, please, and water for the two of us."

He nodded and quickly placed our steaming bowls on the counter.

I tossed him a gold double, and he tried to give it back. "You always overpay. I'll take no more than a gold single today."

"I take care of those who treat me well, and you let Tindra use your fire," I said. "That must be worth something."

"Then I'll give you a silver single as change," he countered.

"Give it to someone who needs it. Who knows? Someday it could be me."

"I don't see how that happens, Sire."

I rubbed the scar on my face. "I never thought I'd wear a traitor's brand."

He shook his head, and said, "You didn't deserve it," then went back to work.

The first spoonful of stew burned my tongue. Tindra returned, rosy-cheeked and smiling, as I waited for the meal to cool. "Feel better?" I asked.

"Much," she said, taking the seat across from me and sniffing the stew. "This will help too."

Once the liquid cooled, the tasty stew went quickly. Tindra slurped the last of hers, then asked, "While we're here, want to check on your armor?"

Someone called my name when we stepped out of the butcher shop, hand in hand. Turning toward the voice, I saw Svan frantically waving, running toward us.

"What's wrong?" I asked.

"A runner back from the battle...waiting outside your quarters."

"Good news?" I asked.

"Wouldn't say but he didn't look upset."

Guess that's a good sign. Hairs on my arm stood tall as warmth spread through my body. "You know where Roi lives?"

"I do, Sire."

"Tell him I need him at my quarters to hear the report. Deliver the same message to General Jomar."

"With all haste, my lord."

Tindra squeezed my hand. "Do you want me in the meeting? If not, I can check on your armor and save you a trip later."

"Go see Thorgault," I said. "I need Roi focused on the report, not glaring at you."

"Right," she said. "After I'm done here, I'll visit Kurt and Aerison."

"Let Aerison know I'll come talk to him as soon as I can."

"Consider it done," she said, smiling. "Hope it's good news."

I nodded. "Thank you."

She let go of my hand and wove her way through the crowded market.

I shouldered past people who wouldn't move out of my way.

Ingo hurried to meet me when I entered the courtyard. "Sire, his name's Bolverk. He's tired, dead on his feet."

The warrior, axes hanging from his belt, leaned against my quarters with his head down and eyes closed.

Crossing the courtyard, I noticed dried blood around a jagged slice along the outside of his left sleeve. "You didn't mention he's injured."

"He said the bandage stopped the bleeding."

I nodded. "Send for Abi after I take him inside."

"I'll see to it myself."

Crossing the rest of the way to my quarters, I called out to Bolverk. "Join me inside."

The warrior's head snapped up, and he looked me in the eye. "Oh...of course, Sire. After you."

I led him to the meeting room. "Have a seat. Do you need something to drink?"

"Tell me where the water is, my lord. I'll get some myself."

"Nonsense. You're wounded and tired. Sit."

"I can't ask my king to serve me."

"I order you to sit," I said. "You can tell me everything when I get back."

He looked from me to the chairs and nodded.

When I returned, his head rested on his hands with his eyes closed, and he was breathing the shallow breath of sleep.

I gently put a mug of water nearby before placing the pitcher in the middle of the table.

He didn't move.

Deciding it best to let him rest, I left to stand near the front door to greet Roi and Jomar.

General Jomar arrived first. "Good news, I hope."

"Don't know yet. Bolverk's sleeping at my meeting table. He arrived exhausted and hurt. Once Roi arrives, we'll wake him and get his report."

Jomar nodded and stepped away from the door.

Roi walked in a short time later.

"In the meeting room," I said. "Let's see what he has to say."

We entered the meeting room and sat across the table from Bolverk. Jomar cleared his throat.

The warrior opened his eyes and raised his head. Blinking as he looked around the room, he settled his gaze on the general. Bolverk jumped from his chair. "Beg pardon, General Jomar, sir. I didn't mean to fall asleep on duty."

"Have a seat. Speak freely," I said.

He sat, took a long drink of water, and nodded. "Satra had fought their way inside before we arrived. I saw twenty or thirty dead Satran as we approached a large hole in the wall. At least that many of Nikulas' men were dead or dying when we charged. Fighting in the streets and alleys, we lost ten or fifteen men before we changed tactics. General Gudmann sent fifty or so men around the outside perimeter of the city, forcing Satra into a two-front battle."

He paused for another drink. "It worked but...trapped rats fight hardest. We made them pay, though. Maybe twenty soldiers made it through us and outside the wall. They were all bleeding."

"How many warriors gave chase?" Jomar asked.

"None."

"Why not?" I asked.

"The generals ordered house-to-house searches. Any warrior who could walk and had at least one good arm searched. There isn't an undisturbed cobweb or clump of dust inside Nikulas' wall."

"I sent them with explicit orders to kill every Satran and give chase to any who fled," I said.

I heard the front door open before Roi cleared his throat. "Fitzeirick, your generals seemed concerned about hidden threats. No reason to fault them for being thorough."

"He's right, Sire," Jomar added. "I've spent enough time with both generals to know they take pride in following orders. If they made the decision to stay and search, they had good reason."

Sighing, I shook my head. "While I appreciate your opinions, I gave an order with the expectation it would be followed."

"Fitzeirick," Roi said. "Sending wounded and tired warriors to chase a fleeing force, into a possible trap would be a waste of good men. Plus, you sent the Varian soldiers to catch any of the enemies who got away."

"He's right, Sire," Bolverk said. "When the Varians arrived, they reported killing Satrans on the run. Chased them to the edge of the central forest from what I heard."

"And their losses?" I asked.

"As best I could tell, none."

"Were they sending a report?" I asked.

"No one rode out with me," Bolverk said.

I looked at Roi and Jomar. "Any questions for him?"

"Our losses?" Jomar asked.

Bolverk shook his head. "I wasn't given a count. If I had to guess, I'd say between thirty and fifty dead, maybe twice as many wounded."

"We need more men," I said, frowning and running my fingers through my hair.

"True," Roi said, "but we can have that conversation after Bolverk leaves."

I nodded. "Any more questions?"

Roi shook his head.

Jomar said, "No."

I stood and offered the warrior my hand. "Thank you for your service."

Getting to his feet, he shook my hand. "Doing my duty, Sire."

I nodded. "See the herbalist waiting at my dining table. She'll take care of your arm. Then find a bed and sleep."

He bowed and left the room.

I moved to sit across from my advisers. "Thoughts?"

Chapter 66

"I see no reason to rush headlong into anything," Roi said. "Do not throw men's lives away needlessly."

"More than anything, we need to recruit more warriors if you plan to attack soon," Jomar said.

"We will take the fight to Satra as soon as possible," I said. "Where do we get more men?"

"Can you ask Varia to send more soldiers?" Jomar asked.

I shook my head. "There's unrest in Varia; King Ander's doing everything he can to stave off a civil war. I'll ask, as a last resort, but we can't rely on them until their situation changes. If Ander fails, we may get no support from Varia."

"Sounds like Nikulas is short on men too," Roi said. "And the southern section of his skati isn't an option from what I understand."

"Correct," I said. "What little time I spent south of the capital tells me I don't have any support. Doubt we'll find any volunteers there."

"A few men under my command came from the south. Could we spare them for a few days to try recruiting from there?" Jomar asked.

"Any idea how many we'd get, assuming they are successful?" I asked.

He shrugged. "Ideally, between fifty and a hundred. To tell the truth, I'd expect no more than twenty."

"How did my half-brother get so many warriors?" I demanded.

"After pulling Commander Haldan and his companies from your skati, he convinced everyone Varia could attack at any moment," Jomar said.

"No doubt with Hallfrid's full support," I said.

Jomar nodded.

"Considering Satra has attacked us twice, we should have men lining up to fight," I said.

"You don't have near the support Eirickson did," Jomar said.

I frowned. "Another problem I need to address. Send the men you think will be most successful. Hopefully, they recruit enough to replace our losses. Swelling our ranks would be better."

"Consider it done," Jomar replied.

"Replacing losses is better than nothing," Roi said.

"*If* we can get anyone," I said. "Let's talk battle plan. We need to get an idea of what's waiting for us past the central forest. I can ask half the Varian force to scout the area."

"A two hundred fifty man scouting party?" Jomar asked.

"Does seem large," Roi said. "Hard to move so many men without attracting attention."

I nodded. "But if they come under attack, it's enough to effectively defend themselves and possibly counterattack."

"That many men, moving through a forest...they *will* be noticed," Jomar said. "I'd advise sending twenty of my men to scout, Sire. Position the Varian force near the forest, ready to act on what the scouts find."

"I agree," Roi added. "If the scouts meet resistance, they can run back to the large force, maybe lead the attackers into a trap."

I pressed my lips together, considering the suggestion, then nodded. "Jomar, pick twenty men. Make it known I expect prompt reports on their findings. On their way out, have them stop by The Trader's Cup and let the refugees know they are safe to return home."

"Gladly, Sire. I'll send extra horses to be stationed at Geri's. Messengers can eat and switch mounts there. Should speed up getting word back to the capital."

"Good thinking," I said. "Excellent suggestion. I agree."

"Thank you, Sire. With your permission, I'll leave to ready my men," Jomar said.

"Yes," I said. "Tell your men I said travel safe and swift."

The general stood and bowed before leaving.

"I'm going to recommend caution again," Roi said.

"There's nothing cautious about war."

"Winning at the expense of wasting lives isn't much of a victory. There's no pride in celebrating over a pile of your warrior's bodies."

"And I'll do my best to avoid such a scene, but we *are* going to war."

"Then fix your thoughts on what's best for your country, not your ego or your need for revenge."

"Thank you for the wisdom and clarity. I need to talk to Agrim."

"Do you still need me?"

"You're free to go."

He stood and hurried out of the room.

I wrote my orders for Gudmann and Heming along with directions to send the Varians to support the scouts on a piece of parchment and sealed it. When I left the room, Abi was rolling a bandage on Bolverk's arm.

"Are you sure it's supposed to burn?" Bolverk asked.

Abi sighed. "Yes, because your wound wasn't treated correctly. The swelling must go away before I can stitch it closed, so leave it alone and don't get the bandage wet. Tomorrow, come see me, and I'll work on it more. You'd think our warriors would have enough sense to bring herbalists with them."

Bolverk stood, thanked Abi, and stopped when he saw me.

"Aren't most of them peaceful?" I asked. "I suspect not a single one wants to go to war."

Abi jumped when I spoke. "Sorry, Sire. I didn't mean any—"

"No need to apologize," I said. "You bring up a good point. Perhaps an herbalist or two should accompany the warriors. Might save a few limbs or lives. I'll talk to Agrim about it, see if he thinks he can recruit a few."

"I'll spread the word too," she said. "Bolverk, remember to come to me tomorrow. A cut that long needs stitches."

"I'll be there," Bolverk said. "Sire, am I free to go?"

I nodded. "Find a bed before you fall asleep on your feet."

He bowed and left my home.

"Thank you, Abi, for everything you do."

"Happy to be of service, Sire."

"What do I owe you for treating him?"

"A silver single and a copper single."

"How about a silver double?" I said, reaching into my coin purse.

"I can't change it for you."

"No worry. Use the extra toward the expense of housing Aerison and Kurt."

"Your generosity is appreciated. Feel free to send for me when you need me again."

I followed her outside and asked Sigric if he knew where I could find Captain Agrim. "Home, as far as I know, Sire."

I thanked him and walked to the next building over.

Agrim opened the door shortly after I knocked. "My lord. What can I do for you?"

"I have a couple of things I need to discuss with you."

"Of course. Come in. Need something to drink?"

"Water."

He placed a mug in front of me after I sat. "What's on your mind, Sire?"

"Herbalists."

He cocked his head. "Having a problem with Abi?"

I smiled. "No, but while speaking with her earlier, she brought up an interesting point. Why are there no herbalists traveling with the warriors when they go to battle? If injured warriors were treated sooner and better, maybe lives could be saved."

He nodded. "I agree, but all the herbalists I've dealt with are peaceful."

"I said much the same, but Abi offered to spread word of our need among her peers. Ask around, see if you can recruit a few. They could contribute to our success in defeating Satra."

"Of course. I'll do my best, Sire," he said. "Is that all?"

"Bolverk's injured. I need a messenger to carry my orders back to the battlefield," I said, handing him the parchment.

Agrim smiled and took the orders. "No problem. Consider it done. Anything else?"

"We need more men and someone to train them."

Agrim nodded again, though he said, "I doubt you'll find many willing to fight for you around the capital."

"Jomar said the same. He's sending men south to see if they can recruit from their homeland."

"Are you asking me to train anyone they can get?"

"I *am* asking, unless you want me to order you," I said.

"No, Sire," he said, face blank. "An order won't be necessary. I'll see they get enough training to fight as one of our warriors."

"Not simply fight—anyone can fight...trained or not. I need men who can fight effectively and win."

"Right," he said. "Yes...of course, Sire. I'll...that is, my men...your guard...we'll train them."

"Something wrong? You seem distracted."

"No, nothing's wrong...exactly. At least I don't think there's anything to worry about."

"What aren't you telling me?"

"Nothing you should... You have more important matters to concern yourself with."

I tapped my fingers on the table. "Yet you seem overly bothered. A shared burden is easier to carry. What has you troubled?"

"When you mentioned Bolverk and his injury, it reminded me of a report I received this morning. A rider passed through the southern gate before dawn. Well before

Bolverk arrived. Something about it bothered me, but until now, I hadn't settled on why."

"I'm listening," I said.

"The rider wore Varian clothes, but the guards didn't see their face."

"Varian style is common in Nikulas' holdings," I said. "Could've been anyone. Maybe a trader rushing home when he felt he could leave safely. What am I missing?"

He held up his hand. "Hear me out, Sire. From what I heard, Bolverk rode non-stop as soon as the Satran fled. After having his wound bandaged. Correct?"

"That's right. So?"

"For someone to arrive here ahead of him, they likely left during the fighting." A frown curled his lips. "Did the guard let a Satran enter the capital?"

I fought down a growl as the grimace crossed my face. "Find a messenger to deliver my orders, then meet me at the southern gate. I want an explanation."

Chapter 67

The guards bowed as I approached the gate.

"What brings you, Sire?" Erland asked.

"Which of you manned this post when Bolverk arrived?"

"All of us," he said.

"And all of you were here when the rider before Bolverk entered the capital?"

"Yes, m'lord," he said.

"Did you stop him? Question where he came from and why he was here?"

"We did, Sire," Erland said. "He told us, without hesitation, he was expected."

My brow furrowed. "According to Captain Agrim, no one saw the rider's face."

"The deep hood on Varian cloaks makes it hard to see faces... especially in the dark," a warrior I didn't recognize said.

"And not one of you asked him to show himself?" I asked, sweeping my arm across the group.

"Given his clothing, we assumed he'd come from Nikulas' hall, possibly a Varian soldier," Erland said. "We let him pass without further questions. Had he hesitated or stuttered, we'd have held him longer."

Agrim stopped at the gate, hands on his knees and breathing heavily. "Your orders will leave shortly, Sire," he wheezed.

"Erland tells me everyone here saw the rider this morning," I said.

He nodded and held up his hand, trying to catch his breath.

"Captain Agrim," I said. "You have work to do. We are at war and cannot afford to let people inside these walls on assumptions and confident voices. Make it clear to *every* man guarding *any* gate if they do not know, with absolute certainty, who someone is, that person does not enter until they are identified and their business is made clear. I don't care who it inconveniences; we cannot afford to let Satran agents infiltrate the capital. Understood?"

"Absolutely, Sire," he replied.

"Good," I said. "Pass the word and gather men to search for this stranger."

"Sire?" he questioned. "How—"

"I don't care how," I growled and thrust my finger at him. "*You* are the captain of my guard. How is *your* problem."

"Understood, m'lord," he said, head bowed. "I'll see him found if I have to search every building in the capital personally."

"With haste," I said. "The sooner he's found, the better. Make sure I'm informed immediately upon his capture."

"That goes without saying, my lord," he replied.

"Beginning to wonder if it does. I'll be at Abi's if you need me," I said, before turning to leave.

• • • • ● • ● • • •

Walking to the herbalist's home took longer than normal as I watched for anyone who stood out or looked suspicious. By the time I arrived, most of my frustration had drained away.

When I greeted the Varian soldier standing watch over Abi's door, he told me Tindra had recently left.

"Do you know where she went?"

He nodded. "She went to get some sweet rolls."

I smiled. "Probably from Goran's, to remind them of home. If she returns before I leave, let her know I'm talking with your lieutenant."

"With pleasure."

When I opened the door to Aerison's room, he said, "Back so soon," before he saw me. "Oh, it's you," he said, frowning.

"Sorry to disappoint," I said, smiling.

He chuckled and shook his head. "You're not a disappointment, just not who I expected."

"If I'd known you wanted a treat, I'd have brought something. Instead, I bring a good report on your men. They arrived in time to make a difference in the battle. I'm sending orders for them to move in support of my scouting group set to leave soon."

He nodded. "What's the plan?"

I gave him a summary of what we had in mind.

"Sounds good," he said. "Expect the full support of my men."

"I do," I replied. "One question before I go. Does the Varian army employ herbalists on the battlefield?"

"Thinking of ordering Abi to fight?" he asked, grinning.

"No," I said, grinning at the thought of her wielding anything more deadly than a gardening spade. "But if we have herbalists nearby, wounded men could receive treatment sooner. Might save lives."

"We don't often have fully trained herbalists with us, but it's not uncommon for two or three woodsyths in our companies to have some herbalist training."

"Thank you for confirming what I thought," I said. "When Tindra gets back, will you tell her I went home?"

"As long as she doesn't mind me talking with my mouth full," he said, and laughed.

"I'm sure she'll understand," I said, before leaving.

On the way home, I wondered if Agrim had made any progress. As I turned to look for him, I remembered leaving my hammer at home. *If someone is here to do me harm, I'm not ready to defend myself. Best arm myself before tracking down Agrim.*

Nearing the gate to the courtyard, I heard Otkel loudly explaining to someone I wasn't home, and he didn't know where I'd gone or when I might return.

I stopped outside to listen.

"May I leave word with you for King Fitzeirick?" the man asked. I didn't recognize his voice.

"Again, we may not be on watch when he returns."

"You cannot pass the message on?" the stranger asked.

"We may not be here when the guard changes or they may be called away before King Fitzeirick returns."

The longer they talked, the more naked I felt. *Surely someone won't attack me with two guards at the ready.* I stepped through the gate and saw a balding, dark-haired man, hands on his hips, shaking his head.

"Well met, Otkel," I called out.

He looked past the stranger and smiled. "Sire, well met. He's here to see you."

The stranger wore Varian-styled clothes except dyed gray and brown instead of the usual bright colors.

When he turned, he looked Croian. *Something about him looks vaguely familiar.* His smile deepened wrinkles near the corners of his eyes. "Good to meet you in person. Nikulas told me you're a good man. May I have a few minutes of your time?"

"You have me at a disadvantage," I said. "Who are you?"

He offered his hand. "Sorry, my name is Tore. You and your promised dined at my pub not long ago."

The resemblance is clear now. I shook his hand. "Oh, Roald's grandson. Yes, we had an...interesting evening. When did you arrive?"

"Before first light. Easier to avoid all the fighting in the dark."

"Any trouble entering the capital?" I asked.

"A short delay ... nothing overly troublesome."

No doubt he's the mystery rider. I smiled and nodded. "Glad you made the trip safely. What can I do for you?"

"I'd hoped to speak with our new king for a few moments." He bowed.

"Of course. Please, come inside."

Otkel opened the door. "All is well, Sire?"

I nodded. "Yes. When Tindra arrives, let her know we have company. Also, have someone find Captain Agrim. I want to see him after Tore leaves."

"Of course, Sire," he said.

"Thank you." I led Tore to my meeting room. "I trust you received the letter I sent on your grandfather's passing."

"I did. My sister and I appreciate you contacting us."

"Something to drink?"

He nodded. "Thank you. I'm still a little dry from the ride. Water, if it's no trouble."

"None at all. Give me a moment."

"You have no servants?"

"Life's been too busy to find servants," I replied, before leaving the room.

Chapter 68

"I'm guessing you're not here because of one evening of bad decisions," I said, placing a mug on the table.

He smiled, shook his head, and took a drink. "No, though I hope you don't regret visiting my family's pub."

"Not at all," I said. "But I *am* a bit ashamed of my behavior."

He chuckled. "Nothing was broken, no fights. Trust me, my people have dealt with far worse. I wanted to personally invite you and Lady Tindra to eat with me this evening."

"I have some business to attend to before we dine this evening but see no reason to refuse."

"No doubt starting a war is demanding. I don't mean to keep you from your tasks. I rode here to attend to some business myself and wanted to personally thank you for keeping Satra from taking my home."

"It's my intention to destroy them, grind the entire nation into dust," I said. "I'm looking toward a future where they no longer exist."

He whistled. "A lofty goal, my king. Surely you need reliable support to achieve such a thing."

"Working on it. It seems things are improving in Croy. I hope to increase the strength of my fighting force soon. After Varia stabilizes under their new king, I expect more support. They have a stake in the war too."

He nodded. "Many believe you did the right thing eliminating Hallfrid, but some question the wisdom of killing men under him."

"It was necessary," I said. "Messy but necessary."

He pursed his lips for a moment. "I noticed warriors using Boril and Porsey's quarters. What happened to them?"

"I'd made arrangements to send them to Varia and gave their homes to my guard. A Satran patrol happened across their caravan. Boril's dead and Porsey defected; he's working with Satra out of spite."

Tore frowned. "Sorry to hear Boril's dead. He always seemed to be a decent man but lacked the backbone to stand for what's right. Shame on Porsey, but he's always been a snake. Wouldn't bother me one bit to hear he died...suffered and died screaming would be even better. I've always suspected he's the reason my parents disappeared. Never could prove it, though."

"I couldn't prove Porsey was behind a lot of my troubles either. Perhaps if Boril had stood up to him, I'd have kept him around," I said. "How did you know about Hallfrid and not Boril and Porsey?"

He grinned. "Same way I knew about your evening at The Sneaky Bear. I have people who make a decent living keeping me informed, but they travel no faster than horses. I do appreciate you not sending your guards hunting a certain servant. I'm told you wear the knife on occasion."

The thin, pale arm offering me the seax came to mind. I couldn't keep the shock from my face. "You're behind that?"

He tilted his head. "I contributed. My sister thought a knife sent the wrong message, that you'd see it as a threat. It seemed to me, and others, you were a man who'd appreciate the utility of a quality blade. We hope it serves you well."

"A fine weapon it is. What's expected in return?"

He raised his hands. "Nothing."

I shook my head. "I have some experience with groups who operate in secret. They always want something. When do I find out what you want?"

"It is a gift—a token of thanks, nothing more."

"In that case, tell your sister it is appreciated."

He nodded. "You mentioned some business needing your attention, so I propose we hold any further discussion until dinner."

"Seems risky to chance spoiling a fine meal with a disagreement."

He gave me a toothy grin. "I dare say our wants, needs...goals are similar. Also, I appreciate good food too much to chance spoiling a meal, especially in my own pub."

I nodded. "What time?"

He pursed his lips for a moment. "I'll be at the Bear the rest of the evening, at least. Must make sure my most trusted people are still trustworthy."

"Tindra and I will come as early as we can."

He tilted his head toward me. "I look forward to meeting the woman ready to serve you and Croy as queen."

"She's spent most of her life working for Varia. King Ander valued her counsel and service highly. Tindra has proven herself to me many times over. Given her strengths and experience, no doubt she'll make a fine queen."

"Sounds promising. I look forward to getting a measure of her myself," he said, before standing and offering his hand again. "For Croy's future prosperity."

Odd phrase. Maybe it's just his way of saying he'd like to meet her. I stood. "Can't think of a better thing to shake on."

"Good," he replied. "I'll see myself out."

As soon as I heard the door close, I sighed and slumped back in the chair. *Guess that's a couple of mysteries solved...and a whole new one to consider. Where is Agrim?*

After a quick trip to the bedroom to slip the seax onto my belt, I went searching for the captain of my guard and found him stomping away from the west gate, red-faced.

"I have good news," I said.

"Could use some, m'lord. Seems even *my* men don't understand why they should do their job to the best of their ability."

"I'm sure you'll make them see the error in their thinking," I said. "I met the stranger."

"You look none the worse for the meeting. He's not a threat?"

"Doesn't appear to be the case. It's Roald's grandson, Tore, here to check on some business concerns."

"Are you sure, Sire? Tore's here? In the capital?" he asked, scratching his head.

"I can't be completely certain, never met him before. I spoke with an older-looking, balding man resembling Roald. You sound concerned. Why?"

"Sounds like him." Agrim pressed his lips together. "Guess he thinks it's safe with Hallfrid gone."

"He mentioned the former general. Porsey too. Didn't have much good to say about either of them."

"Understandable," he said, "considering everyone suspects those two made his parents disappear. Never found evidence to prove it, though."

"Tindra and I are dining with him this evening. I'll make sure to tell you anything I think you need to know."

"You'll eat well," Agrim said, and chuckled.

"Keep after the guards. This time, it wasn't a disaster, but I don't want to think about what could happen."

"I'll make sure of it, Sire, or they'll run around the capital two times."

"Carry on then," I said.

He bowed before hurrying toward the center of town.

I strode home, determined to get some rest.

• • • • • • • • • • •

Lips pressing against my cheek woke me.

Someone grabbed my hand when I pushed them away.

"Not the welcome I expected," Tindra said.

A candle flared to life.

Shading my eyes, I glared at her. "Your fault for sneaking up on a sleeping man."

"I thought you'd enjoy being awoken by a kiss. Many people do, you know."

I blinked and scratched my head. "You mean I'm not the first man you've woken with a kiss?"

"I hate to tell you," she said, smiling, "but I don't remember who the first man I woke with a kiss was."

I sighed. "As long as I'm the last."

She nodded. "You are."

Getting out of bed, I stretched. "Good. Ready for dinner?"

"Where are we going?"

"The Sneaky Bear."

"Are you sure it's a good idea to go back there so soon?"

"Tore's in town and invited us to be his guests. I couldn't turn down a personal invitation, especially considering he's the one who gave me the seax."

"Oh," she said. "Did you ask him why?"

I nodded. "He represents a group of people doing business in Croy. The knife's meant as a token of their thanks."

Her eyes opened wide. "Did he tell you anything else about them?"

"Other than mentioning we had common interests, no."

"I must admit, I'm intrigued. How do you want me to act?"

"You're accompanying me as my promised and the future queen of Croy to a meeting with a potentially powerful ally," I said. "Act accordingly."

"And if my spion instincts tell me we need to interrogate him?" she asked, crossing her arms.

"How many interrogations did Queen Ines take part in?"

She shrugged. "None, as far as I know."

"Sounds like the exact number of interrogations you should plan to be involved with," I said, pointing at her.

"You're taking all the fun out of it," she said, frowning.

"I suspect you'll find ways to amuse yourself."

"Good to know you still have faith in me," she said. "I'll change into a long sleeve shirt; it's better to look elegant. Puts the target at ease."

I shook my head. "You're letting your past show again."

She smiled, reaching for the bottom of her shirt. "My past made me who I am."

"As has mine," I said, securing the knife to my belt, "but I still know how to behave."

"Have you forgotten?" she asked, before pulling on a long-sleeved, black shirt. "I'm working on being regal."

Chapter 69

Kalfken smiled and bowed low when we entered the pub. "Good to see you again, Sire. Tore told me to escort you to his private dining room."

The few people seated in the great room watched as we followed the host to a door in the far-left corner. He opened it and stepped aside to let us pass.

We entered an elegant dining room, greatly influenced by Varian style, lit by two large chandeliers hanging from a high ceiling. Brightly colored tapestries decorated the walls while a long, intricately crafted table dominated the middle of the room. Matching, dark, wooden chairs with bright, fabric cushions skirted the length of the table with a gold and silver gilded throne at the head.

"Please, take a seat. Would you like something to drink while you wait?" Kalfken asked.

"Tea, for me, please," I said.

"Same," Tindra added.

He nodded. "I will inform the master you have arrived," he said, before closing the door.

"Remind you of home?" I asked, as we sat near the throne.

"I don't mind the colors, and the chairs are comfortable. However, the throne..." Tindra paused and shook her head. "Seems to me someone has a rather high opinion of themselves."

I nodded. "It is a bit much. Tore didn't seem the extravagant sort when I met him earlier."

"Perhaps it's for show. Maybe he normally entertains people easily impressed by such a display."

We turned to the door when it opened. A young woman entered, head bowed, carrying a wooden pitcher and two mugs. With haste and near silence, she served our drinks and left the room.

Before I'd emptied my mug, Tore entered the room. Tindra and I stood as he walked the length of the table. I offered him my hand when he got close.

"I'm glad you accepted my invitation," he said, shaking my hand. "I needed a break from reviewing business records."

Tindra curtsied. "Thank you for inviting us."

Tore frowned. "You were not addressed. Fitzeirick, I thought you said she had served the Varian crown."

"For years," I said. "Is there a prob—"

"Yet she didn't stay quiet until spoken to," he said, interrupting me.

"At no time has a Varian woman been expected to stay silent," Tindra said.

"All cultured women know their place," he said, tapping his foot on the floor. "Perhaps you're not the woman my king believes you to be. Present yourself."

"Excuse me," Tindra said, shifting to a combative posture. "I don't answer to you."

"Tore," I said, crossing my arms. "Watch your tone. You *are* addressing the future queen of Croy."

He nodded. "As a leader among the trade guild, I have the right to judge her worth for myself. It's possible she isn't suited for serving you and the country. Your father presented several women to us before we declared Jani suitable. Eirickson had an eye for women below his stature. Many of us expected we'd have to arrange an acceptable wife for him by now, were he still alive."

"I am *not* my father."

The air cooled as Tindra took a deep breath.

Her hand felt uncomfortably warm when I took it. "And we don't recognize any trade guild in Croy."

"Don't recognize—" Tore sputtered. "Yet you constantly overpay at the market and left your purse in my pub. If that's not a show of support, I don't know what is."

I nodded. "My actions were to support people mistreated by some of my warriors and to help those less fortunate than myself."

"As for coming here...a mistake we won't repeat again," Tindra said.

He glared at her before fixing his eyes on me. "Though I hold Nikulas in high regard, I now believe his opinion of you is wrong. You're trying to buy influence and loyalty. The mark of a desperate, insecure man. A strong, worthy leader would recognize that my status gives me the authority to judge every woman for purpose. How could you not know this tradition? It seems you're not the man I thought you to be."

Tindra squeezed my hand, and the heat coursing through her rose.

"I am my own man," I said, wishing the table and walls were stone. "As king, I pass judgments, and I find you wanting."

He clapped his hands together. "It's clear now. I assumed too much after finding out your mentor took a wife who'd been properly trained."

I glared at him. "You have no idea what you are talking about. Grima was wronged. Roi saved her and Einns."

"Wronged?" He laughed. "You know nothing of her past, do you? You have no idea who fathered her boy."

"It's none of my concern. Roi doesn't care about her past or who her son's father is. He's raising Einns as his own and is proud to do so."

"I should hope he does a better job with that boy than he did with you. Any descendant of Eirick's should know, and honor, *all* the traditions of Croy."

"I've learned some of our traditions aren't worth honoring," I said. "Best if you learn to let go of them too."

"So much you don't know, young king," he said, shaking his head, "and so much I could tell you. Of course, information isn't free."

"Give me the seax. He'll tell us everything we want to know before I'm finished," Tindra said, an angry edge in her voice.

I tossed the sheathed knife onto the table, knocking over the pitcher and spilling tea. "No," I said. "We're leaving—and some gifts aren't worth the cost."

Tore nodded, stepped aside, and swept his arm toward the door. "Of course. You're free to go as you see fit but listen carefully. If you leave, I can make your reign difficult, possibly render it completely ineffective. Stay. Hear me out. We both want a prosperous and powerful Croy."

I looked him in the eye. "You claim to know so much, yet you feel safe threatening me. The last man to do so is dead, along with his supporters. I'm guessing you think you're a man of great power and influence, but you are not so powerful compared to a king."

"You make a point, but not the one you intended. A king is only as powerful as those who support him allow. How will Croy fight without tradesmen? Will your warriors syth their own weapons and armor? You may get along fine without servants or a proper wife, but your army requires food. Who supplies them if the tradesmen don't?"

"That's treason," Tindra said, reaching for the knife.

A hole opened in the table, dropping the knife to the floor. "I'm simply pointing out that power, strength, comes in different forms. Fitzeirick, call your woman to heel. Remind her servants best do their job in silence."

"I am no one's servant," she growled.

Tore shook his head and his lips twisted into a sneer. "You are to be queen which is nothing more than the highest-ranked servant to her king and country. If you do not serve, what use are you...other than decoration."

Tindra's hand struck his face so quickly, I wasn't sure I saw her move. "Consider yourself lucky I'm unarmed."

"Leave the capital as soon as your business is finished," I said, poking him in the chest. "And don't come back."

He stepped back. "Fitzeirick, I'm willing to overlook her behavior once. It's obvious she hasn't been taught civilized behavior. You need me, the support I represent. Send her away. Let's you and I sit, eat, and discuss how to move beyond this impasse. We must work together for Croy's future."

"I'd rather throw myself to the fire than share a table with you," I said, and led Tindra out of the pub.

Chapter 70

"I'm going to find Agrim," I said, as we walked. "You're free to come with me or go home if you'd rather."

"We're safer together," she said. "I've never met another Croian who disrespects women like that."

"Another relic from my father and half-brother."

"And what he said about Grima...who *is* Einns' father?"

I shook my head. "Kurt said he knew, offered to tell me. I turned him down. It's Roi's business, not mine."

"I'll ask Kurt."

"Don't. It's none of my business."

"What if it should be?"

"Why? What is Einns going to do? Can he raise a force against me? Is he going to side with the Satran invaders?"

"Seems unlikely, but—"

"Then it isn't anything I need to be worried about," I growled.

"You need to keep an eye on Tore," she said, after a moment of silence.

"Why do you think I'm looking for Agrim?"

"What's Agrim going to do to keep him from turning the tradesmen against you?"

"Nothing," I said. "I want him to make sure Tore leaves."

Tindra stopped. "Then how are you going to keep him from making good on his threat, assuming he can?"

I smiled. "I'm going to see Kurt after I talk to Agrim."

"Why?"

"To make him Kurt's problem. If his council wants to operate in Croy, I'm going to let him know he has competition. Firmly embedded, powerful competition."

"I thought you didn't want them operating in Croy."

I shrugged. "Better the criminal you know as an ally than the one you've made an enemy."

"I don't know if I should feel proud or concerned," she said, "but the sooner you finish this business, the sooner we eat."

I chuckled, took her hand, and headed for Agrim's house.

No one answered when I knocked on his door.

After pounding on it and yelling for the captain of my guard, Engli rushed out of the barracks. "He's not there, Sire."

"Where is he?"

"He said to send for him at General Jomar's quarters if he's needed."

"Thank you," I said, before turning to Tindra. "Coming?"

"I'm feeling underdressed without my sword."

"I'll go with you and get my hammer. Never know what a man like Tore may try."

"You need to talk with Roi about this," she said, as we left the courtyard. "False rumors can be more powerful than the truth."

"What am I going to say? 'Roi, people want to tell me who Einns' real father is. Is there something I should know about him? Is he a threat?' That would just start another argument. One that might fracture our friendship."

"But Tore said 'any descendant of Eirick's'—"

"He was talking about me," I said, cutting her off.

"Listen," she growled. "What if you're not the last of Eirick's blood?"

I sighed. "Einns is too young to be Eirick's and Eirickson wouldn't leave his son with some woman at The Trader's Cup. My half-brother's vanity wouldn't allow him to let his child live like that." I shook my head. "Besides, Grima isn't telling anyone. Why would Tore's claim have any credibility?"

"We know little about Tore and less about how much influence he has. Kurt claims to know something about the boy too."

"I think Kurt wanted to confuse me, make me question Roi."

"I'm telling you, in my experience, this is something you should talk to—"

"I'm not risking Roi's happiness over a rumor. Especially one from the likes of Kurt or Tore."

"If you can't talk openly with the man you call your mentor and trusted adviser about his wife and her son...what can you talk to him about?"

I shook my finger at her. "I *can* talk to him about anything. I *choose* not to talk to him about this because it's ridiculous, and it's not my problem."

She grabbed my finger. "And if Tore makes it your problem?"

"I'll deal with it should it happen."

"Best if we can keep it from becoming a problem at all. Do you want me to talk to Kurt while you give Agrim his newest assignment?"

"No. If a group of foreign agents are coming to...." I paused, considering my words. "I suppose handle is a good word, this situation for me, then I should be the one asking for their help."

"Understood," she said. "Until I'm queen, I have no reason to request such a thing."

"Even then, I'd trust you to check with me first."

"Of course, my lord," she said, then chuckled.

A flash of lightning caught my eye as I knocked on Jomar's door. Thunder boomed while we waited for an answer. I knocked again as the first raindrops fell.

Jomar opened the door, smelling of ale. "Sire. What an unexpected...surprise. Come in before you get wet."

"Where's Agrim?" I asked, as we stepped inside.

Jomar coughed. "He and I were sharing a drink, discussing the coming war."

"I hope he's not as deep into the drink as you are," I said.

The general scratched his head and pointed down a hallway. "I'm not sure. See for yourself."

Agrim's goofy smile vanished when I walked into the meeting room. He jumped to his feet, swaying for a moment. "Sire. I—I...good to see you this...evening. What brings you? Care to join us?"

"We have a problem," I said. "Tore. I want people watching him until he leaves the capital."

He squinted and ran his fingers through his beard. "You...you were having dinner with him. Was the food that bad?"

Tindra snickered while moving to let Jomar join us.

"I wouldn't know. We never got to eat," I said. "He insulted the queen-to-be and threatened to have the tradesmen cut off our supplies when I demanded an apology."

Agrim muttered something before clearing his throat. "He's loyal to Croy but holds on to old ways. I'm sure he didn't mean anything."

"He wanted Tindra to present herself for his judgment. Claimed being head of the tradesmen's guild gave him the right," I said. "As insulting as *that* was, his threats are all but treason."

Jomar coughed, sat, and drained a mug.

A dull roar filled the room as rain pelted the roof.

Agrim pointed at me. "You said I wouldn't have to spill more Croian blood."

I shook my head. "I'm not telling you to kill him, only to follow him while he's here. I want men watching where he goes, who he talks to...nothing more."

He nodded then grabbed the table to steady himself. "I'll get some...someone on it right away."

"Had I known you were drunk, I'd have given the order myself."

"Not necessary, m'lord. I'm far from too drunk to take care of this." He nodded then swayed. "Consider it done...Sire."

"Do you need us to help you to their barracks?" Tindra asked.

He shook his head and wobbled. "I'll make it."

"Jomar, make sure he does. I have other business to see to. I'll see you in the morning."

"Of course, my king. Travel safe. Sounds like it might be bad outside."

Tindra and I left, hurrying through the pouring rain to Abi's. I didn't see the Varian guard when I knocked on the door.

The door opened quickly. "King Fitzeirick, Lady Tindra," the Varian greeted us. "Well met. Come in out of the rain."

I smiled. "Thank you."

"Abi's cooking. If you head to the kitchen, I'm sure she can make extra for you," he said.

Tindra shrugged when I looked at her.

"Tell her we're eating with Kurt."

She nodded and hurried toward the kitchen.

Looking through Kurt's open door, I saw him sitting at a small table.

"Hope you don't mind dinner company," I said.

"You're not cute enough to be my first choice," he said, with a grin. "Come in anyway."

His eye looked better, still swollen but on the way to recovery. The stitches on his cheek brought emphasis to the angry, red wound they held shut. "Abi taking good care of you?"

He nodded. "She seems concerned about my cheek, though. Says something doesn't look right about the cut."

"No doubt she's already working on a treatment," I said, sitting across from him. "I'll give you something to take your mind off her concern. We have a problem."

"We?" he questioned. Crossing his arms, he tilted his head. "Do tell."

"Ever heard of a Croian man named Tore? Lives near Nikulas' hall."

He shook his head. "Can't say I have."

While I was explaining the situation to him, Tindra and Abi came in with our meal. The aroma coming from the bowls smelled like potatoes.

"Good evening, Sire," Abi said.

I nodded. "Good evening. Sorry for dropping by unannounced."

"You are always welcome, my lord. Enjoy your meal."

"You don't know anything about a tradesmen's guild in Croy?" Kurt asked, after Abi left the room.

"Nothing like Tore claims to control," I said. "Certainly no groups operating in secret."

"You think they're planning to work against you?" he asked.

"We have to consider the possibility," Tindra said.

Kurt looked at her. "Going by what Fitzeirick said, Tindra, I'm surprised this man survived the meeting."

"If he wasn't a woodsyth, he wouldn't be breathing now," she said.

"Regardless," I said, "he's a problem...one I need your expertise in dealing with."

"Are you willing to overlook any questionable occurrences?" Kurt asked.

I nodded. "So long as there's no blood in the streets. I'm trying to improve the situation here. Murder in the open won't help."

"Exactly why I'm not sending for Sabast," he said.

"Good," Tindra muttered.

"However...I am hurting for trustworthy messengers," he said.

"I'll see you get what you need," I said. "Have your message and instructions ready to go at first light."

"Will do," he said. "You understand this will take time. My people will have to do some digging, figure out how this guild operates. I have no problem ordering Tore's death, but I expect a single death won't solve your problem. Honestly, sounds like a great business opportunity...if we play our cards right."

"No blood in the streets," I repeated, pointing at him.

"Discrete." He nodded. "We can do this quietly, but it won't be quick. I'll do my best to make sure the only people who know anything changed are either on our side or dead."

"That's all I ask," I said. "The soup wasn't bad...definitely filling."

"I'd eat it again," Tindra commented.

"I'm sure I'll eat it at least once more before I'm well enough to travel," Kurt said, frowning.

"At least you're around to recover," I said, "it could've been worse."

"I'll never forget the sight of Porsey's family being hacked to death," he said, and shivered.

"I hope it doesn't disturb your sleep. I wasn't sending them to slaughter."

His frown deepened as he shook his head. "I know. Doesn't make it any better."

"I'm done," Tindra said, dropping her spoon into her bowl.

"Me too, and I have another stop before we get home. Thank you again, Kurt. Sleep well."

"I should be thanking you," he said. "After all, you're the one bringing an attractive business opportunity to my attention."

"Take care, Kurt," Tindra said, as we left the room.

We were both dripping wet by the time we reached the compound. I sent Tindra home to dry and get a fire going as I turned to the guard barracks.

Drops of water jumped off my arm as I pounded on the door.

Sigric opened the door. "Sire, come in out of the rain."

"I need Svan or Sibbi," I said, as he closed the door behind me.

"Wait by the fire. I'll get them."

The chill faded by the time the two lieutenants arrived, both wet.

"Sire, what can we do for you?" Svan asked.

"Has Agrim made it here yet?" I asked.

They looked at each other. "Yes," Svan said.

"Good. You have men watching Tore now?"

"Yes," Sibbi said.

"That's all I need to know for now. I need a messenger—someone who will follow directions perfectly. I suspect the ride will end in Varia somewhere."

"Bior," Sibbi said. "It'll give him something to do."

"He's recovered?" I asked.

"Well enough to complain he can't do anything because he hasn't recovered enough to fight," Sibbi replied.

"With the Satran pushed back through the forest, I doubt he'll have to fight anyone. Tell him to be at Abi's no later than first light tomorrow. He's to meet with Kurt for directions. Make it clear to him that he does what he's told to the best of his ability, no questions asked."

Sibbi nodded.

"It is vitally important Kurt's message gets to the right people."

"Understood," he said. "Bior follows orders well."

"I trust he will."

"Anything else, Sire?" Svan asked.

"Nothing I can think of," I said. "Good evening, men."

"Rest well, my lord," Svan said.

Chapter 71

The rain slacked as I entered my home. Ingo and Lopt stood at their post, dripping wet and looking miserable.

Tindra's clothes lay spread on the floor in front of the fireplace and her boots sat nearby, but I didn't see her. Calling her name, she yelled from the bedroom.

I laid my clothes out to dry, left my boots next to hers, and walked to my room. A single candle burned on the small table, giving just enough light to see her in bed, covers pulled up to her chin.

"It's warmer with you in here," she said, smiling.

I smiled back, climbed into bed, and snuggled up to her. The candle went out as we warmed each other.

I woke having trouble breathing. For a moment, I panicked before realizing Tindra's arm rested on my throat. She mumbled something as I carefully moved it and drifted back to sleep. A slamming door woke me next.

Coughing as I sat up, I found Tindra wasn't next to me. In the middle of pulling on pants, the bedroom door opened. Light behind the intruder made it hard to see their face. I pushed my will into the stone floor and forced rock around their feet.

"Let me go!" Tindra shouted. "We have a problem."

I blinked a couple of times and shook my head before releasing her. "What could be wrong this early in the day?"

"Tore has more influence and power than I feared."

"What do you mean?" I asked.

"Hungry?"

Still foggy from waking up, it took a moment to understand what she asked. "Breakfast would be nice. What does that have to do with Tore?"

"Where would you like to eat this morning?"

I'm not going to play this game much longer. "Why are you changing the subject after telling me something's wrong?"

The candle on the table burst into flame. "Britt turned pale and hid when she saw me. Goran was near tears when he asked me to leave. I went to Grith's. He refused to serve me."

"They can't do that," I said. "You're my promised. Refusing you is almost the same as refusing me."

"It's Tore's doing. He made good on his threat. The tradesmen cut off our supplies."

I finished dressing. "That quickly? You can't be sure."

"There is no doubt. Thorgault told me Tore gave the order to deny us, specifically, service."

"They can't refuse service to their king. That's—"

"Treason. What are you going to do? Kill them all?"

I shook my head. "No. They're all decent people, and I...no, I'm not going to harm any of them."

"And Tore knows it. Trust me, they're more scared of him than they are of you."

I sat on the floor and held my head in my hands. "I didn't think Tore would follow through on his threat. And this quickly. I'm trying to get us ready to destroy Satra, and now this. What am I going to do?"

She sat next to me and took my hand. "You answered that question last night. Let Kurt handle this problem while you work on the bigger problem."

"While this secret guild tries to starve us into submission?"

Tindra chuckled. "Roi won't let you starve, and I'm not above stealing a meal if I must."

I looked at her. "The queen-to-be will not steal food."

She shrugged. "It's not my first choice."

"I hope Roi's ready for visitors this morning," I said, getting to my feet.

Our boots squished in the mud as we walked to Roi's. The faint smell of bread, no doubt something Einns cooked for breakfast earlier, hung in the damp air when I knocked on the door.

Roi opened the door and smiled when he saw me. "We weren't expecting you. Come in."

I thanked him as we walked inside.

"Something to drink?" Grima asked, from the wash basin.

"Water would be good," I said.

"Same," Tindra added.

"What brings you?" Roi asked.

"A problem," I said. "And we're looking for something to eat."

He cocked his head and pointed to the table. "Sit. There's a little left from breakfast. It's cold, I'm afraid. Einns is out, gathering things for lunch."

"Anything's better than going hungry," I said.

He brought a tray with half a loaf of bread and a nearly empty pot of sticky, boiled grains. "Why didn't you eat before you came?"

"Like I said, I have a problem. I have nothing to cook at home and no one will sell me or Tindra anything."

"What do you mean?" he asked, placing the tray in front of us.

Tindra grabbed a roll.

I followed her lead and told Roi about the encounter with Tore between bites.

He shook his head. "What he's doing...it's treason. What are you going to do?"

"I'm not executing anyone," I said, "so in the short term, there's not much I can do."

"I won't let you starve," he said.

"I know you won't, but I can't eat every meal here until this is taken care of."

"You two are always welcome in our home," Grima said, sitting next to Roi.

"But I don't want to wear out our welcome. We can eat with my guard or in the warriors' barracks."

"But that doesn't solve the problem forever," Roi said.

"I've got Kurt working on the solution."

"Kurt?" he asked. "Are you sure?"

"Better the criminal you know than the one trying to starve you," I said, grinning. "His people are going to have a presence in Croy—nothing I can do about it except use them to my advantage. Kurt sees this and everything as a business opportunity. He won't abuse people, and he won't let his agents take the fight to the streets. Tore and his people vanish, and their replacements are loyal to Kurt."

"The whole idea doesn't sit right with me."

I shrugged. "What else should I do? Apologize to Tore, ask him to forgive me for not letting him insult my promised? That doesn't make me a king; it makes me his subordinate."

"I've insulted Tindra," Roi said. "What's my punishment?"

"You've given your honest opinion but never treated her like a cut of meat to be inspected. You've never treated her like a lowly servant to be judged for purpose," I replied then smiled. "Your punishment is to sign our marriage agreement."

His expression went neutral. "Maybe you should kill me now."

I couldn't keep my eyes from widening.

He laughed. "I'll sign but with verbal protest."

Grima snickered before I chuckled at his joke.

"Your protest is, and will be, appropriately noted," I said, grinning.

"Good to know you still listen to me," he replied, after catching his breath. "What are your plans for the rest of the day?"

"We need to work your shoulder," Tindra said.

"I guess I'm going to get some exercise," I said. "But I'd like to get an update on Tore at some point."

"Want me to look into it?" Roi asked.

"Not right now," I said. "I don't know how deep Tore's resentment runs. The last thing you need is him deciding to cut you off too."

"Fine, but it won't hurt to keep my ears open. Never know who might talk."

I nodded. "True, but don't contact him."

"As you wish."

"Tindra, we best get going. I want to talk to Agrim before we train."

Chapter 72

We left and made our way to the compound. Tindra headed to get her sword while I knocked on Agrim's door.

"He's not there," Kodren said, when he walked out of the barracks.

"Where is he?"

"At the training grounds, working with new recruits from the south," he said.

"That's where I'll go next. Thank you."

"Of course, Sire," he said, and left the compound.

I hurried into my quarters and grabbed the sling for my hammer.

"Where are you going?" Tindra asked, as I buckled the straps.

"Agrim's on the training grounds."

"Oh. In that case, I'll get my belt."

After the familiar click of the magnets in the sling fixing the metal-cased stone hammer to my back, the weight brought a feeling of comfort. "Ready?" I asked.

Tindra drew her sword about halfway out of the scabbard, pushed it back in, and shifted her belt a little. After another half-draw, she nodded. "Let's go."

Considering the amount I figured he drank the night before, Agrim looked none the worse for it as he led about a dozen recruits through spear fighting.

We walked behind him, and I asked, "Have room for us?"

He flinched and turned, nearly tripping over his feet. "Sire, I...of course, but I doubt you two need these lessons."

"We don't," I said, "but I need to work my shoulder so I'm ready to fight if necessary."

"Sire, with all due respect, I hope that day never comes."

I nodded. "I'm not looking forward to it, but better to be ready and not needed than needed and not ready."

"You're welcome to stay, if you like, m'lord. Maybe work behind these men so you're not a distraction," he said.

"We can do that," I said.

Agrim turned back to the group. "High thrust! Make your king proud."

We moved to the back of the group, and Tindra led me in stretches and movements to work my shoulders. Other than occasional odd pulls and an annoying tightness around the healed wound, I felt good.

We worked up quite a sweat by the time Agrim called the lunch break and led us to the warrior mess hall. After instructing the new men on the process of getting food, he noticed us standing in line. "I didn't expect you to eat with us."

"Why wouldn't we eat with them...well, you, specifically," I said. "I need to know about a certain situation."

"We'll have more privacy in the general's hall."

"I don't mind eating with my men," I said, "but this is a sensitive conversation. Let's go."

Entering the general's hall, we received sandwiches and bowls of hot stew, then sat at a table in the corner.

"From what I know, Tore hasn't left his pub since I sent men to watch him."

"Did he have any visitors?" I asked.

"No way to know for sure."

"Going by what I found out this morning, either he left or had visitors," I said.

"Thought you were leaving this to my men."

"I am, but when one goes to buy breakfast and none of the shops will sell them food..." I shrugged. "Questions get asked."

"You were refused service at his order?"

"I was," Tindra said.

"That's treason, Sire. What are you going to do?"

"Openly? Nothing," I said. "I have moves being made, but they're going to take time. Until the local tradesmen see fit to serve me again, we're eating here, in the warrior's mess, or at Roi's."

"Or in my home or with the guard. You're more than welcome. Does this change anything for those watching him?"

I shook my head. "Their order stands. When he steps out of his pub, the only path he follows takes him outside the wall, and he doesn't come back in."

"I'm sure we'd have no trouble dragging him out of The Sneaky Bear, Sire," Agrim said.

"As much as I'd like that, I'm afraid it would send the wrong message. People feared Eirickson; I want them to respect me."

"Understood."

"Now, you spent time with Jomar yesterday. Do you know if the scouts left and, if not, when they will?" I asked.

"They leave at first light tomorrow. Jomar decided to delay them to give the Varian soldiers time to get in position."

"He's probably right," I said, "but I need another messenger now. Also, we need to plan a supply caravan for the Varians. They'll run low sooner or later."

"Where do you need a message delivered?"

"First to The Trader's Cup, then to the warriors we left in the southeast. The scouts were supposed to tell the refugees they could return home. A messenger can do it and tell the warriors they can return once the people are settled."

Agrim nodded. "I'll send a messenger for you as soon as possible. How many wagons for the caravan?"

"Won't know how many wagons we'll need until we see what supplies we can gather...assuming the Tore problem doesn't get worse."

"And if it does?"

"If he forces my hand, he'll join my half-brother at the bottom of a hole I'd rather not reopen."

"Speaking of unpleasant activities," Agrim said, "it's time to get the recruits moving. Are you two going to join the run?"

Tindra shrugged when I looked at her.

I chuckled. "Why not? Running with the Varian soldiers got me ready for battle."

Much like my runs in the Varian capital, I kept to the back of the pack while she set the pace.

After one trip around the city, we returned to the training grounds. Agrim instructed the recruits on how to clean and maintain armor, a subject Tindra and I knew plenty about, so we left the group to bathe before finding some dinner.

"At least Tore can't keep us from bathing," Tindra said, as we left the public bathhouse.

"True," I said. "Hard to—"

"Sire," someone called out, ahead of us.

Tindra wrapped her hand around her sword as I looked for whoever wanted my attention.

Chapter 73

A raised hand waved, and again, someone called for me.

I pushed my way through the crowd, hauling Tindra behind me until we reached a short, thin young man. "What can I do for you?"

"Captain Agrim sent me to find you, said you needed a messenger."

"I do. Come with us."

"It will be my pleasure, Sire," he said.

"I'm going to talk to Thorgault some more, if you don't mind," Tindra said.

"Don't cause more trouble."

"When have I ever caused more trouble?" she replied. "That you know of at least."

I shook my head as she smiled at me and walked away. *Occasionally, she's not cute enough for her potential to give me a headache.*

We hurried to my meeting room, and I wrote three notes. A quick apology and thank you to Geri, the message to be spread among the displaced families, and orders for the warrior's return. After sealing them, I gave the messenger clear instructions.

"I will see these are delivered as quickly as possible," he said, before bowing.

"Travel swift and safe. I doubt you'll run into any Satran but keep your eyes open."

"Of course," he said, and left.

I heard someone shouting outside as I went to get some water. Hurrying to the door, I recognized the voice.

"...all the stubborn, stone-headed, cowardly... He was paid long before this nonsense," Tindra ranted.

Stepping outside, both guards were staring at her, nodding.

"If he had a backbone, he'd stand up to—"

"Tindra," I said. "Calm yourself. I think you're scaring my guards. What are you talking about?"

She growled. "I'll tell you inside."

Heading straight for a drink of water, she sighed after draining a mug. "Thorgault's finished your armor, but he wouldn't give it to me because of Tore."

"Is that why you went to talk to him?"

She nodded. "He'd nearly finished the last time I saw him. I wanted to surprise you. Plus, I wanted to make sure you were comfortable wearing it before you decide to ride off into battle."

I hugged her. "I'm not leaving tomorrow, and this will all get sorted." I kissed the top of her head. "Don't worry. I won't go to battle without armor. I'm not chomping at the bit to fight, but it's nice to know you care."

She hugged me tighter before stepping back. Grabbing my beard, she pulled my face to hers. "Of course I care. I risked my life, promised Crum my family's lives, for you. I don't want to think about what I'd be doing if I hadn't taken your side."

"I haven't forgotten what you've done, but I also haven't forgotten you've always seen me as a way out. Regardless, it's nice to hear you say you care."

"If you don't know by now that you mean more than a way out to me, we're going to have trouble," she said. "How do I know you care about me?"

"I've argued with Roi, several times, defending you when he says you're bad for me. You live in my home, share my bed. Think back to how I kept you away in Varia. I believe my actions speak for themselves."

"I can appreciate actions," she said, "but words are nice too from time to time."

I hugged her again. "I care about you. I'm glad to have you in my life and as my promised. I'll be proud to have you as my queen when the day comes."

"I'm being patient, but as you said, Croy needs a queen. Will we marry before you take the battlefield?"

"It won't be safe for your parents to travel while Satra holds land near the central forest. They certainly can't travel from the pass in the far east."

"I'm willing to sacrifice their presence if necessary."

"And I can't justify or plan a proper ceremony and celebration while preparing for war." I paused and laughed as a thought crossed my mind. "Right now, I can't get anyone to sell me food or drink anyway."

She shook her head and sat at the table. "So, I am to continue being the queen-to-be until Kurt's people fix this whole Tore situation? Or until you've conquered the twice-conquered lands a third time? All the while, if you die, who takes the throne?"

"I'd prefer if Roi took my place, should I die."

"But you have nothing making his claim to the throne official."

"Ruling's been much more difficult than I expected."

Tindra laughed.

"I wasn't trying to be funny."

She nodded. "I know, but ruling isn't supposed to be easy."

"It was when I was only a skald."

"You had little responsibility then. Now, you're the head of the entire country. But we're getting off the important subject. You need to make some proclamations."

"I guess we're eating with Roi this evening. He'll help me figure out the best way to handle this problem."

"Roi, twice in one day...such fun for me," Tindra said, through a forced smile.

"Protest too much and he might not sign our marriage agreement."

"I can be diplomatic," she said.

"From your display outside, I wonder if you've forgotten what that word means," I said.

Crossing her arms, she glared at me. "I was nothing less than courteous to Thorgault. Didn't let my temper flare until I reached our courtyard."

"Best to keep a smile on your face while we're in public," I said, holding my hand out for her. "No reason to let Tore know he's causing us any real difficulty."

"I agree," she said, taking my hand. "Let's go bathe then enjoy dinner with friends."

• • • **•** • **•** • • •

Grima opened the door as we approached, and the familiar smell of Einns' cooking poured out. "I had a feeling we'd see you again today," she said, smiling. "Come in, sit. Dinner will be ready soon."

"I really hate to be a burden," I said.

She shook her head. "You could never be a burden. Besides, I haven't made any friends since we arrived. It's nice to have company."

"It's tough being a woman with power," Tindra said, as we took our seats at the table. "As the wife of King Fitzeirick's top adviser, people are either scared of you or they'll try to manipulate you."

She shook her head. "No one's close enough to me to worry about. Haven't made any friends since returning to Croy. Besides, my sewing keeps me busy. Plus I have a son to raise, a husband to care for, and a home to look after. Those mean more to me than any power I may have because of my marriage."

"Trust me," Tindra said. "Once this war is over, your life will change."

I took Tindra's hand. "Let's not put the cart in front of the horse. No one's going to force Grima's involvement in court matters."

"And if they try, I'll refuse. I want no part of such business," she said, putting her hands on her hips.

Tindra squeezed my hand.

"Let me know if anyone bothers you. I'll make sure they know to leave you alone ...assuming Roi doesn't make it clear first," I said, before looking around the room. "Where is he?"

"Out," she said, "seeing to something. He'll be back before long. He never misses a meal."

"Something he and I have in common," I said, as the door opened.

"I thought I heard a familiar voice," Roi said, closing the door. "Still can't find anyplace else to eat?" He hurried to the table and kissed Grima.

"Einns' cooking will always be my first choice," I said.

"Agreed," Tindra added.

"Good," Roi said, "because I'd hate to think you only visit when it's official business."

"Well...there is another reason I'm here," I said. "But you and I can discuss my concerns after we eat."

"Sounds good," Roi said, before turning toward Einns. "Unless I miss my guess, he's putting the finishing touches on the meal now."

Grima's son looked our way and gave a wide, childish grin.

I studied his face as he walked toward the table. *No doubt he's Croian, but does he resemble anyone I know? He has Grima's hair and eyes. Nothing remarkable about his nose. Strong chin but all that means is his father could be one of thousands of men. I doubt he's my father's last son. I see no reason to worry.*

He placed a covered pot to the table. "Let it sit while I get bowls and spoons."

"Milk or water?" Grima asked.

"We should finish the jug of milk before it sours," Einns said.

"Milk it is," she said, "unless someone wants water."

He lifted the lid with a flourish, spreading the steam across the table. It carried a sweet, spicy, earthy scent and made my mouth water. One by one, he filled each bowl with a thick, brown stew. I noticed pieces of potato, carrot, and dark, red beet mixed with some meat each time he emptied the ladle.

Grima set a mug of milk next to each bowl.

"Enjoy," Einns said, as he sat.

I stirred the thick broth, enjoying the smell drifting up from the bowl, before scooping a heaping spoonful into my mouth. The beets had their typical sweet taste, but it mixed with a peppery spice and the flavor of goat and rabbit. A carrot crunched between my teeth, adding its mild sweetness to the mix. As I chewed, chunks of potato released bursts of spice they had soaked up. The warm, creamy milk eased the burn while adding a new flavor to the mix. "Einns, I need to find new words to tell you how good this is."

"Hmmm," Tindra grunted, as she nodded.

Grima smiled and patted him on the head. "I never thought my boy would cook for a king."

"I'll let him lay out the kitchen in my castle if I ever get one built," I said, before taking another bite.

"Thank you, sir," Einns blurted out, wide-eyed.

"You will, in due time," Roi said, before chuckling and patting his son on the shoulder.

"The bedroom and bath are mine to lay out," Tindra said.

"No argument from me," I replied, before Roi could say anything. "Grima is there an area you'd like to oversee?"

She looked at me and blinked several times. "Will Roi and I have to live there?"

"Live there? No," I said. "But you're more than welcome to stay as much as you'd like. Maybe think about how you'd like your guest quarters to look."

"Roi and I will talk about it," she said, smiling weakly.

"Roi, what part will you play?" I asked.

He smiled. "Someone has to follow you and fix your mistakes."

Tindra snickered.

I nodded. "You've been doing it all my life. Why change now?"

Even Einns laughed.

I eyed him for a moment then joined the group. *If I can't laugh at myself, I shouldn't laugh at anyone.*

Chapter 74

By the time everyone had their fill, the milk was gone along with most of the stew.

Roi stretched his arms over his head and groaned, "I ate too much."

"We still have business to discuss," I said. "Don't fall asleep on me."

"I have no interest in your business," Grima said, "I'll help Einns clean this mess."

"If you don't mind, I'll help too...as much as I can, anyway," Tindra said.

"We'd enjoy your company, Lady Tindra," Einns said, lifting the pot.

Roi belched as they left the table. "What business do we need to go over?"

"Tindra and I were discussing who should lead Croy if I die?"

He looked at me, opened and closed his mouth a couple of times, and blurted, "What?"

I shook my head. "Right now, I have no queen, no heir, so who leads if I fall?"

He shrugged. "I'd advise you to not go fight."

"For all I know, I still have enemies inside our borders. Also, it's possible I can't lead a battle from inside these walls."

"Trust your guard and our generals."

I nodded. "I do, but what would the warriors think if I send them out to fight and don't involve myself?"

"The smart ones would realize you are a wise leader, ensuring the stability of Croy."

"I want the men fighting for me, for Croy, to know I'm willing to risk my life alongside them to win...to make my country and Varia safe."

Roi put his head in his hands, and muttered, "Why am I your favored adviser when you don't listen to me?"

"I always listen to you, but I don't always agree with what you have to say."

"The outcome doesn't change," he said, shaking his head. "Back on subject, are you asking me who I think should be designated to wear the crown should you fall?"

"Not exactly, but close enough. What's your thought?"

"Look to our generals. Goodman has served Croy the longest. He's used to leading people," he said.

"They are used to leading warriors ... men trained to follow orders.

"How is that different than your expectations as king?" he countered.

"A king needs to have more understanding and compassion. Which is why I had someone else in mind as first choice."

"Not Tindra," he muttered, crossing his arms.

"No...at least not until we're married."

"Who?" he asked.

"You."

Roi's eyes flew open. "What makes you think—No, I'm not the right person to rule in your place. I'm no leader of men."

"How can you say such a thing? Without your guidance, I wouldn't be who I am today."

"Exactly my point. I'm an adviser, a mentor. That doesn't make me a good choice to lead a nation."

"Why not? You're wise, stone steady, and you love this country and our people as much as I do. We share a similar vision for its future. You know Crum and..." I stopped, pausing to choose my words carefully, "you two can work together...maybe not well, all the time, but better than two people who don't know each other at all."

He rolled his eyes. "When you put it that way, how could anyone turn down such an attractive offer? I even get to work with Crum." His sarcastic tone grew deeper. "A man who threw his morals to the fire so long ago he can't even find the ashes." He laughed. "I still can't believe he's ruling Varia. Always figured we'd find him dead, in some alley, with a jealous man's knife in his—"

"He's different. He found the woman to fill the hole in his heart," I said, tapping my finger on my chest. "Think about Crum. When would he ever pass up a chance to entertain a new group of people? He didn't darken a single tavern door in Varia. Searching for me, learning to love Jesca, he grew up."

Tindra and Grima came to the table. "I hate to interrupt," Tindra said, "but I need some air, and Grima offered to join me. We shouldn't be long."

I nodded. "Be safe."

"Of course," Tindra said.

Grima kissed Roi, and said, "Einns is going to finish cleaning and go to bed," before they headed outside.

"Now, I'll write the proclamation. Your name won't be the only one given as a successor. The general's names will follow in order of service. After you, the generals, and Agrim sign, it will be official."

"Once this is in place, you'll use it as an excuse to rush off into battle," he said.

"I don't want to fight. This simply provides for a stable Croy should I die of any cause before I marry. Once the marriage is official, the queen rules in the event I die."

"And when she dies?"

"If we have no heir, it falls back to you," I replied, smiling.

"Fine. I'll accept the responsibility," he said, frowning. "Are we through planning for your death?

"We are," I said. "Now to the second subject of potential contention—my wedding."

"I don't trust her." He glared at me. "What do you see in her?"

"She challenges me. She's smart, observant, and dedicated. She has enough experience in Varia's royal court to know how to watch my back and notice even the most subtle attempt to manipulate me. She's trying to better herself and scared she can't."

"But she's not Aesa."

I chuckled. "No, she isn't. As much as I loved Aesa and miss her still, I don't want Tindra to be her. She'll never replace Aesa in my heart or memories. On the other hand, I'm not sure Aesa could rule the entire nation at my side."

"I hear you saying you think Tindra's the right woman to be your queen, but I've never heard you say you love her."

I shook my head. "Not like I did Aesa. Tindra and I, we had...to call it a rocky start is an understatement. Now, we're good for each other."

"Good for each other is not a reason to marry."

I nodded. "As I've said before, people have married for worse reasons. In this case, I also have to plan for the future of Croy."

"What does she have to do with Croy's future?"

"I've destroyed the old court structure," I said. "The queen will help build a new court over time. Any Croian woman I married would choose advisers, ladies, and servants from their families, friends, or in exchange for favors. Tindra's choices will be based on merit. We'll build a stronger government with far less corruption than before."

"You have an admirable goal, but surely there are other, less tainted, choices for a wife and queen."

"Now, who isn't listening?" I said, smiling. "Even if I wanted to select a different queen, I can't deal with a line of women fighting for my attention, scheming against each other, while running a war. Tindra knows when to help and when to let me be. You don't know it, but she cares what you think of her."

"Of course she does. If I like her, it makes it easier for her to manipulate you."

"No, she doesn't want to damage the relationship you and I have. She understands how much I value your guidance and support. Get to know her, not the idea you have of her." Shaking my head, I closed my eyes for a moment. "Especially since Tindra and Grima need to be seen together."

"Why?"

"You're my adviser, my closest ally and confidant. Our wives need to be comfortable around each other. Grima even said she hasn't made any friends since coming here. Tindra can be her friend. Even if you don't trust her, you do trust your wife."

The door slammed open.

Agrim rushed in with Tindra and Grima close behind.

After a deep breath, he said, "Sire, I'm sorry for disturbing you but...we don't know where Tore is."

Orn and Vald hurried in as he spoke.

I stood, blinking as the words took hold in my mind. "What do you mean?"

The guards bowed before Orn spoke. "Sire, it's our fault. We were watching his pub, the last place anyone had seen him. One of the serving girls walked out and gave us food along with word that Tore had left."

"And you believed her?" I asked.

"Of course not, Sire," he replied. "We searched the building, every dusty cranny. The entire time Kalfken followed us, insisting Tore was gone."

"You should have seen the look on his face when I threatened to have the entire guard come tear The Sneaky Bear apart," Vald said.

I rubbed my forehead. "Agrim, you will visit the gates, personally and see if Tore left. Until we know, beyond any doubt, that he's gone, I want every able warrior searching the city. If they can walk, they can look."

He bowed. "Understood, m'lord."

"And Agrim," I said.

"Yes?"

"I am *not* happy."

He bowed again, lower. "As I expected, my lord. All I ask is you not take it out on my men. This is my responsibility. I failed."

"We'll talk later."

"Yes, Sire," he said, and left, taking Orn and Vald with him.

"What are you going to do to him?" Grima asked.

I smiled. "I haven't decided yet, but nothing severe. Until he learns of his fate, his fear will likely be a worse punishment. If it motivates him to prove he's worthy of his title, so much the better."

Roi clapped. "Well played, Fitzeirick."

I gave him a single nod. "Thank you."

Tindra yawned. "Enough excitement for me. I think I'm ready for bed."

"In that case," I said, "Grima, thank you again for the hospitality. Roi, I plan to write the decree tomorrow. Thank you for your support."

Grima took Roi's hand. "Fitzeirick, I can't thank you enough for what you've done for us. It's comforting to know you're a better man than your father."

I cocked my head, trying to understand what she meant.

Tindra took my hand and pulled me toward the door. "Goodnight. Sleep well."

Knowing Tore had evaded my guards, I pushed my talent into the ground to watch for anyone following us.

Tindra led me inside, closed the door, and squeezed my hand. "Grima doesn't want to be involved in court matters because of her history. You're not the last of Eirick's blood. Einns *is* Eirickson's son."

Ice flowed through my body, gathering into a ball in my stomach.

She squeezed my hand. "I didn't ask, I swear."

I sighed and shook my head. "You expect me to believe Grima simply blurted out his father's name?"

"No," she said. "We were talking as we walked. I decided to tell her people were claiming to know who Einns' father was. I didn't want a rumor to catch her off guard."

"Fine, you didn't ask, but you started the conversation...after I told you not to concern yourself."

"To protect her and her son, yes. I know what rumors can do to people. She asked if you knew. I said you didn't want to know because you felt it wasn't your concern. Then she told me Eirickson was his father."

"How is that possible?" I asked. "Geri told us Olver left them with him to settle a debt."

"A lie repeated until it's accepted as truth."

"It doesn't make any sense," I said, shaking my head again. "Eirickson sent his son with some woman to Geri's to cover up...what?"

"Not some woman. A servant girl who caught his eye...Grima. Eirick had no problem with his son using her for his pleasure but ordered her killed as soon as he heard she was with child. Your half-brother paid Olver to kill her. He couldn't bring himself to murder an innocent mother. Instead, he took the coin and hid her."

"And he picked The Trader's Cup, an inn no more than a day's ride from the capital, as the best hiding place?" I asked, then added, "Of course, knowing him, it *was* the best idea he had."

Tindra chuckled. "He knew Geri would keep her hidden...safe. Probably helped that he gave Geri half of the money."

"Assuming this is true," I said, "and I'm not admitting I believe it, does Einns know?"

"No, and Grima doesn't want him to...ever."

"Eirickson didn't know he had a son." *Not sure if that makes me feel sorry for him or not.*

"Grima said she never saw him again."

I sighed and shook my head. "Why would she tell you all this?"

"Roi told her about me, what I am—was. Maybe she decided I could be trusted to keep secrets. Maybe the secret became a burden for her, and she figured a shared burden was easier to bear." Tindra hugged me as I closed my eyes and rubbed my forehead. "She let me tell you because you need to know. He *is* your blood, your family."

"And family helps family," I said, nodding.

"Considering your father and half-brother, you must have learned that from your mother," she said, before laughing.

"I'm better than them. I have to do something for him."

"You're already planning to make him head cook. He'll lead a better life because of you."

"Is that right for my...half-nephew?" I shook my head to clear the confusion. "My blood to serve me?"

"He doesn't know. It's his mother's wish that he never does."

"The more I think about this, the more I chance a headache," I said. "I'm going to bed."

She stepped back and smiled. "Go ahead. I'll join you soon."

All things considered, I'm not going to ask what she's going to do before coming to bed.

Chapter 75

A loud banging woke me.

I bolted from bed and reached for my hammer.

"Who's beating on the door?" Tindra asked.

"Don't know. But I'm going to find out."

After another set of hard knocks, I opened the door to find Haf standing near the door with Svan behind him, holding Thorgault at sword point.

"Sorry, Sire," Haf said. "The tanner insisted on delivering a message in person."

Squinting against the bright sunlight, I asked, "Is he armed?"

"No, Sire," Haf said.

"Then there's no need for weapons. I'm sure he means no harm. Let him talk."

Svan put his sword away, grabbed Thorgault's arm, and led him to me.

"Sorry ta bother ya, m'lord. I didn't wanna. Tore insisted."

"Where's Tore?" I asked.

He offered me a folded parchment. "Dunno. Said ta bring this and left."

I took the message and opened it.

> *Rest assured, by the time you read this, I will be well on the way home. I hope my people didn't inconvenience you too much. I've left orders for things to return to normal, for now. Remember what I can do. I'll send for you when I return and, hopefully, we can reach an agreement benefiting both of us.*

"So, Tore's gone?" I asked, looking back at Thorgault.

"Can't swear ta it."

What isn't he telling me? "Thorgault, come inside, and let's talk for a moment."

Shuffling his feet, he looked down. "If I hafta."

I stepped toward him and extended my hand. "On my honor, I'm not going to hurt you. I still have questions, and we should be comfortable while we talk."

His calloused hand engulfed mine, gripping it tight with a firm shake. "I'll sit wit ya, m'lord. Talk all ya want. But I don't know much else."

"Svan, tell Agrim to come see me after Thorgault leaves and don't speak a word of what he said."

He nodded. "With all haste."

"Kind tanner, follow me please."

"Course, m'lord."

I closed the door and turned to see Tindra drinking from a cup. She raised an eyebrow.

"I'll explain later," I said, shaking my head.

Thorgault greeted her before we entered my meeting room.

"Thirsty?" I asked, as he took the nearest seat.

He shook his head.

Pressing my lips together tightly, I considered the best question to start with. "Why do you listen to Tore?"

"I got people ta take care of...and Tore knows it."

"He threatened you?"

"Not a threat when ya know he'll do it."

Maybe I should tell Kurt to make it messy. "Why didn't you come to me? Remember what I did when I found out about Vegar."

"I do, but..." He shook his head. "Don't take me wrong, ma king, yur nice and all but ..." He closed his eyes.

"But what?" I demanded.

"Ya can't be everywhere. Tore knows how to hurt us."

"Thorgault, look at me."

Raising his head, he shivered when our eyes met.

"I have men to take care of this sort of problem," I said, pointing toward my guard's barracks. "We can protect you like you did for Fastan. But I can't help you, or anyone, if I don't know there's a problem."

"Ya got men, but Tore's got more, and they're everywhere. Yurs are here, but Fastan's alone. She can't risk comin to ya. Mosta mine live near Nikulas. Guild's got lotsa folks there. Do ya have anyone there, ma king?"

"Officially? You're right; I would have to send men there."

"So, we couldn't take tha chance."

"I understand," I said, smiling and nodding. "Before you go, when can I get my armor?"

"Tore said ta treat ya like I used ta."

"I'll be by sometime before lunch. You're free to go."

He stood and bowed. "Thank ya, m'lord. Didn't wanna treat ya that way. Ya been more than fair ta us."

I nodded. "I have no quarrel with you or them. Understand, I'm not happy about what you did, but I can't fault anyone for doing what they must to survive. But if something like this happens again ... tell me, so I can help. If not, I may not be so forgiving."

"I'll do ma best, m'lord. I'll make sure tha armor's ready ta go soon as I get back ta ma shop."

"Be on your way then," I said, following him out of the room.

"Water?" Tindra asked, offering me a cup after the door closed.

I drank it dry in one long gulp. "Thank you for leaving us alone. I'm not sure he would have talked otherwise. Either way, it's going to be an interesting morning."

"More bad news?"

"Not as such," I said. "Thorgault said I can come get my armor."

She raised an eyebrow.

"Tore left sometime this morning."

Taking a seat at the table, she scratched her head. "Without being noticed? How?"

"That's what I intend to find out."

It took longer than I expected before someone knocked on my door again.

Opening it quickly, I saw Agrim standing, eyes cast down, holding a basket. "Sorry for the delay, Sire. I wanted to bring breakfast."

"Breakfast...very thoughtful. Come in. Today brings new challenges."

"We stand ready to do your bidding," he said, hurrying past me to the table.

Tindra reached inside the basket and pulled out a roll about the size of my fist. Taking a bite, she smiled.

I sat and quickly ate a roll. "You can stop searching for Tore."

"What happened?" he asked.

"According to Thorgault, our quarry left around first light."

"With us searching for him?" he asked, running his fingers through his beard. "That's not possible."

"He gave Thorgault a letter to pass on and permission to provide service to me again before he left. Since the good tanner is terrified of Tore, I believe he's telling the truth."

"Why would anyone be afraid of Tore?" Agrim asked, cocking his head.

"Seems the guild master has no problem harming innocent people to get his way. What would you do to keep those you care about safe?"

Agrim shook his head. "That's worse than anything Vegar did. Why aren't we hunting this guy?"

"I have someone working on the problem already. I need you to concentrate your efforts on a different problem. Tore met with him and left the city undetected."

"I don't understand how, Sire," Agrim said.

Tindra went to get more water as I tapped my finger on the table. "And it's your job to find out. Does Tore have allies among my warriors...men who would look the other way as he moved about? If not, we must find any hidden ways to move about or enter and leave this city."

"We will search with all haste, m'lord," he said.

"To the fire with haste. I want answers, accurate answers."

"Yes, of course, my king. May I leave to get started?"

"The sooner, the better," I said. "Keep me up to date with your findings."

"You will hear from me as soon as I know."

"Thank you again for breakfast," Tindra said, as he left the room.

"Pleasure to be of service, my lady," he replied, and left.

After a long drink, I ate another roll before resting my head on the table. "How am I going to fight a war when people we're watching can move around, come and go, as they please? The security of the capital is vital to our victory."

"Thus, the Varian crown has had spions for generations."

"I have no desire to have spions and no time to recruit them if I did."

"If only you knew someone who could take care of recruiting for you," she said, tapping a finger on her chin.

"I'm sure you'd do a fine job, but I don't want to rule that way."

"You didn't want Kurt to have a presence in Croy, but you've found him a necessary ally. Better to have the resources you need, even if you use them sparingly."

"I'll consider your offer after I've had time to better gather my thoughts."

"Willing to listen to another suggestion?"

"I'll listen. Might not agree."

"Working up a sweat often does a fine job of clearing a troubled mind. You have new armor waiting. It needs breaking in before you do something stone-headed like riding off into battle. Go get it while I change into mine, and we'll train together."

"I can't argue with your thinking. Training would give me something different to think about anyway," I said, and left for Thorgault's shop.

The big tanner greeted me and apologized again for causing so much trouble. After explaining, again, that Tore bore all the blame, I assured Thorgault he had my forgiveness.

My dark armor went on easy and fit well after a minor adjustment to the helmet. I bid him farewell, returning home and wondering what Tindra had planned for me.

The longer I walked, the heavier the armor felt and the hotter I got. By the time I reached the courtyard, sweat stung my eyes.

Chapter 76

Tindra moved in a circle, fighting attackers I couldn't see, and stopped when she noticed me watching. "You look terrible."

"Armor's heavy and hot," I said.

"Take the helmet off. I'll get you some water."

The helmet took my hair with it as I lifted it off my head. The wet mass slapped the back of my neck after falling free of the leather. Wiping my forehead did little to stem the flow of stinging sweat.

"Here," Tindra said, handing me a mug.

Emptying it in one long drink, I handed it back. "More."

She nodded and walked back into the house, returning with a pitcher.

It felt like I drank half the pitcher before pouring the rest over my head. "I haven't done anything but walk in this, and I already need to bathe."

"You need to cut your hair. A shave wouldn't hurt either."

"You've never complained about my hair or beard before."

"And I'm not complaining now...you are."

"I wouldn't say—"

"You walked into the courtyard, drowning in sweat, and swallowed more water in two drinks than I have in two days. If you're not complaining, you should be."

"You insisted I needed a helmet."

"Considering the number of times you've taken blows to the head in the past year or so. It could save your life."

"You would know," I said. "Seeing as you were the last one to knock me out."

She nodded. "And if I'd been sent to kill you, we wouldn't be having this conversation."

"Fine," I said. "I'll get my hair cut and shave."

"I can get the shears and take care of it," Tindra said. "If you'll let me."

"Why not?"

She smiled. "Pull yourself a seat from the ground and take off the top of your armor. I'll be right back."

I watched her leave then fought the stiff leather top to free myself before sything a simple seat in the shade.

Tindra returned, whistling an odd tune. "Ready?"

I shrugged. "Sure. What have I got to lose?"

She stepped behind me and chuckled. "Some skin, maybe an ear if I'm not careful."

"You know exactly what to say to make me question my own judgment."

She laughed and grabbed the hair on the back of my head. After a slight tug, I heard the distinct metallic sound of the shear's blades grinding against each other.

Cool air tickled the back of my neck, bringing welcome relief from the heat.

"Hold still while I trim around your ears," she said.

The grinding sound grew louder with every snip, and I clenched my jaw to keep from flinching.

"Much better," she said, and stepped in front of me. "Close your eyes."

"Why?" I asked, trying to ignore the strange feeling of air on my bare ears.

"Don't want to get loose hair in your eyes."

"Oh," I said, before forcing my eyelids together tightly.

"Relax," she said. "There's nothing to be afraid of."

I let some tension out of my cheeks but held my eyes shut as tight as I could. After several cuts, she said, "Keep them closed. I'm going to work on your beard...who knows how much hair will fly."

"Wonderful," I mumbled.

Bracing for the cold tickle of metal against my skin, I focused on her humming as she tugged and snipped.

If felt like most of the day had passed by the time she said, "I think that's about the best I can do."

Even without touching my face, I could tell it wasn't bare. She left about a finger's width of beard along my chin. "I thought you'd shave me clean."

"I'd considered it, but I decided it would make you look like a child, and I didn't want to deal with your brand. This style looks good on you and should be more comfortable when you're wearing the helmet. Give it a try."

The helmet easily slid onto my head, but now I felt the leather against the back of my neck. "It'll take some getting used to."

"Put the top back on and be ready to work when I get back," she said, leaving to return the shears.

I should have guessed the armor wouldn't go on over the helmet, but I tried anyway and amused the guards watching nearby. After fighting back into the armor, I put the helmet on and got my hammer from inside. Everything settled into place before Tindra returned.

"Feel better?" she asked.

"Don't know yet...won't be sure until after I've moved around a bit."

"We'll start with some stretches," she said. "Heft your hammer and follow my lead."

We moved through a long series of movements, and I fought the stiff leather to keep pace with her. Sweat trickled down the side of my face when she looked at me and smiled. "Remember how to block?"

"I don't think—"

She let loose a scream and came at me, swinging wildly.

I knocked a blow away and stepped back.

"Don't think!" she yelled. "You react too slow when you think." Another battle cry, followed by two quick thrusts, then she hit me hard in the chest. "Be happy the plate is there to protect you."

"I'm a little out of practice."

"Not my fault," she said, "and an enemy won't care."

I'd trained with her enough to anticipate the slash aimed at my knee. I didn't count on her spinning with the block and striking high on my other leg. The thick leather blunted most of the blow, but it still stung. "Ouch. A little rough there."

"You, of all people, should know Satran soldiers fight to their last breath." As soon as her mouth closed, she attacked again.

We fell into a routine with Tindra attacking until I missed a block or made some other mistake, which let her punish me with a hard hit on some part of my body. Eventually, I had to take the helmet off to wipe sweat from my eyes. "I think it's time for lunch."

"We could both use a bath before we eat," Tindra said.

After peeling me out of the armor and putting our weapons away, we gathered fresh clothes and cleaned ourselves in the public bath before stopping by Grith's.

The butcher tensed at our entrance. Before he could say anything, I explained we did not blame him for what Tore made him do. He still apologized and insisted on giving us our food for free.

Returning from our meal, we saw Agrim pacing at our door with Svan and Sibbi standing nearby. The captain jogged to me when we passed through the gate. "Sire, I'd heard you cut your hair. A fine job, if I do say so."

"Thank you," Tindra said.

I shook my head. "Are the three of you here, waiting for me, to compliment my haircut?"

"Oh...no, Sire. I wanted to give you a report."

"What have you learned?"

He frowned. "Svan, Sibbi, and I thoroughly questioned every man involved in the search. We agree that none of them conspired with Tore."

"Then how did he leave his pub, meet with at least one person, and get outside the wall without being seen by anyone?"

"We...I don't know, Sire," he said, scratching his head.

"What are you doing to find out?" Tindra asked.

"Searching for...we're doing our best to find hidden passages, my lady."

I sighed. "Have you questioned Thorgault?"

"No, Sire. I have not. Do you think he's involved?"

"Agrim," I said, thrusting my finger at him and clenching my jaw. "I'm beginning to doubt your abilities."

His shoulders drooped as he looked toward the ground. "Sorry, my lord. I'm not... This is all new to me. I'm doing my best, Sire."

"I believe you, but you're missing the obvious," I said. "Any stonesyths involved in the search?"

"Of course."

"Have them search under the ground around his pub. Look for tunnels," I said. "And question Thorgault. Find out where Tore came from when he entered the tanner's shop."

"As you say, Sire. With all haste," he said, and motioned for his lieutenants to follow him.

"I could help them," Tindra said.

"I won't keep you from it," I said. "I have documents to work on. But if you're going, arm yourself...just in case."

"I know how to take care of myself."

"Never said you didn't. Don't want you to get hurt."

She nodded. "I'll leave after changing into a more appropriate outfit."

Chapter 77

I headed to my meeting room, took a stack of parchment, and prepared to write the order of succession which would leave Roi as ruler of Croy should I die before my wedding.

Tindra walked in, dressed in her armor and sword at her side. She ran her fingers through my hair before gripping it, tilting my head back, and pressing her lips to mine. "For success," she said, smiling when she broke the kiss. "I'll be back before dinner."

"Confidence suits you," I said, kissing her again.

Sparks flashed in her eyes as she nodded. "Hard to feel anything *but* confident wearing this."

"Enjoy the hunt. I doubt you'll do much searching as queen."

As she turned, she said, "As queen, I'll do what I want...unless *you* tell me I can't."

"As if you would listen," I muttered, as the door closed.

Turning my focus to the empty page, I inked my quill and wrote. The feather's tip scratched my wishes across the rough page. In the absence of a queen or recognized blood heir, Roi would take the crown, Grima would be queen, and Einns would be his heir. If Roi wasn't able to rule, the responsibility fell to the most senior Croian general.

Confident the page expressed my order clearly, I set it aside and stared at the next blank page. My hands quivered as I contemplated the next document: my marriage agreement. My mother and Aesa's father had written our agreement. It sat ready for me to sign on our wedding day, binding our families and sealing my commitment to her and our future together.

Of everything Eirickson took from me, losing that future hurts the most.

Normally my mother and Tindra's father would negotiate and write out our marriage agreement. I no longer had a mother, and Mikael lived days away in Varia's capital. Reaching to run my fingers through my beard, I groaned when I remembered Tindra had trimmed it short earlier. Instead, I distracted myself by tickling my nose with the feather end of the quill. *Where do I start?*

After several sneezes, I put fresh ink on the quill and forced words onto the parchment.

> *I, King Fitzeirick of Croy, agree to wed Tindra of Varia, sole daughter of Mikael and Margit, founders of the House of Daufi. This union, once joined, bestows the title of Queen to Tindra, including the authority and responsibility befitting the station.*

I pledge to care for her, keep her safe, and make our future prosperous. I ask for no dowry or other payment.

In exchange, I offer her parents land, in the amount of thirty acres inside the capital's wall and the invitation for her family's chosen representatives to establish a house in Croy, along with the assistance of everyone under my command to ensure its success.

Additionally, I grant status and standing in Croy upon her family. May they enjoy the privileges so entailed.

It seemed too short, but nothing worth adding came to mind. I re-read the document twice, looking for anything offensive to Tindra or her family. Eventually, I convinced myself to put it aside for Tindra to add her pledges later.

Next, I wrote an order asking the generals to return from Nikulas' hall with every warrior healthy enough to travel. After placing my seal at the bottom, I grabbed the orders of succession, placed my seal on them, and left to find a messenger.

Sigric and Skegg stood guarding my door and bowed when I walked out.

Passing the training grounds, I stopped to watch new recruits learning to fight as a group and found General Jomar overseeing the lesson.

"Coming along well?" I asked.

"Most of them learn quick enough," he said. "A few are a little slow to understand. They get special attention in the evening."

"Sounds good to me." I presented the succession document to him. "Sign this, and then I need a messenger to carry documents to Nikulas' holdings."

Jomar looked over the parchment and nodded. "Rest until I return!" he yelled, then turned to me. "I don't have a quill with me, but there should be one in the messengers' barracks. Follow me."

We walked by the stables, stopping at a long building. Jomar opened the door and poked his head inside. "King Fitzeirick needs a rider to go to Nikulas!"

"Coming, sir," someone replied.

"They know it's better to volunteer," he said, stepping back. "Most figure it might earn a promotion someday."

Looking at the man who stepped out, I took him for a stable hand. "You're a messenger?"

He stood up straight before bowing at the waist, long, brown hair spilling forward. "One of the best and proud to serve, m'lord."

"A quill and ink, please," Jomar said, looking around the room.

Someone handed him a small quill with ink on the tip.

The general signed the page and handed it back to me.

I locked eyes with the messenger. "It is of the utmost importance Generals Gudmann and Heming receive these. Wait for them to sign this parchment and return it to my hand."

He nodded. "With all possible haste, Sire."

I handed him the parchments, and he jogged toward the stables.

"Thank you, General," I said. "Get those new men ready as quickly as you can. I want to take the fight to Satra as soon as possible."

"They'll do their job. Maybe not as well as seasoned warriors, but Satra will suffer losses at their hands."

I smiled. "Music to my ears."

He nodded. "May I take leave to continue their training?"

"Of course."

He bowed before turning and hurrying back where we had come.

On the way back home, I decided to look for Tindra and make sure she wasn't causing any trouble. *Considering I told Agrim to visit Thorgault, I'll head there first.*

"Well met, tanner," I said, entering his shop.

He smiled. "How's tha armor, m'lord?"

"Still stiff, but I'll work it out," I said. "If Tindra doesn't kill me first."

The big man laughed and shook his head. "What else can I do fur ya'?"

"Has Tindra or Captain Agrim been here?"

He shook his head. "Haven't seen 'em."

Ugh, what's taking him so long? Guess I'll ask some questions while I'm here. "Where did you meet Tore last?"

"Here...in ma shop."

"Do you know where he came from before he met with you?"

Thorgault pointed toward the square. "Came from out there, walked in jus' like ya did. Don't know where he was b'fore. Maybe talkin' ta other folks."

"But he didn't come from underground? He walked into the square like everyone else?"

He shrugged. "Didn't see him walk in da square, just through ma door. I s'pose he coulda come from under da ground, but he's a woodsyth. They don't usually use da tunnels."

I raised my eyebrows. "What tunnels?"

"Don't know nothin fur certain...jus' rumors and stories pa told me 'fore he died. Claimed there are tunnels all over da place here."

"Did he ever mention why the tunnels were there?"

He nodded. "Said long ago, b'fore Eirick or even his pa, everything was taxed heavy...sometimes more den once. Traders made da tunnels ta hide their stuff, sneak it out ta sell elsewhere."

Maybe we've been looking in the wrong place this whole time. I snapped my fingers. "Thorgault, I hate to be rude, but I need to find Captain Agrim."

"Yur a busy man—no need ta 'pologize. Hope ya find him soon."

I nodded and set off to find the captain of my guard. Thinking about what Thorgault told me, I pushed my talent into the ground to look for signs of tunnels but held my power back, not wanting to feel the unnatural stone lurking well below. *Those can't be the tunnels his father told him about.* As luck would have it, I found Agrim and something underground at almost the same time.

Chapter 78

"Sire," he said, "I'm on my way to talk to Thorgault. Wasn't expecting to find you wandering the streets."

"I'll save you the steps. All he knows is Tore walked into his shop from the square. Doesn't know where he came from or if he met with anyone else. He also said woodsyths don't normally use the tunnels."

"What tunnels?"

"Maybe just rumors and old tales, but his father told him about tunnels used by traders to hide goods and avoid taxes. Have the stonesyths found anything underground?"

"A few hollows, maybe old graves, but nothing I'd call a tunnel."

"Did they search this area?"

"No, we were making our way here."

"I'm standing over something. Move away," I said, sidestepping before tearing open the packed dirt road. Working into the ground, nearly my height, the top of the hollow opened to reveal an empty gopher den.

Several of the guards laughed. After a moment of frustration, I joined them.

"Unless Tore is much smaller than I've heard," Agrim said, "I don't think he used that tunnel, m'lord."

"Right," I said, smiling. "Keep searching while I fix this mess."

"You don't want help?"

"I caused it; I can clean it up. Do you happen to know where Tindra is?" I asked.

He chuckled. "Last I saw her, heading toward The Sneaky Bear."

Knew better than to think she'd stay out of trouble. "Why am I not surprised?" I said. "Good hunting."

"Best of luck to you too, Sire."

Fixing the hole alone took longer but having someone help meant fewer people searching. Finding answers carried more importance than my comfort. After smoothing the ground, I turned toward The Sneaky Bear and hoped for the best.

The closer I got to my destination, the thicker the crowd grew. Crouching, I shoved my fingers into the ground and pushed my voice out with my talent. "Make way for King Fitzeirick."

People shoved against each other, moving randomly away from a voice coming from below them.

Not exactly what I wanted, but at least I can get through now.

Breaking through the edge of a half-circle near the front of the pub, I saw Tindra, sword at the ready and body tensed, facing off against three men. "Kalfken will answer my questions!" she yelled, "even if I have to drag him out of the burning building myself!"

"For the last time, he's not here," a tall, thin man wielding two knives said.

I sighed and sythed dirt up to the knees of all four, locking them in place. "Everyone, drop your weapons. Let's talk calmly."

Tindra glanced over her shoulder and glared at me before putting her sword away. "Let me go."

Fire flickered in her eyes as I took my time walking to her. I wasn't surprised at the heat I felt when brushing her cheek. "A queen-to-be should act more regal. Confidence looks better on you than anger."

"They won't let me in and won't send Kalfken out...even when I asked nicely."

I raised the dirt behind her. "When I release you, sit. Cool off. Don't make me bind you."

She pressed her lips together and glared again before nodding.

Turning toward the men, their weapons at their feet, I felt her sit as the dirt let go of her legs.

"You three *will* do the same."

Each nodded and sat after I released them.

"Now, my promised asked to see Kalfken. You claim he's not here but won't let her see for herself. How do I know you're telling the truth?"

The tall, thin man moved to stand.

"Don't," I barked.

He nodded. "King Fitzeirick, I have no reason to lie but I have clear orders to keep you and anyone associated with you out of this building."

"Tore's order?"

"It is."

"Do you know where he is now?"

"Can't say for certain, but I suspect he's home by now," he said. The other two men nodded.

"Home in Nikulas' holdings, correct?"

"Yes."

I raised a seat for myself. "Where is Kalfken?"

He shrugged. "I don't know...except he's not here."

"And you expect me to trust you, take you at your word?"

He shook his head. "I have no expectations of you, only my orders."

I stared at him until he looked away.

"I give you my word, both as King of Croy and as a man of honor, I will not darken the door of this pub with my shadow. No one under my direct command will bother you any longer. But get word to Tore his troubles have only started."

"Are we free to go?" he asked.

I nodded to him. "Don't touch your weapons until we leave. Tindra, you *will* come with me."

The men stayed seated until we rose and turned away.

"What—" she barked.

"Not a word until we're well away."

She held her tongue until we pushed our way past the thickest part of the crowd. "You let them win."

"I hope they think so."

"What do you mean? We have no answers, and you simply walked away."

"We know, as certain as we can, Tore left the city and headed home."

"I had questions for Kalfken. He could've told us how Tore left without being seen. Now, you've locked all of us out of the pub," she said.

"Not exactly, but that's what they think."

She looked around. "Where are you taking me?"

"I need to pass some information on."

"Telling Agrim about this won't help."

"Please stop talking. Never know who's listening."

"Oh," she said, "right. Sorry, I'm—"

"Not thinking clearly? Losing your touch? Out of practice? Getting soft?"

"Frustrated. I'm frustrated," she said, taking my hand.

As we walked, she looked at me, then over her shoulder several times. Judging by her expression, she wanted to say something but kept quiet. When Abi's home came into view, she gasped. "You're going to talk to Kurt."

"His people aren't under my command," I replied, smiling.

"I... Why didn't I think of it myself?"

"Didn't we cover this earlier?" I asked. "You're out of practice."

"Maybe...but it's your fault."

"How do you figure? I didn't force you to my side," I said. "As I remember it, you insisted on coming."

"Yes, I did. But you don't want spions, so I have no one to teach."

"I thought you were teaching some of the guards what to watch for."

"They're busy with their assigned duties, and I lost interest."

"I'm not going to argue with you," I said. "All the same, you're better off practicing being queen. You weren't doing a good job back there."

The Varian guard nodded as he opened the door for us. We thanked him and walked straight to Kurt's room. Peeking through the half-opened door, I saw a half-eaten salad sitting on the table but no Kurt.

"Maybe he's talking to Aerison?" Tindra suggested.

"As good a place to look as any."

Chapter 79

Approaching Lieutenant Aerison's room, we heard no hint of a conversation through the open door.

Looking in, we found his room empty too.

"Garden?" I asked.

She nodded and led me to the center of the home.

We found the three of them working through a series of movements similar to what Tindra had used with me.

"Well met," I called out, once they quit moving. "Aerison, it's good to see you on your feet. Kurt, you're moving well.

"King Fitzeirick, Tindra...an unexpected yet pleasant surprise," Kurt said, glancing our way. "What brings you?"

"I need a few minutes of your time to discuss a subject of common interest," I said. "Tindra, you could stay and help Abi with Aerison if you'd like."

"Anything for a fellow Varian," she said.

Kurt motioned to the table in the center of the garden, and I poured us cups of odd-smelling tea from the jug sitting on it.

He nodded to me as he took a drink. "New look mean anything?"

"Tindra's doing. I got too hot wearing a helmet."

"Not the most stylish fashion, but it works...on you," he said, smiling. "What's on your mind?"

"Things are returning to normal. Tore's out of the capital, most likely home by now."

"And my men should be there soon, looking for a way into his group."

"We don't know how he got away unseen, and I've agreed that no one under my command will bother his people."

He smiled. "Understood. Tindra's suggestion?"

I chuckled. "No. She threatened to burn his pub to the ground."

"It's not like her to be so direct."

"She's not the woman you remember."

"Losing her touch, it sounds like."

"Changing. Getting used to the idea of being a queen but not at the pace I'd like."

"In my experience, she's more useful as a weapon."

"I have plenty of men to fill that role," I said, shaking my head. "What I need is a queen for my people to look up to, but I'm not going to force her to be anything she doesn't want to—" I interrupted myself with a chuckle. "Probably couldn't force her if I wanted to."

He shrugged. "Use her as you see fit, but giving her a target and letting her do what she does best is a winning strategy."

"Noted. I don't need to know what you're doing with Tore and his group. All I ask is you get word to me when it's settled."

The familiar predator's smile crossed his face. "No reason to tell you what I'm doing since I don't take orders from you."

"Wanted to make sure we understood the situation."

"Better than you know," he said. "Don't concern yourself with Tore any longer. It's simply a matter of time."

"So long as I'm not having trouble, I can wait."

"Patience is a fine quality for a king to practice. It took several embarrassing situations for Ander to learn. Another piece of advice: don't make the same mistake."

"So much unexpected wisdom from a humble Varian trader. Perhaps you'd make a good adviser," I said, smiling.

He laughed and shook his head. "Not interested. I could use a messenger, though, if you know where to find one."

"After dinner?"

"So long as he's ready to leave at first light and willing to wait near Nikulas' hall."

"I'll make sure whoever goes understands what's expected."

"Good enough. If you don't mind, I'd like to get back to stretching. Still have some soreness to work out."

I nodded. "Hope your recovery goes well."

"You two better take a break," Tindra said, with a hint of concern in her voice.

I turned to see if anyone needed help.

Aerison stood, hunched over, hands resting on his knees. "Abi, help me to a chair," he said, between huffing breaths.

The herbalist didn't look too steady on her feet either.

I stood but Tindra waved for me to stay put. Sweat dripped from the tip of her nose as she helped Abi get her countryman to the table.

"I know how frustrating it feels to be out of shape," I said, pouring him a cup of tea.

"Been a soldier all my life...never been this bad. Good to see you decided to see to the mess of hair on your head."

Abi, glistening with sweat, plopped into a chair next to Aerison before pouring a cup of tea for herself. "Whoever cut your hair did a nice job, Sire."

I grinned and pointed toward Tindra.

"I don't need a haircut," Kurt quipped, "but I could use your help, Tindra."

"Of course," she said.

"Come with me," he said. "We're going to need a little space."

They stepped a few paces away. Kurt pointed to several places on his chest then reached around to another spot on his back.

Tindra nodded and grabbed his hand, slowly pulling his arm across his back then over his head into an awkward, uncomfortable-looking position.

While she held it there, he poked and rubbed under his collar bone for a moment then nodded. She let his arm fall to his side.

"Again," he said. "Pull harder this time."

"He's tougher than he looks," Aerison said.

"It's to his advantage for people to assume he's weak," I said. "Probably saved his life when the Satran took him captive."

I heard Kurt moan. "Enough, enough...hold right there."

He pressed his thumb into his chest and pushed it up toward his shoulder, repeating the movement several times before saying, "I'm done. My chest is going to hurt in the morning, but it's worth it."

Tindra let his arm go and walked to my side. "Are we done here?"

"I think we are," I said. "Unless they need us to stay."

"No," Abi said. "But thank you for coming. It was an enjoyable, if tiring, visit."

"True," Aerison said. "Always good to see a friend."

Tindra put her hand on Aerison's shoulder. "It's good to see you on your feet. Don't push yourself too hard, though. I'd hate to see you hurt yourself trying to heal."

"I know how to take care of myself," he said. "I'm sure there will be plenty of battles to fight after I'm sound again."

"As much as I suspect you're right, I'd rather the war be over by then," I said, and turned to leave.

"One rarely gets what one wants," he called out, before we left the garden.

"I need to clean myself before dinner," Tindra said, after we left Abi's house. "Join me?"

"Tempting, but I want to talk to Roi. I'll meet you at home when I'm done, and we'll go eat."

"Sounds good to me," she said, turning toward the bath house. "Have fun with your mentor."

Chapter 80

The smell of hot, fresh bread wrapped around me when Grima opened the door.

"Who...Oh, Fitzeirick! I didn't recognize you with the short hair and beard."

"No problem," I said. "I mistook a bakery for my adviser's house."

She giggled. "Einns is preparing sandwiches for dinner this evening. You and Tindra are always welcome to join us. Will she be here soon?"

"She's cleaning up after working hard, helping with Aerison's and Kurt's recovery at Abi's."

"Oh," she said. "Come in. I'll send food home with you."

"Don't feel obligated. The trade guild stopped holding out on me."

"My son has yet to figure out how to cook small portions," she said. "There will be plenty. Have a seat, and I'll let Roi know you're here."

Roi grabbed my shoulder from behind shortly after Grima went to help Einns with his cooking.

"Why is some short-haired stranger sitting at my table, talking to my wife?"

I chuckled. "You know my voice well enough to recognize me."

"I do, but what brought this on?" he asked, as he sat.

"Got too hot in my new helmet."

He nodded. "All is well otherwise, I hope."

"Could be better. Tore lifted the order for the merchants to refuse serving me then left the capital unseen. I have men looking into how. I stopped by to let you know I wrote the succession proclamation and sent a messenger to the generals guarding Nikulas' holdings. Once it returns, I'll have Agrim sign before you and I sign it together. Oh, I named Einns your heir, should you take the throne."

I couldn't read his expression as he stared at me. Wide eyes said surprise, but his clenched jaw looked more like anger.

"Why?" he asked. "He has less claim to the throne than me."

"You see him as your son." I shrugged. "It felt like the right thing to do, so I did it. You and Grima should talk it over."

"Sorry," he said. "I hadn't... If I'm king, that makes us the royal family. Makes sense he'd be next in line. Even if he isn't my blood."

I nodded. "You probably need to explain it to her anyway, since this only matters if I die without a queen or heir. Regardless, he's followed by the most senior general, then the next...on down the line."

"I can't argue with your thinking."

Grima put a basket on the table. "Pork sandwiches and a small jug of spiced apple ale."

My stomach growled as the smells hit my nose. I smiled at her and called out, "Thank you, Einns."

He turned and bowed before going back to preparing their dinner.

"Too bad you can't stay," she said.

"It's probably for the best. Roi needs to explain what we were discussing. Thank you for dinner. Tindra and I will visit again soon."

"I'm growing to appreciate her...insight," Grima said, after glancing at Roi. "Make sure she knows I said she's always welcome."

Nodding, I said, "I'll pass on the message. Have a good evening."

When I got close to my door, Ivar said, "There's a scout waiting for you inside. Tindra let him in."

"Any idea what he has to report?"

"Didn't ask."

"Get word to General Jomar. Tell him to expect a visitor this evening."

"Of course, Sire," he said, and bowed.

I nodded and walked inside.

"We're in the meeting room!" Tindra yelled, when I closed the door.

I left our dinner on the dining table. As I entered the meeting room, a warrior about my height stood and bowed. "I bring news, Sire."

"What have you seen?"

"About half the central forest is gone," he said, frowning. "They used the trees to build a wall. At first, we thought it was just stone, but our stonesyths found stone and wood twisted together. Going through it will be tough, and take a lot of time. It stretches north and south over two leagues each way. We found one wooden gate on the trade path. Heads and skulls stacked on long spikes above the opening gave a clear warning. The smell and the flies..." He paused and shivered. "I'll never forget them. We backed out and joined the Varian camp. We're waiting for your orders."

As he spoke, I rubbed my chin and tried to figure out how we'd get past the barrier.

"Tell me more about the gate."

He shrugged. "We didn't get too close. It looked like a wide, wooden gate, likely barred on the other side."

"You saw no Satran patrols?"

"No, Sire," he said. "We found no fresh signs of movement."

"Hear any sounds or see smoke? Anything to give us an idea of what's on the other side?"

"We didn't spend much time in one place," he said, "but I can't think of anything specific to report. It seemed quiet. A few of us thought maybe there was no one on the other side."

"Our last defense of Nikulas' holdings must have bloodied them badly," I said, slapping my hand on the table. "It's time to strike."

"I'm going to suggest caution," Tindra said, after clearing her throat.

"Why? We have to take the fight to them if we hope to win."

"I've heard nothing to make me think it's time to charge forward. As a matter of fact, the fortification sounds like a big problem," she said.

I turned to the warrior. "Go tell General Jomar what you told me. Once he's done with you, get some food and sleep. Report back to him for orders after you rest."

He stood and bowed again. "Yes, my lord."

Tindra tapped her fingers on the table until the door closed. "The wall—"

"It's a minor obstacle, raised in haste...out of fear. It must have a weakness. We'll find it and get the army through."

"Are you listening to yourself?" she asked. "What he described took time and a lot of material to build. Satra fears no one. They put heads on spikes. How could you see that as fear?"

"They fear us, so they resort to trying to scare us away."

She pointed at me. "If you won't listen to me, tell Roi. Get his opinion."

I chuckled. "If I tell Roi you advised caution, he'll tell me to attack to spite you. I'll talk to Jomar in the morning. I think he'll agree with me."

She sighed. "Before you do anything, talk to Roi."

"Dinner's on the dining table. Hungry?"

She nodded and stomped out of the room.

After a moment, I followed her to the table. She'd already taken a sandwich and ripped a chunk out of it, chewing fast and hard.

"Something bothering you?" I asked.

The candle flame near her danced angrily as she took a long drink from the jug. "Why are you so eager to get your men killed?"

I pulled out the other sandwich and sat. "I'm not. I *am* eager to rid the world of Satra. I'd prefer none of my warriors fall, but we *will* be fighting a war and men will die."

"If you throw them at that wall, they'll die right there. The war will be lost in the forest."

"You sound like you know something about it."

"I know what a well-planned out defensive structure looks like, and what he described fits. You need more information."

"That's the cautious spion talking," I said, after swallowing a mouthful of pork and bread. "You want to know as much as you can before you act."

"Caution has served me well...kept me alive. Talk to Roi before you do anything."

"Roi knows people," I said. "I'll discuss this with Jomar; he knows battles. Why are you taking Roi's side?"

"He has good insight, and you listen to him."

"If I listened to him, you wouldn't be my promised," I said.

"I never said you didn't have a mind of your own. All I ask is you think before you act, like you've done the entire time I've known you."

"I am. If I wasn't, I wouldn't talk to Jomar before making my final decision."

"And if he agrees, what's your next move?"

"Ramp up our supplies for war while waiting for Gudmann and Heming to return with every fighting man they have. After a day's rest, every warrior, except my guard, rides to join the forces at the central forest."

"Four hundred men, at most, against a wall you know nothing about with a single gate. I couldn't plan a better trap to save my life. If Satra's smart, it will be a slaughter."

"I never said we wouldn't figure out how to deal with the barrier. The scouts reported there were no sounds and no fires. Perhaps we have time to syth holes in it and charge through."

"You can't work stone and wood woven together, can you?"

"No, but many builders work with both."

She shook her head. "How many builders do you have among your warriors?"

"I don't know, but stonesyths can tunnel under it."

"Without knowing how deep the timbers might go?" she asked, raising her eyebrows.

I pointed at her. "Firesyths. The gate's wood, burn it."

Sighing, she smiled. "As much as I enjoy a good blaze, don't you think flames might attract unwanted attention? Plus, for all you know, the gate's wood over stone."

I nodded and tapped a finger on the table, looking for an answer. Pressing my lips together, I snapped my fingers. "Woodsyths make ladders. Warriors scale them at night, open the gate, and the force marches through."

"This is Satra. The barbaric nation who conquered your entire territory. The same people who attacked Nikulas twice, almost winning the second time. If you think it will be as simple as ladders in the dark, I'm going to bed now because you're already dreaming."

I smiled at her joke. "I'm sure you're tired. I have to arrange a messenger for Kurt. I'll join you when I get back."

She left her chair and hugged me from behind. "Please tell me you'll talk to Roi before you make a final decision."

"Only if I need another opinion after talking to Jomar."

She yawned and squeezed tighter for a moment. "I'll likely be asleep when you get back."

"I'll do my best to not disturb you."

Chapter 81

Walking alone, as twilight deepened into darkness, a sense of unease came over me. *A king shouldn't fear for his safety inside the walls of his capital but I have made a few enemies. Still, I can watch out for myself.*

With little more than a thought, my talent flowed into the ground. The familiar comfort using my talent to watch for threats put me at ease.

Inside the messengers' barracks, eight or nine men sat at a long table, eating and playing cards. "Well met, men."

The group stood and bowed. "Well met, Sire."

"My apologies for interrupting your evening. I need a messenger to go to herbalist Abi's house, meet with a Varian man named Kurt, and follow his instructions without question. The ride will be to Nikulas' holdings. You may wait there a while to meet your contact. Anyone volunteer?"

A short, thin, boyish man walked toward me, dropping to one knee at the end of the table. "I'm familiar with the route. My family lives there."

"Travel swift and safe," I said.

"Sire, I haven't heard from them since the attacks. Duty allowing, I'd like to check on their wellbeing."

I nodded. "Provided you do everything asked, take the time you need before returning."

"Thank you, my lord. I'll leave for Abi's after I change clothes and gather supplies."

I nodded and left the building.

As she said, Tindra was asleep, snoring softly, when I got back. She mumbled something when I slid under the cover and rolled to face away from me.

Excitement at the prospect of taking the fight to Satra and starting the process of getting my skati back under Croy's control fought my desire to sleep. *No, I won't be the one spilling their blood, but those barbarians will pay for their horrible actions. Taking my land. Killing my mother, Aesa, and untold numbers of Croy's people. Satra will fall. Every one of them will pay, smashed to dust by the Croian army.*

I fell asleep with visions of celebrating the ultimate defeat of our enemy filling my head and woke to an empty bed.

Where's Tindra? The front door closed while I dressed. Making sure I knew where my hammer was, I opened the door a crack to look for my unexpected guest.

Tindra set a basket in the middle of the dining table.

"Morning," I said, stepping out of the bedroom.

She looked at me and smiled. "I thought you'd like spiced boiled oats and roast rabbit rolls for breakfast."

"Mmm, sounds good. I'll get us bowls and spoons."

The spicy steam burned my nose and brought thoughts of my youth to mind. A spoonful of the traditional Varian breakfast mush almost brought a tear to my eye.

"Hoped it might remind you of simpler times," she said. "After our disagreement last night, I thought it might ground you, keep your thoughts on what's best for Croy."

Nodding as I chewed, the smile crossed my lips all by itself. "Thank you. I needed this." *Being reminded of what the attacks have taken from me makes the importance of crushing Satra clear.*

She returned my smile and handed me a roll. "No need to go to such an important meeting with a plain breakfast."

"Not that I'm in a hurry to leave you, but I'd like to get the discussion underway and give the warrior orders to take back. Do you mind if I take the roll with me?"

She shook her head. "I suspected you might leave without finishing and bought extra. Take them in case anyone else wants a bite."

"Anyone else? You mean Jomar?"

"Right," she said. "I'll wrap them in a cloth to make it easier to carry."

I kissed her as she gave me the bundle and left for the general's barracks. Before knocking on the door, I heard Jomar talking to someone. *Must be the warrior. Good. We can give him the order as soon as we reach a decision.*

Jomar opened the door soon after I knocked. "We were wondering when you were going to get here."

"Tindra said you'd bring a little breakfast," Roi said.

My head whipped toward him. "Why are you here?"

"Tindra stopped by this morning on the way to get breakfast. She said you wanted to meet with me and Jomar to talk about the scout's report. Jomar explained the situation before you arrived."

I frowned and shook my head. "Of all the scheming, underhanded—"

"I take it you didn't expect me to be here?" he asked.

"No, but I shouldn't be surprised."

"Proves one thing," he said.

"What?" I asked.

"She might make a good queen after all."

Closing my eyes, I sighed. "We had a disagreement last night, and I guess we'll have words again today."

"I'll admit, I thought it odd you sent her with the message."

I turned to Jomar. "Having Roi here doesn't change anything. Let's get on with it. Anyone want a rabbit roll? They *are* tasty."

Jomar took a roll, and we all sat at his table. "My first concern is the wall," he said.

"Roi, how did you get past it sneaking into my old skati?" I asked.

"I entered through the eastern passage, not through the central forest."

"So, we have a barrier we know little about," Jomar said, "other than it *will* be challenging to get through."

"Regardless," I said. "According to the report, there doesn't seem to be any activity near the other side. If it's too hard to go through, going under or over the wall are other options."

"Unless the lack of activity is bait for a trap," Roi said.

"Jomar, do you agree?" I asked.

"It *is* suspicious. I'd like to know what's on the other side of the wall."

"I feel the same," I said. "How do we proceed?"

"With caution," Roi said.

"The time for caution has passed," I said. "We can't take the fight to Satra while being cautious."

"But we can't win a war if we lose a large number of men at the wall," Roi said. "The fight will be over before it starts. You're not going to win by throwing bodies at the enemy. You have to be smarter."

"Jomar, your opinion?"

He sat with his eyes closed, took several breaths, and nodded. "The truth? Roi's right. We don't have an overabundance of warriors. Having said that, we have to be aggressive if we're going to take our skati back. I'd suggest a closer look at the wall. Can our stonesyths tunnel under it? If not, using a ladder for a quick look over will let us know what we might face. From there we can decide on the best course."

"If we can tunnel under," I said, "I want our forces on the other side as fast as possible. Send the scout back with the following orders. If they can go under, there's no need to wait; get through and get the gate open. Send word back to the Varian force to take a position in the forest and watch for the gate to open. Once they're through, send word back but push east, killing every Satran they find. If they have to look over the wall, report back what they find before proceeding."

"I hope it's the second option," Roi said.

"If we can safely get two hundred men past the wall, we'll send Gudmann and Heming on their tails and nearly double the force soon," I said.

"Four hundred men, battle ready and well supplied, should be enough to start our offensive," Jomar said. "I'll send the scout back shortly."

"Tell him I wished him swift and safe travels," I said.

"Gladly."

Roi and I left together. I offered him the last roll, but he shook his head.

"You've always been firmly grounded," he said. "Don't let your hatred, your need for revenge, cloud sound judgment."

"If we sit and do nothing, Satra picks us apart one battle after another. Taking back my old territory puts the area's resources under our control," I said. "We will win."

"Keep me informed," he said.

I nodded. "When I want your insight, I'll come to you."

"Arrogance does not look good on you."

"It's not arrogant to be an aggressive leader."

"And it's not weakness for a leader to seek wise, trusted council," he said.

"And I do, but you are not the only man serving in that role. Jomar has enough experience to give me valuable insight."

He put his hand on my shoulder. "Certainly, but does he have Croy's best interest in mind?"

"I have to believe he does or remove him from leadership."

"Even though you didn't appoint him."

"Not everyone serving under my father or half-brother are evil. Those left, I've found to be loyal and useful servants to Croy."

"I hope you're right," he said, shaking his head. "And don't be too hard on Tindra. She did what any decent queen would...what's best for her people."

"Are you changing your mind about her?" I asked.

"No, but I can respect someone's motives without liking their morals," he said, before turning to go home.

Speaking of motives and respect...my promised and I are going to have words when I see her again.

Chapter 82

Entering the courtyard, I found Tindra sat, cross-legged, in the shade of a tree outside the compound wall and waved to me when she saw me. "Come, sit with me."

"No," I said, crossing my arms. "We're going inside to talk."

She cocked her head. "Did your meeting not go well?"

I pointed to our door. "We're not having this conversation in public."

She pursed her lips, got to her feet, and walked ahead of me.

"Sit," I said, pointing toward the table as I closed the door.

"If I'm going to defend myself, I'd rather stand."

"Suit yourself." I sighed. "You shouldn't have invited Roi without telling me."

"Why not?" she asked. "If I'm expected to act like your queen, don't be upset with me when I do."

"You went behind my back," I said, through clenched teeth.

"Are you saying I didn't act in the best interest of Croy?"

"Not as such."

"Then I did my duty to your country and your people," she said, folding her arms across her chest. "Truth be told, I went above and beyond my duty since I'm not yet queen."

"You conspired against me."

"I've forgotten more about conspiracy than you'll ever know," she said. "One can't conspire alone. Even though it seemed like a good idea, I wasn't sure Roi would listen to me anyway, all things considered."

I pointed at her. "Then you manip—"

"Don't you dare accuse me of manipulating you. Had I done so, *you* would have asked Roi to attend the meeting. Manipulation is something I'm good at—exceptionally good if I do say so myself. If I manipulate you, trust me, you *won't* know it."

"So, you lied to Roi."

"I did not say anything false," she said, shaking her head. "I gave him carefully selected truths."

"But—"

"No buts. If you want to be angry with me, put on your armor and bring your hammer. You can give me everything you've got as we dance around the courtyard," she said.

"No. That's a bad idea and a good way for one of us to do something we'd regret. Maybe you did the right thing, and maybe you didn't. I'm going to go for a walk and try to sort this out."

"I'll go with you."

"I'm not happy with you right now. Having you with me isn't going to help clear my head."

She glared at me for a moment then opened her mouth.

"Just don't," I said, turning to leave. "Nothing you say is going to help. I'll be home later."

Leaving the courtyard, I wandered aimlessly, focusing more on my anger than a specific destination. Shouts from the training grounds got enough of my attention for me to wave to the men learning to fight effectively as a unit. For a moment, I considered joining them to vent my frustration on someone else. *No. I didn't cross weapons with Tindra because I didn't want anyone to get hurt. I wouldn't be right risking an innocent.*

Continuing to plod along, my feet took me to Roi and Grima's door. Rubbing my hands together, I contemplated knocking. *I'm not mad at Roi. He'd probably be angry if he knew what Tindra did.*

The door opened, and Roi stepped out. "You look lost. What's wrong?"

"The meeting this morning," I said, shaking my head.

"You're still mad at Tindra for inviting me? Or, maybe, you're upset with me for attending."

"You're always welcome, but in this case, I didn't feel like I needed your opinion."

He nodded. "You made that plain enough. So, did you come here to talk with me about her?"

I shrugged. "Not sure why I ended up here...other than I needed to be away from her."

"Maybe I can help, maybe I can't." He put his hand on my shoulder. "Come inside. Let's talk."

"Thank you for the offer, but there's no need to involve your family in this."

Roi smiled. "Grima's busy upstairs. Einns is out, gathering herbs."

I nodded and followed him inside.

"Have a seat; I'll get some ale."

Roi placed a mug in front of me. "I'll talk to you about anything but don't forget, this is one of the few times I've agreed with Tindra's actions."

I took a long drink. "That's what bothers me. I told her I wasn't going to talk to you about possible strategies because you know people, but Jomar knows battles."

He tapped his finger on the table for a moment. "Not because you expected me to caution you against being too aggressive?"

"Another reason," I said, nodding.

"I have a mind for tactics but not on the scale necessary to conquer Satra. Still, my advice stands. Fitzeirick, I've known you your whole life, and I've never seen you make completely emotional decisions, except when it comes to fighting Satra."

"Can you blame me?" I asked, glaring at him. "You know what they cost me and our country."

"I do, but that doesn't mean you have to make snap decisions and risk paying an even higher price. Are you really mad at Tindra, or is she simply the focus of the frustration and anger rooted in Eirickson's scheming?"

"She went behind my back to do something I would have forbidden had I known her plan," I said, tapping a finger on my mug.

"Were she already queen, would you be angry at her for trying to help?"

Crossing my arms, I looked him in the eyes. "Aren't you mad she manipulated you?"

He took a drink and chuckled. "Give me some credit. I suspected something when she showed up here alone and told me about the meeting."

"Then why play her game?"

"To figure out her scheme...and warn you, if necessary. Now, answer my question."

Closing my eyes, I rubbed the bridge of my nose and considered Roi's question. *I can't fault her for doing what she thought best for my—our country...exactly what I'd expect a queen to do.* "No. I might be irritated by her method, but I'm not angry with her action."

"Then you have your answer ... assuming you still want to marry her."

"You're right, and I do."

He smiled. "Sounds like you and I don't have anything else to discuss. But I'd recommend you talk to Tindra about your expectations. Or risk another disagreement."

I finished the mug. "Like I told her, you know people. Thank you for the insight."

"Anytime, my friend. If she kicks you out, we can find you a place to sleep."

"Tindra will *not* kick me out of my own house."

Roi's laugh followed me out the door.

Entering the courtyard, I spotted Tindra wearing her armor, working through stretches.

I stopped in front of her. "Next time you think about inviting people to one of my meetings, pass it by me first."

She focused on something behind me and didn't speak until she had finished her routine. "I understand why you left but don't expect me to apologize for doing the right thing."

I put my hands on my hips. "I'm not asking for an apology."

She nodded. "Then we're good?"

"What?" I asked, cocking my head.

"You're not angry with me?" she asked, standing in the same pose, eyes still looking past me.

"No." I glanced over my shoulder to make sure someone wasn't behind me.

"Good." Her lips curled into a grin. "Join me for one more set, then we can go inside and talk."

I'd barely had time to set my feet when a man ran into the courtyard. Spotting me, he yelled my name and skidded to a stop a few paces away. "The warriors are returning through the southern gate."

I thanked him and turned to Tindra. "Our talk will have to wait."

She sighed and nodded. "Or we can talk on the way there."

"We could," I said, offering her my hand.

Walking together, hand in hand, I explained what Roi and I discussed and how I understood my anger wasn't completely justified.

As the stream of warriors came into view, she promised to be more mindful of not acting without checking with me first unless she had no other option.

General Gudman rode through the gate as we arrived.

"Well met, General," I called out.

He looked at me. "Sire, I didn't expect you to greet us."

I nodded. "Where's Heming?"

"Not far behind. I'll ride back and get him if you'd like."

"No need," I said. "I can wait."

Heming rode up before Gudmann could respond. "Good to see you, m'lord. No one told me we'd be greeted by the king." He reached into a saddlebag and offered me a page of parchment. "I believe you wanted this back after we signed it."

I took it from him. "Yes, thank you. Did the messenger stay behind?"

"Rode back with us," Heming said.

I nodded. "You two talk with Jomar. He'll let you know what to expect in the coming days."

"Hope he has some fresh food," Gudmann said. "Hard rations wear on an old man."

"I won't disagree," Heming said, "but it's better than riding on an empty stomach."

"Don't want to hear it. I've walked about half the trip on nothing but cattail roots," I said. "Go eat but see Jomar before nightfall."

"We will," Gudmann said. "It's nice to be home."

"Enjoy it while you can," I said. "Your stay may be short."

"We'll do what we must," Heming said.

"On your way then," I said, and waved.

The generals bowed and rode away.

"Speaking of food, lunch?" Tindra asked.

"Sounds good," I said, taking her hand again.

We made small talk over bowls of Grith's lamb stew.

"Drink plenty of water," Tindra said. "You have to work on stretching your armor when we get home."

I'd hoped she'd forget. Frowning, I nodded. "If you insist."

She smiled. "I do."

We returned home and went inside to put on our armor.

Tindra helped me pull on the heavy and stiff leather before slipping into hers.

Once we were outside, she led me through the stretches we'd started earlier.

Several times, the armor resisted my movements. More than once, I lost my balance and fell.

"Do that on the battlefield, and you're a dead man," she commented, after a hard fall.

I decided against giving her the satisfaction of acknowledging she was right.

After several rounds, I took my helmet off to wipe my face.

"You know what we should do before dinner?" Tindra asked.

"No, what?"

"Go for another run."

"That doesn't sound like a good idea," I said.

"On me!" she yelled and headed for the gate out of the courtyard.

I barely had time to shove my helmet on before she got too far away for me to catch. By the time we returned to the compound, I had resorted to sything some stamina from the ground to stay on my feet.

"Tindra, you do know you're not queen yet, don't you?" I said, flopping onto the ground near our door.

"Of course, but why does it matter?"

"Because if I die from this, Roi takes over, not you."

She laughed and shook her head. "You won't die. I bet you thank me...at some point. But let's not worry about the far-off future. I'm sweaty and hungry *now*."

"Me too. Let's get clean and go eat."

I groaned while getting back to my feet. Once inside, we stripped out of our armor, gathered fresh clothes, and went to bathe.

The warm water felt good, but my stomach insisted I needed to eat.

"Do I smell roast goat?" Tindra asked, when we got close to Goran's shop.

Sniffing the air, I nodded. "Smells good."

Goran frowned when we walked in. "Wasn't sure I would see you again, after—."

"Wasn't your fault," I said, smiling. "I can't blame you for doing what you had to do to take care of your family."

He nodded. "Thank you, Sire. I felt horrible for refusing to serve you. I had to stop Britt from sneaking food out to you. She didn't understand it was too risky. She screamed at me then wouldn't talk to me for days."

"Rest assured, that is all behind us now, and I'm taking steps to make sure it never happens again," I said. "What's for dinner?"

Goran smiled. "Britt's trying something new—spicy and sweet goat pie. Interested?"

"Sounds good," I said. "We'll take one each."

"Are you sure?" he asked. "They're big enough to feed two people each."

"I'm hungry enough to eat for two people," I said.

Tindra chuckled. "I'm not quite that hungry, but I'll do my best."

"Two pies and a jug of cinnamon milk. Sit where you like. It'll be right out."

"And water," I said, before taking Tindra's hand and leading her to a table in the corner of the room. As soon as we settled into the seats, Britt hurried to our table with a jug, two cups, and a shining smile. "Well met, King Fitzeirick. I'm so happy you came back. I'll bring your pies out after they cool a little. I'd hate for you to burn your tongue."

"Thank you for your concern," I said.

"And attention to detail," Tindra added.

The young girl curtseyed and rushed back to the kitchen.

"She knows we're to be married, right?" I asked Tindra.

Tindra shrugged. "She does, but a girl wants what a girl wants. Given some time and a cute boy or two, she'll forget you."

"Einns needs to come here for a few days. I can't image what they'd make together."

"He might distract her too much," Tindra said, grinning.

"Might be what she needs to get over her infatuation with me." I took a sip of the thick, cinnamon-flavored milk.

A strange smell, combining honey, cinnamon, and spices, floated from the kitchen. It grew stronger as Britt approached our table, carrying a tray with two large pies. "Enjoy, Sire," she said, setting them in front of us.

I nodded, grabbed a fork, and attacked the meal. Before I knew it, I had devoured my pie and drank over half the milk.

Tindra had about a third of her meal left when she gave up.

I left a gold double on the table, wished Goran and Britt a good evening, and we walked home, holding hands.

Hedin met us at the compound's entrance. "Sire, a messenger returned with a report from the wall. Agrim sent for the generals; they're waiting for you in your meeting room."

Closing my eyes, I squeezed Tindra's hand. *Word back this soon? I'm not sure what to think.* "Thank you. Guess we won't be going straight to bed."

We entered the house and headed to the meeting room. The three generals sat across from the warrior. They stood when we entered the room.

"You may sit and give your report," I said.

The warrior bowed before returning to his seat. "The stonesyths said the wall went too deep to go under safely, so we made a ladder and peeked over near nightfall. I saw a fortress about a bowshot away. Against the darkening sky, I saw men walking along the top of the western wall. The ground between looks nearly impassable. Hills, partial walls, maybe a few pits, scattered randomly about...like a child throwing toys during a tantrum. I'm afraid we'd be dodging arrows from the moment we entered. The barriers would slow horses to a walk and archers would cut down any force trying to cross on foot."

I shivered and looked from one general to the next. "Thoughts?"

Gudmann shook his head.

"Nothing good," Jomar said.

"Darkness would help, but torches would give us away," Heming said.

"If I may," Tindra said. "Scale the wall and move through at night without torches."

"Stumbling about, making all kinds of noise, would attract as much attention as torches," Gudmann said.

"She's right; it can be done," I said. "I survived underground for about nine months in absolute darkness. A moonless night would be about the same condition."

"I doubt we have nine months for others to learn how to move around in the dark," Gudmann said.

"I taught myself how to do it, and blind stonesyths use the same method to move about safely on their own," I said. "How many men would we need to lead our warriors to the fortress?"

Heming shrugged. "Twenty, twenty-five. But what good would it do? They'd be stuck there."

I turned to the messenger. "Could you tell anything about the fortress?"

He shook his head. "Too far away and too dark."

I nodded. "We'll need to get men there to find a way inside. First thing tomorrow, I want thirty of our strongest stonesyth warriors waiting for me in the courtyard. I'll teach them what I know."

"What if Satra attacks again?" Jomar asked.

"The field slows their movement too, and they have to come through the one gate at the central forest. The Varian soldiers waiting there would end any Satran attack quickly," I said. "Unless you have a better idea, I have work to do in the morning."

"I haven't heard how we're getting men through the barrier," Gudmann said.

"As I suggested, our warriors scale the wall," Tindra said.

"They'll make too much noise getting to the ground on the other side," Heming countered.

"Send builders to make holes for our warriors to pass through," I said.

"Maybe," Gudmann said, scratching his chin.

"We have a little time to figure it out," I said. "Warrior, thank you for your service. Generals, I want thirty men in the morning."

They stood, bowed, and made their way out of the room.

I yawned. "I need sleep."

She took my hand, led me to the bedroom, and undressed me.

"Not tonight," I said. "I'm too tired, have too much on my mind."

She smiled and stood on her toes to kiss me. "No obligation."

I kissed her back and got into bed. She crawled over me and kissed me again before putting out the candle. We fell asleep tangled together.

Chapter 83

"The men are waiting in the courtyard. Do you want to eat before you begin the lessons?" she asked, waking me.

"Yes," I said, before stretching and yawning. "Hate for a growling stomach to distract me."

"Good. There are Varian sweet rolls from Goran on the table, along with goat milk."

I thanked her and dressed before going to eat.

"Would you mind running to see if Fastan has any heavy cloth we can use for blindfolds?" I asked, after finishing a roll.

She pointed to a woven sack in the chair nearest me and smiled. "Already taken care of."

"Breakfast and blindfolds, what more could a man want?"

Laughing, she shook her head. "I provide much more than food and teaching supplies."

"Yes, you do," I said, "and I appreciate your efforts. Speaking of...are you planning to help teach?"

"I'd planned to spend time with Grima," she said, "if she's not busy."

"Suit yourself, but with your experience around the blind and sneaking around in the dark, I thought you might have insights I don't."

"Other people pay well for my skills," she said, smiling.

"And I plan to make you queen. Is that not payment enough?"

She pressed her lips together and looked toward the ceiling while tapping a finger on her chin. "Hmmm...it should be just about enough."

"Well, then come help me teach."

"I'd rather not," she said. "It's likely I'd be more of a hindrance than a help. Plus, last time I mingled with a group of fighters, some got offended, and I had to stay with their sergeant to be safe. Grima's company will be more pleasant, I think."

I nodded. "Tell Grima I send my regards," I said, grabbing the sack of blindfolds.

She smiled. "Of course."

I walked out to the sight of thirty men crowding a section of the courtyard.

Some had formed small groups, talking. Others engaged in practice combat.

One, kneeling by himself and making shapes with dirt, caught my eye. *Why isn't he with his fellow warriors? Because he's better than them or worse? Only one way to find out.* "You," I said, dropping the sack. "In the back. On one knee. Step forward."

Standing, his short legs moved quickly as he walked through the crowd. "Yes, Sire," he said, before bowing. As his head tilted forward, the long braid of dark-brown hair fell over his shoulder. His eyes matched the color of his hair when he looked at me.

"Your name?"

"Fastulf, my lord."

"Close your eyes."

He nodded and smashed his eyes shut tightly.

"I want everyone but Fastulf to stand perfectly still, arms at your side. On my command, he'll try to walk to the far side of the crowd, eyes closed the entire time, without touching anyone. Do not help or hinder him. Understand?"

"Aye," they replied in unison.

"Fastulf, go."

"As you say, Sire," he replied, before turning and taking hesitant steps. He missed the first group then walked directly into one of the fighters. Turning back to me, he opened his eyes. "Impossible."

I nodded, took a dark strip of wool cloth from the sack, and tied it over my eyes. "Everyone move, quietly, then stand still again. Do not leave a straight path through the group."

Tracking the movement, I walked as soon as they stopped. Several times I felt feet shift slightly as my talent passed under them. Taking careful steps, I slowly made my way through the jumble of thirty warriors.

"Move again," I said, without turning around, and walked through the group backward when they stopped.

Exiting the crowd, I turned to face them and removed the blindfold. "How many of you figured out what I did?"

No one moved or said anything.

"Anyone feel anything?"

Most of the men nodded.

"Speak," I barked. "You can't learn and I can't teach if we don't have conversations. I can't answer questions if no one asks any."

"Someone sything the ground," a voice from the back of the crowd said.

"Correct, but do you know who?"

"You, Sire?" the voice asked.

"Correct again. Now, do you know why?"

"No," several men said.

I nodded. "If I told you I'd buried two hundred gold doubles in this courtyard, how would you find it?"

"Search for disturbed ground," a man near the front said.

"I'm a stonesyth and can open and close holes in the ground without leaving even the smallest sign. You men better be able to do the same; otherwise, you're wasting my time. If you want the two hundred coins, how would you find it?"

He smiled. "Push my talent into the ground and search for anything unnatural."

"Exactly. You can find—"

"Can we look for the coins now?" another man asked.

I shook my head. "There are no coins buried here, at least as far as I know...I've never searched. Regardless, with a little practice, you can find things sitting on the ground in almost the same way."

"But if it's sitting on the ground, why not simply look for it with your eyes?" he asked.

"What if you're blind?"

"Then I wouldn't be a warrior," he said, and let loose a coarse, cackling laugh.

"What if it's dark as pitch and you have no candle, and your life depends on finding the item as quickly as possible?" I asked.

"Well," he said, pulling his ear, "I guess I'm a dead man."

Several of the warriors chuckled.

"I like a good jest as much as anyone, but it's time to be serious," I said, nodding. "What I'm about to teach you literally saved my life, more than once, and got me out of a nightmare situation. I had to learn it the hard way. Pay attention, and you'll benefit from my experience. We'll start easy. Everyone close your eyes."

I sythed a hole large enough for me to hide in. "Without opening your eyes, point to a recent change in your surroundings."

The ground trembled with energy, even with most of it well below the surface. I felt the ripples as their talents tumbled past the hole. It took longer than I wanted, but each man ended up pointing at the large hole.

"Good," I said. "Without looking, what's different?"

"The pit wasn't there before," someone said.

"Correct." Closing the hole, I made a new one, farther to the side and about half the depth. "Keep your eyes closed and try again. Check the surface, not the depths."

Energy flowed again, most of it closer to the surface. This time a fair amount stopped at the edge of the hole.

Fingers swept past me, stopping in the direction of the new hole. "The hole moved, and it's not as deep," someone called out.

"Better," I said, before closing the hole, "but some of you still searched too deep. Focus on the top of the ground." I pressed my finger into the ground between my feet and took two steps back. "What changed now?"

About half the men pointed to me. "Something disturbed the ground, there," one of them said. The rest still searched; I felt their talent passing well under my feet.

"Everyone open your eyes. If you are pointing, do not drop your arm. Everyone still searching, stop. You still haven't figured out what I'm asking you to do," I said. "The men pointing, line up in front of me."

I gathered blindfolds while waiting for the fourteen men to line up. "Take one and hand the rest down. When you get a blindfold, secure it well. You men not lined up, step back. I'll work with you more in a little while. For now, watch, and you might learn a little as we go. Those of you blindfolded, if you think you're ready, take one step forward."

The line stepped toward me almost in unison.

"Count to ten, out loud, then point at anything moving. Keep your finger on it until you're told to stop. Understand?"

"Aye."

When they hit three, I took slow, heavy steps back and forth in front of the group.

At first, no one moved. Foreheads wrinkled and lips pressed together, but no one raised a hand to point. So much energy flowed through the dirt, dust clouds formed along the top of the ground near where I stood originally. As I passed the left side of the line, I pushed my talent toward them, passing energy under their feet. Heads turned, but no one pointed.

I bit my lip to keep from laughing.

Walking past the men not searching, I nodded to them.

They smiled in return.

Shortly before reaching the right side of the line, I felt a ripple and tripped over a small bump. Stumbling forward, fighting to keep my balance, I fell.

Fastulf pointed at me. A few others pointed soon after.

"Did one of you trip me on purpose?"

"Not on purpose, Sire," he said, removing his blindfold. "I thought I felt a pattern of moved dirt, but I wasn't sure. I wanted to see if the pattern broke when I moved the ground."

"You were tracking my footsteps—that's the idea," I said. "Anyone else notice the same thing?"

"I felt it when you fell," someone said.

"Same," the rest of the pointers added.

"I'm sure some of you are more sensitive than others, but the idea is to look for slight changes. Everyone take off your blindfolds for now, and one at a time, push your talent toward my feet. Tell me what you notice."

"The dirt moved where you're standing," Fastulf said.

"Ignore the dirt. Focus on what my feet are doing to the ground."

He shrugged. "Nothing. You're standing still...nothing's changing."

I lifted one foot "Now? Do you still notice nothing?"

He closed his eyes and furrowed his brow.

"Concentrate. Look for differences under me compared to around or beside where I'm standing."

Fastulf opened his eyes and smiled. "I feel your foot pushing on the ground. Is that what you mean?"

"Exactly," I said, putting my foot down.

"Yes," he said. "I felt your weight shift."

"Blindfold," I said, pointing to Fastulf. "Once it's on, find me and follow with your finger. Everyone else, track my feet with your talent to see if you can feel what's happening."

Chapter 84

Energy circled my feet for several heartbeats before Fastulf pointed at me.

Walking in a tight circle, I retraced my steps behind the line of men. The small warrior kept his finger on me until I jumped away from the left side of the line.

Brow furrowed, his hand dropped while he searched, rising again when I took a step.

"Not bad," I said, stopping in front of him. "With some practice, you'll do well."

He pulled the blindfold down. "How did you move sideways?"

"I jumped, and you didn't search past where you thought I should be. You have to widen your search area, even if you think you know where I'll go."

Pressing his lips together, he raised his eyebrows. "You learned this by yourself?"

I nodded. "If I hadn't, I'd be long dead. Self-preservation is an excellent motivator."

"Makes sense," he said.

"Now, is anyone else getting an understanding of what I'm trying to teach you?"

"We're looking for weight on the ground?" someone asked.

I nodded. "Anything touching the ground presses against it, and you can find where they touch. Learn how to do this well, and no one can sneak up on you, regardless of how quiet they move, because you'll know where they are the moment they enter your search area. Now, I need a volunteer for this group to track while Fastulf and I work with the other men."

Three warriors stepped forward. I pointed to the nearest one. "Your name?"

"Gavid, Sire."

"Thank you, Gavid. Don't make it too hard for them at first. Everyone is still learning."

He bowed. "Of course, my king. Everyone, blindfolds on and try to find me."

"Fastulf, let's work with the other group," I said.

He hurried to my side as I walked to the men who hadn't picked up on the lesson.

"People learn at different rates," I said. "If you doubt your ability to master this skill, I won't blame you for walking out of the courtyard now. You will not be punished or dishonored in any way; you have my word."

Pausing, I looked each warrior in the eye. "I want to impress upon each of you the importance of learning this stonesything skill. I'm preparing you to lead warriors into our first attack on Satra. These lessons will make you the tip of Croy's spear, drawing first blood.

"Those inhuman brutes think they've set a trap between the central forest and their closest fortress. They believe themselves safe and, I'm sure, are planning their next attack on Croian soil. I'm tired of our countrymen getting hurt or killed fighting on our soil; it's time we take the attack to them and force them to defend the territory they soaked in Croian blood. It's time we avenge the deaths of every Croian slaughtered during the Satran invasion. Step forward if you are still willing to accept this responsibility."

As one, the warriors took a step toward me.

Finally, cooperation without threats...or worse. "Good," I said, smiling. "Close your eyes and wait for my command."

Once their eyes were closed, I turned to Fastulf and whispered, "Move away, about ten steps or so, and kneel or sit. I want you to make a bigger target than standing would."

He nodded and moved away, sitting a short distance from the wall.

"Men, push your talent into the ground but go no deeper than a hand's width. Search, across the top of the ground, not down into it. Find where your fellow warrior is sitting and point to him."

Faces twisted, some comically, as the men tried their best to follow the instructions. Faint ripples moved under the ground's surface, and energies tumbled under and around my feet. One by one, the men turned and pointed to Fastulf.

"Good, very good. Now, follow him with your finger. Fastulf, walk."

Jumping to his feet, he took long, slow strides.

Their fingers trailed slightly behind him, but they were getting the hang of it.

When he looked toward me, I motioned for him to change direction.

Nearly as one, the men caught the change.

"Excellent. If each of you can master this skill, we can't lose," I said. "You've earned a lunch break. After you've eaten, return here for more training. As you leave, practice while you walk, pushing your talent around you and reading where things press against the ground."

The men crowded the exit, trying to leave all at once

I decided to let the guards know I'd need their help later. Opening the barracks' door, I spotted Otkel. "Pass the word, I want any guardsmen not on duty, or sleeping from night watch, in the courtyard after lunch."

He nodded. "Of course, Sire. I'll gather them myself."

"Make sure they eat first," I said. "We'll be working until dark, maybe later."

"Understood."

I thanked him and left to get something to eat.

Men crowded the courtyard when I returned. Several fingers followed Fastulf as he walked through the crowd.

Wanted to get here and get the guard prepared first. At least the warriors returned and started practicing.

After a couple of men noticed me, the crowd split to let me pass.

"Glad to see you all came back," I said.

A few men laughed.

"Given the progress we made before lunch, we'll get down to the real challenge and learn how to find and avoid obstacles and enemies. Some guardsmen will be obstacles, and others will, when we get to that point, act as enemies. The goal is to not trip over obstacles as you make your way through. I need the warriors to stand outside the wall, where you cannot see into the courtyard. Go now, exiting in an orderly fashion, please. Make sure you put on a blindfold before you enter."

To their credit, they did a better job of getting through the gate without clogging the passage. Once the last one exited, I motioned for the guards to come near me.

"Stonesyths...make obstacles. Short walls, hills, or shallow pits but nothing too dangerous. I want to trip them up, not hurt them. Once that's done, everyone find someplace to stand or sit among the hazards and block the path. Walking from the gate to the far side of the courtyard without tripping should be a challenge but leave at least one way open. A successful crossing is the goal."

"Aye," they said, and went to work.

I have no idea what the field looks like beyond the central forest, but I don't want those warriors surprised by anything they come across there.

Soon the guards formed an impressive, ragged maze in the courtyard. I stood at the exit, closed my eyes, and sought a path to the entrance. I'd almost given up but worked out two difficult tracks from beginning to end. "Let the first warrior in!" I yelled.

A blindfolded man took a few tentative steps into the courtyard and stopped.

"Ahead of you is a maze of obstacles and some guards blocking the path. Find your way through without tripping or falling," I said.

Jaw clenched, his head moved side to side in short, jerky movements. Turning to his right, he walked confidently toward a pit. Stopping mid-stride, he turned away and followed a safer path. About a third of the way into the challenge, he tripped over a sitting guard.

"Stop," I called out. "Take off your blindfold, turn around, and go back out. You can try again after everyone else has a chance. I'd advise practicing locating and tracking people. If you master finding the hard-to-detect things, the other obstacles come easy."

He bowed before turning to walk out.

"Next."

Two more warriors tried and failed. The fourth found his way to the exit but stopped short of walking out when he felt me standing nearby. "There's no exit," he said.

"I'm standing outside the test," I said, shaking my head. "Come toward me."

He smiled and dipped his head. "Yes, my lord."

I raised his blindfold when he reached me. "Congratulations, you're the first one through."

"Thank you, Sire."

"You're welcome. Take a seat and watch your fellow warriors, but don't do anything to distract or aid them," I said.

He bowed and walked away.

I nodded. "Next."

Agrim approached and stood at my side, watching as three more failed before the next two made it through, then Fastulf entered the courtyard. With little more than a shrug, he rushed into the course.

"He's good," Agrim whispered, as we watched the small warrior avoid obstacles without breaking stride.

"Maybe better than me," I replied. "I think I've found the leader for this group."

Head held high, Fastulf marched to us, bowed, and removed his blindfold.

"Well done," I said. "Wait here a moment."

"Something wrong, Sire?" he asked.

"No."

"But your life is about to get more complicated," Agrim commented.

"What?" Fastulf asked.

"Ignore him," I said, looking sideways at the captain. "He happened to be in the right place at the wrong time, and I put him to work. Captain Agrim, watch the guides and keep them honest while I discuss something with Fastulf."

Agrim chuckled and shook his head. "Have fun."

Fastulf cocked his head but didn't say anything.

"Come with me." I led the warrior inside my home and took a seat at the dining table. "What do I need to know about you?"

"I'm a Croian warrior, ready to fight for my king," he said, squaring his shoulders. "What else matters?"

"Why are you picking up this new skill so quickly?"

He shrugged. "My father's a strong stonesyth, makes a living finding metal in the ground. I'm not as strong but what you asked us to do made sense to me."

I nodded. "Who do you serve under?"

"Commander Leikner, General Jomar."

"What would they say if I asked about you? Any problems I should know about?"

He smirked. "Other than the obvious?"

"Presume I don't know what you're talking about."

"I'm one of the shortest men serving as a warrior. Some say I'm too short to do any good in a fight. I know what I'm capable of—being overlooked doesn't bother me anymore. Makes it easier to go about my business unnoticed, if nothing else."

I nodded. "Confidence and ability always catch my eye. I'd hope to find a leader in this group. You're what I'm looking for."

He snickered and shook his head. "I'm honored, my king, but a thirsty man wouldn't follow me to water."

Pointing outside, I said, "I have twenty-nine other warriors, many struggling to do what you're mastering with ease. You thirty must guide hundreds of men, safely and quietly, across territory meant to slow any attack to a crawl. If this fails, we have no hope of taking the fight to Satra...they will bleed us to death, slowly but surely."

"No doubt, Sire, but that doesn't mean a single warrior will look to me as a leader. I'm not saying I can't do it, but I know they will walk all over me."

"Fastulf, you're the best of the lot. You have more than enough talent to earn their respect." I said. "Don't taunt anyone but don't hide your abilities either."

He put his hands on his hips. "I'm well-practiced at going unnoticed. How do I catch their attention?"

"Attack the course again, in a way your fellow warriors can't overlook. I'll send word to Jomar and make sure you're included in planning for the upcoming attack."

"As you say, Sire." He bowed, put the blindfold back on, and left...walking backward.

By the time I walked outside, Fastulf was a third of the way through.

Agrim and most of the other warriors watched him slack-jawed. "Did you tell him to walk the test backward?"

"I suggested he find a way to make an impression on his fellow guides. He's going to lead them."

"You think his peers will follow him?"

"I think this evening will be an eye-opening event for some," I said. "What's your impression of the rest?"

"Several took five or six tries before finding a way out."

I smiled. "Everyone, blindfolds on. Guards, take new positions."

Once the guards were still, I checked for clear paths. Three this time, with one so difficult I doubted anyone would try it.

"Men, line up and find your way outside the wall. We'll repeat this exercise until it's time for dinner."

Even with several long breaks to change up the obstacles, I decided to let the men leave early because there were only so many ways to use a limited amount of space.

"Be back no later than sunset," I said, watching Tindra enter the courtyard. "We'll have some fun in the dark, so rest, eat, and get back here dressed in your armor. If it makes noise when you move, you'd best figure out how to make it quiet...and have your blindfolds with you."

The men cheered and made their way out.

"If you're going to be prowling around tonight, I want in. Let's eat dinner at Goran's," Tindra said.

"I won't keep you from participating, but don't hurt anyone."

"What makes you think I'd ever do such a thing?"

"Our first encounter."

"Different circumstance," she said, trying to hide a smile. "You were my target."

"And now you're the queen-to-be, not a mercenary."

"I will behave appropriately. Don't worry," she said, with a nod.

I explained the day's events and what I had planned for the evening while we enjoyed a spicy Varian dinner before heading home to prepare.

"I miss my silks," Tindra commented, after pulling her leather armor over her head. "They work so well for moving quietly."

"Once things settle, I'll make sure you get another silk outfit," I said, and fought my way into my still stiff armor.

"You're going to be a busy man once this war is done."

"Instead of being a busy man before it really starts."

Chapter 85

A dozen guards came out of the barracks soon after Tindra and I walked outside.

"Gather round," I said. "Split into four groups of three. Starting at sunset, thirty blindfolded warriors will scatter throughout the southern half of the city with the goal of exiting through the south gate without being caught. It's your job to catch them without simply standing watch at the gate."

Smiles and nods spread through the group. "Sounds easy enough," someone commented.

"The guides will be instructed to surrender without a fight. Collect cloth without hurting anyone...absolutely no weapons. The hunt ends when the moon starts to descend. Go ahead and find your places."

"Are they starting from here?" someone asked.

"I'm not telling you where they're starting. Every blindfold collected is worth a silver single."

After they left, Tindra tapped me on the arm. "What's my job?"

"Doing what you do best. I expect you to collect more blindfolds than the best two-guard teams."

"With thirty guides to share between four patrols and me, I'll have to collect half the cloth...more than half, to best two teams."

"Not up to the challenge?"

She looked toward the ground. "I *am* out of practice, haven't hunted anyone since getting involved in your mission." Pausing, she looked at me with a big smile. "I think you're overestimating your guard. Where are we meeting when the lesson is over?"

"Here."

She nodded and left.

I stood alone in the courtyard, watching the shadows grow longer, and wondered if any of the guides were going to return. It seems they'd taken my advice about quiet armor seriously because I didn't hear them approaching the gate.

"Line up and follow me."

We paraded through the capital to the Varia army campground.

"Two lines. Here," I said, sweeping my hand in front of me.

The warriors hurried into two, even, straight lines.

"On my word, you will secure blindfolds in place and leave this area. A number of my guard are looking for you. Your goal is to pass through the southern gate without being captured. If caught, you will surrender your blindfold without argument or fighting and walk directly to the courtyard. Every guide who makes it through the southern gate will receive two gold doubles when they hand me their blindfold. If I get a credible report of anyone moving without their blindfold in place or fighting the patrols, you will immediately be kicked off this team. Any questions?"

"How many patrols?" a voice from the backline asked.

"I'm not going to tell you."

Several men grumbled.

"May we work in teams?" another asked.

"I don't care, but one man hides easier than a group."

Several of the warriors nodded.

"The exercise is over when the moon starts to descend. Those caught or not at the southern gate by then will be given more training. If you're ready, fasten your blindfolds and head for the southern gate."

One by one, they covered their eyes and started their journey with measured steps.

After waiting for the last of them to fade into the deepening dark, I headed for the southern gate. Twice I had to stop and change my route when I felt guides searching for threats.

Reaching the gate, I found two guardsmen talking with someone standing in the shadows outside the wall. The other four glanced toward them several times as I approached.

"What's wrong? Who's out there?" I asked the closest guard.

"A warrior named Fastulf. Said he's here for you. But he walked up wearing a blindfold. Why would anyone be out in the dark blindfolded?"

I chuckled. "You better hope he's not the last blindfolded warrior you see tonight."

"I beat you here," Fastulf said, stepping into the circle of torchlight and twirling the blindfold on his finger.

"Can't say I'm surprised you're the first, but I didn't expect you to be so fast. Dare I ask how?"

"I'm good at not being noticed."

I nodded and handed him two gold doubles. "Now the hunted can play hunter if you want...but there's a catch."

"I'm listening."

"You can't take a blindfold by yourself. You must find Lady Tindra and hunt with her."

"Sire, what are the odds the queen-to-be will let me hunt with her?"

Grabbing a handful of dirt, I sythed a crude stone with my brand in it. "Present this to her along with the doubles."

"Any chance you'd tell me where to find her?"

I shrugged. "I have no idea. She's hunting in the southern half of the capital, like the rest of the guard. It's on you to find her."

"What happens if I don't?"

"Nothing," I said. "I'm offering you the opportunity to learn from her and show your peers you're not to be overlooked."

He smiled and tied knots in his cloth. "Give me the seal. I hadn't planned on going to bed early anyway."

As soon as his hand closed over the stone, he ran into the night like an arrow flying from a bow.

"What's going on?" a guard asked.

"A test. Practice for the start of our war with Satra."

"You expect our warriors to fight *blindfolded*?" another asked.

"No. It's simply part of the training. Now help me watch for more blindfolded men."

"Yes, Sire."

Watching the moon rise fully above the wall, I began to wonder if Fastulf would be the only guide to avoid capture. Thankfully, a few made their way to the gate, calming my nerves. My confidence grew as more arrived. The hunt ended with nineteen guides, counting Fastulf, arriving safely. To a man, they smiled when I handed them their reward.

"On me," I said. "Let's see who got caught and if anyone gave up."

"I don't see Fastulf here," someone said.

"Bet he gave up," another voice added.

I raised my eyebrows, turned, and left for the courtyard at a jog.

As we approached the gate, I counted twenty-five people gathered around a fire near the center of the yard.

Tindra hurried toward me when I entered the torch-lit gate. She stopped, blocking the way, and put her fist on her hip. "I didn't need any help."

"Never said you did."

"Why did you send him after me?"

"Who went after Lady Tindra?" someone asked.

"Fastulf," I said, waving for him. "Come join the rest of the guides."

He jogged over from the far side of the fire.

A chorus of gasps and 'ooohhhs' erupted behind me.

"Well...he's out," someone commented.

"No, he isn't," I said, turning. "I had an additional challenge for the first man to arrive with his blindfold. Fastulf earned it. In fact, he beat me to the southern gate."

He grinned at my praise.

"Not possible," someone said.

"Are you calling your king a liar?" I asked.

"No, Sire," the voice in the dark replied. "Not at all."

"Good. Now, Tindra, I didn't send him to find you because I doubted your ability. I sent him after you because of your skill in hiding and moving about unnoticed. It gave him a chance to prove he could go beyond what's expected, and he did. How many blindfolds do you have?"

"Does his count?" she asked.

"No, I've already paid for it."

"Six in total," she said. "Four by myself and two with him slowing me down."

"Leaving no more than five to be caught between four patrols. How many silvers am I handing out tonight?"

Two patrols walked behind Tindra. Ortlan raised his hand, and said, "We have three."

Kodren stepped away from his group. "We have two."

"Impressive," I said, smiling. "As long as you ignore Tindra's performance." I reached into my purse and grabbed a handful of coins. "Ortlan, Kodren, come get payment for your groups. I trust you to divide it equally."

They bowed. "Most generous, Sire."

I turned to the guides behind me. "You have proven yourself worthy of the task I have in mind for you. Take tomorrow off, rest, practice on your own...or whatever. Know you will be asked to test yourself in the field...soon. Fastulf, stay here. The rest are free to go."

The short guide bowed. "Yes, my lord."

The others bowed and turned to leave as I addressed the circle of men around the fire.

"The eleven who were captured: be back after noon. We will train together for two days, testing again on the second night. This is your last chance to lead the first attack on Satra. The warriors who lead our charge will be honored and rewarded. Do you understand?"

"Yes, Sire," they shouted.

"You are dismissed." I waited until the courtyard cleared before turning to Fastulf.

"I'm calling a planning meeting with the generals in the morning, after breakfast, and you will attend."

"As you say, Sire," he said.

Taking two more coins from my purse, I held out my hand.

"I cannot take more, my king," he said.

"You earned it, same as the other hunters."

"Following Lady Tindra taught me more than coins are worth."

"Flattery?" Tindra said. "Maybe you're smarter than I thought."

He smiled and looked away.

I chuckled. "Smart or lucky—either way, be here with the generals tomorrow."

"Yes, Sire."

"Go get some sleep; you earned it," I said.

"Thank you, my king," he said, before bowing and leaving the courtyard.

Chapter 86

Tindra grabbed my hand, and I flinched at the heat coming off her. "Let's get to bed," she said, with a breathy edge on her voice.

Rather than risk a firesyth's fury, I let her drag me inside. We made it to the bed but didn't fall asleep for quite a while.

. . . ● . ● . ● . .

My attempt at untangling myself from Tindra woke her.

"Morning," she said, smiling.

"You look happy."

"Happy, satisfied...some of each." Her stomach growled. "And hungry," she said, laughing.

"We both could use a meal," I said. "Goran's?"

"Spicy food after last night? You don't have to ask me twice," she said, and crawled over me to get out of bed.

I shook my head before getting up and dressing.

"Let's find Agrim before we eat," I said. "I need him to gather the generals."

Goran served us sandwiches made of spiced bread and scrambled eggs with cinnamon milk to drink. I didn't care for how the milk and eggs tasted together, but Tindra seemed to love it.

We arrived to find Agrim standing outside our door with Fastulf.

"The generals are here, m'lord. Fastulf came with them, but you didn't say anything about anyone else attending this morning," he said.

"He's here at my invitation. The leader of the guides needs to know what's going on."

Agrim nodded. "Of course, Sire."

"Thank you for your attention to detail," I said, and we walked inside. "Tindra, would you mind getting water for everyone?"

"Of course not," she replied. "Am I to attend the meeting too?"

"Yes. You may notice things I overlook. Fastulf, sit with the generals."

"Yes, m'lord," he said, as we entered the meeting room.

The generals stood before I sat. "I'm glad you could make it, given the short notice. I wasn't sure how well the test would go last night, but I'm happy to say the results were mostly positive. Because of his ability and performance, Fastulf is leading the guides. I want each of you to make his authority clear to your men. Any mission involving his company, make sure he knows all the details."

"Understood," Jomar said. "I'll pass the word. Other than his promotion, what else are we here to discuss?"

Tindra entered carrying a tray with cups, placed it on the table, and sat to my right.

"I wanted to let you three know how things are progressing and what people we need ready to start the next part of the attack plan."

"Heard last night's results were mixed, at best," Gudmann said.

"True," I said, "but the exercise wasn't a failure. We have nineteen guides ready now and eleven promising prospects. I'll know more two nights from now."

"What do we do until then?" General Heming asked.

"Find builders. No less than five, but more would be better. I want them at the central forest wall by tomorrow morning. Their only job is to study the wall and find the best way through. They will open holes for the guides to lead warriors and soldiers through."

"To be slaughtered by archers on the other side?" Gudmann asked.

"No, they'll go through at night and guide their men quietly, through the maze, to the fortress," I said.

"To be slaughtered the next morning," Heming said.

"Each guide is a strong stonesyth. Once the teams reach the fortress, they open holes in the western wall, with the woodsyths' help if necessary, and the attack starts. As long as we have at least one more solid stonesyth and a couple of good woodsyths in each group, the plan should work."

"How many fighters can the guides take?" Jomar asked.

I scratched my chin for a moment. "Fastulf, how many men can you lead across?"

He shrugged. "Maybe none; I've never tried."

"If a force of one hundred and fifty, attacking unexpectedly, can't kill enough Satran to let the rest of your men cross the broken ground and back them up, this plan is doomed to fail," Tindra said. "Plan for five per guide."

"What makes you so sure?" Jomar asked.

"Call it professional instinct," she replied, smiling. "I've planned similar actions before, only with far fewer men on both sides."

I pointed to Fastulf. "Can you guide five warriors through obstacles?"

"Can't say, for certain, Sire," he said, "None of us have tried."

"You're their leader," Tindra said. "Best make sure they're ready for the task."

His face lost some color, but he nodded.

"Assuming these men can do what's needed, how soon will we put this plan in motion?" Gudmann asked.

"Until I'm confident I have thirty capable guides, ready to get a force in position, we won't make a move," I said. "If all goes well, three days. Prepare everything with that goal in mind."

"And if this doesn't go well?" Gudmann asked, frowning.

"I'm willing to listen to other strategies," I said. "Think it over. Call a meeting if any of you have a better idea. Things can change until we have men through the wall, then we're committed."

"Agreed," Jomar said. The other generals nodded.

"Generals, again, thank you for your time. You're free to go," I said. "Fastulf, stay."

"Yes, Sire?"

"Two things. First, meet with the other guides. Get them used to seeing you, praise them when they do the right thing, and correct them when they don't. Get everyone together and help the eleven who aren't doing as well as they could be. You're a leader—their leader. Act like it, but don't abuse your new authority. If they resent you, they won't follow you."

He nodded.

"Second, I'm going to write a letter for King Crum of Varia. He needs to know we plan to attack soon. Perhaps I can convince him to send more men or, at least, put pressure on our enemy from the eastern passage. Wait for me to finish, then get it to a messenger for delivery. I don't expect a quick response, so let the messenger know he isn't expected to wait for a reply."

"I'm glad to be of service, m'lord."

Tindra collected the cups while I put quill to parchment. It didn't take long to write and seal the letter.

Fastulf stood when I handed it to him.

"Remember, this goes directly to King Crum of Varia."

"Your words from my mouth," Fastulf said, and hurried from the room.

Chapter 87

I found Tindra sitting at the dining table. "I didn't want to leave without letting you know I'd be visiting Grima," she said.

"You don't have to check in with me," I said.

She stood and smiled. "But I know you worry when I disappear."

"You do have a way of getting into mischief," I said, grinning. "Still, you're just as good at getting out of trouble as you are causing it. I'm going to ask Kurt if he's heard anything from his people in Nikulas' hall. It would be inconvenient, to say the least, if Tore decided to cause trouble again this close to launching our first attack. I'll find you at Roi and Grima's after I'm done at Abi's."

"Tell everyone I said hello," she said, before kissing me.

I followed her out with a smile on my face.

The ever-present Varian guard greeted me as I knocked on Abi's door. "I hear my fellow soldiers will be on the move soon," he said.

I nodded. "Should things go according to plan, yes. Will you join them?"

"My orders are to guard Lieutenant Aerison. Until I hear different, this is where I stay."

"Your commitment is admirable," I said.

He bowed. "Thank you, King Fitzeirick."

Abi opened the door. "Yes, how may I help — Oh, my king...I wasn't expecting you. What can I do for you this morning?"

"I came to see Kurt."

"Oh. I saw him walking toward the garden after breakfast. Come in. I'm sure he'll be happy to see you."

I followed her inside, and the guard closed the door behind us.

"Here," I said, offering her three gold doubles.

"You don't owe me anything, m'lord."

"You're treating two people and feeding a Varian soldier because of me. This is to cover the cost."

"I don't mind the company," she said, shrugging. "Gives me something to do besides tending my garden and waiting for someone to get sick."

"Still, you're serving me and deserve payment. Take it, or leave it somewhere for you to find later."

She nodded and took the coins. "Only because you insist, my king."

"Believe me, you've earned it," I replied, and headed toward the center of her home.

Kurt sat alone at the table, writing something.

"Well met, Kurt," I called out.

He turned and waved me over. "Well met. Didn't expect to see you today."

"I had some questions for you before putting plans in motion."

"Well," he said, dropping his quill, "since you're here, I don't need to get a message to you. I'm leaving for Varia after lunch."

"Answers one of my questions. Not that I'm trying to run you out of Croy. You're welcome to stay as long as you need but returning to Varia is necessary, I'm sure."

"It's well past time for me to return home," he said. "What's on your mind?"

"Any news on Tore?"

He shrugged. "People are working to make sure he doesn't cause you more trouble, but these things take time. They *can* work faster, but then it won't be discreet."

"No," I said, closing my eyes. "Unless Tore or his people start openly working against me, I'd rather your efforts stay hidden."

He nodded. "Anything else?"

"Satra has built walls and barriers. My warriors can't simply march into battle without falling to archers before the fight even starts. We have a solid plan to get through the barriers, but we'll need those boats you mentioned before to ensure our victory. How soon can you have people making them?"

He shook his head. "When I get back, my priority is getting a feel for what's changed. Varia has a new king and queen, in case you forgot, and I have no idea if they're causing problems."

"Crum shouldn't be cause for concern, and Jesca's too kind to stir up much trouble."

"I doubt your friend is still the same man you grew up with. As far as I'm concerned, Jesca's an unknown, but I hope you're right. Regardless, neither have any experience being in power. That can lead to problems."

"Assuming they aren't in your way," I said. "When could we have the boats?"

"It won't take long to get woodsyths who know how to best make transport boats from Varia to your coast, a week or less...depending on the weather. Gathering wood shouldn't take much longer. The slow part of the process is training your men to use them."

I pressed my lips together and nodded. "What if Varians, some of your men, used them—not to go into battle for me but to transport my warriors."

Another shrug. "I doubt the rest of the council leadership would agree with risking more of our resources, and you'd have to talk King Crum into risking more Varian lives in Croy's war."

"I can't speak for your peers, but Crum knows this isn't only my war. Croy's loss means Varia falls not long after."

"Don't ask me to commit to anything more...not until I know how things are back home."

I nodded. "Understood. I won't delay your return. When you see Crum, tell him I wished him well and apologized again for missing his wedding party."

"*If* I see him," he said.

"Travel safe and swift."

"Thank you, and best of luck when you attack."

I thanked him and left Abi's to stop by Roi's house, hoping I wasn't walking into a fight.

Knocking on the door, Grima opened it and smiled. "It's good to see you. Tindra said you might stop by. Please come in."

The smell of roasting meat hit me as I entered.

"Lunch will be ready soon. You're more than welcome to join us," she said, closing the door.

"I appreciate the invitation, but I have to eat an early lunch. Important training this afternoon, and I have to be there for it."

She nodded. "The life of a king, I guess."

Einns stood near a small goat roasting over a bed of coals. Tindra wasn't far from him, staring at the low flames.

He said something to her, and the fire rose in the middle of the open pit.

"Is Roi here?" I asked, taking a seat at the table.

Tindra looked over her shoulder and winked at me.

"He's out back, washing after slaughtering the goat," Grima said. "Would you like something to drink?"

"Water would be fine, thank you," I said, before looking at my nephew. *If only I could tell him.* "Einns, will the meat be ready soon?"

Taking his knife from his belt, he peeled a slice from the goat's ribs and took a bite. "Close enough that I could make you a plate now if you want, sir."

"If it's not too much trouble," I said.

"I need to sit for a moment," Tindra said. "I'll take it to him."

"Thank you, Lady Tindra," he said.

The door opened as Grima handed me a cup.

"Smells like lunchtime," Roi said, carrying a bundle of clothes. "And we have another guest. Glad you could join us, Fitzeirick."

"I won't be here long," I said. "I want to be there for the second training course for the guides."

"Does this have anything to do with guards hunting in packs the other night?" Roi asked.

I nodded. "First test, nineteen passed. I'm giving the other eleven a chance to practice and test again. If they don't make it, I have to find more men and start the training again."

"And why are you doing this?" he asked.

"Our enemy took half the central forest and built a wall. Well away, on the other side, stands another wall. Between is a maze of hills, pits, and broken ground designed to slow our advance and let their archers pick us apart.

"I'm training thirty stonesyths to guide warriors quietly and safely through in the dark. Once they reach the far wall, they'll syth holes through it and launch a surprise attack."

Roi tapped his finger on his chin for a moment. "Without seeing exactly what you're talking about, the plan sounds rock solid."

"The generals seem to agree," Tindra added, as she put a plate of steaming goat meat in front of me.

Roi looked toward the kitchen. "Where's mine?"

"Still cooking," Einns said. "But not much longer."

"Fitzeirick is on a schedule," Grima said. "You can wait."

Roi laughed and shook his head.

"And I'm a guest," I added, before putting a slice of the meat in my mouth. "Excellent cooking, as usual, Einns...but I have a question."

Under the table, Tindra's foot tapped mine.

"Yes, sir?" the boy replied, facing me.

"Most boys around your age are preparing for a future in the army or looking for adventure, but you put all your energy into cooking. I'd like to know why."

Grima's posture relaxed, and she sighed quietly.

"I do it because it makes other people happy, sir."

"A noble goal," I said, nodding, "but what makes you happy?"

"I liked helping in the kitchen at The Trader's Cup, first because it was easier than the rest of my chores, but then I saw how a warm meal changed the people staying there. It made me feel good to see them smile."

Grima moved next to her son and put a hand on his shoulder.

"Then Roi came for us, and I wanted to thank him, and cooking was what I knew best. At first, I wasn't very good at it, though."

"But you learned," Roi said, nodding.

Einns looked down for a moment. "And going into Varia let me try new things. I got even better at making good food."

"And now you serve meals to a king," I said, smiling. "Not many people can say that, certainly not at your age. I can't wait to see what you make as you keep practicing."

"Thank you, Sire."

Grima wiped a tear from her eye and hugged her son for a moment.

"How's Kurt doing?" Tindra asked, taking a piece from my plate.

"He's leaving for Varia this afternoon. Wants to get home and see if Crum has messed with his life."

"That boy's probably too busy trying to keep the crown on his head to cause anyone any problems," Roi said.

"Not quite what I said, but close enough," I said, nodding.

"And the other problem?" Tindra asked.

"He has people on it," I said, shrugging. "Advised patience if I wanted to keep everything quiet. I also asked him about the boats. He couldn't commit to anything until he got a feel for things in Varia."

Grima brought two more plates to the table. One for Roi and another for Tindra.

"No," Tindra said, pushing the meal away. "You eat, Grima. I'll get a plate for myself."

"Wouldn't be much of a host, or a friend, if I didn't take care of my guests," Grima replied, before stepping away.

"Speaking of hosts and friends," I said, glancing at my empty plate. "I don't mean to be rude, but I need to get back to the courtyard and get things ready for the guides."

"I'll come after I finish eating," Tindra said.

"Take your time," I said.

"Hope all goes well," Roi said, as I left the table.

Stopping at the door, I turned to look at him. "You're welcome to stop by later and watch. Who knows? You might learn something."

He chuckled as I closed the door.

Chapter 88

A large group of men crowded the courtyard. Stopping at the gate, I took a quick headcount and came up with thirty, along with the guards I expected. *An entire company? Why are they here?*

"Guides." Fastulf's voice rose over the crowd. "King Fitzeirick should be here soon. We must prove we're ready for whatever he throws at us."

"Aye!"

Interesting. "Fastulf!" I yelled. "A word."

The guides turned to face me and bowed before parting to let their leader through. He rushed to me, bowing again when he got close. "Yes, Sire?"

"I expected the eleven men who needed extra training. Why is everyone here?" I asked.

"We talked," he started, pausing to look over his shoulder, "and decided all of us could use more time to practice and train, m'lord."

I smiled, clapped my hands together, and looked past Fastulf to the guides. "In that case, I'm glad all of you came back. Shows you understand how important your role will be in starting the war. Of course, this isn't what I had planned for, but it presents the opportunity for a better test.

"Fastulf, break your company into two teams. Make sure the eleven men who failed the first test are part of both. One team will make the course, and the other will try to beat it. Guards, you will not be needed today. You are dismissed to find other duties."

Someone near the barracks groaned, but I didn't hear any other protest.

While Fastulf split his men, I moved to stand near my home and watch the proceedings. Once he had them in two lines, I cleared my throat. "Front line, stay in the courtyard. Rear line, wait outside. Fastulf, stand at the gate to make sure no one watches, then make sure they are blindfolded and send them in once the course is ready."

After they left, I looked down the row in front of me. "You know what to do. No dangerous obstacles, and make sure there's at least one path through."

The smooth courtyard quickly turned into a maze of pits, hills, and rough ground, with men blocking most of the otherwise open paths.

"Fastulf, we're ready," I called out.

I watched as the guides made their way, more confidently this time, through the obstacles. After the last man made it through, I sent the first group out, and the second group remade the course. Each time we changed groups, the exercise became more difficult, but both groups rose to the challenges. During one of the changes, Tindra dodged her way through the course and stood at my side.

"Didn't expect you to stay at Roi and Grima's so long," I said, before giving her a quick kiss.

"I left not long after you did and managed to catch Kurt before he left. Then I went to visit Aerison before taking care of some other business."

"What other business?" I asked, looking at her sideways.

"You're not the only one with concerns," she said. "If anything comes up that I can't handle, I'll let you know."

I frowned at her for a moment, then turned to watch the guides find their way through the latest course.

Dusk had taken over from daylight when I called an end to the training. "You did well today," I said. "Expect a harder test when you come back tomorrow."

The men bowed and left the courtyard.

"Svan," I said. "Tomorrow evening, gather as many guards as we can spare to hunt the guides and get word to the generals. I need three companies of warriors tomorrow after dinner. I'll let them know where tomorrow."

"I'll make sure it happens," he said, smiling.

Tindra took my hand. "I don't know about you, but I could use a bath before we eat."

"I had the same thought. Dinner at Grith's?"

"Sounds good," she said.

Returning home clean and full of mutton sandwiches and roast potatoes, I undressed and flopped onto the bed. Sleep took me before Tindra put out the candle.

Something brushed against my lips, then pressed. Opening my eyes, Tindra filled my vision.

"I have breakfast," she said, after another kiss. "Goran had scrambled eggs and spiced pork."

I shuffled my way to the table.

"You'll be relieved to know Britt no longer has eyes for you," Tindra said, as I sat in front of a plate piled high with food.

"Oh?" I replied, raising my eyebrows as I lifted my fork. "Anyone I might know?"

She nodded and tried to fight a smile. "Someone we both know, very well. Met him over a bundle of Varian spices in the marketplace."

I swallowed. "The only person we both know well who also buys spices is Einns."

"And he let her have the last bunch," Tindra said, smiling. "Grima has raised quite the gentleman, it seems."

"How do you know about this?" I asked, brow furrowed.

"Britt talked with me while I waited for a fresh batch of eggs." She shrugged.

I sighed. "Does Goran know? Do I need to say anything to Roi and Grima?"

"Relax," she said, putting her hand on my shoulder. "I can take care of any problems that may arise."

"I know how you usually take care of problems," I said, patting her hand. "That doesn't help me relax."

"Don't be stone-headed. I have many skills." She kissed me on the head. "A queen-to-be needs opportunities to be diplomatic. That's my plan, should I need to step into any situation between our friends."

"Sounds like a good idea," I said, kissing her hand. "Speaking of plans. After I finish eating, I'm going to spend the day making sure preparations are going well. This evening is the, hopefully, final test for the guides. Are you interested in playing in the dark?"

"Maybe." She kissed my head again. "Are you going to send Fastulf to slow me down again?"

"No," I said. "I don't have any special tests in mind this time."

"Then I'll be more than happy to test our men," she said, moving to sit across from me.

"Any idea what you'll do until then?" I asked. "You're more than welcome to join me in making the rounds."

"As much as I would enjoy spending the day with you, I have several things demanding my attention too. Let's meet at Grith's for dinner before the sun sets."

"Part of me wants to know what you're up to; the other is afraid to ask," I said, eyeing her suspiciously as I got to my feet.

"I'm not doing anything you should be concerned about," she said, through a thinly disguised smile. "If you'd feel better, send a guard to accompany me and report my activities back to you."

"Not necessary," I said, stopping behind her and tilting her head back for a kiss. "I trust you. See you at Grith's."

"Good. See you there. Hope your day goes smoothly."

Knowing our attack could be no more than a few days away filled me with a need to make sure everything was as ready as it could be. Nervous energy powered my footsteps to find one of my generals.

General Jomar did his best to address my concerns when I spoke with him. When I told him I needed the two companies to be ready at the Varian campground at sunset, he reminded me not to get ahead of myself in planning. His exact words, "You still have eleven guides who haven't passed their test."

I thanked him for his counsel, stopped by Fastan's shop for a large sack of blindfolds, and dropped them off at home before continuing my trek to meet with most of the people involved with preparing supplies for Croy's army to go to war; quartermasters, wagon builders, blacksmiths, tanners, horse groomsmen, and more. To a man, they gave their word that all would be ready when they were called upon. I didn't know if I should be proud or skeptical. *Nothing ever goes as planned, especially with this many people involved.*

Despite the assurance, doubt weighed on my mind as I made my way to Grith's to eat with my queen-to-be. Tindra wasn't there when I arrived, but she showed up soon after two bowls of squirrel and rabbit stew hit the table.

Tindra told me about her day, including stopping by Goran's again both to talk to him about Einns and arrange for a Varian dinner to be delivered to Aerison and his guard.

I confessed my concern over how smoothly all the preparations seemed to be going.

She nodded as I spoke, then smiled and took my hand. "I'm not saying you're wrong to have doubts but remember, it's easy to get everything gathered and have everyone working toward the same goal at first. Keeping focus, and morale, after the fighting starts is when the difficult work begins. Surprise attacks have a good chance of being successful—that's why they happen. How you manage defeat and motivate your men to push on...that's what really matters. The side which carries the most determination to win will be the victor."

"I see the wisdom in what you're saying," I said, returning her smile. "What I'm not sure of is how to put your words into action."

She chuckled. "Fitzeirick, since I've known you, the one thing you haven't lacked is determination. You'll figure it out."

"Thank you for the confidence. I appreciate your support." I squeezed her hand.

She squeezed back. "Doing what any queen worthy of the title would do for her king."

"But you are not yet queen," I said. *Though I'm beginning to wonder why I'm waiting.*

She closed her eyes for a moment. "I promised my support to you before we left Varia to overthrow Eirickson. You still need my help, and I keep my promises. No matter what challenge you face, I will be at your side."

I nodded. "Speaking of challenges...I have guides to test. We'd best get going."

Chapter 89

We returned home to a crowded courtyard. Thirty guides stood in two lines, and I counted a dozen guards clustered near their barracks.

"Tindra, guardsmen, guides," I said. "The same rules as last time with one change. This time, the guides may leave the city walls through any existing opening and meet me outside the south gate. Hunters, I ask that you actively search for the guides, do not simply stand in view of the gates and wait for them to come to you. Guides, remember if you are caught, do not resist and do no harm."

"Wait," Tindra said. "They don't have to go through the city to the southern gate?"

"Correct. Any existing way out is an option."

"So, because they failed the first test, you're making this one easier?" she asked.

"I can see how you might make such an assumption, but this test will be at least as difficult as the first."

"If you insist," she muttered, under her breath.

"Any other questions from the hunters?" I asked.

I took their silence as a 'no' and dismissed them to find their positions.

"I need to get something from inside, then we'll go to the starting point," I said, and retrieved blindfolds for the warriors.

Murmurs started behind me when the camp came into view.

"Line up in front of your fellow warriors," I said. "Anyone who thought tonight's test would be easier is mistaken. While blindfolded, you will each lead two warriors out of the capital while avoiding the hunters. To pass the test, you must arrive with your blindfold in place and at least one warrior. This is practice for what you will do on the battlefield. Understood?"

A hesitant chorus of 'ayes' answered.

With a nod, I continued. "Warriors, there is one rule...do not fight if you are captured. Is this clear?"

They answered with more enthusiasm.

"Guides, get two blindfolds, select the warriors you want with you, and discuss strategy including how to stay with you. When you are ready, put the blindfolds on."

Once everyone had their eyes covered, I cleared my throat. "I hope to see each of you at the southern gate before the moon reaches the top of its climb."

After the last trio faded into the darkness, I made my way to the southern gate.

"No one beat you here tonight, m'lord," one of the guards said.

"I'm not surprised," I replied. "This time the guides are leading two warriors while avoiding capture. Plus, there are more hunters involved."

Another guard whistled. "Stumbling around, blindfolded, in the dark, *and* leading two other men without getting caught. Sounds like you're asking the impossible, Sire."

I chuckled. "It won't be easy, but I've done something similar in a far more dangerous environment."

"Sounds like an interesting story," someone behind me said.

I turned to him. "It's not something I care to talk about. I made a bad decision and ended up in a horrible situation, not much else to say."

"Understood, Sire," he said, with a nod. "The rumors are hard to believe anyway."

"No doubt most are false, at best misleading, depending on the source," I said.

"But you did vanish for most of a year," another guard said. "Everyone knows that's true."

I nodded. "Nine months, and I lost everything but myself. But now is not the time to discuss history. I'm working toward better days for Croy and Varia."

"Sorry if I misspoke, m'lord."

"No offense taken," I said. "Now, everyone, help me watch for guides. They could come from almost anywhere."

Checking the area around me, I felt the first guide's talent press against mine. Soon after, he hurried through the gate with two warriors on his heels. "Is King Fitzeirick here yet?" he asked, blindfold still in place.

"Yes," I said.

He pulled off the blindfold and handed it to me. "But I'm the first one here?"

"You are," I said, "and with both warriors. Well done. Have a seat, rest. I'm sure you're tired."

He chuckled for a moment. "Fastulf owes me a gold double."

"Your leader is paying for success?" I asked.

"No, Sire. He and I had a wager on who would get here first and if they would arrive before you. Had I beat him and you, I'd get two gold doubles."

I nodded and returned to checking for more guides.

After a short time, two groups arrived, walking from the west. More showed up as the evening passed. Eventually, the entire company reached me, and Fastulf made a show of paying his debt. Fourteen warriors were captured, but all the guides passed the test.

"I'm certainly not disappointed. Quite the opposite. I have thirty guides ready to take a force and launch our first attack. Warriors, thank you for your time. I hope you enjoyed yourselves. What you did tonight is but a taste of what will happen on the battlefield. Prepare to ride out soon. I'll meet with the generals early tomorrow, so be ready to go on short notice."

"We'd go now if you sent us, Sire," Fastulf said, saluting.

"I think I'd better let you all get some rest first," I said, returning his salute. "I give you leave. Go back to the barracks, and sleep well."

The guides cheered and clapped each other on the back. The warriors who had accompanied them saluted before giving their congratulations as I left to go home.

The hunters were there, waiting on me, with the captured warriors. Tindra stood, talking to three warriors and the other two sat on the ground, outside the group.

"Did you catch these three?" I asked her.

"No," she said. "Came up empty-handed tonight. Wanted to know how they felt about the evening's activity."

"And?" I asked.

"Challenging," one warrior said. "I never considered how difficult it is to get around in the dark, even in someplace familiar."

"It's hard when you can't see what or who is near," another added.

"I know, all too well," I said. "I appreciate everyone's efforts this evening. Know that you have contributed to our success in the coming war. You're free to return to your barracks. I hope you rest well."

A chorus of thanks filled the courtyard before everyone left.

"It's hard to go to sleep frustrated," Tindra said, and took my hand.

"I'll do what I can to help you get over it," I said, leading her to the bedroom.

Chapter 90

I woke before Tindra, dressed quietly, and left for Goran's to get breakfast. *No sense in meeting with the generals on an empty stomach.*

Along the way, I tried to work out how the battle would go. I expected victory, but at what cost? Nothing in my experience gave me any insight. From there, my mind wandered to the future. *Should I marry Tindra now, just in case? We're living like we're already wed. What would change? It would make her queen, give her more authority...more power. If I didn't want her to be at my side, I'd have sent her away long ago.*

Goran greeted me with a smile, and Britt happily loaded my arms with a bounty of boiled grains and roast deer.

• • • ● • ● • • •

Tindra walked out of the bedroom as I placed the food on the table.

Someone knocked on the door.

"You have a meeting after this, right?" she asked.

I cocked my head. "Yes, but I haven't sent Agrim to get anyone."

The man at the door bowed when I opened it. "Beg pardon, Sire. I hate to disturb you this early, but I've just returned from Varia with word from King Crum," he said, offering me a sealed parchment.

Tindra snickered. "'King Crum' sounds so funny," she whispered.

I glanced back at her and took the message. "No need to apologize. Thank you for your service."

"Anytime, m'lord," he replied, bowing again before turning away.

I closed the door and read the message carefully.

"Well? What does his royal Crumness have to say?" she asked, as I returned to the table.

Shaking my head, I said. "Not the best news. No more men to me, but he's tripled patrols to keep Satra from entering Varia and told me to consider the far eastern passage closed. He said he'll meet me there to talk after our warriors free my old skati."

"I hear Ander's influence in his decision."

"How so? Ander seemed ready, almost eager, to support the war."

"Before he lost his wife and gave up the crown," Tindra said. "Taking those events into account, it makes sense he'd advise Crum to protect Varia without risking more than necessary."

"At least Satra won't have anywhere to go but south, back to their country."

"Knowing where the enemy can run to, if they retreat, makes things somewhat easier."

I nodded. "And I can let the generals know what to expect."

After quickly finishing my meal, I left for Agrim's quarters. "Captain, find the generals and Fastulf. Bring them to my meeting room. Let them know I expect action soon."

"I'll have them there as quickly as possible, Sire."

When I returned home, Tindra was cleaning dishes. "Join me in the meeting room when you're done. I want you to know what's going on."

"Shouldn't be long," she said, smiling.

I hadn't been seated long enough to get comfortable when she entered and took her place on my right.

Taking her hand, I looked at her and thought about the future again. *Do it. It's the right thing for Croy and for you.* "Are you willing to wed without your parents being here?"

Her eyes opened wide, and she smiled, squeezing my hand. "Are you serious?"

I smiled. "I wouldn't joke about this."

Her expression changed, her smile turning to a frown. "You're leaving with the guides."

"No, I don't intend to," I said. "I want to enjoy my wife and hear reports of my warrior's victories. I am sorry your parents can't be here, and that we don't have time for a proper celebration. Once the war is won, we'll have a wedding party for the ages. I promise."

"I'm not sure I believe you're not planning to leave, but I *will* hold you to your promise," she said, her frown turning back into a smile.

"I'll do my best to not disappoint you."

The front door opened, and Agrim led everyone into the room.

I greeted them and told them about the message from Varia.

"Not ideal but good to know," Jomar said.

"It does make things a little easier," Gudmann added.

"It's better than nothing, I said, nodding. "Now, if you haven't heard, while not perfect, I consider last night's test successful. We have thirty guides trained and ready to lead our men safely through the hazards to start our attack. I believe we're ready, and I'm certain we've given our enemy too much time to plan their next attack. The sooner our forces move, the better. Any questions or comments? Speak freely," I said.

"I spoke with my men last night. Ten of us can lead more than five men," Fastulf said. "Should we increase the size of the force we're taking across?"

"I'd rather not spread ourselves too thin. If the initial attack fails, we need fighting men ready to stop a Satran charge," I said.

Gudmann cleared his throat. "This all sounds good, assuming it works. If it doesn't, do we have another plan?"

"I am working on another way to move warriors into their country. However, it depends on resources and support from Varia, which won't happen soon enough to be useful now," I said. "I wouldn't discourage anyone from finding other options, so long as it doesn't delay our first attack."

Gudmann grunted and looked to his peers. They nodded in agreement.

"Fastulf, how soon could you have your men ready to leave?" I asked.

He looked me in the eyes. "This afternoon, if that's what you need, Sire."

Gudmann flinched and opened his eyes wide.

"Take the rest of today to gather supplies and be ready to leave at first light tomorrow. When you get to the wall, work with the builders. Make sure you can get through the wall to start our attack the following evening," I said.

He nodded.

"Generals, ready all of our forces to leave with the guides so everyone can be well-rested before the attack. Send word when the guides are through the wall. If the attack must be delayed, I want to know why. Make sure you send a messenger to report on the battle's outcome.

"Leave enough horses at The Trader's Cup to supply messengers riding back and forth. If Geri complains, tell him I'll pay whatever price he names. Prepare the men to take the fight to the Satran."

"Should the surprise fail, at what point do we retreat?" Jomar asked.

"I trust your judgment. Fight hard but fight smart," I said.

"We will," Gudmann said. "Assuming the best and we end up pushing Satra back, how far do we go?"

"As far east as you feel safe, given the number of men you have. News of our forces smashing Satra against the cliffs of the eastern passage and liberating my homeland would please me greatly. Should they run back across their border, do not follow them into Satra. We'll take the war to their country when we have more men and resources in place. You have my assurance; it will happen but not before we are ready."

"Gather information along the way, if you can," Tindra said. "The more we know about them, the better off we are."

"Of course," Jomar said.

"Care for any Croians you find. It's likely they were treated worse than slaves. One exception to this order is Porsey, the traitor. He betrayed his own family to save his skin and gave our enemy information about us. His life is worth less than nothing; kill him without remorse."

"I'll spread the word myself," Heming said.

"Good," I said. "Impress on every man, Croian or Varian, we can—we will—win. Everyone will be better off with the nation of Satra reduced to dust. Make them a terrible memory and nothing more."

The generals nodded.

"You have much to prepare and not long to get it done. Go, and do Croy proud," I said.

They stood, bowed, and hurried out of the room.

Chapter 91

"Have you issued all the orders needed for today?" Tindra asked.

I scratched my chin. "I believe I have, yes."

"Does anything else need your attention?" She grinned.

"Nothing comes to mind," I said, studying her face for a hint of what she had in mind. "Everyone assures me they are ready to go to war."

She took my hand. "Then what did you have planned for the rest of your day?"

"I'm beginning to wonder what you had planned for the rest of my day," I said, squeezing her hand.

She raised her eyebrows. "I've seen so little of Croy. Can we take a break from all the planning and meetings and just get away for a while? Go someplace, relax, and enjoy some peace together...before the battle begins and you get caught up in running the war, I mean."

"Where did you want to go?" I asked, cocking my head.

"You took Kurt to a beach south of the capital, right?"

"I did, yes. We could ride there and be back for dinner if that's what you had in mind."

She smiled. "It is. I'll head to the market for food to take with us. You get horses and meet me at the gate to the courtyard."

"As much as I like how that sounds, what will my leaders think of me riding out to take a break while they work on getting their men ready to wade into battle?"

Tindra sighed. "Sometimes, you are not devious enough for your own good. Should anyone ask, we are scouting the shore for the best place to launch Kurt's boats in case they are needed as the war advances."

Closing my eyes for a moment, I nodded before smiling. "That would work. Let's do it."

Tindra leaned in for a quick kiss then hurried away.

Shaking my head at her enthusiasm and cunning, I set off for the stable to get Andale and a horse for Tindra.

Dodging through the chaos around the stables left no doubt the generals had everyone preparing to leave. After several attempts to find a stable hand to get our horses and the tack to ride them, I gave up and took care of the task myself.

Andale was his usual, patient self. There wasn't much to pick from when it came to finding a horse for Tindra. I chose a white and chestnut mare that looked like the best of a group of green mounts. She snorted and stomped while I cinched the saddle in place and came close to biting me before I got the bridle and reins secured. *Fiery and willful, much like the woman who will ride her.* Smiling at my own humor, I mounted Andale and led the rowdy mare away from the stable.

Making your way through a crowd on horseback is different than on foot. Workers, intent on completing their assigned task, don't pay much attention to who they are approaching or walking past—even if it's their king. Put the same king on a horse, and they are eager to get out of the way instead of risk being knocked down and trampled.

Tindra stood at the gate, a basket hanging from the crook in her right arm, wearing a shirt I hadn't seen before. The light-colored fabric looked smooth, almost shiny, when it moved as she turned to look my way.

"What took so long?" she asked, when I got close.

"Everyone is busy getting ready for tomorrow. I had to tack the horses myself. That color looks good on you. What's it made of?"

"After the last attack on Nikulas' hall, some of the traders have gotten desperate. I managed to get enough raw silk from one to have Fastan make this shirt. I'd rather it been dyed, but Fastan hadn't worked with silk before and didn't want to risk ruining what little I could get. I do miss my black silks, but Grima gave it to a friend in Varia before she left."

The mention of the black, silk outfit brought to mind the first time I met Tindra. She attacked me after I'd fought with a bully from my childhood that I happened across again in Varia. Tired and injured, I did the best I could to defend myself against Tindra's rapid strikes and fluid fighting style. In the end, she knocked me out and bound me hand and foot. "I like that color," I said, rubbing the back of my head.

She rubbed her hand along the sleeve and grinned. "I love the way it feels."

"Ready to go?" I asked.

She nodded and held the basket out toward me. "Hold this. I haven't tried to mount a horse since I lost my hand."

"Oh," I said, taking our lunch. *Maybe I chose the wrong horse.* "Hadn't thought of that. Give it a try. If you can't get on, I'll help you up."

To my surprise, she only needed three hops to get in the saddle.

Tindra took the reins.

"You might want to—"

Before I could finish warning her, she clicked her tongue and put her heels to the horse's flank. The mare bucked once before taking off at a full gallop. Tindra's yelp did nothing to stop the horse.

Andale, built for endurance and not speed, wasn't able to keep pace with Tindra's speeding mount. Before they vanished from sight, Tindra yelled, "Whoa!" loud enough for her voice to echo off the buildings around us, and the mare skidded to a stop.

I stopped beside her to a glare that could start a bonfire. "Sorry. I tried—"

"To get me killed?" Tindra screeched, still pulling the reins tight. "A warning would have been nice."

"You poked the horse before I could finish," I argued. "Let me guide you back to the stable, and we'll find a different horse."

"No, we've wasted enough time. I'm on this one, and I can deal with it now that I know what to expect...but you keep our food, just in case."

"If you insist," I said, raising my eyebrows.

"It will be fine," she replied. "I've overcome worse challenges. This horse isn't going to get the better of me. Let's try this again."

I got Andale to a fast walk, ready to run if Tindra's horse bolted again.

The mare snorted and whinnied when Tindra clicked her tongue and went straight to a trot at the slightest tap of a boot. "Better," Tindra muttered. "But someone needs to teach this thing some manners."

I'm guessing it'll be you. "Keep working on her," I said. "We've got a ways to go before we reach the water."

Andale had no trouble keeping pace with the fiery mare as we headed for the south gate, waving to many of the people we passed along the way.

The mare, which Tindra had taken to calling 'Forvar'—a Varian word I wasn't familiar with—balked at passing through the gate leading out of the capital. Tindra yelled at her and kicked her heels into the horse's flank. Again, the mare responded by running at full speed. Thankfully there was little traffic through the opening, and no one was injured.

Making sure to secure the basket in the crook of my elbow, I snapped Andale's reins, and we did our best to keep the galloping duo in sight. The guards at the gate stood slack-jawed as I rode through. My heart pounded as Tindra sped away.

She screamed, "You want to run, Forvar? Let's run!" and kicked both heels into the ill-behaved animal.

Seeing she seemed to be in control gave me a little relief. I slowed Andale to a trot and resigned myself to catching her when she stopped. *Doubt the horse will gallop to the coast.*

Hurrying past the trees and open spaces south of the capital, I noticed a few homesteads growing in areas that were unsettled a short time ago. Without stopping to see what the people were doing, I took it to be a good sign.

My eyes swept back and forth across the horizon ahead, hoping to spot my fiancée as I kept riding at a brisk pace. The longer I rode without seeing them, the more concern I felt. *Did the horse run to the coast? More likely, it veered off the path and carried Tindra into a stand of trees or threw her in a field and ran off.* I bellowed her name, hoping to hear her respond.

A faint reply came from ahead. I put my heels to Andale and galloped to find her still mounted, letting the mare graze in a grassy strip between the path and a clump of trees.

"What happened?" I asked.

"Forvar and I came to an understanding. I wouldn't let her stop until she didn't want to run anymore. Now, she knows I'm in charge. I see you kept our lunch with you, impressive. How much longer until we reach the water?"

I glanced at the basket before looking at Tindra again. "We're about halfway there. You decided to name her Forvar?"

"Seems fitting," Tindra said, nodding and patting the horse's neck.

"What's it mean?"

She smiled. "Stubborn, stone-headed, willful."

"Good name. You want to keep her?"

"I do," she said, clicked her tongue, and flicked the reins. "Now, let's get to the shore."

"You sure?" I asked, as Forvar walked toward the path.

"Yes. She'll behave now," Tindra said.

I moved Andale to ride beside her, heading south at a leisurely pace.

Between explaining to Tindra that I didn't know much about this part of Croy, beyond the stories of rafts being dashed to pieces against the rocky section of the beach when the waves washed high enough, carrying on with small talk, and making observations of the land around us, we reached the shore as the sun passed its highest point in the sky.

"Let's find a place to let the horses rest while we eat lunch," Tindra said, looking around as we rode onto the sand.

"Didn't do much scouting for places to eat when I rode here with Kurt," I said, and tilted my head toward a group of men sitting in the shade of some trees several paces from where the water met the land. "Plus, the locals didn't seem too friendly."

Tindra pursed her lips as her hand went to her hip, where her sword's hilt would have been. "You should have mentioned that before we left. We would have come armed."

"I doubt they'll attack us. We'll just head away from them. Come on." I turned Andale left and rode toward the mountains separating the western part of Croy from our lands to the east. We found an overhang casting a shadow on the sand and dismounted to let our horses roam while we ate.

Tindra took the basket, sat with her back against the stone, and removed a small cloth bundle. Unwrapping the food inside, she handed me two small loaves of bread. "Those are for you; I have one. Also, there's plenty of wine for the two of us." She held up a small, wooden bottle with a cork stopper. "Open this for me, then I'll give you yours."

I sat next to her, and we enjoyed our meal together. Biting into the bread, I found it stuffed with a spiced fowl. *A fruity wine wouldn't have been my first choice, but it isn't bad.*

"Didn't know Grith sold wine," I said, spraying a few crumbs from my lips.

"He doesn't," Tindra said. "Grima told me about a vintner she and Roi favored, and this seemed like a good occasion to try his wine. It's an interesting change."

"And enjoyable enough, much like the scenery."

"Agreed," Tindra said, nodding. "The cool breeze and sound of the waves are exactly what I needed before our lives get complicated again."

"Things are going to get better," I said. "Maybe not as soon as I'd like, but I have to believe Croy and Varia will prosper together in a future without Satra."

"Speaking of the future, have you ever considered living around here?"

"Shouldn't a king live in his capital city?" I asked.

"But kings can have more than one castle. The rulers of Varia have for generations."

"Interesting," I said, scratching my chin. "I'll have to think about that."

"It would make for a nice getaway," Tindra said, pressing her shoulder against mine. "From time to time."

After a couple more bottles of wine—the more I drank, the better it tasted—I wondered if we would safely make it home before dark. We stumbled and staggered, hand in hand, to where the horses munched in a patch of grass, well north of our secluded dining area.

Tindra couldn't mount Forvar without my help, and I had trouble getting on Andale without falling over. Carefully, and with more fortune on our side than we deserved, we made it back to the nearly empty stables without falling out of our saddles. A lone stableboy took our mounts and offered to find someone to help us get home. We turned him down and headed to Goran's for dinner.

After a quick meal, and lots of water, we made our way home steadier on our feet and fell into bed together.

Chapter 92

I woke to near darkness and carefully slid out of bed.

Tindra rolled over as I dressed. Her eyes fluttered as I did my best to dress quietly. Reaching for my hammer, I knocked it over, and the handle thunking against the floor woke her.

She bolted upright. "What are you doing?"

"Going—"

"I knew it," she said, and candles burst into bright flames. "You're going out with the warriors."

Closing my eyes, I shook my head. "No, I'm not. I told you I'm staying, and I am."

"Then why are you taking your hammer?"

"I'm going to the southern gate to show my support. Don't you think I should be armed to see Croy's army off?"

"Oh. Yes," she said, looking away from me. "Wait for me. I'll join you."

"I don't want to miss their exit. Come when you're ready."

She nodded, and I left the room.

Passing the meeting room, I had an idea and took a moment to grab the marriage agreement.

A faint, orange glow and wispy, golden clouds in the eastern sky greeted me. I jogged to the gate, hoping to catch the warriors on their way out.

"Have they already left?" I asked one of the guards.

"Who, Sire?"

"The warriors. Have they left for the battlefield?"

"No, my king. At least, they haven't passed through *this* gate."

"Good," I said, with a sigh of relief. "I'd hoped to see them off."

As the words left my mouth, I heard the dull thunder of horse hooves on stone. When the front of the line got into sight, I held my hammer across my chest, saluting as they passed.

The men returned my gesture and nodded.

Nearly half the warriors had passed before Tindra arrived.

"Sorry I'm so late," she said, drawing her sword and laying it across her chest. "Had to find a way past the parade."

"You made it. Showing your support is what counts."

The generals, riding at the rear ahead of the supply wagons, smiled when they saw us and returned our salutes before bowing in their saddles.

After the supply wagons passed, I put my hammer away.

Tindra sheathed her sword before taking my hand. "You want to go with them; I know it."

I didn't answer, afraid my own words would convince me to leave. Instead, I clicked my hammer into the sling on my back, squeezed Tindra's hand, and turned to walk away.

"Where are we going?" she asked.

"We just witnessed one part of Croy's future, and I've decided it's time to secure another part," I said, releasing her hand and putting my arm across her shoulders to pull her close to me.

"I'm glad you're thinking about the future, but that doesn't tell me where we're going."

"Wanted to surprise you," I said, producing the parchment I'd taken on the way out of our house. "We're going to Roi's so he can sign our wedding agreement. Assuming you're ready."

Her eyes opened wide and hugged me for a moment, then stepped back. "I thought...I mean, I *am* ready, but I...I didn't think you were."

I nodded. "Been thinking about it a lot. We're all but married now...right?"

"True."

"I keep saying we'll marry when the time is right," I said, taking her hand. "What makes this the wrong time? Other than I'm starting a war. When will it end? Will the time be right then?"

She smiled, eyes shining. "The only time we have is right now."

"My point, right now...let's give Croy the queen it needs."

She nodded and kissed me. "I'm ready to be the queen you need. Let's go."

Hand in hand, we hurried to my mentor's house. If I didn't know better, I'd say our feet never touched the ground.

Chapter 93

Roi answered soon after I knocked. "Didn't expect to see you this morning. Come in. Grima and Einns are in the market getting fresh eggs for breakfast. Have you eaten?"

"We didn't come looking for food, though we haven't eaten," I said, reaching for the agreement. "Today is meant to be a happy day because Tindra and I will be married."

I slapped the parchment on the table. "Sign, please."

He looked from me to the page and back then tilted his head.

"You agreed," I said.

"You can't get married without a celebration," he said, smiling

"We've agreed to celebrate later," Tindra said. "After the war, when it's safe for my parents to come."

"It doesn't have to be a big event. Let me find Grima and Einns. I'll sign, and the celebration will start."

"Roi," I said, putting my hands on my hips, "we don't want a party right now. Sign our agreement, and we'll be on our way."

He sighed. "Grima will skin me if she finds out I let you two leave before she got back. I'll sign if you promise to stay here while I go find her."

Tindra nodded when I glanced at her. "Yes. We'll wait."

After gathering his quill and ink, he signed the agreement and hurried out.

Tindra and I kissed and held each other tight. The feeling was nearly overwhelming. Satisfying, comforting warmth flowed between us. All the frustration from everything that had gone wrong since I declared myself King of Croy faded behind this one thing going right.

Together, we will shape Croy's future. No challenge will stop the two of us from building on this foundation.

"I still think he's up to something," she said, resting her cheek against my chest.

I kissed the top of her head. "You mean other than insisting we celebrate?"

The door flew open, and a blur vaguely resembling Grima rushed toward us and pulled Tindra away from me, into a hug. "If I'd known ahead of time, I would've made you a dress," Grima said, before turning to me. "You have to tell me things!"

"I decided this morning," I said. "Wasn't time to tell anyone but Tindra."

Roi, loaded with baskets, followed Einns, carrying several baskets of his own, to the cooking area. Dropping his burden, Einns bowed. "Congratulations, King Fitzeirick and Queen Tindra. I didn't plan to make a wedding breakfast. If you want, I'll go find everything to make sweet cakes."

"Einns, you don't have to do anything special. We weren't expecting a celebration."

"No celebration? You have to eat and drink and dance," Grima said.

Roi chuckled. "Speaking of which, I have to go back and get the mead. Couldn't carry it while being a pack mule."

"I wish he'd have asked first," I said, as the door closed. "I'm not sure I can stomach much mead. And—"

Tindra wagged her finger at me. "Don't say it."

"Don't say what?" Grima asked.

"He was about to say, 'I don't dance,' even though we *have* danced together," Tindra said, smiling.

"Don't listen to her," I said.

"You can't deny we danced," Tindra said. "Our performance gathered quite a bit of attention, as I recall."

"I'm not denying anything, but in my defense, I *was* coerced and a little drunk," I said.

"Coerced? Perhaps, but you chose the number of drinks, not me. Also, I did most of the dancing, so from a certain point of view, there is *some* truth to your statement," Tindra said.

"Doesn't matter anyway," I said. "There's no band. Can't dance without music."

"True," Grima said, frowning. "Still, we can have a good time. Tindra, come with me."

An awkward silence settled in the room as Einns went to work.

I sat at the table and looked at him. *What should I say?* "Don't go to any trouble. We'll be happy with whatever you were planning to make for your parents."

He nodded but kept his focus on preparing the meal.

I can tell him the truth about us without giving anything away. "You're family, you know." I held my breath.

He turned to me. "Not really. Roi said you're like his son, but I know he's not your father. Still, it makes me happy to have a home and people like Roi and you making sure my mother and I are taken care of."

"Because you both deserve it. Anything you need, you let me know. I'll make sure you get it."

He turned back to his work. "Thank you, sir. I will."

"You know there's a place for you in my castle once it's built." *I have to take care of family.*

"With my mother and Roi, sure."

"Also as my head cook."

"It would be an honor."

"One you've earned," I said. "And it's important to have someone trustworthy cooking. Might keep me from getting poisoned."

Grima walked into the room, interrupting the conversation, and announced, "I present to you, Queen Tindra of Croy."

Tindra sauntered in behind her, firesyth grace adding a seductive appeal to each step, wearing a simple, white dress. Grima had pulled her dark hair back, emphasizing the curve of her cheeks. With a smile reaching from ear to ear, my wife glowed. Sparks danced in her amber eyes. She paused and spun around once before continuing to me.

"You should wear your hair pulled back more often," I said, and kissed her.

"Can't braid it with only one hand," she said.

"Then we'll have to find you a lady to help."

Roi walked in, hefting a barrel.

"Need some help?" I asked.

He shook his head and carried it to a small table in the corner before looking Tindra up and down. "My wife's clothes look good on you."

She laughed. "I make everything I wear look good."

He shook his head, grabbed mugs from a nearby shelf, and opened the tap on the barrel. After passing them around, he lifted his high. "To the king and queen of Croy, long may they live."

I took a small sip of the sweet drink and tapped him on the shoulder. "I have to know why you're suddenly happy at the idea of our marriage."

He glanced toward Grima. "We talked. Tindra's been good for her, offered to help her adjust to this new life. Since they've become friends, Grima seems happier...so I suppose she might be good for you too."

"And, with a queen, you're not next in line for the crown," I said.

"Another good reason to change my mind."

I hugged him. "Even though we don't always agree, I appreciate you watching out for me. I hope you keep doing it for many years."

He clapped his hand on my back. "So long as I draw breath."

Grima pulled him away. "You two stop being so serious. This is a day for smiles and laughter."

I looked into Tindra's eyes, and the world stopped. *I love her.*

"We don't have to dance," she whispered.

I couldn't say anything, so I pulled her to me and kissed her—hard.

She met my force, eager to let me know she felt the same way.

After a few thumping heartbeats, we swayed to music no one else heard.

Someone laughed, another voice cheered, but we kept moving together. I danced, leading my wife in the first moments of our life together.

Tindra melted against me, and heat poured off her. Looking into her shiny eyes, I saw the fire my body felt.

Blinking an uncomfortable tear out of my eye, I looked around the room as the world intruded into my refuge

Roi and Grima danced nearby. Einns watched us from a few paces away. After emptying his mug, he set the table. Wooden plates thunking against the tabletop got everyone else's attention.

I floated to the table, holding Tindra's hand. Someone piled my plate high with thin slices of pork.

"Enjoy," Roi said, and we all dug in.

After a couple of bites, Tindra raised her mug. "My compliments to the cook."

We all showed our agreement by taking a drink.

Einns blushed before looking down.

Tindra stopped eating shortly before I'd had my fill.

"I believe it's time for us to go home," I said. "Einns, thank you again for an excellent meal."

"I'm glad you enjoyed it, sir."

Grima rushed to my side and hugged me. "So very happy for you."

I barely had time to thank her before Roi pulled me away and stared into my eyes. "Keep your head, and don't let her control you," he said, just above a whisper.

"You sure you've changed your mind?"

"Enough to be happy for you, but not enough to fully trust a snake to be anything but what she is," he replied.

"She's not who she was. Give it time. You'll see."

Walking home, arm-in-arm, Tindra's white dress and skipping steps gathered a lot of attention. Several women pointed and whispered as we passed.

"I'd guess we're starting some rumors," I said quietly.

"Good. I love rumors. They're so much fun."

I shook my head and tried to not laugh while smiling and nodding to everyone who looked our way.

Ivar and Hedin stood guard at our door.

"Pass the word. The queen and I are not to be disturbed until tomorrow morning at the earliest," I said.

"The queen?" Hedin asked.

Ivar shook his head. "Hedin's always been a little slow. I'll explain it to him."

Tindra chucked as I led her inside.

We spent the rest of the day close to each other, talking, laughing, touching, dancing, and loving—generally behaving as if we hadn't already been living together. When we couldn't keep our eyes open any longer, we collapsed into bed and fell asleep tangled together. Visions of a happy, prosperous future for us, our family, and our country wove into a tapestry of joyful dreams.

To the reader:

Thank you for reading this novel. I encourage you to leave a review at your preferred book retailer. If you enjoyed my story, please recommend it to your friends.

You are welcome to follow me on social media at:
www.facebook.com/JAGuynnAuthor
www.twitter.com/JAGuynnAuthor

Also follow my publisher at:
www.facebook.com/3220Group

Other titles by J.A. Guynn

Branded Book 1: Skald
Branded Book 3: Conqueror
Water Princess: Through the Storm